# The Shaving
# of Shagpat

# The Shaving of Shagpat

## George Meredith

MINT EDITIONS

*The Shaving of Shagpat* was first published in 1856.

This edition published by Mint Editions 2021.

ISBN 9781513278445 | E-ISBN 9781513278902

Published by Mint Editions®

 MINT
EDITIONS

minteditionbooks.com


Publishing Director: Jennifer Newens
Design & Production: Rachel Lopez Metzger
Project Manager: Micaela Clark
Typesetting: Westchester Publishing Services

# Contents

# THE THWACKINGS

It was ordained that Shibli Bagarag, nephew to the renowned Baba Mustapha, chief barber to the Court of Persia, should shave Shagpat, the son of Shimpoor, the son of Shoolpi, the son of Shullum; and they had been clothiers for generations, even to the time of Shagpat, the illustrious.

Now, the story of Shibli Bagarag, and of the ball he followed, and of the subterranean kingdom he came to, and of the enchanted palace he entered, and of the sleeping king he shaved, and of the two princesses he released, and of the Afrite held in subjection by the arts of one and bottled by her, is it not known as 'twere written on the finger-nails of men and traced in their corner-robes? As the poet says:

> *Ripe with oft telling and old is the tale,*
> *But 'tis of the sort that can never grow stale.*

Now, things were in that condition with Shibli Bagarag, that on a certain day he was hungry and abject, and the city of Shagpat the clothier was before him; so he made toward it, deliberating as to how he should procure a meal, for he had not a dirhem in his girdle, and the remembrance of great dishes and savoury ingredients were to him as the illusion of rivers sheening on the sands to travellers gasping with thirst.

And he considered his case, crying, "Surely this comes of wandering, and 'tis the curse of the inquiring spirit! for in Shiraz, where my craft is in favour, I should be sitting now with my uncle, Baba Mustapha, the loquacious one, cross-legged, partaking of seasoned sweet dishes, dipping my fingers in them, rejoicing my soul with scandal of the Court!"

Now, he came to a knoll of sand under a palm, from which the yellow domes and mosques of the city of Shagpat, and its black cypresses, and marble palace fronts, and shining pillars, and lofty carven arches that spanned half-circles of the hot grey sky, were plainly visible. Then gazed he awhile despondingly on the city of Shagpat, and groaned in contemplation of his evil plight, as is said by the poet:

> *The curse of sorrow is comparison!*
> *As the sun casteth shade, night showeth star,*
> *We, measuring what we were by what we are,*
> *Behold the depth to which we are undone.*

Wherefore he counselleth:

> *Look neither too much up, nor down at all,*
> *But, forward stepping, strive no more to fall.*

And the advice is excellent; but, as is again said:

> *The preacher preacheth, and the hearer heareth,*
> *But comfort first each function requireth.*

And "wisdom to a hungry stomach is thin pottage," saith the shrewd reader of men. Little comfort was there with Shibli Bagarag, as he looked on the city of Shagpat the clothier! He cried aloud that his evil chance had got the better of him, and rolled his body in the sand, beating his breast, and conjuring up images of the profusion of dainties and the abundance of provision in Shiraz, exclaiming, "Well-a-way and woe's me! this it is to be selected for the diversion of him that plotteth against man." Truly is it written:

> *On different heads misfortunes come:*
> *One bears them firm, another faints,*
> *While this one hangs them like a drum*
> *Whereon to batter loud complaints.*

And of the three kinds, they who bang the drum outnumber the silent ones as do the billows of the sea the ships that swim, or the grains of sand the trees that grow; a noisy multitude.

Now, he was in the pits of despondency, even as one that yieldeth without further struggle to the waves of tempest at midnight, when he was ware of one standing over him,—a woman, old, wrinkled, a very crone, with but room for the drawing of a thread between her nose and her chin; she was, as is cited of them who betray the doings of Time,

> *Wrinkled at the rind, and overripe at the core,*

and every part of her nodded and shook like a tree sapped by the waters, and her joints were sharp as the hind-legs of a grasshopper; she was indeed one close-wrecked upon the rocks of Time.

Now, when the old woman had scanned Shibli Bagarag, she called to him, "O thou! what is it with thee, that thou rollest as one reft of his wits?"

He answered her, "I bewail my condition, which is beggary, and the lack of that which filleth with pleasantness."

So the old woman said, "Tell me thy case."

He answered her, "O old woman, surely it was written at my birth that I should take ruin from the readers of planets. Now, they proclaimed that I was one day destined for great things, if I stood by my tackle, I, a barber. Know then, that I have had many offers and bribes, seductive ones, from the rich and the exalted in rank; and I heeded them not, mindful of what was foretold of me. I stood by my tackle as a warrior standeth by his arms, flourishing them. Now, when I found great things came not to me, and 'twas the continuance of sameness and satiety with Baba Mustapha, my uncle, in Shiraz,—the tongue-wagger, the endless tattler,—surely I was advised by the words of the poet to go forth in search of what was wanting, and he says:

> 'Thou that dreamest an Event,
> While Circumstance is but a waste of sand,
> Arise, take up thy fortunes in thy hand,
> And daily forward pitch thy tent.'

Now, I passed from city to city, proclaiming my science, holding aloft my tackle. Wullahy! many adventures were mine, and if there's some day propitiousness in fortune, O old woman, I'll tell thee of what befell me in the kingdom of Shah Shamshureen: 'tis wondrous, a matter to draw down the lower jaw with amazement! Now, so it was, that in the eyes of one city I was honoured and in request, by reason of my calling, and I fared sumptuously, even as a great officer of state surrounded by slaves, lounging upon clouds of silk stuffs, circled by attentive ears: in another city there was no beast so base as I. Wah! I was one hunted of men and an abomination; no housing for me, nought to operate upon. I was the lean dog that lieth in wait for offal. It seemeth certain, O old woman, that a curse hath fallen on barbercraft in these days, because of the Identical, whose might I know not. Everywhere it is growing in disrepute; 'tis languishing! Nevertheless till now I have preserved my tackle, and I would descend on yonder city to exercise it, even for a livelihood, forgetting awhile great things, but that I dread men may have changed there also,—and there's no stability in them, I call Allah (whose name be praised!) to witness; so should I be a thing unsightly, subject to hateful castigation; wherefore is it that I am in that state described by the poet, when,

> *'Dreading retreat, dreading advance to make,*
> *Round we revolve, like to the wounded snake.'*

Is not my case now a piteous one, one that toucheth the tender corner in man and woman?"

When she that listened had heard him to an end, she shook her garments, crying, "O youth, son of my uncle, be comforted! for, if it is as I think, the readers of planets were right, and thou art thus early within reach of great things—nigh grasping them."

Then she fell to mumbling and reciting jigs of verse, quaint measures; and she pored along the sand to where a line had been drawn, and saw that the footprints of the youth were traced along it. Lo, at that sight she clapped her hands joyfully, and ran up to the youth, and peered in his face, exclaiming, "Great things indeed! and praise thou the readers of planets, O nephew of the barber, they that sent thee searching the Event thou art to master. Wullahy! have I not half a mind to call thee already Master of the Event?"

Then she abated somewhat in her liveliness, and said to him, "Know that the city thou seest is the city of Shagpat, the clothier, and there's no one living on the face of earth, nor a soul that requireth thy craft more than he. Go therefore thou, bold of heart, brisk, full of the sprightliness of the barber, and enter to him. Lo, thou'lt see him lolling in his shop-front to be admired of this people—marvelled at. Oh! no mistaking of Shagpat, and the mole might discern Shagpat among myriads of our kind; and enter thou to him gaily, as to perform a friendly office, one meriting thanks and gratulations, saying, 'I will preserve thee the Identical!' Now he'll at first feign not to understand thee, dense of wit that he is! but mince not matters with him, perform well thy operation, and thou wilt come to great things. What say I? 'tis certain that when thou hast shaved Shagpat thou wilt have achieved the greatest of things, and be most noteworthy of thy race, thou, Shibli Bagarag, even thou! and thou wilt be Master of the Event, so named in anecdotes and histories and records, to all succeeding generations."

At her words the breast of Shibli Bagarag took in a great wind, and he hung his head a moment to ponder them; and he thought, "There's provokingness in the speech of this old woman, and she's one that instigateth keenly. She called me by my name! Heard I that? 'Tis a mystery!" And he thought, "Peradventure she is a Genie, one of an ill tribe, and she's luring me to my perdition in this city! How if that be so?" And again he thought, "It cannot be! She's probably the Genie that presided over my birth, and promised me dower of great things through the mouths of the readers of planets."

Now, when Shibli Bagarag had so deliberated, he lifted his sight, and lo, the old woman was no longer before him! He stared, and rubbed his eyes, but she was clean gone. Then ran he to the knolls and eminences that were scattered about, to command a view, but she was nowhere visible. So he thought, "'Twas a dream!" and he was composing himself to despair upon the scant herbage of one of those knolls, when as he chanced to gaze down the city below, he saw there a commotion and a crowd of people flocking one way; he thought, "'Twas surely no dream? come not Genii, and go they not, in the fashion of that old woman? I'll even descend on yonder city, and try my tackle on Shagpat, inquiring for him, and if he is there, I shall know I have had to do with a potent spirit. Allah protect me!"

So, having shut together the clasps of resolve, he arose and made for the gates of the city, and entered it by the principal entrance. It was a fair city, the fairest and chief of that country; prosperous, powerful; a mart for numerous commodities, handicrafts, wares; round it a wild country and a waste of sand, ruled by the lion in his wrath, and in it the tiger, the camelopard, the antelope, and other animals. Hither, in caravans, came the people of Oolb and the people of Damascus, and the people of Vatz, and they of Bagdad, and the Ringheez, great traders, and others, trading; and there was constant flow of intercourse between them and the city of Shagpat. Now as Shibli Bagarag paced up one of the streets of the city, he beheld a multitude in procession following one that was crowned after the manner of kings, with a glittering crown, clad in the yellow girdled robes, and he sporting a fine profusion of hair, unequalled by all around him, save by one that was a little behind, shadowed by his presence. So Shibli Bagarag thought, "Is one of this twain Shagpat? for never till now have I seen such rare growths, and 'twere indeed a bliss to slip the blade between them and those masses of darkness that hang from them." Then he stepped before the King, and made himself prominent in his path, humbling himself; and it was as he anticipated, the King prevented his removal by the slaves that would have dragged him away, and desired a hearing as to his business, and what brought him to the city, a stranger.

Thereupon Shibli Bagarag prostrated himself and cried, "O great King, Sovereign of the Time! surely I am one to be looked on with the eye of grace; and I am nephew to Baba Mustapha, renowned in Shiraz, a barber;—I a barber, and it is my prayer, O King of the Age, that thou take me under thy protection and the shield of thy fair will, while I perform good work in this city by operating on the unshorn."

When he had spoken, the King made a point of his eyebrows, and exclaimed, "Shiraz? So they hold out against Shagpat yet, aha? Shiraz! that nest of them! that reptile's nest!" Then he turned to his Vizier beside him, and said, "What shall be done with this fellow?"

So the Vizier replied, "'Twere well, O King, he be summoned to a sense of the loathsomeness of his craft by the agency of fifty stripes."

The King said, "'Tis commanded!"

Then he passed forward in his majesty, and Shibli Bagarag was ware of the power of five slaves upon him, and he was hurried at a quick pace through the streets and before the eyes of the people, even to the common receptacle of felons, and there received from each slave severally ten thwacks with a thong: 'tis certain that at every thwack the thong took an airing before it descended upon him. Then loosed they him, to wander whither he listed; and disgust was strong in him by reason of the disgrace and the severity of the administration of the blows. He strayed along the streets in wretchedness, and hunger increased on him, assailing him first as a wolf in his vitals, then as it had been a chasm yawning betwixt his trunk and his lower members. And he thought, "I have been long in chase of great things, and the hope of attaining them is great; yet, wullahy! would I barter all for one refreshing meal, and the sense of fulness. 'Tis so, and sad is it!" And he was mindful of the poet's words,—

> *Who seeks the shadow to the substance sinneth,*
> *And daily craving what is not, he thinneth:*
> *His lean ambition how shall he attain?*
> *For with this constant foolishness he doeth,*
> *He, waxing liker to what he pursueth,*
> *Himself becometh what he chased in vain!*

And again:

*Of honour half my fellows boast,—*
*A thing that scorns and kills us:*
*Methinks that honours us the most*
*Which nourishes and fills us.*

So he thought he would of a surety fling far away his tackle, discard barbercraft, and be as other men, a mortal, forgotten with his generation. And he cried aloud, "O thou old woman! thou deceiver! what halt thou obtained for me by thy deceits? and why put I faith in thee to the purchase of a thwacking? Woe's me! I would thou hadst been but a dream, thou crone! thou guileful parcel of belabouring bones!"

Now, while he lounged and strolled, and was abusing the old woman, he looked before him, and lo, one lolling in his shop-front, and people standing outside the shop, marking him with admiration and reverence, and pointing him out to each other with approving gestures. He who lolled there was indeed a miracle of hairiness, black with hair as he had been muzzled with it, and his head as it were a berry in a bush by reason of it. Then thought Shibli Bagarag, "'Tis Shagpat! If the mole could swear to him, surely can I." So he regarded the clothier, and there was naught seen on earth like the gravity of Shagpat as he lolled before those people, that failed not to assemble in groups and gaze at him. He was as a sleepy lion cased in his mane; as an owl drowsy in the daylight. Now would he close an eye, or move two fingers, but of other motion made he none, yet the people gazed at him with eagerness. Shibli Bagarag was astonished at them, thinking, "Hair! hair! There is might in hair; but there is greater might in the barber! Nevertheless here the barber is scorned, the grower of crops held in amazing reverence." Then thought he, "'Tis truly wondrous the crop he groweth; not even King Shamshureen, after a thousand years, sported such mighty profusion! Him I sheared: it was a high task!—why not this Shagpat?"

Now, long gazing on Shagpat awoke in Shibli Bagarag fierce desire to shear him, and it was scarce in his power to restrain himself from flying at the clothier, he saying, "What obstacle now? what protecteth him? Nay, why not trust to the old woman? Said she not I should first essay on Shagpat? and 'twas my folly in appealing to the King that brought on me that thwacking. 'Tis well! I'll trust to her words. Wullahy! will it not lead me to great things?"

So it was, that as he thought this he continued to keep eye on Shagpat, and the hunger that was in him passed, and became a ravenous vulture that flew from him and singled forth Shagpat as prey; and there was no help for it but in he must go and state his case to Shagpat, and essay shearing him.

Now, when he was in the presence, he exclaimed, "Peace, O vendor of apparel, unto thee and unto thine!"

Shagpat answered, "That with thee!"

Said Shibli Bagarag, "I have heard of thee, O thou wonder! Wullahy! I am here to render homage to that I behold."

Shagpat answered, "'Tis well!"

Then said Shibli Bagarag, "Praise my discretion! I have even this day entered the city, and it is to thee I offer the first shave, O tangle of glory!"

At these words Shagpat darkened, saying gruffly, "Thy jest is offensive, and it is unseasonable for staleness and lack of holiness."

But Shibli Bagarag cried, "No jest, O purveyor to the outward of us! but a very excellent earnest."

Thereat the face of Shagpat was as an exceeding red berry in a bush, and he said angrily, "Have done! no more of it! or haply my spleen will be awakened, and that of them who see with more eyes than two."

Nevertheless Shibli Bagarag urged him, and he winked, and gesticulated, and pointed to his head, crying, "Fall not, O man of the nicety of measure, into the trap of error; for 'tis I that am a barber, and a rarity in this city, even Shibli Bagarag of Shiraz! Know me nephew of the renowned Baba Mustapha, chief barber to the Court of Persia. Languishest thou not for my art? Lo! with three sweeps I'll give thee a clean poll, all save the Identical! and I can discern and save it; fear me not, nor distrust my skill and the cunning that is mine."

When he had heard Shibli Bagarag to a close, the countenance of Shagpat waxed fiery, as it had been flame kindled by travellers at night in a thorny bramble-bush, and he ruffled, and heaved, and was as when dense jungle-growths are stirred violently by the near approach of a wild animal in his fury, shouting in short breaths, "A barber! a barber! Is't so? can it be? To me? A barber! O thou, thou reptile! filthy thing! A barber! O dog! A barber? What? when I bid fair for the highest honours known? O sacrilegious wretch! monster! How? are the Afrites jealous, that they send thee to jibe me?"

Thereupon he set up a cry for his wife, and that woman rushed to him from an inner room, and fell upon Shibli Bagarag, belabouring him.

So, when she was weary of this, she said, "O light of my eyes! O golden crop and adorable man! what hath he done to thee?"

Shagpat answered, "'Tis a barber! and he hath sworn to shave me, and leave me not save shorn!"

Hardly had Shagpat spoken this, when she became limp with the hearing of it. Then Shibli Bagarag slunk from the shop; but without the crowd had increased, seeing an altercation, and as he took to his heels they followed him, and there was uproar in the streets of the city and in the air above them, as of raging Genii, he like a started quarry doubling this way and that, and at the corners of streets and open places, speeding on till there was no breath in his body, the cry still after him that he had bearded Shagpat. At last they came up with him, and belaboured him each and all; it was a storm of thwacks that fell on the back of Shibli Bagarag. When they had wearied themselves in this fashion, they took him as had he been a stray bundle or a damaged bale, and hurled him from the gates of the city into the wilderness once more.

Now, when he was alone, he staggered awhile and then flung himself to the earth, looking neither to the right nor to the left, nor above. All he could think was, "O accursed old woman!" and this he kept repeating to himself for solace; as the poet says:

> 'Tis sure the special privilege of hate,
> To curse the authors of our evil state.

As he was thus complaining, behold the very old woman before him! And she wheezed, and croaked, and coughed, and shook herself, and screwed her face into a pleasing pucker, and assumed womanish airs, and swayed herself, like as do the full moons of the harem when the eye of the master is upon them. Having made an end of these prettinesses, she said, in a tone of soft insinuation, "O youth, nephew of the barber, look upon me."

Shibli Bagarag knew her voice, and he would not look, thinking, "Oh, what a dreadful old woman is this! just calling on her name in detestation maketh her present to us." So the old woman, seeing him resolute to shun her, leaned to him, and put one hand to her dress, and squatted beside him, and said, "O youth, thou hast been thwacked!"

He groaned, lifting not his face, nor saying aught. Then said she, "Art thou truly in search of great things, O youth?"

Still he groaned, answering no syllable. And she continued, "'Tis surely in sweet friendliness I ask. Art thou not a fair youth, one to entice a damsel to perfect friendliness?"

Louder yet did he groan at her words, thinking, "A damsel, verily!" So the old woman said, "I wot thou art angry with me; but now look up, O nephew of the barber! no time for vexation. What says the poet?—

> *'Cares the warrior for his wounds*
> *When the steed in battle bounds?'*

Moreover:

> *'Let him who grasps the crown strip not for shame,*
> *Lest he expose what gain'd it blow and maim!'*

So be it with thee and thy thwacking, O foolish youth! Hide it from thyself, thou silly one! What! thou hast been thwacked, and refusest the fruit of it—which is resoluteness, strength of mind, sternness in pursuit of the object!"

Then she softened her tone to persuasiveness, saying, "'Twas written I should be the head of thy fortune, O Shibli Bagarag! and thou'lt be enviable among men by my aid, so look upon me, and (for I know thee famished) thou shalt presently be supplied with viands and bright wines and sweetmeats, delicacies to cheer thee."

Now, the promise of food and provision was powerful with Shibli Bagarag, and he looked up gloomily. And the old woman smiled archly at him, and wriggled in her seat like a dusty worm, and said, "Dost thou find me charming, thou fair youth?"

He was nigh laughing in her face, but restrained himself to reply, "Thou art that thou art!"

Said she, "Not so, but that I shall be." Then she said, "O youth, pay me now a compliment!"

Shibli Bagarag was at a loss what further to say to the old woman, for his heart cursed her for her persecutions, and ridiculed her for her vanities. At last he bethought himself of the saying of the poet, truly the offspring of fine wit, where he says:

> *Expect no flatteries from me,*
> *While I am empty of good things;*
> *I'll call thee fair, and I'll agree*
> *Thou boldest Love in silken strings,*
> *When thou hast primed me from thy plenteous store!*

GEORGE MEREDITH

*But, oh! till then a clod am I:*
*No seed within to throw up flowers:*
*All's drouthy to the fountain dry:*
*To empty stomachs Nature lowers:*
*The lake was full where heaven look'd fair of yore!*

So, when he had spoken that, the old woman laughed and exclaimed, "Thou art apt! it is well said! Surely I excuse thee till that time! Now listen! 'Tis written we work together, and I know it by divination. Have I not known thee wandering, and on thy way to this city of Shagpat, where thou'lt some day sit throned? Now I propose to thee this—and 'tis an excellent proposal—that I lead thee to great things, and make thee glorious, a sitter in high seats, Master of an Event?"

Cried he, "A proposal honourable to thee, and pleasant in the ear."

She added, "Provided thou marry me in sweet marriage."

Thereat he stared on vacancy with a serious eye, and he could scarce credit her earnestness, but she repeated the same. So presently he thought, "This old hag appeareth deep in the fountain of events, and she will be a right arm to me in the mastering of one, a torch in darkness, seeing there is wisdom in her as well as wickedness. The thwackings?— sad was their taste, but they're in the road leading to greatness, and I cannot say she put me out of that road in putting me where they were. Her age?—shall I complain of that when it is a sign she goeth shortly altogether?"

As he was thus debating he regarded the old woman stealthily, and she was in agitation, so that her joints creaked like forest branches in a wind, and the puckers of her visage moved as do billows of the sea to and fro, and the anticipations of a fair young bride are not more eager than what was visible in the old woman. Wheedlingly she looked at him, and shaped her mouth like a bird's bill to soften it; and she drew together her dress, to give herself the look of slimness, using all fascinations. He thought, "'Tis a wondrous old woman! Marriage would seem a thing of moment to her, yet is the profit with me, and I'll agree to it." So he said, "'Tis a pact between us, O old woman!"

Now, the eyes of the old woman brightened when she heard him, and were as the eyes of a falcon that eyeth game, hungry with red fire, and she looked brisk with impatience, laughing a low laugh and saying, "O youth, I must claim of thee, as is usual in such cases, the kiss of contract."

So Shibli Bagarag was mindful of what is written,

*If thou wouldst take the great leap, be ready for the little jump,*

and he stretched out his mouth to the forehead of the old woman. When he had done so, it was as though she had been illuminated, as when light is put in the hollow of a pumpkin. Then said she, "This is well! this is a fair beginning! Now look, for thy fortune will of a surety follow. Call me now sweet bride, and knocker at the threshold of hearts!"

So Shibli Bagarag sighed, and called her this, and he said, "Forget not my condition, O old woman, and that I am nigh famished."

Upon that she nodded gravely, and arose and shook her garments together, and beckoned for Shibli Bagarag to follow her; and the two passed through the gates of the city, and held on together through divers streets and thoroughfares till they came before the doors of a palace with a pillared entrance; and the old woman passed through the doors of the palace as one familiar to them, and lo! they were in a lofty court, built all of marble, and in the middle of it a fountain playing, splashing silvery. Shibli Bagarag would have halted here to breathe the cool refreshingness of the air, but the old woman would not; and she hurried on even to the opening of a spacious Hall, and in it slaves in circle round a raised seat, where sat one that was their lord, and it was the Chief Vizier of the King.

Then the old woman turned round sharply to Shibli Bagarag, and said, "How of thy tackle, O my betrothed?"

He answered, "The edge is keen, the hand ready."

Then said she, "'Tis well."

So the old woman put her two hands on the shoulders of Shibli Bagarag, saying, "Make thy reverence to him on the raised seat; have faith in thy tackle and in me. Renounce not either, whatsoever ensueth. Be not abashed, O my bridegroom to be!"

Thereupon she thrust him in; and Shibli Bagarag was abashed, and played foolishly with his fingers, knowing not what to do. So when the Chief Vizier saw him he cried out, "Who art thou, and what wantest thou?"

Now, the back of Shibli Bagarag tingled when he heard the Vizier's voice, and he said, "I am, O man of exalted condition, he whom men know as Shibli Bagarag, nephew to Baba Mustapha, the renowned of Shiraz; myself barber likewise, proud of my art, prepared to exercise it."

Then said the Chief Vizier, "This even to our faces! Wonderful is the audacity of impudence! Know, O nephew of the barber, thou art among them that honour not thy art. Is it not written, For one thing thou shaft be crowned here, for that thing be thwacked there? So also it is written, The tongue of the insolent one is a lash and a perpetual castigation to him. And it is written, O Shibli Bagarag, that I reap honour from thee, and there is no help but that thou be made an example of."

So the Chief Vizier uttered command, and Shibli Bagarag was ware of the power of five slaves upon him; and they seized him familiarly, and placed him in position, and made ready his clothing for the reception of fifty other thwacks with a thong, each several thwack coming down on him with a hiss, as it were a serpent, and with a smack, as it were the mouth of satisfaction; and the people assembled extolled the Chief Vizier, saying, "Well and valiantly done, O stay of the State! and such-like to the accursed race of barbers."

Now, when they had passed before the Chief Vizier and departed, lo! he fell to laughing violently, so that his hair was agitated and was as a sand-cloud over him, and his countenance behind it was as the sun of the desert reflected ripplingly on the waters of a bubbling spring, for it had the aspect of merriness; and the Chief Vizier exclaimed, "O Shibli Bagarag, have I not made fair show?"

And Shibli Bagarag said, "Excellent fair show, O mighty one!" Yet knew he not in what, but he was abject by reason of the thwacks.

So the Vizier said, "Thou lookest lean, even as one to whom Fortune oweth a long debt. Tell me now of thy barbercraft: perchance thy gain will be great thereby?"

And Shibli Bagarag answered, "My gain has been great, O eminent in rank, but of evil quality, and I am content not to increase it." And he broke forth into lamentations, crying in excellent verse:—

> *Why am I thus the sport of all—*
> *A thing Fate knocketh like a ball*
> *From point to point of evil chance,*
> *Even as the sneer of Circumstance?*
> *While thirsting for the highest fame,*
> *I hunger like the lowest beast:*
> *To be the first of men I aim*
> *And find myself the least.*

Now, the Vizier delayed not when he heard this to have a fair supply set before Shibli Bagarag, and meats dressed in divers fashions, spiced, and coloured, and with herbs, and wines in golden goblets, and slaves in attendance. So Shibli Bagarag ate and drank, and presently his soul arose from its prostration, and he cried, "Wullahy! the head cook of King Shamshureen could have worked no better as regards the restorative process."

Then said the Chief Vizier, "O Shibli Bagarag, where now is thy tackle?"

And Shibli Bagarag winked and nodded and turned his head in the manner of the knowing ones, and he recited the verse:

> 'Tis well that we are sometimes circumspect,
> And hold ourselves in witless ways deterred:
> One thwacking made me seriously reflect;
> A SECOND turned the cream of love to curd:
> Most surely that profession I reject
> Before the fear of a prospective THIRD.

So the Vizier said, "'Tis well, thou turnest verse neatly" And he exclaimed extemporaneously:

> If thou wouldst have thy achievement as high
>
> As the wings of Ambition can fly:
> If thou the clear summit of hope wouldst attain,
> And not have thy labour in vain;
> Be steadfast in that which impell'd, for the peace
> Of earth he who leaves must have trust:
> He is safe while he soars, but when faith shall cease,
> Desponding he drops to the dust.

Then said he, "Fear no further thwacking, but honour and prosperity in the place of it. What says the poet?—

> 'We faint, when for the fire
> There needs one spark;
> We droop, when our desire
> Is near its mark.'

How near to it art thou, O Shibli Bagarag! Know, then, that among this people there is great reverence for the growing of hair, and he that is hairiest is honoured most, wherefore are barbers creatures of especial abhorrence, and of a surety flourish not. And so it is that I owe my station to the esteem I profess for the cultivation of hair, and to my persecution of the clippers of it. And in this kingdom is no one that beareth such a crop as I, saving one, a clothier, an accursed one!— and may a blight fall upon him for his vanity and his affectation of solemn priestliness, and his lolling in his shop-front to be admired and marvelled at by the people. So this fellow I would disgrace and bring to scorn,—this Shagpat! for he is mine enemy, and the eye of the King my master is on him. Now I conceive thy assistance in this matter, Shibli Bagarag,—thou, a barber."

When Shibli Bagarag heard mention of Shagpat, and the desire for vengeance in the Vizier, he was as a new man, and he smelt the sweetness of his own revenge as a vulture smelleth the carrion from afar, and he said, "I am thy servant, thy slave, O Vizier!" Then smiled he as to his own soul, and he exclaimed, "On my head be it!"

And it was to him as when sudden gusts of perfume from garden roses of the valley meet the traveller's nostril on the hill that overlooketh the valley, filling him with ecstasy and newness of life, delicate visions. And he cried, "Wullahy! this is fair; this is well! I am he that was appointed to do thy work, O man in office! What says the poet?—

> '*The destined hand doth strike the fated blow:*
> *Surely the arrow's fitted to the bow!*'

And he says:

> '*The feathered seed for the wind delayeth,*
> *The wind above the garden swayeth,*
> *The garden of its burden knoweth,*
> *The burden falleth, sinketh, soweth.*'"

So the Vizier chuckled and nodded, saying, "Right, right! aptly spoken, O youth of favour! 'Tis even so, and there is wisdom in what is written:

> '*Chance is a poor knave;*
> *Its own sad slave;*
> *Two meet that were to meet:*
> *Life's no cheat.*'"

Upon that he cried, "First let us have with us the Eclipser of Reason, and take counsel with her, as is my custom."

Now, the Vizier made signal to a slave in attendance, and the slave departed from the Hall, and the Vizier led Shibli Bagarag into a closer chamber, which had a smooth floor of inlaid silver and silken hangings, the windows looking forth on the gardens of the palace and its fountains and cool recesses of shade and temperate sweetness. While they sat there conversing in this metre and that, measuring quotations, lo! the old woman, the affianced of Shibli Bagarag—and she sumptuously arrayed, in perfect queenliness, her head bound in a circlet of gems and gold, her figure lustrous with a full robe of flowing crimson silk; and she wore slippers embroidered with golden traceries, and round her waist a girdle flashing with jewels, so that to look on she was as a long falling water in the last bright slant of the sun. Her hair hung disarranged, and spread in a scattered fashion off her shoulders; and she was younger by many moons, her brow smooth where Shibli Bagarag had given the kiss of contract, her hand soft and white where he had taken it. Shibli Bagarag was smitten with astonishment at sight of her, and he thought, "Surely the aspect of this old woman would realise the story of Bhanavar the Beautiful; and it is a story marvellous to think of; yet how great is the likeness between Bhanavar and this old woman that groweth younger!"

And he thought again, "What if the story of Bhanavar be a true one; this old woman such as she—no other?"

So, while he considered her, the Vizier exclaimed, "Is she not fair—my daughter?"

And the youth answered, "She is, O Vizier, that she is!"

But the Vizier cried, "Nay, by Allah! she is that she will be." And the Vizier said, "'Tis she that is my daughter; tell me thy thought of her, as thou thinkest it."

And Shibli Bagarag replied, "O Vizier, my thought of her is, she seemeth indeed as Bhanavar the Beautiful—no other."

Then the Vizier and the Eclipser of Reason exclaimed together, "How of Bhanavar and her story, O youth? We listen!"

So Shibli Bagarag leaned slightly on a cushion of a couch, and narrated as followeth.

# AND THIS IS THE STORY OF BHANAVAR THE BEAUTIFUL

K now that at the foot of a lofty mountain of the Caucasus there lieth a deep blue lake; near to this lake a nest of serpents, wise and ancient. Now, it was the habit of a damsel to pass by the lake early at morn, on her way from the tents of her tribe to the pastures of the flocks. As she pressed the white arch of her feet on the soft green-mossed grasses by the shore of the lake she would let loose her hair, looking over into the water, and bind the braid again round her temples and behind her ears, as it had been in a lucent mirror: so doing she would laugh. Her laughter was like the falls of water at moonrise; her loveliness like the very moonrise; and she was stately as a palm-tree standing before the moon.

This was Bhanavar the Beautiful.

Now, the damsel was betrothed to the son of a neighbouring Emir, a youth comely, well-fashioned, skilled with the bow, apt in all exercises; one that sat his mare firm as the trained falcon that fixeth on the plunging bull of the plains; fair and terrible in combat as the lightning that strideth the rolling storm; and it is sung by the poet:

> *When on his desert mare I see*
> *My prince of men,*
> *I think him then*
> *As high above humanity*
> *As he shines radiant over me.*
>
> *Lo! like a torrent he doth bound,*
> *Breasting the shock*
> *From rock to rock:*
> *A pillar of storm, he shakes the ground,*
>
> *His turban on his temples wound.*
>
> *Match me for worth to be adored*
> *A youth like him*
> *In heart and limb!*
> *Swift as his anger is his sword;*
> *Softer than woman his true word.*

Now, the love of this youth for the damsel Bhanavar was a consuming passion, and the father of the damsel and the father of the youth looked fairly on the prospect of their union, which was near, and was plighted as the union of the two tribes. So they met, and there was no voice against their meeting, and all the love that was in them they were free to pour forth far from the hearing of men, even where they would. Before the rising of the sun, and ere his setting, the youth rode swiftly from the green tents of the Emir his father, to waylay her by the waters of the lake; and Bhanavar was there, bending over the lake, her image in the lake glowing like the fair fulness of the moon; and the youth leaned to her from his steed, and sang to her verses of her great loveliness ere she was wistful of him. Then she turned to him, and laughed lightly a welcome of sweetness, and shook the falls of her hair across the blushes of her face and her bosom; and he folded her to him, and those two would fondle together in the fashion of the betrothed ones (the blessing of Allah be on them all!), gazing on each other till their eyes swam with tears, and they were nigh swooning with the fulness of their bliss. Surely 'twas an innocent and tender dalliance, and their prattle was that of lovers till the time of parting, he showing her how she looked best—she him; and they were forgetful of all else that is, in their sweet interchange of flatteries; and the world was a wilderness to them both when the youth parted with Bhanavar by the brook which bounded the tents of her tribe.

It was on a night when they were so together, the damsel leaning on his arm, her eyes toward the lake, and lo! what seemed the reflection of a large star in the water; and there was darkness in the sky above it, thick clouds, and no sight of the heavens; so she held her face to him sideways and said, "What meaneth this, O my betrothed? for there is reflected in yonder lake a light as of a star, and there is no star visible this night."

The youth trembled as one in trouble of spirit, and exclaimed, "Look not on it, O my soul! It is of evil omen."

But Bhanavar kept her gaze constantly on the light, and the light increased in lustre; and the light became, from a pale sad splendour, dazzling in its brilliancy. Listening, they heard presently a gurgling noise as of one deeply drinking. Then the youth sighed a heavy sigh and said, "This is the Serpent of the Lake drinking of its waters, as is her wont once every moon, and whoso heareth her drink by the sheening of that light is under a destiny dark and imminent; so know I my days are numbered, and it was foretold of me, this!" Now the youth sought to dissuade Bhanavar from gazing on the light, and he flung his whole body before her eyes, and clasped her head upon his breast, and clung about her, caressing her; yet she slipped from him, and she cried, "Tell me of this serpent, and of this light."

So he said, "Seek not to hear of it, O my betrothed!"

Then she gazed at the light a moment more intently, and turned her fair shape toward him, and put up her long white fingers to his chin, and smoothed him with their softness, whispering, "Tell me of it, my life!"

And so it was that her winningness melted him, and he said, "Bhanavar! the serpent is the Serpent of the Lake; old, wise, powerful; of the brood of the sacred mountain, that lifteth by day a peak of gold, and by night a point of solitary silver. In her head, upon her forehead, between her eyes, there is a Jewel, and it is this light."

Then she said, "How came the Jewel there, in such a place?"

He answered, "'Tis the growth of one thousand years in the head of the serpent."

She cried, "Surely precious?"

He answered, "Beyond price!"

As he spake the tears streamed from him, and he was shaken with grief, but she noted nought of this, and watched the wonder of the light, and its increasing, and quivering, and lengthening; and the light was as an arrow of beams and as a globe of radiance. Desire for the Jewel waxed in her, and she had no sight but for it alone, crying, "'Tis a Jewel exceeding in preciousness all jewels that are, and for the possessing it would I forfeit all that is."

So he said sorrowfully, "Our love, O Bhanavar? and our hopes of espousal?"

But she cried, "No question of that! Prove now thy passion for me, O warrior! and win for me that Jewel."

Then he pleaded with her, and exclaimed, "Urge not this! The winning of the Jewel is worth my life; and my life, O Bhanavar—surely its breath is but the love of thee."

So she said, "Thou fearest a risk?"

And he replied, "Little fear I; my life is thine to cast away. This Jewel it is evil to have, and evil followeth the soul that hath it."

Upon that she cried, "A trick to cheat me of the Jewel! thy love is wanting at the proof."

And she taunted the youth her betrothed, and turned from him, and hardened at his tenderness, and made her sweet shape as a thorn to his caressing, and his heart was charged with anguish for her. So at the last, when he had wept a space in silence, he cried, "Thou hast willed it; the Jewel shall be thine, O my soul!"

Then said he, "Thou hast willed it, O Bhanavar! and my life is as a grain of sand weighed against thy wishes; Allah is my witness! Meet me therefore here, O my beloved, at the end of one quarter-moon, even beneath the shadow of this palm-tree, by the lake, and at this hour, and I will deliver into thy hands the Jewel. So farewell! Wind me once about with thine arms, that I may take comfort from thee."

When their kiss was over the youth led her silently to the brook of their parting—the clear, cold, bubbling brook—and passed from her sight; and the damsel was exulting, and leapt and made circles in her glee, and she danced and rioted and sang, and clapped her hands, crying, "If I am now Bhanavar the Beautiful how shall I be when that Jewel is upon me, the bright light which beameth in the darkness, and needeth to light it no other light? Surely there will be envy among the maidens and the widows, and my name and the odour of my beauty will travel to the courts of far kings."

So was she jubilant; and her sisters that met her marvelled at her and the deep glow that was upon her, even as the glow of the Great Desert when the sun has fallen; and they said among themselves, "She is covered all over with the blush of one that is a bride, and the bridegroom's kiss yet burneth upon Bhanavar!"

So they undressed her and she lay among them, and was all night even as a bursting rose in a vase filled with drooping lilies; and one of the maidens that put her hand on the left breast of Bhanavar felt it full, and the heart beneath it panting and beating swifter than the ground is struck by hooves of the chosen steed sent by the Chieftain to the city of his people with news of victory and the summons for rejoicing.

Now, the nights and the days of Bhanavar were even as this night, and she was as an unquiet soul till the appointed time for the meeting with her lover had come. Then when the sun was lighting with slant beam the green grass slope by the blue brook before her, Bhanavar arrayed herself and went forth gaily, as a martial queen to certain conquest; and of all the flowers that nodded to the setting,—yea, the crimson, purple, pure white, streaked-yellow, azure, and saffron, there was no flower fairer in its hues than Bhanavar, nor bird of the heavens freer in its glittering plumage, nor shape of loveliness such as hers. Truly, when she had taken her place under the palm by the waters of the lake, that was no exaggeration of the poet, where he says:

> *Snows of the mountain-peaks were mirror'd there*
> *Beneath her feet, not whiter than they were;*
> *Not rosier in the white, that falling flush*
> *Broad on the wave, than in her cheek the blush.*

And again:

> *She draws the heavens down to her,*
> *So rare she is, so fair she is;*
> *They flutter with a crown to her,*
> *And lighten only where she is.*

And he exclaims, in verse that applieth to her:

> *Exquisite slenderness!*
> *Sleek little antelope!*
> *Serpent of sweetness!*
> *Eagle that soaringly*
> *Wins me adoringly!*
> *Teach me thy fleetness,*
> *Vision of loveliness;*
> *Turn to my tenderness!*

Now, when the sun was lost to earth, and all was darkness, Bhanavar fixed her eyes upon an opening arch of foliage in the glade through which the youth her lover should come to her, and clasped both hands across her bosom, so shaken was she with eager longing and expectation. In her hunger for his approach, she would at whiles pluck up the herbage about her by the roots, and toss handfuls this way and that, chiding the peaceful song of the nightbird in the leaves above her head; and she was sinking with fretfulness, when lo! from the opening arch of the glade a sudden light, and Bhanavar knew it for the Jewel in the fingers of her betrothed, by the strength of its effulgence. Then she called to him joyfully a cry of welcome, and quickened his coming with her calls, and the youth alighted from his mare and left it to pasture, and advanced to her, holding aloft the Jewel. And the Jewel was of great size and purity, round, and all-luminous, throwing rays and beams everywhere about it, a miracle to behold,—the light in it shining, and as the very life of the blood, a sweet crimson, a ruby, a softer rose, an amethyst of tender hues: it was a full globe of splendours, showing like a very kingdom of the Blest; and blessed was the eye beholding it! So when he was within reach of her arm, the damsel sprang to him and caught from his hand the Jewel, and held it before her eyes, and danced with it, and pressed it on her bosom, and was as a creature giddy with great joy in possessing it. And she put the Jewel in her bosom, and looked on the youth to thank him for the Jewel with all her beauty; for the passion of a mighty pride in him who had won for her the Jewel exalted Bhanavar, and she said sweetly, "Now hast thou proved to me thy love of me, and I am thine, O my betrothed,—wholly thine. Kiss me, then, and cease not kissing me, for bliss is in me."

But the youth eyed her sorrowfully, even as one that hath great yearning, and no power to move or speak.

So she said again, in the low melody of deep love-tones, "Kiss me, O my lover! for I desire thy kiss."

Still he spake not, and was as a pillar of stone.

And she started, and cried, "Thou art whole? without a hurt?" Then sought she to coax him to her with all the softness of her half-closed eyes and budded lips, saying, "'Twas an idle fear! and I have thee, and thou art mine, and I am thine; so speak to me, my lover! for there is no music like the music of thy voice, and the absence of it is the absence of all sweetness, and there is no pleasure in life without it."

So the tenderness of her fondling melted the silence in him, and presently his tongue was loosed, and he breathed in pain of spirit, and his words were the words of the proverb:

He that fighteth with poison is no match for the
prick of a thorn.

And he said, "Surely, O Bhanavar, my love for thee surpasseth what is told of others that have loved before us, and I count no loss a loss that is for thy sake." And he sighed, and sang:

*Sadder than is the moon's lost light,*
*Lost ere the kindling of dawn,*
*To travellers journeying on,*

*The shutting of thy fair face from my sight.*
*Might I look on thee in death,*
*With bliss I would yield my breath.*

*Oh! what warrior dies*
*With heaven in his eyes?*
*O Bhanavar! too rich a prize!*
*The life of my nostrils art thou,*
*The balm-dew on my brow;*

*Thou art the perfume I meet as I speed o'er the plains,*
*The strength of my arms, the blood of my veins.*

Then said he, "I make nothing matter of complaint, Allah witnesseth! not even the long parting from her I love. What will be, will be: so was it written! 'Tis but a scratch, O my soul! yet am I of the dead and them that are passed away. 'Tis hard; but I smile in the face of bitterness."

Now, at his words the damsel clutched him with both her hands, and the blood went from her, and she was as a block of white marble, even as one of those we meet in the desert, leaning together, marking the wrath of the All-powerful on forgotten cities. And the tongue of the damsel was dry, and she was without speech, gazing at him with wide-open eyes, like one in trance. Then she started as a dreamer wakeneth, and flung herself quickly on the breast of the youth, and put up the sleeve from his arm, and beheld by the beams of the quarter-crescent that had risen through the leaves, a small bite on the arm of the youth her betrothed, spotted with seven spots of blood in a crescent; so she knew that the poison of the serpent had entered by that bite; and she loosened herself to the violence of her anguish, shrieking the shrieks of despair, so that the voice of her lamentation was multiplied about and made many voices in the night. Her spirit returned not to her till the crescent of the moon was yellow to its fall; and lo! the youth was sighing heavy sighs and leaning to the ground on one elbow, and she flung herself by him on the ground, seeking for herbs that were antidotes to the poison of the serpent, grovelling among the grasses and strewn leaves of the wood, peering at them tearfully by the pale beams, and startling the insects as she moved. When she had gathered some, she pressed them and bruised them, and laid them along his lips, that were white as the ball of an eye; and she made him drink drops of the juices of the herbs, wailing and swaying her body across him, as one that seeketh vainly to give brightness again to the flames of a dying fire. But now his time was drawing nigh, and he was weak, and took her hand in his and gazed on her face, sighing, and said, "There is nothing shall keep me by thee now, O my betrothed, my beautiful! Weep not, for it is the doing of fate, and not thy doing. So ere I go, and the grave-cloth separates thy heart from my heart, listen to me. Lo, that Jewel! it is the giver of years and of powers, and of loveliness beyond mortal, yet the wearing of it availeth not in the pursuit of happiness. Now art thou Queen over the serpents of this lake: it was the Queen-serpent I slew, and her vengeance is on me here. Now art thou mighty, O Bhanavar! and look to do well by thy tribe, and that from which I spring, recompensing my father for his loss, pouring ointment on his affliction, for great is the grief of the old man, and he loveth me, and is childless."

Then the youth fell back and was still; and Bhanavar put her ear to his mouth, and heard what seemed an inner voice murmuring in him, and it was of his infancy and his boyhood, and of his father the Emir's first gift to him, his horse Zoora, in old times. Presently the youth revived somewhat, and looked upon her; but his sight was glazed with a film, and she sang her name to him ere he knew her, and the sad sweetness of her name filled his soul, and he replied to her with it weakly, like a far echo that groweth fainter, "Bhanavar! Bhanavar! Bhanavar!" Then a change came over him, and the pain of the poison and the passion of the death-throe, and he was wistful of her no more; but she lay by him, embracing him, and in the last violence of his anguish he hugged her to his breast. Then it was over, and he sank. And the twain were as a great wave heaving upon the shore; lo, part is wasted where it falleth; part draweth back into the waters. So was it!

Now the chill of dawn breathed blue on the lake and was astir among the dewy leaves of the wood, when Bhanavar arose from the body of the youth, and as she rose she saw that his mare Zoora, his father's first gift, was snuffing at the ear of her dead master, and pawing him. At that sight the tears poured from her eyelids, and she sobbed out to the mare, "O Zoora! never mare bore nobler burden on her back than thou in Zurvan my betrothed. Zoora! thou weepest, for death is first known to thee in the dearest thing that was thine; as to me, in the dearest that was mine! And O Zoora, steed of Zurvan my betrothed, there's no loveliness for us in life, for the loveliest is gone; and let us die, Zoora, mare of Zurvan my betrothed, for what is dying to us, O Zoora, who cherish beyond all that which death has taken?"

So spake she to Zoora the mare, kissing her, and running her fingers through the long white mane of the mare. Then she stooped to the body of her betrothed, and toiled with it to lift it across the crimson saddle-cloth that was on the back of Zoora; and the mare knelt to her, that she might lay on her back the body of Zurvan; when that was done, Bhanavar paced beside Zoora the mare, weeping and caressing her, reminding her of the deeds of Zurvan, and the battles she had borne him to, and his greatness and his gentleness. And the mare went without leading. It was broad light when they had passed the glade and the covert of the wood. Before them, between great mountains, glimmered a space of rolling grass fed to deep greenness by many brooks. The shadow of a mountain was over it, and one slant of the rising sun, down a glade of the mountain, touched the green tent of the Emir, where it stood a little apart from the others of his tribe. Goats and asses of the tribe were pasturing in the quiet, but save them nothing moved among the tents, and it was deep peacefulness. Bhanavar led Zoora slowly before the tent of the Emir, and disburdened Zoora of the helpless weight, and spread the long fair limbs of the youth lengthwise across the threshold of the Emir's tent, sitting away from it with clasped hands, regarding it. Ere long the Emir came forth, and his foot was on the body of his son, and he knew death on the chin and the eyes of Zurvan, his sole son. Now the Emir was old, and with the shock of that sight the world darkened before him, and he gave forth a groan and stumbled over the sunken breast of Zurvan, and stretched over him as one without life. When Bhanavar saw that old man stretched over the body of his son, she sickened, and her ear was filled with the wailings of grief that would arise, and she stood up and stole away from the habitations of the tribe, stricken with her guilt, and wandered beyond the mountains, knowing not whither she went, looking on no living thing, for the sight of a thing that moved was hateful to her, and all sounds were sounds of lamentation for a great loss.

Now, she had wandered on alone two days and two nights, and nigh morn she was seized with a swoon of weariness, and fell forward with her face to the earth, and lay there prostrate, even as one that is adoring the shrine; and it was on the sands of the desert she was lying. It chanced that the Chieftain of a desert tribe passed at midday by the spot, and seeing the figure of a damsel unshaded by any shade of tree or herb or tent-covering, and prostrate on the sands, he reined his steed and leaned forward to her, and called to her. Then as she answered nothing he dismounted, and thrust his arm softly beneath her and lifted her gently; and her swoon had the whiteness of death, so that he thought her dead verily, and the marvel of her great loveliness in death smote the heart on his ribs as with a blow, and the powers of life went from him a moment as he looked on her and the long dark wet lashes that clung to her colourless face, as at night in groves where the betrothed ones wander, the slender leaves of the acacia spread darkly over the full moon. And he cried, "'Tis a loveliness that maketh the soul yearn to the cold bosom of death, so lovely, exceeding all that liveth, is she!"

After he had contemplated her longwhile, he snatched his sight from her, and swung her swiftly on the back of his mare, and leaned her on one arm, and sped westward over the sands of the desert, halting not till he was in the hum of many tents, and the sun of that day hung a red half-circle across the sand. He alighted before the tent of his mother, and sent women in to her. When his mother came forth to the greetings of her son, he said no word, but pointed to the damsel where he had leaned her at the threshold of her tent. His mother kissed him on the forehead, and turned her shoulder to peer upon the damsel. But when she had close view of Bhanavar, she spat, and scattered her hair, and stamped, and cried aloud, "Away with her! this slut of darkness! there's poison on her very skirts, and evil in the look of her."

Then said he, "O Rukrooth, my mother! art thou lost to charity and the uses of kindliness and the laws of hospitality, that thou talkest this of the damsel, a stranger? Take her now in, and if she be past help, as I fear; be it thy care to give her decent burial; and if she live, O my mother, tend her for the love of thy son, and for the love of him be gentle with her."

While he spake, Rukrooth his mother knelt over the damsel, as a cat that sniffeth the suspected dish; and she flashed her eyes back on him, exclaiming scornfully, "So art thou befooled, and the poison is already in thee! But I will not have her, O my son! and thou, Ruark, my son, neither shalt thou have her. What! will I not die to save thee from a harm? Surely thy frown is little to me, my son, if I save thee from a harm; and the damsel here is—I shudder to think what; but never lay shadow across my threshold dark as this!"

Now, Ruark gazed upon his mother, and upon Bhanavar, and the face of Bhanavar was as a babe in sleep, and his soul melted to the parted sweetness of her soft little curved red lips and her closed eyelids, and her innocent open hands, where she lay at the threshold of the tent, unconscious of hardness and the sayings of the unjust. So he cried fiercely, "No paltering, O Rukrooth, my mother: and if not to thy tent, then to mine!"

When she heard him say that in the voice of his anger, Rukrooth fixed her eyes on him sorrowfully, and sighed, and went up to him and drew his head once against her heart, and retreated into the tent, bidding the women that were there bring in the body of the damsel.

It was the morning of another day when Bhanavar awoke; and she awoke in a dream of Zoora, the mare of Zurvan her betrothed, that was dead, and the name of Zoora was on her tongue as she started up. She was on a couch of silk and leopard-skins; at her feet a fair young girl with a fan of pheasant feathers. She stared at the hangings of the tent, which were richer than those of her own tribe; the cloths, and the cushions, and the embroideries; and the strangeness of all was pain to her, she knew not why. Then wept she bitterly, and with her tears the memory of what had been came back to her, and she opened her arms to take into them the little girl that fanned her, that she might love something and be beloved awhile; and the child sobbed with her. After a time Bhanavar said, "Where am I, and amongst whom, my child, my sister?"

And the child answered her, "Surely in the tent of the mother of Ruark, the chief, even chief of the Beni-Asser, and he found thee in the desert, nigh dead. 'Tis so; and this morning will Ruark be gone to meet the challenge of Ebn Asrac, and they will fight at the foot of the Snow Mountains, and the shadow of yonder date-palm will be over our tent here at the hour they fight, and I shall sing for Ruark, and kneel here in the darkness of the shadow."

While the child was speaking there entered to them a tall aged woman, with one swathe of a turban across her long level brows; and she had hard black eyes, and close lips and a square chin; and it was the mother of Ruark. She strode forward toward Bhanavar to greet her, and folded her legs before the damsel. Presently she said, "Tell me thy story, and of thy coming into the hands of Ruark my son."

Bhanavar shuddered. So Rukrooth dismissed the little maiden from the chamber of the tent, and laid her left hand on one arm of Bhanavar, and said, "I would know whence comest thou, that we may deal well by thee and thy people that have lost thee."

The touch of a hand was as the touch of a corpse to Bhanavar, and the damsel was constrained to speak by a power she knew not of, and she told all to Rukrooth of what had been, the great misery, and the wickedness that was hers. Then Ruark's mother took hold of Bhanavar a strong grasp, and eyed her long, piteously, and with reproach, and rocked forward and back, and kept rocking to and fro, crying at intervals, "O Ruark! my son! my son! this feared I, and thou art not the first! and I saw it, I saw it! Well-away! why came she in thy way, why, Ruark, my son, my fire-eye? Canst thou be saved by me, fated that thou art, thou fair-face? And wilt thou be saved by me, my son, ere thy story be told in tears as this one, that is as thine to me? And thou wilt seize a jewel, Ruark, O thou soul of wrath, my son, my dazzling Chief, and seize it to wear it, and think it bliss, this lovely jewel; but 'tis an anguish endless and for ever, my son! Woe's me! an anguish is she without end."

Rukrooth continued moaning, and the thought that was in the mother of Ruark struck Bhanavar like a light in the land of despair that darkly illumineth the dreaded gulfs and abysses of the land, and she knew herself black in evil; and the scourge of her guilt was upon her, and she cursed herself before Rukrooth, and fawned before her, abasing her body. So Rukrooth was drawn to the damsel by the violence of her self-accusing and her abandonment to grief, and lifted her, and comforted her, and after awhile they had gentle speech together, and the two women opened their hearts and wept. Then it was agreed between them that Bhanavar should depart from the encampment of the tribe before the return of Ruark, and seek shelter among her own people again, and aid them and the tribe of Zurvan, her betrothed, by the might of the Jewel which was hers, fulfilling the desire of Zurvan. The mind of the damsel was lowly, and her soul yearned for the blessing of Rukrooth.

Darkness hung over the tent from the shadow of the date-palm when Bhanavar departed, and the blessing of Rukrooth was on her head. She went forth fairly mounted on a fresh steed; beside her two warriors of them that were left to guard the encampment of the tribe of Ruark in his absence; and Rukrooth watched at the threshold of her tent for the coming of Ruark.

When it was middle night, and the splendour of the moon was beaming on the edge of the desert, Bhanavar alighted to rest by the twigs of a tamarisk that stood singly on the sands. The two warriors tied the fetlocks of their steeds, and spread shawls for her, and watched over her while she slept. And the damsel dreamed, and the roaring of the lion was hoarse in her dream, and it was to her as were she the red whirlwind of the desert before whom all bowed in terror, the Arab, the wild horsemen, and the caravans of pilgrimage; and none could stay her, neither could she stay herself, for the curse of Allah was on men by reason of her guilt; and she went swinging great folds of darkness across kingdoms and empires of earth where joy was and peace of spirit; and in her track amazement and calamity, and the whitened bones of noble youths, valorous chieftains. In that horror of her dream she stood up suddenly, and thrust forth her hands as to avert an evil, and advanced a step; and with the act her dream was cloven and she awoke, and lo! it was sunrise; and where had been two warriors of the Beni-Asser, were now five, and besides her own steed five others, one the steed of Ruark, and Ruark with them that watched over her: pale was the visage of the Chief. Ruark eyed Bhanavar, and signalled to his followers, and they, when they had lifted the damsel to her steed and placed her in their front, mounted likewise, and flourished their lances with cries, and jerked their heels to the flanks of their steeds, and stretched forward till their beards were mixed with the tossing manes, and the dust rose after them crimson in the sun. So they coursed away, speeding behind their Chief and Bhanavar; sweet were the desert herbs under their crushing hooves! Ere the shadow of the acacia measured less than its height they came upon a spring of silver water, and Ruark leaped from his steed, and Bhanavar from hers, and they performed their ablutions by that spring, and ate and drank, and watered their steeds. While they were there Bhanavar lifted her eyes to Ruark, and said, "Whither takest thou me, O my Chief?"

His brow was stern, and he answered, "Surely to the dwelling of thy tribe."

Then she wept, and pulled her veil close, murmuring, "'Tis well!"

They spake no further, and pursued their journey toward the mountains and across the desert that was as a sea asleep in the blazing heat, and the sun till his setting threw no shade upon the sands bigger than what was broad above them. By the beams of the growing moon they entered the first gorge of the mountains. Here they relaxed the swiftness of their pace, picking their way over broken rocks and stunted shrubs, and the mesh of spotted creeping plants; all around them in shadow a freshness of noisy rivulets and cool scents of flowers, asphodel and rose blooming in plots from the crevices of the crags. These, as the troop advanced, wound and widened, gradually receding, and their summits, which were silver in the moonlight, took in the distance a robe of purple, and the sides of the mountains were rounded away in purple beyond a space of emerald pasture. Now, Ruark beheld the heaviness of Bhanavar, and that she drooped in her seat, and he halted her by a cave at the foot of the mountains, browed with white broom. Before it, over grass and cresses, ran a rill, a branch from others, larger ones, that went hurrying from the heights to feed the meadows below, and Bhanavar dipped her hand in the rill, and thought, "I am no more as thou, rill of the mountain, but a desert thing! Thy way is forward, thy end before thee; but I go this way and that; my end is dark to me; not a life is mine that will have its close kissing the cold cheeks of the saffron-crocus. Cold art thou, and I— flames! They that lean to thee are refreshed, they that touch me perish." Then she looked forth on the stars that were above the purple heights, and the blushes of inner heaven that streamed up the sky, and a fear of meeting the eyes of her kindred possessed her, and she cried out to Ruark, "O Chief of the Beni-Asser, must this be? and is there no help for it, but that I return among them that look on me basely?"

Ruark stooped to her and said, "Tell me thy name."

She answered, "Bhanavar is my name with that people."

And he whispered, "Surely when they speak of thee they say not Bhanavar solely, but Bhanavar the Beautiful?"

She started and sought the eye of the Chief, and it was fixed on her face in a softened light, as if his soul had said that thing. Then she sighed, and exclaimed, "Unhappy are the beautiful! born to misery! Allah dressed them in his grace and favour for their certain wretchedness! Lo, their countenances are as the sun, their existence as the desert; barren are they in fruits and waters, a snare to themselves and to others!"

Now, the Chief leaned to her yet nearer, saying, "Show me the Jewel."

Bhanavar caught up her hands and clenched them, and she cried bitterly, "'Tis known to thee! She told thee, and there be none that know it not!"

Arising, she thrust her hand into her bosom, and held forth the Jewel in the palm of her white hand. When Ruark beheld the marvel of the Jewel, and the redness moving in it as of a panting heart, and the flashing eye of fire that it was, and all its glory, he cried, "It was indeed a Jewel for queens to covet from the Serpent, and a prize the noblest might risk all to win as a gift for thee."

Then she said, "Thy voice is friendly with me, O Ruark! and thou scornest not the creature that I am. Counsel me as to my dealing with the Jewel."

Surely the eyes of the Chief met the eyes of Bhanavar as when the brightest stars of midnight are doubled in a clear dark lake, and he sang in measured music:

> *"Shall I counsel the moon in her ascending?*
> *Stay under that tall palm-tree through the night;*
> *Rest on the mountain-slope*
> *By the couching antelope,*
> *O thou enthroned supremacy of light!*
> *And for ever the lustre thou art lending,*
> *Lean on the fair long brook that leaps and leaps,—*
> *Silvery leaps and falls.*
> *Hang by the mountain walls,*
> *Moon! and arise no more to crown the steeps,*
> *For a danger and dolour is thy wending!*

And, O Bhanavar, Bhanavar the Beautiful! shall I counsel thee, moon of loveliness,—bright, full, perfect moon!—counsel thee not to ascend and be seen and worshipped of men, sitting above them in majesty, thou that art thyself the Jewel beyond price? Wah! What if thou cast it from thee?—thy beauty remaineth!"

And Bhanavar smote her palms in the moonlight, and exclaimed, "How then shall I escape this in me, which is a curse to them that approach me?"

And he replied:

> *Long we the less for the pearl of the sea*
> *Because in its depths there's the death we flee?*
> *Long we the less, the less, woe's me!*
> *Because thou art deathly,—the less for thee?*

She sang aloud among the rocks and the caves and the illumined waters:

*Destiny! Destiny! why am I so dark?*
*I that have beauty and love to be fair.*
*Destiny! Destiny! am I but a spark*
*Track'd under heaven in flames and despair?*
*Destiny! Destiny! why am I desired*
*Thus like a poisonous fruit, deadly sweet?*
*Destiny! Destiny! lo, my soul is tired,*
*Make me thy plaything no more, I entreat!*

Ruark laughed low, and said, "What is this dread of Rukrooth my mother which weigheth on thee but silliness! For she saw thee willing to do well by her; and thou with thy Jewel, O Bhanavar, do thou but well by thyself, and there will be no woman such as thou in power and excellence of endowments, as there is nowhere one such as thou in beauty." Then he sighed to her, "Dare I look up to thee, O my Queen of Serpents?" And he breathed as one that is losing breath, and the words came from him, "My soul is thine!"

When she heard him say this, great trouble was on the damsel, for his voice was not the voice of Zurvan her betrothed; and she remembered the sorrow of Rukrooth. She would have fled from him, but a dread of the displeasure of the Chief restrained her, knowing Ruark a soul of wrath. Her eyelids dropped and the Chief gazed on her eagerly, and sang in a passion of praises of her; the fires of his love had a tongue, his speech was a torrent of flame at the feet of the damsel. And Bhanavar exclaimed, "Oh, what am I, what am I, who have slain my love, my lover!—that one should love me and call on me for love? My life is a long weeping for him! Death is my wooer!"

Ruark still pleaded with her, and she said in fair gentleness, "Speak not of it now in the freshness of my grief! Other times and seasons are there. My soul is but newly widowed!"

Fierce was the eye of the Chief, and he sprang up, crying, "By the life of my head, I know thy wiles and the reading of these delays: but I'll never leave thee, nor lose sight of thee, Bhanavar! And think not to fly from me, thou subtle, brilliant Serpent! for thy track is my track, and thy condition my condition, and thy fate my fate. By Allah! this is so."

Then he strode from her swiftly, and called to his Arabs. They had kindled a fire to roast the flesh of a buffalo, slaughtered by them from among a herd, and were laughing and singing beside the flames of the fire. So by the direction of their Chief the Arabs brought slices of sweet

GEORGE MEREDITH

buffalo-flesh to Bhanavar, with cakes of grain: and Bhanavar ate alone, and drank from the waters before her. Then they laid for her a couch within the cave, and the aching of her spirit was lulled, and she slept there a dreamless sleep till morning.

By the morning light Bhanavar looked abroad for the Chief, and he was nowhere by. A pang of violent hope struck through her, and she pressed her bosom, praying he might have left her, and climbed the clefts and ledges of the mountain to search over the fair expanse of pasture beyond, for a trace of him departing. The sun was on the heads of the heavy flowers, and a flood of gold down the gorges, and a delicate rose hue on the distant peaks and upper dells of snow, which were as a crown to the scene she surveyed; but no sight of Ruark had she. And now she was beginning to rejoice, but on a sudden her eye caught far to east a glimpse of something in motion across an even slope of the lower hills leaning to the valley; and it was a herd that rushed forward, like a black torrent of the mountains flinging foam this way and that, and after the herd and at the sides of the herd she distinguished the white cloaks and scarfs and glittering steel of the Arabs of Ruark. Presently she saw a horseman break from the rest, and race in a line toward her. She knew this one for Ruark, and sighed and descended slowly to meet him. The greeting of the Chief was sharp, his manner wild, and he said little ere he said, "I will see thee under the light of the Jewel, so tie it in a band and set it on thy brow, Bhanavar!"

Her mouth was open to intercede with his desire, but his forehead became black as night, and he shouted in the thunder of his lion-voice, "Do this!"

She took the Jewel from its warm bed in her bosom, and held it, and got together a band of green weeds, and set it in the middle of the band, and tied the band on her brow, and lifted her countenance to the Chief. Ruark stood back from her and gazed on her; and he would have veiled his sight from her, but his hand fell. Then the might of her loveliness seized Bhanavar likewise, and the full orbs of her eyes glowed on the Chief as on a mirror, and she moved her serpent figure scornfully, and smiled, saying, "Is it well?"

And he, when he could speak, replied, "'Tis well! I have seen thee! for now can I die this day, if it be that I am to die. And well it is! for now know I there is truly no place but the tomb can hold me from thee!"

Bhanavar put the Jewel from her brow into her bosom, and questioned him, "What is thy dread this day, O my Chief?"

He answered her gravely, "I have seen Rukrooth my mother while I slept; and she was weeping, weeping by a stream, yea, a stream of blood; and it was a stream that flowed in a hundred gushes from her own veins. The sun of this dawn now, seest thou not? 'tis overcrimson; the vulture hangeth low down yonder valley." And he cried to her, "Haste! mount with me; for I have told Rukrooth a thing; and I know that woman crafty in the thwarting of schemes; such a fox is she where aught accordeth not with her forecastings, and the judgment of her love for me! By Allah! 'twere well we clash not; for that I will do I do, and that she will do doth she."

So the twain mounted their steeds, and Ruark gathered his Arabs and placed them, some in advance, some on either side of Bhanavar; and they rode forward to the head of the valley, and across the meadows, through the blushing crowds of flowers, baths of freshest scents, cool breezes that awoke in the nostrils of the mares neighings of delight; and these pranced and curvetted and swung their tails, and gave expression to their joy in many graceful fashions; but a gloom was on Ruark, and a quick fire in his falcon-eye, and he rode with heels alert on the flanks of his mare, dashing onward to right and left, as do they that beat the jungle for the crouching tiger. Once, when he was well-nigh half a league in front, he wheeled his mare, and raced back full on Bhanavar, grasping her bridle, and hissing between his teeth, "Not a soul shall have thee save I: by the tomb of my fathers, never, while life is with us!"

And he taunted her with bitter names, and was as one in the madness of intoxication, drunken with the aspect of her matchless beauty and with exceeding love for her. And Bhanavar knew that the dread of a mishap was on the mind of the Chief.

Now, the space of pasture was behind them a broad lake of gold and jasper, and they entered a region of hills, heights, and fastnesses, robed in forests that rose in rounded swells of leafage, each over each—above all points of snow that were as flickering silver flames in the farthest blue. This was the country of Bhanavar, and she gazed mournfully on the glades of golden green and the glens of iron blackness, and the wild flowers, wild blossoms, and weeds well known to her that would not let her memory rest, and were wistful of what had been. And she thought, "My sisters tend the flocks, my mother spinneth with the maidens of the tribe, my father hunteth; how shall I come among them but strange? Coldly will they regard me; I shall feel them shudder when they take me to their bosoms."

She looked on Ruark to speak with him, but the mouth of the Chief was set and white; and even while she looked, cries of treason and battle arose from the Arabs that were ahead, hidden by a branching wind of the way round a mountain slant. Then the eyes of the Chief reddened, his nostrils grew wide, and the darkness of his face was as flame mixed with smoke, and he seized Bhanavar and hastened onward, and lo! yonder were his men overmatched, and warriors of the mountains bursting on them from an ambush on all sides. Ruark leapt in his seat, and the light of combat was on him, and he dug his knees into his mare, and shouted the war-cry of his tribe, lifting his hands as it were to draw down wrath from the very heavens, and rushed to the encounter. Says the poet:

*Hast thou seen the wild herd by the jungle galloping close?*
*With a thunder of hooves they trample what heads may oppose:*
*Terribly, crushingly, tempest-like, onward they sweep:*
*But a spring from the reeds, and the panther is sprawling in air,*
*And with muzzle to dust and black beards foam-lash'd, here and there,*
*Scatter'd they fly, crimson-eyed, track'd with blood to the deep.*

Such was the onset of Ruark, his stroke the stroke of death; and ere the echoes had ceased rolling from that cry of his, the mountain-warriors were scattered before him on the narrow way, hurled down the scrub of the mountain, even as dead leaves and loosened stones; so like an arm of lightning was the Chief!

Now Ruark pursued them, and was lost to Bhanavar round a slope of the mountain. She quickened her pace to mark him in the glory of the battle, and behold! a sudden darkness enveloped her, and she felt herself in the swathe of tightened folds, clasped in an arm, and borne rapidly she knew not whither, for she could hear and see nothing. It was to her as were she speeding constantly downward in darkness to the lower realms of the Genii of the Caucasus, and every sense, and even that of fear, was stunned in her. How long an interval had elapsed she knew not, when the folds were unwound; but it was light of day, and the faces of men, and they were warriors that were about her, warriors of the mountain; but of Ruark and his Arabs no voice. So she said to them, "What do ye with me?"

And one among them, that was a youth of dignity and grace, and a countenance like morning on the mountains, answered, "The will of

Rukrooth, O lady! and it is the plight of him we bow to with Rukrooth, mother of the Desert-Chief."

She cried, "Is he here, the Prince, that I may speak with him?"

The same young warrior made answer, "Not so; forewarned was he, and well for him!"

Bhanavar drew her robe about her and was mute. Ere the setting of the moon they journeyed on with her; and continued so three days and nights through the defiles and ravines and matted growths of the mountains. On the fourth dawn they were on the summit of a lofty mountain-rise; below them the sun, shooting a current of gold across leagues of sea. Then he that had spoken with Bhanavar said, "A sail will come," and a sail came from under the sun. Scarce had the ship grated shore when the warriors lifted Bhanavar, and waded through the water with her, and placed her unwetted in the ship, and one, the fair youth among the warriors, sprang on board with her, remaining by her. So the captain pushed off, and the wind filled the sails, and Bhanavar was borne over the lustre of the sea, that was as a changing opal in its lustre, even as a melted jewel flowing from the fingers of the maker, the Almighty One. The ship ceased not sailing till they came to a narrow strait, where the sea was but a river between fair sloping hills alight with towers and palaces, opening a way to a great city that was in its radiance over the waters of the sea as the aspect of myriad sheeny white doves breasting the wave. Hitherto the young warrior had held aloof in coldness of courtesy from Bhanavar; but now he sat by her, and said, "The bond between my prince and Rukrooth is accomplished, and it was to snatch thee from the Chief of the Beni-Asser and bring thee even to this city."

Bhanavar exclaimed, "Allah be praised in all things, and his will be done!"

The youth continued, "Thou art alone here, O lady, exposed to the perils of loneliness; surely it were well if I linger with thee awhile, and see to thy welfare in this city, even as a brother with a sister; and I will deal honourably by thee."

Bhanavar looked on the young warrior and blushed at his exceeding sweetness with her; the soft freshness of his voice was to her as the blossom-laden breeze in the valleys of the mountains, and she breathed low the words of her gratitude, saying, "If I am not a burden, let this be so."

Then said he, "Know me by my name, which is Almeryl; and that we seem indeed of one kin, make known unto me thine."

She replied, "Ill-omened is it, this name of Bhanavar!"

The youth among warriors gazed on her a moment with the fluttering eye of bashfulness, and said, "Can they that have marked thee call thee other than Bhanavar the Beautiful?"

She remembered that Ruark had spoken in like manner, and the curse of her beauty smote her, and she thought, "This fair youth, he hath not a mother to watch over him and ward off souls of evil. I dread there will come a mishap to him through me; Allah shield him from it!" And she sought to dissuade him from resting by her, but he cried, "'Tis but a choice to dwell with thee or with the dogs in the street outside thy door, O Bhanavar!"

Now, the ship sailed close up to the quay, and cast anchor there in the midst of other ships of merchandise. Almeryl then threw a robe over his mountain dress and spoke with the captain apart, and he and Bhanavar took leave of the captain, and landed on the quay among the porters, and of these one stepped forward to them and shouted cheerily, "Where be the burdens and the bales, O ye, fair couple fashioned in the eye of elegant proportions? Ye twin palm-trees, male and female! Wullahy! broad is the back of your servant."

Almeryl beckoned to him that he should follow them, and he followed them, blessing the wind that had brought them to that city and the day. So they passed through the streets and lanes of the city, and the porter pointed out this house and that house wanting an occupant, and Almeryl fixed on one in an open thoroughfare that had before it a grass-plot, and behind a garden with fountains and flowers, and grass-knolls shaded by trees; and he paid down the half of its price, and had it furnished before nightfall sumptuously, and women in it to wait on Bhanavar, and stuffs and goods, and scents for the bath,—all luxuries whatsoever that tradesmen and merchants there could give in exchange for gold. Then Almeryl dismissed the porter in Allah's name, and gladdened his spirit with a gift over the due of his hire that exalted him in the eyes of the porter, and the porter went from him, exclaiming, "In extremity Ukleet is thy slave!" and he sang:

> *Shouldst thou see a slim youth with a damsel arriving,*
> *Be sure 'tis the hour when thy fortune is thriving;*
> *A generous fee makes the members so supple*
> *That over the world they could carry this couple.*

Now so it was that the youth Almeryl and the damsel Bhanavar abode in the city they had come to weeks and months, and life to either of them as the flowing of a gentle stream, even as brother and sister lived they, chastely, and with temperate feasting. Surely the youth loved her with a great love, and the heart of Bhanavar turned not from him, and was won utterly by his gentleness and nobleness and devotion; and they relied on each other's presence for any joy, and were desolate in absence, as the poet says:

> *When we must part, love,*
> *Such is my smart, love,*
> *Sweetness is savourless,*
> *Fairness is favourless!*
> *But when in sight, love,*
> *We two unite, love,*
> *Earth has no sour to me;*
> *Life is a flower to me!*

And with the increase of every day their passion increased, and the revealing light in their eyes brightened and was humid, as is sung by him that luted to the rage of hearts:

> *Evens star yonder*
> *Comes like a crown on us,*
> *Larger and fonder*
> *Grows its orb down on us;*
> *So, love, my love for thee*
> *Blossoms increasingly;*
> *So sinks it in the sea,*
> *Waxing unceasingly.*

On a night, when the singing-girls had left them, the youth could contain himself no more, and caught the two hands of Bhanavar in his, saying, "This that is in my soul for thee thou knowest, O Bhanavar! and 'tis spoken when I move and when I breathe, O my loved one! Tell me then the cause of thy shunning me whenever I would speak of it, and be plain with thee."

For a moment Bhanavar sought to release herself from his hold, but the love in his eyes entangled her soul as in a net, and she sank forward to him, and sighed under his chin, "'Twas indeed my very love of thee that made me."

The twain embraced and kissed a long kiss, and leaned sideways together, and Bhanavar said, "Hear me, what I am."

Then she related the story of the Serpent and the Jewel, and of the death of her betrothed. When it was ended, Almeryl cried, "And was this all?—this that severed us?" And he said, "Hear what I am."

So he told Bhanavar how Rukrooth, the mother of Ruark, had sent messengers to the Prince his father, warning him of the passage of Ruark through the mountains with one a Queen of Serpents, a sorceress, that had bewitched him and enthralled him in a mighty love for her, to the ruin of Ruark; and how the Chief was on his way with her to demand her in marriage at the hands of her parents; and the words of Rukrooth were, "By the service that was between thee and my husband, and by the death he died, O Prince, rescue the Chief my son from this damsel, and entrap her from him, and have her sent even to the city of the inland sea, for no less a distance than that keepeth Ruark from her."

And Almeryl continued, "I questioned the messengers myself, and they told me the marvel of thy loveliness and the peril to him that looked on it, so I swore there was no power should keep me from a sight of thee, O my loved one! my prize! my life! my sleek antelope of the hills! Surely when my father appointed the warriors to lie in wait for thy coming, I slipped among them, so that they thought it ordered by him I should head them. The rest is known to thee, O my fountain of blissfulness! but the treachery to Ruark was the treachery of Ebn Asrac, not of such warriors as we; and I would have fallen on Ebn Asrac, had not Ruark so routed that man without faith. 'Twas all as I have said, blessed be Allah and his decrees!"

Bhanavar gazed on her beloved, and the bridal dew overflowed her underlids, and she loosed her hair to let it flow, part over her shoulders, part over his, and in sighs that were the measure of music she sang:

> *I thought not to love again!*
> *But now I love as I loved not before;*
> *I love not; I adore!*
> *O my beloved, kiss, kiss me! waste thy kisses like a rain.*
> *Are not thy red lips fain?*

*Oh, and so softly they greet!*
*Am I not sweet?*
*Sweet must I be for thee, or sweet in vain:*
*Sweet to thee only, my dear love!*
*The lamps and censers sink, but cannot cheat*
*These eyes of thine that shoot above*
*Trembling lustres of the dove!*
*A darkness drowns all lustres: still I see*
*Thee, my love, thee!*
*Thee, my glory of gold, from head to feet!*
*Oh, how the lids of the world close quite when our lips meet!*

Almeryl strained her to him, and responded:

*My life was midnight on the mountain side;*
*Cold stars were on the heights:*
*There, in my darkness, I had lived and died,*
*Content with nameless lights.*
*Sudden I saw the heavens flush with a beam,*
*And I ascended soon,*
*And evermore over mankind supreme,*
*Stood silver in the moon.*

And he fell playfully into a new metre, singing:

*Who will paint my beloved*
*In musical word or colour?*
*Earth with an envy is moved:*
*Sea-shells and roses she brings,*
*Gems from the green ocean-springs,*
*Fruits with the fairy bloom-dews,*
*Feathers of Paradise hues,*
*Waters with jewel-bright falls,*
*Ore from the Genii-halls:*
*All in their splendour approved;*
*All; but, match'd with my beloved,*
*Darker, and denser, and duller.*

Then she kissed him for that song, and sang:

GEORGE MEREDITH

*Once to be beautiful was my pride,*
*And I blush'd in love with my own bright brow:*
*Once, when a wooer was by my side,*
*I worshipp'd the object that had his vow:*
*Different, different, different now,*
*Different now is my beauty to me:*
*Different, different, different now!*
*For I prize it alone because prized by thee.*

Almeryl stretched his arm to the lattice, and drew it open, letting in the soft night wind, and the sound of the fountain and the bulbul and the beam of the stars, and versed to her in the languor of deep love:

*Whether we die or we live,*
*Matters it now no more:*
*Life has nought further to give:*
*Love is its crown and its core.*
*Come to us either, we're rife,—*
*Death or life!*

*Death can take not away,*
*Darkness and light are the same:*
*We are beyond the pale ray,*
*Wrapt in a rosier flame:*
*Welcome which will to our breath;*
*Life or death!*

So did these two lovers lute and sing in the stillness of the night, pouring into each other's ears melodies from the new sea of fancy and feeling that flowed through them.

Ere they ceased their sweet interchange of tenderness, which was but one speech from one soul, a glow of light ran up the sky, and the edge of a cloud was fired; and in the blooming of dawn Almeryl hung over Bhanavar, and his heart ached to see the freshness of her wondrous loveliness; and he sang, looking on her:

*The rose is living in her cheeks,*
*The lily in her rounded chin;*
*She speaks but when her whole soul speaks,*

*And then the two flow out and in,*
*And mix their red and white to make*
*The hue for which I'd Paradise forsake.*

*Her brow from her black falling hair*
*Ascends like morn: her nose is clear*
*As morning hills, and finely fair*
*With pearly nostrils curving near*
*The red bow of her upper lip;*
*Her bosom's the white wave beneath the ship.*

*The fair full earth, the enraptured skies,*
*She images in constant play:*
*Night and the stars are in her eyes,*
*But her sweet face is beaming day,*
*A bounteous interblush of flowers:*
*A dewy brilliance in a dale of bowers.*

Then he said, "And this morning shall our contract of marriage be written and witnessed?"

She answered, "As my lord willeth; I am his."

Said he, "And it is thy desire?"

She nestled to him and dinted his bare arm with the pearls of her mouth for a reply.

So that morning their contract of marriage was written, and witnessed by the legal number of witnesses in the presence of the Cadi, with his license on it endorsed; and Bhanavar was the bride of Almeryl, he her husband. Never was youth blessed in a bride like that youth!

Now, the twain lived together the circle of a full year of delightful marriage, and love lessened not in them, but was as the love of the first day. Little cared they, having each other, for the loneliness of their dwelling in that city, where they knew none save the porter Ukleet, who went about their commissions. Sometimes to amuse themselves with his drolleries, they sent for him, and were bountiful with him, and made him drink with them on the lawn of their garden leaning to an inlet of the sea; and then he would entertain them with all the scandal and gossip of the city, and its little folk and great. When he was outrageously extravagant in these stories of his, Bhanavar exclaimed, "Are such things, now? can it be true?"

GEORGE MEREDITH

And he nodded in his conceit, and replied loftily, "'Tis certain, O my Prince and Princess! ye be from the mountains, unused to the follies and dissipations of men where they herd; and ye know them not, men!"

The lamps being lit in the garden to the edges of the water, where they lay one evening, Ukleet, who had been in his briskest mood, became grave, and put his forefinger to the side of his nose and began, "Hear ye aught of the great tidings? Wullahy! no other than the departure of the wife of Boolp, the broker, into darkness. 'Tis of Boolp ye hire this house, and had ye a hundred houses in this city ye might have had them from Boolp the broker, he that's rich; and glory to them whom Allah prospereth, say I! And I mention this matter, for 'tis certain now Boolp will take another wife to him to comfort him, for there be two things beloved of Boolp, and therein manifesteth he taste and the discernment of excellence, and what is approved; and of these two things let the love of his hoards of the yellow-skinned treasure go first, and after that attachment to the silver-skinned of creation, the fair, the rapturous; even to them! So by this see ye not Boolp will yearn in his soul for another spouse? Now, O ye well-matched pair! what a chance were this, knew ye but a damsel of the mountains, exquisite in symmetry, a moon to enrapture the imagination of Boolp, and in the nature of things herit his possessions! for Boolp is an old man, even very old."

They laughed, and cried, "We know not of such a damsel, and the broker must go unmarried for us."

When next Ukleet sat before them, Almeryl took occasion to speak of Boolp again, and said, "This broker, O Ukleet, is he also a lender of money?"

Ukleet replied, "O my Prince, he is or he is not: 'tis of the maybes. I wot truly Boolp is one that baiteth the hook of an emergency."

The brows of the Prince were downcast, and he said no more; but on the following morning he left Bhanavar early under a pretext, and sallied forth from the house of their abode alone.

Since their union in that city they had not been once apart, and Bhanavar grieved and thought, "Waneth his love for me?" and she called her women to her, and dressed in this dress and that dress, and was satisfied with none. The dews of the bath stood cold upon her, and she trembled, and fled from mirror to mirror, and in each she was the same surpassing vision of loveliness. Then her women held a glass to her, and she examined herself closely, if there might be a fleck upon her anywhere, and all was as the snow of the mountains on her round limbs sloping in the curves of harmony, and the faint rose of the dawn on slants of snow was their hue. Twining her fingers and sighing, she thought, "It is not that! he cannot but think me beautiful." She smiled a melancholy smile at her image in the glass, exclaiming, "What availeth it, thy beauty? for he is away and looketh not on thee, thou vain thing! And what of thy loveliness if the light illumine it not, for he is the light to thee, and it is darkness when he's away."

Suddenly she thought, "What's that which needeth to light it no other light? I had well-nigh forgotten it in my bliss, the Jewel!" Then she went to a case of ebony-wood, where she kept the Jewel, and drew it forth, and shone in the beam of a pleasant imagination, thinking, "'Twill surprise him!" And she robed herself in a robe of saffron, and set lesser gems of the diamond and the emerald in the braid of her hair, and knotted the Serpent Jewel firmly in a band of gold-threaded tissue, and had it woven in her hair among the braids. In this array she awaited his coming, and pleased her mind with picturing his astonishment and the joy that would be his. Mute were the women who waited on her, for in their lives they had seen no such sight as Bhanavar beneath the beams of the Jewel, and the whole chamber was aglow with her.

Now, in her anxiety she sent them one and one repeatedly to look forth at the window for the coming of the Prince. So, when he came not she went herself to look forth, and stretched her white neck beyond the casement. While her head was exposed, she heard a cry of some one from the house in the street opposite, and Bhanavar beheld in the house of the broker an old wrinkled fellow that gesticulated to her in a frenzy. She snatched her veil down and drew in her head in anger at him, calling to her maids, "What is yonder hideous old dotard?"

And they answered, laughing, "'Tis indeed Boolp the broker, O fair mistress and mighty!"

To divert herself she made them tell her of Boolp, and they told her a thousand anecdotes of the broker, and verses of him, and the constancy of his amorous condition, and his greediness. And Bhanavar was beguiled of her impatience till it was evening, and the Prince returned to her. So they embraced, and she greeted him as usual, waiting what he would say, searching his countenance for a token of wonderment; but the youth knew not that aught was added to her beauty, for he looked nowhere save in her eyes. Bhanavar was nigh weeping with vexation, and pushed him from her, and chid him with lack of love and

GEORGE MEREDITH

weariness of her; and the eye of the Prince rose to her brow to read it, and he saw the Jewel. Almeryl clapped his hands, crying, "Wondrous! And this thy surprise for me, my fond one? beloved of mine!" Then he gazed on her a space, and said, "Knowest thou, thou art terrible in thy beauty, Bhanavar, and hast the face of lightning under that Jewel of the Serpent?"

She kissed him, whispering, "Not lightning to thee! Yet lovest thou Bhanavar?"

He replied, "Surely so; and all save Bhanavar in this world is the darkness of oblivion to me."

When it was the next morning, Almeryl rose to go forth again. Ere he had passed the curtain of the chamber Bhanavar caught him by the arm, and she was trembling violently. Her visage was a wild inquiry: "Thou goest?—and again? There is something hidden from me!"

Almeryl took her to his heart, and caressed her with fond flatteries, saying, "Ask but what is beating under these two pomegranates, and thou learnest all of me."

But she stamped her foot, crying, "No! no! I will hear it! There's a mystery."

So he said, "Well, then, it is this only; small matter enough. I have a business with the captain of the vessel that brought us hither, and I must see him ere he setteth sail; no other than that, thou jealous, watchful star! Pierce me with thine eyes; it is no other than that."

She levelled her lids at him till her lustrous black eyelashes were as arrows, and mimicked him softly, "No other than that?"

And he replied, "Even so."

Then she clung to him like a hungry creature, repeating, "Even so," and let him go. Alone, she summoned a slave, a black, and bade him fetch to her without delay Ukleet the porter, and the porter was presently ushered in to her, protesting service and devotion. So, she questioned him of Almeryl, and the Prince's business abroad, what he knew of it. Ukleet commenced reciting verses on the ills of jealousy, but Bhanavar checked him with an eye that Ukleet had seen never before in woman or in man, and he gaped at her helplessly, as one that has swallowed a bone. She laughed, crying, "Learn, O thou fellow, to answer my like by the letter."

Now, what she heard from Ukleet when he had recovered his wits, was that the Prince had a business with none save the lenders of money. So she spake to Ukleet in a kindly tone, "Thou art mine, to serve me?"

He was as one fascinated, and delivered himself, "Yea, O my mistress! with tongue-service, toe-service, back-service, brain-service, whatso pleaseth thy sweet presence."

Said she, "Hie over to the broker opposite, and bring him hither to me."

Ukleet departed, saying, "To hear is to obey."

She sat gazing on the Jewel and its counterchanging splendours in her hand, and the thought of Almeryl and his necessity was her only thought. Not ten minutes of the hour had passed before the women waiting on her announced Ukleet and the broker Boolp. Bhanavar gave little heed to the old fellow's grimaces, and the compliments he addressed her, but handed him the Jewel and desired his valuation of its worth. The face of Boolp was a keen edge when he regarded Bhanavar, but the sight of the Jewel sharpened it tenfold, and he tossed his arms, exclaiming, "A jewel, this!"

So Bhanavar cried to him, "Fix a price for it, O thou broker!"

And Boolp, the old miser, debated, and began prating,

"O lady! the soul of thy slave is abashed by a double beam, this the jewel of jewels, thou truly of thy sex; and saving thee there's no jewel of worth like this one, and together ye be—wullahy! never felt I aught like this since my espousal of Soolka that's gone, and 'twas nothing like it then! Now, O my Princess, confess it freely—this is but a pretext, this valuation of the Jewel, and Ukleet our go-between; and leave the rewarding of him to me. Wullahy! I can be generous, and my days of favour with fair ladies be not yet over. Blessed be Allah for this day! And thinkest thou those eyes fell on me with discriminating observation ere my sense of perception was struck by thee? Not so, for I had noted thee, O moon of hearts, from my window yonder."

In this fashion Boolp the broker went on prating, and bowing, and screwing the corners of his little acid eyes to wink the wink of common accord between himself and Bhanavar. Meantime she had spoken aside to one of her women, and a second black slave entered the chamber, bearing in his hand a twisted scourge, and that slave laid it on the back of Boolp the broker, and by this means he was brought quickly to the valuation of the Jewel. Then he named a sum that was a great sum, but not the value of the Jewel to the fiftieth part, nay nor the five-hundredth part, of its value; and Ukleet remonstrated with him, but he was resolute, saying, "Even that sum leaves me a beggar."

So Bhanavar said, "My desire is for immediate payment of the money, and the Jewel is thine for that sum."

GEORGE MEREDITH

Now the broker went to fetch the money, and returned with it in bags of gold one-half the amount, and bags of silver one-third, and the remainder in writing made due at a certain period for payment. And he groaned and handed her the money, and took the Jewel in his hands; exclaiming, "In the name of Allah!"

That evening, when it was dark and the lamps lit in the chamber, and the wine set and the nosegay, Almeryl asked of Bhanavar to see her under the light of the Jewel. She warded him with an excuse, but he was earnest with her. So she feigned that he teased her, saying, "'Tis that thou art no longer content with me as I am, O my husband!" Then she said, "Wert thou successful in thy dealings this day?"

His arm slackened round her, and he answered nothing. So she cried, "Fie on thee, thou foolish one! and what is thy need of running over this city? Know I not thy case and thine occasion, O my beloved? Surely I am Queen of Serpents, a mistress of enchantments, a diviner of things hidden, and I know thee. Here, then, is what thou requirest, and conceal not from me thy necessity another time, my husband!"

Upon that she pointed his eye to the money-bags of gold and of silver. Almeryl was amazed, and asked her, "How came these? for I was at the last extremity, without coin of any kind."

She answered, "How, but by the Serpents!"

And he exclaimed, "Would that I might work as that porter worketh, rather than this!"

Now, seeing he bewailed her use of the powers of the Jewel, Bhanavar fell between his arms, and related to him her discovery of his condition, and how she disposed of the Jewel to the broker, and of the scourging of Boolp; and he praised her, and clave to her, and they laughed and delighted their souls in plenteousness, and bliss was their portion; as the poet says,

> *Bliss that is born of mutual esteem*
> *And tried companionship, I truly deem*
> *A well-based palace, wherein fountains rise*
> *From springs that have their sources in the skies.*

So were they for awhile. It happened that one day, that was the last day of the year since her wearing of the Jewel, Ukleet said to them, "Be wary! the Vizier Aswarak hath his eye on you, and it is no cool one. I say nothing: the wise are discreet in their tellings of the great. 'Tis certain the broker Boolp forgetteth not his treatment here."

They smiled, turning to each other, and said, "We live innocently, we harm no one, what should we fear?"

During the night of that day Bhanavar awoke and kissed the Prince; and lo! he shuddered in his sleep as with the grave-cold. A second time she was awakened on the breast of Almeryl by a dream of the Serpents of the Lake Karatis—the lake of the Jewel; and she stood up, and there was in the street a hum of voices, and she saw there before the house armed men with naked steel in their hands. Scarce had she called Almeryl to her, when the outer door of their house was forced, and she shrieked to him, "'Tis thou they come for: fly, O my Prince, my husband! the way of the garden is clear."

But he said sadly, "Nay, what am I? it is thou they would win from me. I'll leave thee not in this life."

So she cried, "O my soul, then together!—but I shall hinder thee, and be a burden to thy flight."

And she called on the All-powerful for aid, and ran with him into the garden of the house, and lo! by the water side at the end of the garden a boat full of armed soldiers with scimitars. So these fell upon them, and bound them, and haled them into the house again, where was the dark Vizier Aswarak, and certain officers of the night watch with a force. The Vizier cried when he saw them, "I accuse thee, Prince Almeryl, of being here in the city of our lord the King, to conspire against him and his authority."

Almeryl faced the Vizier firmly, and replied, "I knew not in my life I had made an enemy; but there is one here who telleth that of me."

The Vizier frowned, saying, "Thou deniest this? And thou here, and thy father at war with the sovereignty of our lord the King!"

Almeryl beheld his danger, and he said, "Is this so?"

Then cried the Vizier, "Hear him! is not that a fair simulation?" So he called to the guard, "Shackle him!" When that was done, he ordered the house to be sacked, and the women and the slaves he divided for a spoil, but he reserved Bhanavar to himself: and lo! twice she burst away from them that held her to hang upon the lips of Almeryl, and twice was she torn from him as a grape-bunch is torn from the streaming vine, and the third time she swooned and the anguish of life left her.

Now, Bhanavar was borne to the harem of the Vizier, and for days she suffered no morsel of food to enter her mouth, and was dying,

GEORGE MEREDITH

had not the Vizier in the cunning of his dissimulation fed her with distant glimpses of Almeryl, to show her he yet lived. Then she thought, "While my beloved liveth, life is due to me"; and she ate and drank and reassumed her fair fulness and the queenliness that was hers; but the Vizier had no love of her, and respected her, considering in his mind, "Time will exhaust the fury of this tigress, and she is a fruit worth the waiting for. Wullahy! I shall have possessed her ere the days of over-ripening."

There was in the harem of the Vizier a mountain-girl that had been brought there in her childhood, and trained to play upon the lute and accompany her voice with the instrument. To this little damsel Bhanavar gave her heart, and would listen all day, as in a trance, to her luting, till the desire to escape from that bondage and gather tidings of Almeryl mastered her, and she persuaded one of the blacks of the harem with a bribe to procure her an interview with the porter Ukleet. So at a certain hour of the night Ukleet was introduced into the garden of the harem, and he was in the darkness of that garden a white-faced porter with knees that knocked the dread-march together; but Bhanavar strengthened his soul, and he said to her, "'Twas the doing of Boolp the broker: and he whispered the Vizier of thee and thy beauty, O my mistress! Surely thy punishment and this ruin is but part payment to Boolp of the price of the Jewel, the great Jewel that's in the hands of the Vizier."

Then she questioned him: "And Almeryl, the Prince, my husband, what of him?"

Ukleet was dumb, and Bhanavar asked to hear no more. Surely she was at the gates of pale spirits within an hour of her interview with Ukleet, and there was no blessedness for her save in death, the stiffer of ills, the drug that is infallible. As is said:

> *Dark is that last stage of sorrow*
> *Which from Death alone can borrow*
> *Comfort:—*

Bhanavar would have died then, but in a certain pause of her fever the Vizier stood by her. She looked at him long as she lay, and the life in her large eyes was ebbing away slowly; but there seemed presently a check, as an eddy comes in the stream, and the light of intelligence flowed like a reviving fire into her eyes, and her heart quickened with desire of life while she looked on the Vizier. So she passed the pitch of that fever, and bloomed anew in her beauty, and cherished it, for she had a purpose.

Now, there was rejoicing in the harem of the Vizier Aswarak when Bhanavar arose from the couch; and the Vizier exulted, thinking, "I have tamed this wild beauty, or she had reached death in that extremity." So he allowed Bhanavar greater freedom and indulgences, and Bhanavar feigned to give her soul to the pleasures women delight in, and the Vizier buried her in gems and trinkets and costly raiment, robes of exquisite silks, the choicest of Samarcand and China; and he permitted her to make purchases among certain of the warehouses of the city and the shops of the tradesmen, jewellers and others, so that she went about as she would, but for the slaves that attended her and the overseer of the harem. This continued, and Aswarak became urgent with her, and to remove suspicion from him she named a day from that period when she would be his. Meantime she contrived to see Ukleet the porter frequently, and within a week of her engagement with the Vizier she gazed from a lattice-window of the harem, and beheld in the garden, by the beams of the moon, Ukleet, and he was looking as on the watch for her. So she sent to him the little mountain-girl she loved, but Ukleet would tell her nothing; then went she herself, greeting him graciously, for his service was other than that of self-seeking.

Ukleet said, "O Lady, mistress of hearts, moon of the tides of will! 'tis certain I was thy slave from the hour I beheld thee first, and of the Prince, thy husband; Allah rest his soul! Now these be my tidings. Wullahy! the King is one maddened with the reports I've spread about of thy beauty, yea! raging. And I have a friend in his palace, even an under-cook, acute in the interpreting of wishes. There was he always gabbling of thy case, O my Princess, till the head-cook seized hold on it, and so it went to the chamberlain, thence to the chief of the eunuchs, and from him in a natural course, to the King. Now from the King the tracking of this tale went to the under-cook down again, and from him to me. So was I summoned to the King, and the King discoursed with me—I with him, in fair fluency; he in exclamations of desire to have sight of thee, I in expatiation on that he would see when he had his desire. Now in this have I not done thee a service, O sovereign of fancies?"

Bhanavar mused and said, "On the after-morrow I pass through the city to make a selection of goods, and I shall pass at noon by the great mosque, on my way to the shop of Ebn Roulchook, the King's jeweller, beyond the meat-market. Of a surety, I know not how my lord the King may see me."

Said the porter, "'Tis enough! on my head be it." And he went from her, singing the song:

> *How little a thing serves Fortune's turn*
> *When she's intent on doing!*
> *How easily the world may burn*
> *When kings come out a-wooing!*

Now, ere she set forth on the after-morrow to make her purchases, Bhanavar sent word to the Vizier Aswarak that she would see him, and he came to her drunken with alacrity, for he augured favourably that her reluctance was melting toward him: so she said, "O my master, my time of mourning is at an end, and I would look well before thee, even as one worthy of being thy bride; so bestow on me, I pray thee, for my wearing that day, the jewels that be in thy treasury, the brightest and clearest of them, and the largest."

The Vizier Aswarak replied, and he was one in great satisfaction of soul, "All that I have are thine. Wullahy! and one, a marvel, that I bought of Boolp the broker, that had it from an African merchant." So he commanded the box wherein he had deposited the Jewel to be brought to him there in the chamber of Bhanavar, and took forth the Serpent Jewel between his forefinger and thumb, and laughed at the eager eyes of Bhanavar when she beheld it, saying, "'Tis thine! thy bridal gift the day I possess thee."

Bhanavar trembled at the sight of the Jewel, and its redness was to her as the blood of Zurvan and Almeryl. She stretched her hand out for it and cried, "This day, O my lord, make it mine."

So the Vizier said, "Nay, what I have spoken will I keep to; it has cost me much."

Bhanavar looked at him, and uttered in a soft tone, "Truly it has cost thee much."

Then she exclaimed, as in play, "See me, how I look by its beam." And in her guile she snatched the Jewel from him, and held it to her brow. Then Aswarak started from her and feared her, for the red light of the Jewel glowed, and darkened the chamber with its beam, darkening all save the lustre that was on the visage of Bhanavar. He shouted, "What's this! Art thou a sorceress?"

She removed the Jewel, and ceased glaring on him, and said, "Nothing but thy poor slave!"

Then he coaxed her to give him the Jewel, and she would not; he commanded her peremptorily, and she hesitated; so he grasped her tightened hand, and his face loured with wrath; yet she withheld the Jewel from him laughing; and he was stirred to extreme wrath, and drew from his girdle the naked scimitar, and menaced her with it. And he looked mighty; but she dreaded him little, and stood her full height before him, daring him, and she was as the tigress defending a cub from a wilder beast. Now when he was about to call in the armed slaves of the palace, she said, "I warn thee, Vizier Aswarak! tempt me not to match them that serve me with them that serve thee."

He ground his teeth in fury, crying, "A conspiracy! and in the harem! Now, thou traitress! the logic of the lash shall be tried upon thee." And he roared, "Ho! ye without there! ho!"

But ere the slaves had entered Bhanavar rubbed the Jewel on her bosom, muttering, "I have forborne till now! Now will I have a sacrifice, though I be it." And rubbing the Jewel, she sang,

> *Hither! hither!*
> *Come to your Queen;*
> *Come through the grey wall,*
> *Come through the green!*

There was heard a noise like the noise of a wind coming down a narrow gorge above falling waters, a hissing and a rushing of wings, and behold! Bhanavar was circled by rings and rings of serpent-folds that glowed round her, twisted each in each, with the fierceness of fire, she like a flame rising up white in the midst of them. The black slaves, when they had lifted the curtain of the harem-chamber, shrieked to see her, and Aswarak crouched at her feet with the aspect of an angry beast carved in stone. Then Bhanavar loosed on either of the slaves a serpent, saying, "What these have seen they shall not say." And while the sweat dropped heavily from the forehead of Aswarak, she stepped out of the circle of serpents, singing,

> *Over! over!*
> *Hie to the lake!*
> *Sleep with the left eye,*
> *Keep the right awake.*

Then the serpents spread with a great whirr, and flew through the high window and the walls as they had come, and she said to the Vizier, "What now? Fearest thou? I have spared thee, thou that madest me desolate! and thy slaves are a sacrifice for thee. Now this I ask: Where lies my beloved, the Prince my husband? Speak nothing of him, save the place of his burial!"

So he told her, "In the burial-ground of the great prison."

She rolled her eyes on the Vizier darkly, exclaiming, "Even where the felons lie entombed, he lieth!" And she began to pant, pale with what she had done, and leaned to the floor, and called,

> *Yellow stripe, with freckle red,*
> *Coil and curl, and watch by my head.*

And a serpent with yellow stripes and red freckles came like a javelin down to her, and coiled and curled round her head, and she slept an hour. When she arose the Vizier was yet there, sitting with folded knees. So she sped the serpent to the Lake Karatis, and called her women to her, and went to an inner room, and drew an outer robe and a vest over that she had on, and passed the Vizier, and said, "Art thou not rejoiced in thy bride, O Aswarak? 'Twas a wondrous clemency, hers! Now but four more days and thou claimest her. Say nothing of what thou hast seen, or thou wilt shortly see nothing further to say, my master."

So she left the Vizier sitting still in that chamber, and mounted a mule, attended by slaves on foot before and behind her, and passed through the streets till she came to the shop of Ebn Roulchook. The King was in disguise at the extremity of the shop, and while she examined this and that of the precious stones, Bhanavar for a moment made bare the beauty, of her face, and love's fires took fast hold of the King, and he cried, "I marvel not at the eloquence of the porter."

Now, she made Ebn Roulchook bring to her a circlet of gold, with a hollow in the frontal centre, and fit into that hollow the Serpent Jewel. So, while she laughed and chatted with her women Bhanavar lifted the circlet, and made her countenance wholly bare even to the neck and the beginning slope of the bosom, and fixed the circlet to her head with the Jewel burning on her brow. Then when he beheld the glory of excelling loveliness that she was, and the splendour in her eyes under the Jewel, the King shouted and parted with his disguise, and Ebn Roulchook and the women and slaves with Bhanavar fled to the courtyard that was behind the shop, leaving Bhanavar alone with the King. Surely Bhanavar returned not to the dwelling of the Vizier.

Now, the King Mashalleed espoused Bhanavar, and she became his queen and ruled him, and her word was the dictate of the land. Then caused she the body of Almeryl, with the severed head of the Prince, to be disinterred, and entombed secretly in the palace; and she had lamps lit in the vault, and the pall spread, and the readers of the Koran to read by the tomb; and then she stole to the tomb hourly, in the day and in the night, wailing of him and her utter misery, repeating verses at the side of the tomb, and they were,

*Take me to thee!*
*Like the deep-rooted tree,*
*My life is half in earth, and draws*
*Thence all sweetness; oh may my being pause*
*Soon beside thee!*

*Welcome me soon!*
*As to the queenly moon,*
*Man's homage to my beauty sets;*
*Yet am I a rose-shrub budding regrets:*
*Welcome me soon.*

*Soul of my soul!*
*Have me not half, but whole.*
*Dear dust, thou art my eyes, my breath!*
*Draw me to thee down the dark sea of death,*
*Soul of my soul!*

And she sang:

*Sad are they who drink life's cup*
*Till they have come to the bitter-sweet:*
*Better at once to toss it up,*
*And trample it beneath the feet;*
*For venom-charged as serpents' eggs*
*'Tis then, and knows not other change.*
*Early, early, early, have I reached the dregs*
*Of life, and loathe and love the bittersweet, revenge!*

GEORGE MEREDITH

Then turned she aside, and sang musingly:

> *I came to his arms like the flower of the spring,*
> *And he was my bird of the radiant wing:*
> *He flutter'd above me a moment, and won*
> *The bliss of my breast as a beam of the sun,*
> *Untouch'd and untasted till then—*

The voice in her throat was like a drowning creature, and she rose up, and chanted wildly:

> *I weep again?*

> *What play is this? for the thing is dead in me long since:*
> *Will all the reviving rain*
> *Of heaven bring me back my Prince?*
> *But I, when I weep, when I weep,*
> *Blood will I weep!*
> *And when I weep,*
> *Sons for fathers shall weep;*
> *Mothers for sons shall weep;*
> *Wives for husbands shall weep!*
> *Earth shall complain of floods red and deep,*
> *When I weep!*

Upon that she ran up a secret passage to her chamber and rubbed the Jewel, and called the serpents, to delight her soul with the sight of her power, and rolled and sported madly among them, clutching them by the necks till their thin little red tongues hung out, and their eyes were as discoloured blisters of venom. Then she arose, and her arms and neck and lips were glazed with the slime of the serpents, and she flung off her robes to the close-fitting silken inner vest looped across her bosom with pearls, and whirled in a mazy dance-measure among them, and sang melancholy melodies, making them delirious, fascinating them; and they followed her round and round, in twines and twists and curves, with arched heads and stiffened tails; and the chamber swam like an undulating sea of shifting sapphire lit by the moon of midnight. Not before the moon of midnight was in the sky ceased Bhanavar sporting with the serpents, and she sank to sleep exhausted in their midst.

Such was the occupation of the Queen of Mashalleed when he came not to her. The women and slaves of the palace dreaded her, and the King himself was her very slave.

Meanwhile the plot of her unforgivingness against Aswarak ripened: and the Vizier beholding the bride he had lost Queen of Mashalleed his master, it was as she conceived, that his heart was eaten with jealousy and fierce rage. Bhanavar as she came across him spake mildly, and gave him gentle looks, sad glances, suffering not his fires to abate, the torment of his love to cool. Each night he awoke with a serpent in his bed; the beam of her beauty was as the constant bite of a serpent, poisoning his blood, and he deluded his soul with the belief that Bhanavar loved him notwithstanding, and that she was seized forcibly from him by the King. "Otherwise," thought he, "why loosed she not a serpent from the host to strangle me even as yonder black slaves?" Bhanavar knew the mind of Aswarak, and considered, "The King is cunning and weak, a slave to his desires, and in the bondage of the jewel, my beauty. The Vizier is unscrupulous, a hatcher of intrigues; but that he dreads me and hopes a favour of me, he would have wrought against me ere now. 'Tis then a combat 'twixt him and me. O my soul, art thou dreaming of a fair youth that was the bliss of thy bosom night and day, night and day? The Vizier shall die!"

One morning, and it was a year from the day she had become Queen of Mashalleed, Bhanavar sprang up quickly from the side of the King; and he was gazing on her in amazement and loathing. She flew to her chamber, chasing forth her women, and ran to a mirror. Therein she saw three lines that were on her brow, lines of age, and at the corners of her mouth and about her throat a slackness of skin, the skin no longer its soft rosy white, but withered brown as leaves of the forest. She shrieked, and fell back in a swoon of horror. When she recovered, she ran to the mirror again, and it was the same sight. And she rose from swooning a third time, and still she beheld the visage of a hag; nothing of beauty there save the hair and the brilliant eyes. Then summoned she the serpents in a circle, and the number of them was that of the days in the year: and she bared her wrist and seized one, a gray-silver with sapphire spots, and hissed at him till he hissed, and foam whitened the lips of each. Thereupon she cried:

> *Treble-tongue and throat of hell,*
> *What is come upon me, tell!*

GEORGE MEREDITH

And the Serpent replied,

> *Jewel Queen! beauty's price!*
> *'Tis the time for sacrifice!*

She grasped another, one of leaden colour, with yellow bars and silver crescents, and cried:

> *Treble-tongue and throat of fire,*
> *Name the creature ye require!*

And the Serpent replied:

> *Ruby lip! poison tooth!*
> *We are hungry for a youth.*

She grasped another that writhed in her fingers like liquid emerald, and cried:

> *Treble-tongue and throat of glue!*
> *How to know the one that's due?*

And the Serpent replied:

> *Breast of snow! baleful bliss!*
> *He that wooing wins a kiss.*

She clutched one at her elbow, a hairy serpent with yellow languid eyes in flame-sockets and livid-lustrous length—a disease to look on, and cried:

> *Treble-tongue and throat of gall!*
> *There's a youth beneath the pall.*

And the Serpent replied:

> *Brilliant eye! bloody tear!*
> *He has fed us for a year.*

She squeezed that hairy serpent till her finger-points whitened in his neck, and he dropped lifelessly, crying:

> *Treble-tongues and things of mud!*
> *Sprang my beauty from his blood?*

And the Serpents rose erect, replying:

> *Yearly one of us must die;*
> *Yearly for us dieth one;*
> *Else the Queen an ugly lie*
> *Lives till all our lives be done!*

Bhanavar stood up, and hurried them to Karatis. When she was alone she fell toward the floor, repeating, "'Tis the Curse!" Suddenly she thought, "Yet another year my beauty shall be nourished by my vengeance, yet another! And, O Vizier, the kiss shall be thine, the kiss of doom; for I have doomed thee ere now. Thou, thou shalt restore me to my beauty: that only love I now my Prince is lost."

So she veiled her face in the close veil of the virtuous, and despatched Ukleet, whom she exalted in the palace of the King, to the Vizier; and Ukleet stood before Aswarak, and said, "O Vizier, my mistress truly is longing for you with excessive longing, and in what she now undergoeth is forgotten an evil done by you to her; and she bids you come and concert with her a scheme deliberately as to the getting rid of this tyrant who is an affliction to her, and her life is lessened by him."

The Vizier was deceived by his passion, and he chuckled and exclaimed, "My very dream! and to mind me of her, then, she sent the serpents! Wullahy, in the matter of women, wait! For, as the poet declareth:

> *"Tis vanity our souls for such to vex;*
> *Patience is a harvest of the sex.'*

And they fret themselves not overlong for husbands that are gone, these young beauties. I know them. Tell the Queen of Serpents I am even hers to the sole of my foot."

So it was understood between them that the Vizier should be at the gate of the garden of the palace that night, disguised; and the Vizier

GEORGE MEREDITH

rejoiced, thinking, "If she have not the Jewel with her, it shall go ill with me, and I foiled this time!"

Ukleet then proceeded to the house of Boolp the broker, fronting the gutted ruins where Bhanavar had been happy in her innocence with Almeryl, the mountain prince, her husband. Boolp was engaged haggling with a slave-merchant the price of a fair slave, and Ukleet said to him, "Yet awhile delay, O Boolp, ere you expend a fraction of treasure, for truly a mighty bargain of jewels is waiting for you at the palace of my lord the King. So come thither with all your money-bags of gold and silver, and your securities, and your bonds and dues in writing, for 'tis the favourite of the King requireth you to complete a bargain with her, and the price of her jewels is the price of a kingdom."

Said Boolp, "Hearing is compliance in such a case."

And Ukleet continued, "What a fortune is yours, O Boolp! truly the tide of fortune setteth into your lap. Fail not, wullahy! to come with all you possess, or if you have not enough when she requireth it to complete the bargain, my mistress will break off with you. I know not if she intend even other game for you, O lucky one!"

Boolp hitched his girdle and shrugged, saying, "'Tis she will fail, I wot,—she, in having therewith to complete the bargain between us. Wa! wa!—there! I've done this before now. Wullahy! if she have not enough of her rubies and pearls to outweigh me and my gold, go to, Boolp will school her! What says the poet?—

> 'Earth and ocean search, East, West, and North, to the South,
> None will match the bright rubies and pearls of her mouth.'"

"Aha! what? O Ukleet! And he says:

> 'The lovely ones a bargain made
> With me, and I renounced my trade,
> Half-ruined; "Ah!" said they, "return and win!
> To even scales ourselves we will throw in!"'

How so? But let discreetness reign and security flourisheth!"
Ukleet nodded at him, and repeated the distich:

> Men of worth and men of wits
> Shoot with two arrows, and make two hits.

So he arranged with Boolp the same appointment as with the Vizier, and returned to Queen Bhanavar.

Now, in the dark of night Aswarak stood within the gate of the palace-garden of Mashalleed that was ajar, and a hand from a veiled figure reached to him, and he caught it, in the fulness of his delusion, crying, "Thou, my Queen?" But the hand signified silence, and drew him past the tank of the garden and through a court of the palace into a passage lit with lamps, and on into a close-curtained chamber, and beyond a heavy curtain into another, a circular passage descending between black hangings, and at the bottom a square vault draped with black, and in it precious woods burning, oils in censers, and the odour of ambergris and myrrh and musk floating in clouds, and the sight of the Vizier was for a time obscured by the thickness of the incenses floating. As he became familiar with the place, he saw marked therein a board spread at one end with viands and wines, and the nosegay in a water-vase, and cups of gold and a service of gold,— every preparation for feasting mightily. So the soul of Aswarak leapt, and he cried, "Now unveil thyself, O moon of our meeting, my mistress!"

The voice of Bhanavar answered him, "Not till we have feasted and drunken, and it seemeth little in our eyes. Surely the chamber is secure: could I have chosen one better for our meeting, O Aswarak?"

Upon that he entreated her to sit with him to the feast, but she cried, "Nay! delay till the other is come."

Cried he, "Another?"

But she exclaimed, "Hush!" and saying thus went forward to the foot of the passage, and Boolp was there, following Ukleet, both of them under a weight of bags and boxes. So she welcomed the broker, and led him to the feast, he coughing and wheezing and blinking, unwitting the vexation of the Vizier, nor that one other than himself was there. When Boolp heard the voice of the Vizier, in astonishment, addressing him, he started back and fell upon his bags, and the task of coaxing him to the board was as that of haling a distempered beast to the water. Then they sat and feasted together, and Ukleet with them; and if Aswarak or Boolp waxed impatient of each other's presence, he whispered to them, "Only wait! see what she reserveth for you." And Bhanavar mused with herself, "Truly that reserved shall be not long coming!" So they drank, and wine got the mastery of Aswarak, so that he made no secret of his passion, and began to lean to her and verse extemporaneously in her ear; and she stinted not in her replies, answering to his urgency in girlish guise, sighing behind the veil, as if under love's influence. And the Vizier pressed close, and sang:

> 'Tis said that love brings beauty to the cheeks
> Of them that love and meet, but mine are pale;
> For merciless disdain on me she wreaks,
> And hides her visage from my passionate tale:
> I have her only, only when she speaks.
> Bhanavar, unveil!
>
> I have thee, and I have thee not! Like one
> Lifted by spirits to a shining dale
> In Paradise, who seeks to leap and run
> And clasp the beauty, but his foot doth fail,
> For he is blind: ah! then more woful none!
> Bhanavar, unveil!

He thrust the wine-cup to her, and she lifted it under her veil, and then sang, in answer to him:

> My beauty! for thy worth
> Thank the Vizier!
>
> He gives thee second birth:
> Thank the Vizier!
>
> His blooming form without a fault:
> Thank the Vizier!
>
> Is at thy foot in this blest vault:
> Thank the Vizier!
>
> He knoweth not he telleth such a truth,
> Thank the Vizier!
>
> That thou, thro' him, spring'st fresh in blushing youth:
> Thank the Vizier!

*He knoweth little now, but he shall soon be wise:*
*Thank the Vizier!*

*This meeting bringeth bloom to cheeks and lips and eyes:*
*Thank the Vizier!*

*O my beloved in this blest vault, if I love thee for aye,*
*Thank the Vizier!*

*Thine am I, thine! and learns his soul what it has taught—to die,*
*Thank the Vizier!*

Now, Aswarak divined not her meaning, and was enraptured with her, and cried, "Wullahy! so and such thy love! Thine am I, thine! And what a music is thy voice, O my mistress! 'Twere a bliss to Eblis in his torment could he hear it. Life of my head! and is thy beauty increased by me? Nay, thou flatterer!" Then he said to her, "Away with these importunate dogs! 'tis the very hour of tenderness! Wullahy! they offend my nostril: stung am I at the sight of them."

She rejoined,—

*O Aswarak! star of the morn!*
*Thou that wakenest my beauty from night and scorn,*
*Thy time is near, and when 'tis come,*
*Long will a jackal howl that this thy request had been dumb.*
*O Aswarak! star of the morn!*

So the Vizier imaged in his mind the neglect of Mashalleed from these words, and said, "Leave the King to my care, O Queen of Serpents, and expend no portion of thy power on him; but hasten now the going of these fellows; my heart is straitened by them, and I, wullahy! would gladly see a serpent round the necks of either."

She continued,—

*O Aswarak! star of the morn!*
*Lo! the star must die when splendider light is born;*
*In stronger floods the beam will drown:*
*Shrink, thou puny orb, and dread to bring me my crown,*
*O Aswarak! star of the morn!*

Then said she, "Hark awhile at those two! There's a disputation between them."

So they hearkened, and Ukleet was pledging Boolp, and passing the cup to him; but a sullenness had seized the broker, and he refused it, and Ukleet shouted, "Out, boon-fellow! and what a company art thou, that thou refusest the pledge of friendliness? Plague on all sulkers!"

And the broker, the old miser, obstinate as are the half-fuddled, began to mumble, "I came not here to drink, O Ukleet, but to make a bargain; and my bags be here, and I like not yonder veil, nor the presence of yonder Vizier, nor the secresy of this. Now, by the Prophet and that interdict of his, I'll drink no further."

And Ukleet said, "Let her not mark your want of fellowship, or 'twill go ill with you. Here be fine wines, spirited wines! choice flavours! and you drink not! Where's the soul in you, O Boolp, and where's the life in you, that you yield her to the Vizier utterly? Surely she waiteth a gallant sign from you, so challenge her cheerily."

Quoth Boolp, "I care not. Shall I leave my wealth and all I possess void of eyes? and she so that I recognise her not behind the veil?"

Ukleet pushed the old miser jeeringly: "You not recognise her? Oh, Boolp, a pretty dissimulation! Pledge her now a cup to the snatching of the veil, and bethink you of a fitting verse, a seemly compliment,— something sugary."

Then Boolp smoothed his head, and was bothered; and tapped it, and commenced repeating to Bhanavar:

> *I saw the moon behind a cloud,*
> *And I was cold as one that's in his shroud:*
> *And I cried, Moon!—*

Ukleet chorused him, "Moon!" and Boolp was deranged in what he had to say, and gasped,—

> *Moon! I cried, Moon!—and I cried, Moon!*

Then the Vizier and Ukleet laughed till they fell on their backs; so Bhanavar took up his verse where he left it, singing,—

*And to the cry*
*Moon did make fair the following reply:*
*"Dotard, be still! for thy desire*
*Is to embrace consuming fire."*

Then said Boolp, "O my mistress, the laws of conviviality have till now restrained me; but my coming here was on business, and with me my bags, in good faith. So let us transact this matter of the jewels, and after that the song of—

*'Thou and I*
*A cup will try,'*

even as thou wilt."

Bhanavar threw aside her outer robe and veil, and appeared in a dress of sumptuous blue, spotted with gold bees; her face veiled with a veil of gauzy silver, and she was as the moon in summer heavens, and strode mar jestically forward, saying, "The jewels? 'tis but one. Behold!"

The lamps were extinguished, and in her hand was the glory of the Serpent Jewel, no other light save it in the vaulted chamber.

So the old miser perked his chin and brows, and cried wondering, "I know it, this Jewel, O my mistress."

She turned to the Vizier, and said, lifting the red gloom of the Jewel on him, "And thou?"

Aswarak ate his under-lip.

Then she cried, "There's much ye know in common, ye two."

Thereupon Bhanavar passed from the feast on to the centre of the vault, and stood before the tomb of Almeryl, and drew the cloth from it; and they saw by the glow of the Jewel that it was a tomb. When she had mounted some steps at the side of the tomb, she beckoned them to come, crying, in a voice of sobs, "This which is here, likewise ye may know."

So they came with the coldness of a mystery in their blood, and looked as she looked intently over a tomb. The lid was of glass, and through the glass of the lid the Jewel flung a dark rosy ray on the body of Almeryl lying beneath it.

Now, the miser was perplexed at the sight; but Aswarak stepped backward in defiance, bellowing, "'Twas for this I was tricked to come here! Is't fooling me a second time? By Allah! look to it; not a second time will Aswarak be fooled."

GEORGE MEREDITH

Then she ran to him, and exclaimed, "Fooled? For what cam'st thou to me?"

And he, foaming and grinding his breath, "Thou woman of wiles! thou serpent! but I'll be gone from here."

So she faltered in sweetness, knowing him doomed, and loving to dally with him in her wickedness, "Indeed if thou cam'st not for my kiss—"

Then said the Vizier, "Yet a further guile! Was't not an outrage to bring me here?"

She faltered again, leaning the fair length of her limbs on a couch, "'Tis ill that we are not alone, else could these lips convince thee well: else indeed!"

And the Vizier cried, "Chase then these intruders from us, O thou sorceress, and above all serpents in power! for thou poisonest with a touch; and the eye and the ear alike take in thy poisons greedily. Thou overcomest the senses, the reason, the judgment; yea, vindictiveness, wrath, suspicions; leading the soul captive with a breath of thine, as 'twere a breeze from the gardens of bliss."

Bhanavar changed her manner a little, lisping, "And why that starting from the tomb of a dead harmless youth? And that abuse of me?"

He peered at her inquiringly, echoing "Why?"

And she repeated, as a child might repeat it, "Why that?"

Then the Vizier smote his forehead in the madness of utter perplexity, changing his eye from Bhanavar to the tomb of Almeryl, doubting her truth, yet dreading to disbelieve it. So she saw him fast enmeshed in her subtleties, and clapped her hands crying, "Come again with me to the tomb, and note if there be aught I am to blame in, O Aswarak, and plight thyself to me beside it."

He did nothing save to widen his eye at her somewhat; and she said, "The two are yonside the tomb, and they hear us not, and see us not by this light of the Jewel; so come up to it boldly with me; free thy mind of its doubt, and for a reconcilement kiss me on the way."

Aswarak moved not forward; but as Bhanavar laid the Jewel in her bosom he tore the veil from her darkened head, and caught her to him and kissed her. Then Bhanavar laughed and shouted, "How is it with thee, Vizier Aswarak?"

He was tottering, and muttered, "'Tis a death-chill hath struck me even to my marrow."

So she drew the Jewel forth once more, and rubbed it ablaze, and the noise of the Serpents neared; and they streamed into the vault and under it in fiery jets, surrounding Bhanavar, and whizzing about her till in their velocity they were indivisible; and she stood as a fountain of fire clothed in flashes of the underworld, the new loveliness of her face growing vivid violet like an incessant lightning above them. Then stretched she her two hands, and sang to the Serpents:—

*Hither, hither, to the feast!*
*Hither to the sacrifice!*
*Virtue for my sake hath ceased:*
*Now to make an end of Vice!*

*Twisted-tail and treble-tongue,*
*Swelling length and greedy maw!*
*I have had a horrid wrong;*
*Retribution is the law!*

*Ye that suck'd my youthful lord,*
*Now shall make another meal:*
*Seize the black Vizier abhorr'd;*
*Seize him! seize him throat and heel!*

*Set your serpent wits to find*
*Tortures of a new device:*
*Have him! have him heart and mind!*
*"Hither to the sacrifice"*

Then she whirled with them round and round as a tempest whirls; and when she had wound them to a fury, lo, she burst from the hissing circle and dragged Ukleet from the vault into the passage, and blocked the entrance to the vault. So was Queen Bhanavar avenged.

Now, she said to Ukleet, "Ransom presently the broker,—him they will not harm," and hastened to the King that he might see her in her beauty. The King reclined on cushions in the harem with a fair slave-girl, newly from the mountains, toying with the pearls in her locks. Then thought Bhanavar, "Let him not slight me!" So she drew a rose-coloured veil over her face and sat beside Mashalleed. The King continued his fondling with the girl, saying to her, "Was there no destiny foretold of thy coming to the palace of the King to rule it, O Nashta, starbeam in the waters! and hadst thou no dream of it?"

Bhanavar struck the King's arm, but he noticed her not, and Nashta laughed. Then Bhanavar controlled her trembling and said, "A word, O King! and vouchsafe me a hearing."

The King replied languidly, still looking on Nashta, "'Tis a command that the voice of none that are crabbed and hideous be heard in the harem, and I find comfort in it, O Nashta! but speak thou, my fountain of sweet-dropping lute-notes!"

Bhanavar caught the King's hand and said, "I have to speak with thee; 'tis the Queen. Chase from us this little wax puppet a space."

The King disengaged his hand and leaned it over to Nashta, who began playing with it, and fitting on it a ring, giggling. Then, as he answered nothing, Bhanavar came nearer and slapped him on the cheek. Mashalleed started to his feet, and his hand grasped his girdle; but that wrathfulness was stayed when he beheld the veil slide from her visage. So he cried, "My Queen! my soul!"

She pointed to Nashta, and the King chid the girl, and sent her forth lean with his shifted displeasure, as a kitten slinks wet from a fish-pond where it had thought to catch a great fish. Then Bhanavar exclaimed, "There was a change in thy manner to me before that creature."

He sought to dissimulate with her, but at last he confessed, "I was truly this morning the victim of a sorcery."

Thereupon she cried, "And thou went angered to find me not by thee on the couch, but one in my place, a hag of ugliness. Hear then the case, O Mashalleed! Surely that old crone had a dream, and it was that if she slept one night by the King she would arise fresh in health from her ills, and with powers lasting a year to heal others of all maladies with a touch. So she came to me, petitioning me to bring this about. O my lord the King, did I well in being privy to her desire?"

The King could not doubt this story of Bhanavar, seeing her constant loveliness, and the arch of her flashing brow, and the oval of her cheek and chin smooth as milk. So he said, "O my Queen! I had thought to go, as I must, gladly; but how shall I go, knowing thy truth, thy beauty unchanged; thee faithful, a follower of the injunctions of the Prophet in charitable deeds?"

Cried she, "And whither goeth my lord, and on what errand?"

He answered, "The people of a province southward have raised the standard of revolt and mocked my authority; they have been joined by certain of the Arab chiefs subject to my dominion, and have defeated my armies. 'Tis to subdue them I go; yea, to crush them. Yet, wallaby! I know not. Care I if kingdoms fall away, and nations, so that I have thee? Nay, let all pass, so that thou remain by me."

Bhanavar paced from him to a mirror, and frowned at the reflection of her fairness, thinking, "Such had he spoken to the girl Nashta, or another, this King!" And she thought, "I have been beloved by the noblest three on earth; I will ask no more of love; vengeance I have had. 'Tis time that I demand of my beauty nothing save power, and I will make this King my stepping-stone to power, rejoicing my soul with the shock of armies."

Now, she persuaded Mashalleed to take her with him on his expedition against the Arabs; and they set forth, heading a great assemblage of warriors, southward to the land bordering the Desert. The King credited the suggestions of Bhanavar, that Aswarak had disappeared to join the rebels, and pressed forward in his eagerness to inflict a chastisement signal in swiftness upon them and that traitor; so eagerly Mashalleed journeyed to his army in advance, that the main body, with Bhanavar, was left by him long behind. She had encouraged him, saying, "I shall love thee much if thou art speedy in winning success." The Queen was housed on an elephant, harnessed with gold, and with silken purple trappings; from the rose-hued curtains of her palanquin she looked on a mighty march of warriors, filling the extent of the plains; all day she fed her sight on them. Surely the story of her beauty became noised among the guards of her person that rode and ran beneath the royal elephant, till the soldiers of Mashalleed spake but of the beauty of the Queen, and Bhanavar was as a moon shining over that sea of men.

Now, they had passed the cultivated fields, and were halting by the ford of a river bordering the Desert, when lo! a warrior on the yonside, riding in a cloud of dust, and his shout was, "The King Mashalleed is defeated, and flying." Then the Captains of the host witnessed to the greatness of Allah, and were troubled with a dread, fearing to advance; but Bhanavar commanded a horse to be saddled for her, and mounted it, and plunged through the ford singly; so they followed her, and all day she rode forward on horseback, touching neither food nor drink. By night she was a league beyond the foremost of them, and fell upon the King encamped in the Desert, with the loose remnant of his forces. Mashalleed, when he had looked on her, forgot his affliction, and stood up to embrace her, but Bhanavar spurned him, crying, "A time for this in the time of disgrace?" Then she said, "How came it?"

He answered, "There was a Chief among the enemy, an Arab, before the terror of whom my people fled."

Cried she, "Conquer him on the morrow, and till then I eat not, drink not, sleep not."

On the morrow Mashalleed again encountered the rebels, and Bhanavar, seated on her elephant, from a sand-hillock under a palm, beheld the prowess of the Arab Chief and the tempest of battle that he was. She thought, "I have seen but one mighty in combat like that one, Ruark, the Chief of the Beni-Asser." Thereupon she coursed toward the King, even where the arrows gloomed like locusts, thick and dark in the air aloof, and said, "The victory is with yonder Chief! Hurl on him three of thy sons of valour."

The three were selected, and made onslaught on this Chief, and perished under his arm.

Bhanavar saw them fall, and exclaimed, "Another attack on him, and with thrice three!"

Her will was the mandate of Mashalleed, and these likewise were ordered forth, and closed on the Chief, but he darted from their toils and wheeled about them, spearing them one by one till the nine were in the dust. Bhanavar compressed her dry lips and muttered to the King, "Head thou a body against him."

Mashalleed gathered round his standard the chosen of his warriors, and smoothed his beard, and headed them. Then the Chief struck his lance behind him, and stretched rapidly a half-circle across the sand, and halted on a knoll. When they neared him he retreated in a further half-circle, and continued this wise, wasting the fury of Mashalleed, till he stood among his followers. There, as the King hesitated and prepared to retreat, he and the others of the tribe levelled their lances and hung upon his rear, fretting them, slaughtering captains of the troop. When Mashalleed turned to face his pursuer, the Chief was alone, immovable on his mare, fronting the ranks. Then Bhanavar taunted the King, and he essayed the capture of that Chief a second time and a third, and it was each time as the first. Bhanavar looked about her with rapid eyes, murmuring, "Oh, what a Chief is he! Oh that a cloud would fall, a smoke arise, to blind these hosts, that I might sling my serpents on him unseen, for I will not be vanquished, though it be by Ruark!" So she drew to the King, and the altercation between them was fierce in the fury of the battle, he saying, "'Tis a feint of the Chief, this challenge; and I must succour the left of my army by the well, that he is overmatching with numbers"; and she, "If thou head them not, then will I, and thou shalt behold a woman do what thou durst not, and lose her love and win her scorn." While they spake the Arabs they looked on seemed to flutter and waver, and the Chief was backing to them, calling to them as 'twere words of shame to rally them. Seeing this, Mashalleed charged against the Chief once more, and lo! the Arabs opened to receive him, closing on his band of warriors like waters whitened by the storm on a fleet of swift-scudding vessels: and there was a dust and a tumult visible, such as is seen in the darkness when a vessel struck by the lightning-bolt is sinking—flashes of steel, lifting of hands, rolling of horsemen and horses. Then Bhanavar groaned aloud, "They are lost! Shame to us! only one hope is left-that 'tis Ruark, this Chief!" Now, the view of the plain cleared, and with it she beheld the army of Mashalleed broken, the King borne down by a dust of Arabs; so she unveiled her face and rode on the host with the horsemen that guarded her, glorious with a crown of gold and the glowing Jewel on her brow. When she was a javelin's flight from them the Arabs shouted and paused in terror, for the light of her head was as the sun setting between clouds of thunder; but that Chief dashed forward like a flame beaten level by the wind, crying, "Bhanavar; Bhanavar!" and she knew the features of Ruark; so she said, "Even I!" And he cried again, "Bhanavar! Bhanavar!" and was as one stricken by a shaft. Then Bhanavar threw on him certain of the horsemen with her, and he suffered them without a sign to surround him and grasp his mare by the bridle-rein, and bring him, disarmed, before the Queen. At sight of Ruark a captive the Arabs fell into confusion, and lost heart, and were speedily chased and scattered from the scene like a loose spray before the wind; but Mashalleed the King rejoiced mightily and praised Bhanavar, and the whole army of the King praised her, magnifying her.

Now, with Ruark she interchanged no syllable, and said not farewell to him when she departed with Mashalleed, to encounter other tribes; and the Chief was bound and conducted a prisoner to the city of the inland sea, and cast into prison, in expectation of Death the releaser, and continued there wellnigh a year, eating the bitter bread of captivity. In the evening of every seventh day there came to him a little mountain girl, that sat by him and leaned a lute to her bosom, singing of the mountain and the desert, but he turned his face from her to the wall. One day she sang of Death the releaser, and Ruark thought, "'Tis come! she warneth me! Merciful is Allah!" On the morning that followed Ukleet entered the cell, and with him three slaves, blacks, armed with scimitars. So Ruark stood up and bore witness to his faith, saying, "Swift with the stroke!" but Ukleet exclaimed, "Fear not! the end is not yet."

Then said he, "Peace with thee! These slaves, O Chief, excelling in martial qualities! surely they're my retinue, and the retinue of them of my rank in the palace; and where I go they go; for the exalted have more shadows than one! yea, three have they in my case, even very grimly black shadows, whereon the idle expend not laughter, and whoso joketh in their hearing, 'tis, wullahy! the last joke of that person. In such-wise are the powerful known among men, they that stand very prominent in the beams of prosperity! Now this of myself; but for thee—of a surety the Queen Bhanavar, my mistress, will be here by the time of the rising of the moon. In the name of Allah!" Saying that he departed in his greatness, and Ruark watched for her that rose in his soul as the moon in the heavens.

Meanwhile Bhanavar had mused, "'Tis this day, the day when the Serpents desire their due, and the King Mashalleed they shall have; for what is life to him but a treachery and a dalliance, and what is my hold on him but this Jewel of the Serpents? He has had the profit of beauty, and he shall yield the penalty: my kiss is for him, my serpent-kiss. And I will release Ruark, and espouse him, and war with kings, sultans, emperors, infidels, subduing them till they worship me."

She flashed her figure in the glass, and was lovely therein as one in the light of Paradise; but ere she reached the King Mashalleed, lo! the hour of the Serpents had struck, and her beauty melted from her as snow melts from off the rock; and she was suddenly haggard in utter uncomeliness, and knew it not, but marched, smiling a grand smile, on to the King. Now as Mashalleed lifted his eyes to her he started amazed, crying, "The hag again!" and she said, "What of the hag, O my lord the King?" Thereat he was yet more amazed, and exclaimed, "The hag of ugliness with the voice of Bhanavar! Has then the Queen lent that loathsomeness her voice also?"

Bhanavar chilled a moment, and looked on the faces of the women present, and they were staring at her, the younger ones tittering, and among them Nashta, whom she hated. So she cried, "Away with ye!" But the King commanded them, "Stay!" Then the Queen leaned to him, saying, "I will speak with my lord alone"; whereat he shrank from her, and spat. Ice and flame shivered through the blood of Bhanavar, yet such was her eagerness to give the kiss to Mashalleed, that she leaned to him, still wooing him to her with smiles. Then the King seized her violently, and flung her over the marble floor to the very basin of the fountain, and the crown that was on her brow fell and rolled to the feet of Nashta. The girl lifted it, laughing, and was in the act of fitting it to her fair head amid the chuckles of her companions, when a slap from the hand of Bhanavar spun her twice round, and she dropped to the marble insensible. The King bellowed in wrath, and ran to Nashta, crying to the Queen, "Surrender that crown to her, foul hag!" But Bhanavar had bent over the basin of the fountain, and beheld the image of her change therein, and was hurrying from the hall and down the corridors of the palace to the private chamber. So he made bare the steel by his side, and followed her with a number of the harem guard, menacing her, and commanding her to surrender the crown with the Jewel. Ere she could lay hand on a veil, he was beside her, and she was encompassed. In that extremity Bhanavar plucked the Jewel from her crown, and rubbed it, calling the Serpents to her. One came, one only, and that one would not move from her to sling himself about the neck of Mashalleed, but whirled round her, hissing:

*Every hour a serpent dies,*
*Till we have the sacrifice:*
*Sweeten, sweeten, with thy kiss,*
*Quick! a soul for Karatis.*

Surely the King bit his breath, marvelling, and his fury became an awful fear, and he fell back from her, molesting her no further. Then she squeezed the serpent till his body writhed in knots, and veiled herself, and sprang down a secret passage to the garden, and it was the time of the rising of the moon. Coolness and soothingness dropped on her as a balm from the great light, and she gazed on it murmuring, as in a memory:

*Shall I counsel the moon in her ascending?*
*Stay under that dark palm-tree through the night,*
*Rest on the mountain slope,*
*By the couching antelope,*
*O thou enthroned supremacy of light!*
*And for ever the lustre thou art lending*
*Lean on the fair long brook that leaps and leaps,*
*Silvery leaps and falls:*

GEORGE MEREDITH

*Hang by the mountain-walls,*
*Moon! and arise no more to crown the steeps,*
*For a danger and dolour is thy wending!*

And she panted and sighed, and wept, crying, "Who, who will kiss me or have my kiss now, that I may indeed be as yonder beam? Who, that I may be avenged on this King? And who sang that song of the ascending of the moon, that comes to me as a part of me from old times?" As she gazed on the circled radiance swimming under a plume of palm leaves, she exclaimed, "Ruark! Ruark the Chief!" So she clasped her hands to her bosom, and crouched under the shadows of the garden, and fled through the garden gates and the streets of the city, heavily veiled, to the prison where Ruark awaited her within the walls and Ukleet without. The Governor of the prison had been warned by Ukleet of her coming, and the doors and bars opened before her unchallenged, till she stood in the cell of Ruark; her eyes, that were alone unveiled, scanned the countenance of the Chief, the fevered lustre-jet of his looks, and by the little moonlight in the cell she saw with a glance the straw-heap and the fetters, and the black-bread and water untasted on the bench—signs of his misery and desire for her coming. So she greeted him with the word of peace, and he replied with the name of the All-Merciful. Then said she, "O Ruark, of Rukrooth thy mother tell me somewhat."

He answered, "I know nought of her since that day. Allah have her in his keeping!"

So she cried, "How? What say'st thou, Ruark? 'tis a riddle."

Then he, "The oath of Ruark is no rope of sand! He swore to see her not till he had set eyes on Bhanavar."

She knelt by the Chief, saying in a soft voice, "Very greatly the Chief of the Beni-Asser loved Bhanavar." And she thought, "Yea! greatly and verily love I him; and he shall be no victim of the Serpents, for I defy them and give them other prey." So she said in deeper notes, "Ruark! the Queen is come hither to release thee. O my Chief! O thou soul of wrath! Ruark, my fire-eye! my eagle of the desert! where is one on earth beloved as thou art by Bhanavar?" The dark light in his eyes kindled as light in the eyes of a lion, and she continued, "Ruark, what a yoke is hers who weareth this crown! He that is my lord, how am I mated to him save in loathing? O my Chief, my lion! hadst thou no dream of Bhanavar, that she would come hither to unbind thee and lift thee beside her, and live with thee in love and veilless loveliness,—thine?

Yea! and in power over lands and nations and armies, lording the infidel, taming them to submission, exulting in defiance and assaults and victories and magnanimities—thou and she?" Then while his breast heaved like a broad wave, the Queen started to her feet, crying, "Lo, she is here! and this she offereth thee, Ruark!"

A shrill cry parted from her lips, and to the clapping of her hands slaves entered the cell with lamps, and instruments to strike off the fetters from the Chief; and they released him, and Ruark leaned on their shoulders to bear the weight of a limb, so was he weakened by captivity; but Bhanavar thrust them from the Chief, and took the pressure of his elbow on her own shoulder, and walked with him thus to the door of the cell, he sighing as one in a dream that dreameth the bliss of bliss. Now they had gone three paces onward, and were in the light of many lamps, when behold! the veil of Bhanavar caught in the sleeve of Ruark as he lifted it, and her visage became bare. She shrieked, and caught up her two hands to her brow, but the slaves had a glimpse of her, and said among themselves, "This is not the Queen." And they murmured, "'Tis an impostor! one in league with the Chief." Bhanavar heard them say, "Arrest her with him at the Governor's gate," and summoned her soul, thinking, "He loveth me, the Chief! he will look into my eyes and mark not the change. What need I then to dread his scorn when I ask of him the kiss: now must it be given, or we are lost, both of us!" and she raised her head on Ruark, and said to him, "my Chief, ere we leave these walls and join our fates, wilt thou plight thyself to me with a kiss?"

Ruark leapt to her like the bounding leopard, and gave her the kiss, as were it his whole soul he gave. Then in a moment Bhanavar felt the blush of beauty burn over her, and drew the veil down on her face, and suffered the slaves to arrest her with Ruark, and bring her before the Governor, and from the Governor to the King in his council-chamber, with the Chief of the Beni-Asser.

Now, the King Mashalleed called to her, "Thou traitress! thou sorceress! thou serpent!"

And she answered under the veil, "What, O my lord the King! and wherefore these evil names of me?"

Cried he, "Thou thing of guile! and thou hast pleaded with me for the life of the Chief thus long to visit him in secret! Life of my head I but Mashalleed is not one to be fooled."

So she said, "'Tis Bhanavar! hast thou forgotten her?"

Then he waxed white with rage, exclaiming, "Yea, 'tis she! a serpent

GEORGE MEREDITH

in the slough! and Ukleet in the torture hath told of thee what is known to him. Unveil! unveil!"

She threw the veil from her figure, and smiled, for Mashalleed was mute, the torrent of invective frozen on his mouth when he beheld the miracle of beauty that she was, the splendid jewel of throbbing loveliness. So to scourge him with the bitter lash of jealousy, Bhanavar turned her eyes on Ruark, and said sweetly, "Yet shalt thou live to taste again the bliss of the Desert. Pleasant was our time in it, O my Chief!" The King glared and choked, and she said again, "Nor he conquered thee, but I; and I that conquered thee, little will it be for me to conquer him: his threats are the winds of idleness."

Surely the world darkened before the eyes of Mashalleed, and he arose and called to his guard hoarsely, "Have off their heads!" They hesitated, dreading the Queen, and he roared, "Slay them!"

Bhanavar beheld the winking of the steel, but ere the scimitars descended, she seized Ruark, and they stood in a whizzing ring of serpents, the sound of whom was as the hum of a thousand wires struck by storm-winds. Then she glowed, towering over them with the Chief clasped to her, and crying:

> *King of vileness! match thy slaves*
> *With my creatures of the caves.*

And she sang to the Serpents:

> *Seize upon him! sting him thro'!*
> *Thrice this day shall pay your due.*

But they, instead of obeying her injunction, made narrower their circle round Bhanavar and the Chief. She yellowed, and took hold of the nearest Serpent horribly, crying:

> *Dare against me to rebel,*
> *Ye, the bitter brood of hell?*

And the Serpent gasped in reply:

> *One the kiss to us secures:*
> *Give us ours, and we are yours.*

Thereupon another of the Serpents swung on, the feet of Ruark, winding his length upward round the body of the Chief; so she tugged at that one, tearing it from him violently, and crying:

*Him ye shall not have, I swear!*
*Seize the King that's crouching there.*

And that Serpent hissed:

*This is he the kiss ensures:*
*Give us ours, and we are yours.*

Another and another Serpent she flung from the Chief, and they began to swarm venomously, answering her no more. Then Ruark bore witness to his faith, and folded his arms with the grave smile she had known in the desert; and Bhanavar struggled and tussled with the Serpents in fierceness, strangling and tossing them to right and left. "Great is Allah!" cried all present, and the King trembled, for never was sight like that seen, the hall flashing with the Serpents, and a woman-serpent, their Queen, raging to save one from their fury, shrieking at intervals:

*Never, never shall ye fold,*
*Save with me the man I hold.*

But now the hiss and scream of the Serpents and the noise of their circling was quickened to a slurred savage sound and they closed on Ruark, and she felt him stifling and that they were relentless. So in the height of the tempest Bhanavar seized the Jewel in the gold circlet on her brow and cast it from her. Lo! the Serpents instantly abated their frenzy, and flew all of them to pluck the Jewel, chasing the one that had it in his fangs through the casement, and the hall breathed empty of them. Then in the silence that was, Bhanavar veiled her face and said to the Chief, "Pass from the hall while they yet dread me. No longer am I Queen of Serpents."

But he replied, "Nay! said I not my soul is thine?"

She cried to him, "Seest thou not the change in me? I was bound to those Serpents for my beauty, and 'tis gone! Now am I powerless, hateful to look on, O Ruark my Chief!"

He remained still, saying, "What thou hast been thou art."

She exclaimed, "O true soul, the light is hateful to me as I to the light; but I will yet save thee to comfort Rukrooth, thy mother."

So she drew him with her swiftly from the hall of the King ere the King had recovered his voice of command; but now the wrath of the All-powerful was upon her and him! Surely within an hour from the flight of the Serpents, the slaves and soldiers of Mashalleed laid at his feet two heads that were the heads of Ruark and Bhanavar; and they said, "O great King, we tracked them to her chamber and through to a passage and a vault hung with black, wherein were two corpses, one in a tomb and one unburied, and we slew them there, clasping each other, O King of the age!"

Mashalleed gazed upon the head of Bhanavar and sighed, for death had made the head again fair with a wondrous beauty, a loveliness never before seen on earth.

# The Betrothal

Now, when Shibli Bagarag had ceased speaking, the Vizier smiled gravely, and shook his beard with satisfaction, and said to the Eclipser of Reason, "What opinest thou of this nephew of the barber, O Noorna bin Noorka?"

She answered, "O Feshnavat, my father, truly I am content with the bargain of my betrothal. He, Wullahy, is a fair youth of flowing speech." Then she said, "Ask thou him what he opineth of me, his betrothed?"

So the Vizier put that interrogation to Shibli Bagarag, and the youth was in perplexity; thinking, "Is it possible to be joyful in the embrace of one that hath brought thwackings upon us, serious blows?" Thinking, "Yet hath she, when the mood cometh, kindly looks; and I marked her eye dwelling on me admiringly!" And he thought, "Mayhap she that groweth younger and counteth nature backwards, hath a history that would affect me; or, it may be, my kisses—wah! I like not to give them, and it is said,

*'Love is wither'd by the withered lip';*

and that,

*'On bones become too prominent he'll trip.'*

Yet put the case, that my kisses—I shower them not, Allah the All-seeing is my witness! and they be given daintily as 'twere to the leaf of a nettle, or over-hot pilau. Yet haply kisses repeated might restore her to a bloom, and it is certain youth is somehow stolen from her, if the Vizier Feshnavat went before her, and his blood be her blood; and he is powerful, she wise. I'll decide to act the part of a rejoicer, and express of her opinions honeyed to the soul of that sex."

Now, while he was thus debating he hung his head, and the Vizier awaited his response, knitting his brows angrily at the delay, and at the last he cried, "What! no answer? how's this? Shall thy like dare hold debate when questioned of my like? And is my daughter Noorna bin Noorka, thinkest thou, a slave-girl in the market,—thou haggling at her price, O thou nephew of the barber?"

So Shibli Bagarag exclaimed, "O exalted one, bestower of the bride!

surely I debated with myself but for appropriate terms; and I delayed to select the metre of the verse fitting my thoughts of her, and my wondrous good fortune, and the honour done me."

Then the Vizier, "Let us hear: we listen."

And Shibli Bagarag was advised to deal with illustrations in his dilemma, by-ways of expression, and spake in extemporaneous verse, and with a full voice:

> *The pupils of the Sage for living Beauty sought;*
> *And one a Vision clasped, and one a Model wrought.*
> *"I have it!" each exclaimed, and rivalry arose:*
> *"Paint me thy Maid of air!" "Thy Grace of clay disclose."*
> *"What! limbs that cannot move!" "What! lips that melt away!"*
> *"Keep thou thy Maid of air!" "Shroud up thy Grace of clay!"*
> *'Twas thus, contending hot, they went before the Sage,*
> *And knelt at the wise wells of cold ascetic age.*
> *"The fairest of the twain, O father, thou record":*

He answered, "Fairest she who's likest to her lord."
Said they, "What fairer thing matched with them might prevail?"
The Sage austerely smiled, and said, "Yon monkey's tail."

> *'Tis left for after-time his wisdom to declare:*
> *That's loveliest we best love, and to ourselves compare.*
> *Yet lovelier than all hands shape or fancies build,*
> *The meanest thing of earth God with his fire hath filled.*

Now, when Shibli Bagarag ceased, Noorna bin Noorka cried, "Enough, O wondrous turner of verse, thou that art honest!" And she laughed loudly, rustling like a bag of shavings, and rolling in her laughter.

Then said she, "O my betrothed, is not the thing thou wouldst say no other than—

> *'Each to his mind doth the fairest enfold,*
> *For broken long since was Beauty's mould';*

and, 'Thou that art old, withered, I cannot flatter thee, as I can in no way pay compliments to the monkey's tail of high design; nevertheless the Sage would do thee honour'? So read I thy illustration, O keen of wit! and thou art forgiven its boldness, my betrothed,—Wullahy! utterly so."

Now, the youth was abashed at her discernment, and the kindliness of her manner won him to say:

> *There's many a flower of sweetness, there's many a gem of earth*
> *Would thrill with bliss our being, could we perceive its worth.*
> *O beauteous is creation, in fashion and device!*
> *If I have fail'd to think thee fair, 'tis blindness is my vice.*

And she answered him:

> *I've proved thy wit and power of verse,*
> *That is at will diffuse and terse:*
> *Lest thou commence to lie—be dumb!*
> *I am content: the time will come!*

Then she said to the Vizier Feshnavat, "O my father, there is all in this youth, the nephew of the barber, that's desirable for the undertaking; and his feet will be on a level with the task we propose for him, he the height of man above it. 'Tis clear that vanity will trip him, but honesty is a strong upholder; and he is one that hath the spirit of enterprise and the mask of dissimulation: gratitude I observe in him; and it is as I thought when I came upon him on the sand-hill outside the city, that his star is clearly in a web with our star, he destined for the Shaving of Shagpat."

So the Vizier replied, "He hath had thwackings, yet is he not deterred from making further attempt on Shagpat. I think well of him, and I augur hopefully. Wullahy! the Cadi shall be sent for; I can sleep in his secresy; and he shall perform the ceremonies of betrothal, even now and where we sit, and it shall be for him to write the terms of contract: so shall we bind the youth firmly to us, and he will be one of us as we are, devoted to the undertaking by three bonds—the bond of vengeance, the bond of ambition, and that of love."

Now, so it was that the Vizier despatched a summons for the attendance of the Cadi, and he came and performed between Shibli Bagarag and Noorna bin Noorka ceremonies of betrothal, and wrote terms of contract; and they were witnessed duly by the legal number of witnesses, and so worded that he had no claim on her as wife till such time as the Event to which he bound himself was mastered. Then the fees being paid, and compliments interchanged, the Vizier exclaimed, "Be ye happy! and let the weak cling to the strong; and be ye two to one in this world, and no split halves that betray division and stick not together when the gum is heated." Then he made a sign to the Cadi and them that had witnessed the contract to follow him, leaving the betrothed ones to their own company.

So when they were alone Noorna gazed on the youth wistfully, and said in a soft tone, "Thou art dazed with the adventure, O youth! Surely there is one kiss owing me: art thou willing? Am I reduced to beg it of thee? Or dream'st thou?"

He lifted his head and replied, "Even so."

Thereat he stood up languidly, and went to her and kissed her. And she smiled and said, "I wot it will be otherwise, and thou wilt learn swiftness of limb, brightness of eye, and the longing for earthly beatitude, when next I ask thee, O my betrothed!"

Lo! while she spake, new light seemed in her; and it was as if a splendid jewel were struggling to cast its beams through the sides of a crystal vase smeared with dust and old dirt and spinnings of the damp spider. He was amazed, and cried, "How's this? What change is passing in thee?"

She said, "Joy in thy kiss, and that I have 'scaped Shagpat."

Then he: "Shagpat? How? had that wretch claim over thee ere I came?"

But she looked fearfully at the corners of the room and exclaimed, "Hush, my betrothed! speak not of him in that fashion, 'tis dangerous; and my power cannot keep off his emissaries at all times." Then she said, "O my betrothed, know me a sorceress ensorcelled; not that I seem, but that I shall be! Wait thou for the time and it will reward thee. What! thou think'st to have plucked a wrinkled o'erripe fruit,—a mouldy pomegranate under the branches, a sour tamarind? 'Tis well! I say nought, save that time will come, and be thou content. It is truly as I said, that I have thee between me and Shagpat; and that honoured one of this city thought fit in his presumption to demand me in marriage at the hands of my father, knowing me wise, and knowing the thing that transformed me to this, the abominable fellow! Surely my father entertained not his proposal save with scorn; but the King looked favourably on it, and it is even now matter of reproach to Feshnavat, my father, that he withholdeth me from Shagpat."

Quoth Shibli Bagarag, "A clothier, O Noorna, control the Vizier! and demand of him his daughter in marriage! and a clothier influence the King against his Vizier!—'tis, wullahy! a riddle."

She replied, "'Tis even so, eyes of mine, my betrothed! but thou know'st not Shagpat, and that he is. Lo! the King, and all of this city save we three, are held in enchantment by him, and made foolish by one hair that's in his head."

Shibli Bagarag started in his seat like one that shineth with a discovery, and cried, "The Identical!"

Then she, sighing, "'Tis that indeed! but the Identical of Identicals, the chief and head of them, and I, woe's me! I, the planter of it."

So he said, "How so?"

But she cried, "I'll tell thee not here, nor aught of myself and him, and the Genie held in bondage by me, till thou art proved by adventure, and we float peacefully on the sea of the Bright Lily: there shalt thou see me as I am, and hear my story, and marvel at it; for 'tis wondrous, and a manifestation of the Power that dwelleth unseen."

So Shibli Bagarag pondered awhile on the strange nature of the things she hinted, and laughter seized him as he reflected on Shagpat, and the whole city enchanted by one hair in his head; and he exclaimed, "O Noorna, knoweth he, Shagpat, of the might in him?"

She answered, "Enough for his vain soul that homage is paid to him, and he careth not for the wherefore!"

Shibli Bagarag fixed his eyes on the deep-flowered carpets of the floor, as if reading there a matter quaintly written, and smiled, saying, "What boldness was mine—the making offer to shear Shagpat, the lion in his lair, he that holdeth a whole city in enchantment! Wah! 'twas an instance of daring!"

And Noorna said, "Not only an entire city, but other cities affected by him, as witness Oolb, whither thou wilt go; and there be governments and states, and conditions of men remote, that hang upon him, Shagpat. 'Tis even so; I swell not his size. When thou hast mastered the Event, and sent him forth shivering from thy blade like the shorn lamb, 'twill be known how great a thing has been achieved, and a record for the generations to come; choice is that historian destined to record it!"

Quoth he, looking eagerly at her, "O Noorna, what is it in thy speech affecteth me? Surely it infuseth the vigour of wine, old wine; and I shiver with desire to shave Shagpat, and spin threads for the historian to weave in order. I, wullahy! had but dry visions of the greatness destined for me till now, my betrothed! Shall I master an Event in shaving him, and be told of to future ages? By Allah and his Prophet (praise be to that name!), this is greatness! Say, Noorna, hadst thou foreknowledge of me and my coming to this city?"

So she said, "I was on the roofs one night among the stars ere moonrise, O my betrothed, and 'twas close on the rise of this very month's moon. The star of our enemy, Shagpat, was large and red, mine as it were menaced by its proximity, nigh swallowed in its haughty beams and the steady overbearings of its effulgence. 'Twas so as it had long been, when suddenly, lo! a star from the upper heaven that shot down between them wildly, and my star took lustre from it; and the star of Shagpat trembled like a ring on a tightened rope, and waved and flickered, and seemed to come forward and to retire; and 'twas presently as a comet in the sky, bright,—a tadpole, with large head and lengthy tail, in the assembly of the planets. This I saw: and that the stranger star was stationed by my star, shielding it, and that it drew nearer to my star, and entered its circle, and that the two stars seemed mixing the splendour that was theirs. Now, that sight amazed me, and my heart in its beating quickened with the expectation of things approaching. Surely I rendered praise, and pressed both hands on my bosom, and watched, and behold! the comet, the illumined tadpole, was becoming restless beneath the joint rays of the twain that were dominating him; and he diminished, and lashed his tail uneasily, half madly, darting as do captured beasts from the fetters that constrain them. Then went there from thy star—for I know now 'twas thine—a momentary flash across the head of the tadpole, and again another and another, rapidly, pertinaciously. And from thy star there passed repeated flashes across the head of the tadpole, till his brilliance was as 'twere severed from him, and he, like drossy silver, a dead shape in the conspicuous heavens. And he became yellow as the rolling eyes of sick wretches in pain, and shrank in his place like pale parchment at the touch of flame; dull was he as an animal fascinated by fear, and deprived of all power to make head against the foe, darkness, that now beset him, and usurped part of his yet lively tail, and settled on his head, and coated part of his body. So when this tadpole, that was once terrible to me, became turbaned, shoed, and shawled with darkness, and there was little of him remaining visible, lo! a concluding flash shot from thy star, and he fell heavily down the sky and below the hills, into the sea, that is the Enchanted Sea, whose Queen is Rabesqurat, Mistress of Illusions. Now when my soul recovered from amazement at the marvels seen, I arose and went from the starry roofs to consult my books of magic, and 'twas revealed to me that one was wandering to a junction with my destiny, and that by his means the great aim would of a surety be accomplished—Shagpat Shaved! So my purpose was to discover him; and I made calculations, and summoned them that serve me to search for such a youth as thou art; fairly, O my betrothed, did I preconceive thee. And so it was that I traced a magic line from the sand-hills to the city, and from the outer hills to the sand-hills; and whoso approached by that line I knew was he marked out as my champion, my betrothed,—a youth destined for great things. Was I right? The egg hatcheth. Thou art already proved by thwackings, seasoned to the undertaking, and I doubt not thou art he that will finish with that tadpole Shagpat, and sit in the high seat, thy name an odour in distant lands, a joy to the historian, the Compiler of Events, thou Master of the Event, the greatest which time will witness for ages to come."

When she had spoken Shibli Bagarag considered her words, and the knowledge that he was selected by destiny as Master of the Event inflated him; and he was a hawk in eagerness, a peacock in pride, an ostrich in fulness of chest, crying, "O Noorna bin Noorka! is't really so? Truly it must be, for the readers of planets were also busy with me at the time of my birth, interpreting of me in excessive agitation; and the thing they foretold is as thou foretellest. I am, wullahy! marked: I walk manifest in the eye of Providence."

Thereupon he exulted, and his mind strutted through the future of his days, and down the ladder of all time, exacting homage from men, his brethren; and 'twas beyond the art of Noorna to fix him to the present duties of the enterprise: he was as feathered seed before the breath of vanity.

Now, while the twain discoursed, she of the preparations for shaving Shagpat, he of his completion of the deed, and the honours due to him as Master of the Event, Feshnavat the Vizier returned to them from his entertainment of the Cadi; and he had bribed him to silence with a mighty bribe. So he called to them—

"Ho! be ye ready to commence the work? and have ye advised together as to the beginning? True is that triplet:

> 'Whatever enterprize man hath,
> For waking love or curbing wrath,
> 'Tis the first step that makes a path.'

GEORGE MEREDITH

And how have ye determined as to that first step?"

Noorna replied, "O my father! we have not decided, and there hath been yet no deliberation between us as to that."

Then he said, "All this while have ye talked, and no deliberation as to that! Lo, I have drawn the Cadi to our plot, and bribed him with a mighty bribe; and I have prepared possible disguises for this nephew of the barber; and I have had the witnesses of thy betrothal despatched to foreign parts, far kingdoms in the land of Roum, to prevent tattling and gabbling; and ye that were left alone for debating as to the great deed, ye have not yet deliberated as to that! Is't known to ye, O gabblers, aught of the punishment inflicted by Shahpesh, the Persian, on Khipil, the Builder?—a punishment that, by Allah!"

Shibli Bagarag said, "How of that punishment, O Vizier?"

And the Vizier narrated as followeth.

# And this is the Punishment of Shahpesh, the Persian, on Khipil, the Builder

They relate that Shahpesh, the Persian, commanded the building of a palace, and Khipil was his builder. The work lingered from the first year of the reign of Shahpesh even to his fourth. One day Shahpesh went to the riverside where it stood, to inspect it. Khipil was sitting on a marble slab among the stones and blocks; round him stretched lazily the masons and stonecutters and slaves of burden; and they with the curve of humorous enjoyment on their lips, for he was reciting to them adventures, interspersed with anecdotes and recitations and poetic instances, as was his wont. They were like pleased flocks whom the shepherd hath led to a pasture freshened with brooks, there to feed indolently; he, the shepherd, in the midst.

Now, the King said to him, "O Khipil, show me my palace where it standeth, for I desire to gratify my sight with its fairness."

Khipil abased himself before Shahpesh, and answered, "'Tis even here, O King of the age, where thou delightest the earth with thy foot and the ear of thy slave with sweetness. Surely a site of vantage, one that dominateth earth, air, and water, which is the builder's first and chief requisition for a noble palace, a palace to fill foreign kings and sultans with the distraction of envy; and it is, O Sovereign of the time, a site, this site I have chosen, to occupy the tongues of travellers and awaken the flights of poets!"

Shahpesh smiled and said, "The site is good! I laud the site! Likewise I laud the wisdom of Ebn Busrac, where he exclaims:

> 'Be sure, where Virtue faileth to appear,
> For her a gorgeous mansion men will rear;
> And day and night her praises will be heard,
> Where never yet she spake a single word.'"

Then said he, "O Khipil, my builder, there was once a farm servant that, having neglected in the seed-time to sow, took to singing the richness of his soil when it was harvest, in proof of which he displayed the abundance of weeds that coloured the land everywhere. Discover to me now the completeness of my halls and apartments, I pray thee, O Khipil, and be the excellence of thy construction made visible to me!"

Quoth Khipil, "To hear is to obey."

He conducted Shahpesh among the unfinished saloons and imperfect courts and roofless rooms, and by half erected obelisks, and columns pierced and chipped, of the palace of his building. And he was bewildered at the words spoken by Shahpesh; but now the King exalted him, and admired the perfection of his craft, the greatness of his labour, the speediness of his construction, his assiduity; feigning not to behold his negligence.

Presently they went up winding balusters to a marble terrace, and the King said, "Such is thy devotion and constancy in toil, Khipil, that thou shaft walk before me here."

He then commanded Khipil to precede him, and Khipil was heightened with the honour. When Khipil had paraded a short space he stopped quickly, and said to Shahpesh, "Here is, as it chanceth, a gap, O King! and we can go no further this way."

Shahpesh said, "All is perfect, and it is my will thou delay not to advance."

Khipil cried, "The gap is wide, O mighty King, and manifest, and it is an incomplete part of thy palace."

Then said Shahpesh, "O Khipil, I see no distinction between one part and another; excellent are all parts in beauty and proportion, and there can be no part incomplete in this palace that occupieth the builder four years in its building: so advance, do my bidding."

Khipil yet hesitated, for the gap was of many strides, and at the bottom of the gap was a deep water, and he one that knew not the motion of swimming. But Shahpesh ordered his guard to point their arrows in the direction of Khipil, and Khipil stepped forward hurriedly, and fell in the gap, and was swallowed by the water below. When he rose the second time, succour reached him, and he was drawn to land trembling, his teeth chattering. And Shahpesh praised him, and said, "This is an apt contrivance for a bath, Khipil O my builder! well conceived; one that taketh by surprise; and it shall be thy reward daily when much talking hath fatigued thee."

Then he bade Khipil lead him to the hall of state. And when they were there Shahpesh said, "For a privilege, and as a mark of my approbation, I give thee permission to sit in the marble chair of yonder throne, even in my presence, O Khipil."

Khipil said, "Surely, O King, the chair is not yet executed."

And Shahpesh exclaimed, "If this be so, thou art but the length of thy measure on the ground, O talkative one!"

Khipil said, "Nay, 'tis not so, O King of splendours! blind that I am! yonder's indeed the chair."

And Khipil feared the King, and went to the place where the chair should be, and bent his body in a sitting posture, eyeing the King, and made pretence to sit in the chair of Shahpesh, as in conspiracy to amuse his master.

Then said Shahpesh, "For a token that I approve thy execution of the chair, thou shalt be honoured by remaining seated in it up to the hour of noon; but move thou to the right or to the left, showing thy soul insensible of the honour done thee, transfixed thou shalt be with twenty arrows and five."

The King then left him with a guard of twenty-five of his body-guard; and they stood around him with bent bows, so that Khipil dared not move from his sitting posture. And the masons and the people crowded to see Khipil sitting on his master's chair, for it became rumoured about. When they beheld him sitting upon nothing, and he trembling to stir for fear of the loosening of the arrows, they laughed so that they rolled upon the floor of the hall, and the echoes of laughter were a thousand-fold. Surely the arrows of the guards swayed with the laughter that shook them.

Now, when the time had expired for his sitting in the chair, Shahpesh returned to him, and he was cramped, pitiable to see; and Shahpesh said, "Thou hast been exalted above men, O Khipil! for that thou didst execute for thy master has been found fitting for thee."

Then he bade Khipil lead the way to the noble gardens of dalliance and pleasure that he had planted and contrived. And Khipil went in that state described by the poet, when we go draggingly, with remonstrating members,

> *Knowing a dreadful strength behind,*
> *And a dark fate before.*

They came to the gardens, and behold, these were full of weeds and nettles, the fountains dry, no tree to be seen—a desert. And Shahpesh cried, "This is indeed of admirable design, O Khipil! Feelest thou not the coolness of the fountains?—their refreshingness? Truly I am grateful to thee! And these flowers, pluck me now a handful, and tell me of their perfume."

Khipil plucked a handful of the nettles that were there in the place of flowers, and put his nose to them before Shahpesh, till his nose was reddened; and desire to rub it waxed in him, and possessed him, and became a passion, so that he could scarce refrain from rubbing it even in the King's presence. And the King encouraged him to sniff and enjoy their fragrance, repeating the poet's words:

> *Methinks I am a lover and a child,*
> *A little child and happy lover, both!*
> *When by the breath of flowers I am beguiled*
> *From sense of pain, and lulled in odorous sloth.*
> *So I adore them, that no mistress sweet*
> *Seems worthier of the love which they awake:*
> *In innocence and beauty more complete,*
> *Was never maiden cheek in morning lake.*
> *Oh, while I live, surround me with fresh flowers!*
> *Oh, when I die, then bury me in their bowers!*

And the King said, "What sayest thou, O my builder? that is a fair quotation, applicable to thy feelings, one that expresseth them?"

Khipil answered, "'Tis eloquent, O great King! comprehensiveness would be its portion, but that it alludeth not to the delight of chafing."

Then Shahpesh laughed, and cried, "Chafe not! it is an ill thing and a hideous! This nosegay, O Khipil, it is for thee to present to thy mistress. Truly she will receive thee well after its presentation! I will have it now sent in thy name, with word that thou followest quickly. And for thy nettled nose, surely if the whim seize thee that thou desirest its chafing, to thy neighbour is permitted what to thy hand is refused."

The King set a guard upon Khipil to see that his orders were executed, and appointed a time for him to return to the gardens.

At the hour indicated Khipil stood before Shahpesh again. He was pale, saddened; his tongue drooped like the tongue of a heavy bell, that when it soundeth giveth forth mournful sounds only: he had also the look of one battered with many beatings. So the King said, "How of the presentation of the flowers of thy culture, O Khipil?"

He answered, "Surely, O King, she received me with wrath, and I am shamed by her."

And the King said, "How of my clemency in the matter of the chafing?"

Khipil answered, "O King of splendours! I made petition to my neighbours whom I met, accosting them civilly and with imploring, for I ached to chafe, and it was the very raging thirst of desire to chafe that was mine, devouring eagerness for solace of chafing. And they chafed me, O King; yet not in those parts which throbbed for the chafing, but in those which abhorred it."

Then Shahpesh smiled and said, "'Tis certain that the magnanimity of monarchs is as the rain that falleth, the sun that shineth: and in this spot it fertilizeth richness; in that encourageth rankness. So art thou but a weed, O Khipil! and my grace is thy chastisement."

Now, the King ceased not persecuting Khipil, under pretence of doing him honour and heaping favours on him. Three days and three nights was Khipil gasping without water, compelled to drink of the drought of the fountain, as an honour at the hands of the King. And he was seven days and seven nights made to stand with stretched arms, as they were the branches of a tree, in each hand a pomegranate. And Shahpesh brought the people of his court to regard the wondrous pomegranate shoot planted by Khipil, very wondrous, and a new sort, worthy the gardens of a King. So the wisdom of the King was applauded, and men wotted he knew how to punish offences in coin, by the punishment inflicted on Khipil the builder. Before that time his affairs had languished, and the currents of business instead of flowing had become stagnant pools. It was the fashion to do as did Khipil, and fancy the tongue a constructor rather than a commentator; and there is a doom upon that people and that man which runneth to seed in gabble, as the poet says in his wisdom:

> *If thou wouldst be famous, and rich in splendid fruits,*
> *Leave to bloom the flower of things, and dig among the roots.*

Truly after Khipil's punishment there were few in the dominions of Shahpesh who sought to win the honours bestowed by him on gabblers and idlers: as again the poet:

> *When to loquacious fools with patience rare*
> *I listen, I have thoughts of Khipil's chair:*
> *His bath, his nosegay, and his fount I see,—*
> *Himself stretch'd out as a pomegranate-tree.*
> *And that I am not Shahpesh I regret,*

GEORGE MEREDITH

*So to inmesh the babbler in his net.*
*Well is that wisdom worthy to be sung,*
*Which raised the Palace of the Wagging Tongue!*

And whoso is punished after the fashion of Shahpesh, the Persian, on Khipil the Builder, is said to be one "in the Palace of the Wagging Tongue" to this time.

# THE GENIE KARAZ

Now, when the voice of the Vizier had ceased, Shibli Bagarag exclaimed, "O Vizier, this night, no later, I'll surprise Shagpat, and shave him while he sleepeth: and he shall wake shorn beside his spouse. Wullahy! I'll delay no longer, I, Shibli Bagarag."

Said the Vizier, "Thou?"

And he replied, "Surely, O Vizier! thou knowest little of my dexterity."

So the Vizier laughed, and Noorna bin Noorka laughed, and he was at a loss to interpret the cause of their laughter. Then said Noorna, "O my betrothed, there's not a doubt among us of thy dexterity, nor question of thy willingness; but this shaving of Shagpat, wullahy! 'tis longer work than what thou makest of it."

And he cried, "How? because of the Chief of Identicals planted by thee in his head?"

She answered, "Because of that; but 'tis the smallest opposer, that."

Then the Vizier said, "Let us consult."

So Shibli Bagarag gave ear, and the Vizier continued, "There's first, the Chief of Identicals planted by thee in the head of that presumptuous fellow, O my daughter! By what means shall that be overcome?"

She said, "I rank not that first, O Feshnavat, my father; surely I rank first the illusions with which Rabesqurat hath surrounded him, and made it difficult to know him from his semblances, whenever real danger threateneth him."

The Vizier assented, saying, "Second, then, the Chief of Identicals?"

She answered, "Nay, O my father; second, the weakness that's in man, and the little probability of his finishing with Shagpat at one effort; and there is but a sole chance for whoso attempteth, and if he faileth, 'tis forever he faileth."

So the Vizier said, "Even I knew not 'twas so grave! Third, then, the Chief of Identicals?"

She replied, "Third! which showeth the difficulty of the task. Read ye not, first, how the barber must come upon Shagpat and fix him for his operation; second, how the barber must be possessed of more than mortal strength to master him in so many strokes; third, how the barber must have a blade like no other blade in this world in sharpness, in temper, in velocity of sweep, that he may reap this crop which flourisheth on Shagpat, and with it the magic hair which defieth edge of mortal blades?"

Now, the Vizier sighed at the words, saying, "Powerful is Shagpat. I knew not the thing I undertook. I fear his mastery of us, and we shall be contemned—objects for the red finger of scorn."

Noorna turned to Shibli Bagarag and asked, "Do the three bonds of enterprise—vengeance, ambition, and love—shrink in thee from this great contest?"

Shibli Bagarag said, "'Tis terrible! on my head be it!"

She gazed at him a moment tenderly, and said, "Thou art worthy of what is in store for thee, O my betrothed! and I think little of the dangers, in contemplation of the courage in thee. Lo, if vengeance and ambition spur thee so, how will not love when added to the two?"

Then said she, "As to the enchantments and spells that shall overreach him, and as to the blade wherewith to shear him?"

Feshnavat exclaimed, "Yonder's indeed where we stumble and are tripped at starting."

But she cried, "What if I know of a sword that nought on earth or under resisteth, and before the keen edge of which all Illusions and Identicals are as summer grass to the scythe?"

They both shouted, "The whereabout of that sword, O Noorna!"

So she said, "'Tis in Aklis, in the mountains of the Koosh; and the seven sons of Aklis sharpen it day and night till the adventurer cometh to claim it for his occasion. Whoso succeedeth in coming to them they know to have power over the sword, and 'tis then holiday for them. Many are the impediments, and they are as holes where the fox haunteth. So they deliver to his hand the sword till his object is attained, his Event mastered, smitten through with it; and 'tis called the Sword of Events. Surely, with it the father of the Seven vanquished the mighty Roc, Kroojis, that threatened mankind with ruin, and a stain of the Roc's blood is yet on the hilt of the sword. How sayest thou, O Feshnavat,—shall we devote ourselves to get possession of that Sword?"

So the Vizier brightened at her words, and said, "O excellent in wisdom and star of counsel! speak further, and as to the means."

Noorna bin Noorka continued, "Thou knowest, O my father, I am proficient in the arts of magic, and I am what I am, and what I shall be, by its uses. 'Tis known to thee also that I hold a Genie in bondage, and can utter ten spells and one spell in a breath. Surely my services to the youth in his attainment of the Sword will be beyond price! Now to reach

Aklis and the Sword there are three things needed—charms: and one is a phial full of the waters of Paravid from the wells in the mountain yon-side the desert; and one, certain hairs that grow in the tail of the horse Garraveen, he that roameth wild in the meadows of Melistan; and one, that the youth gather and bear to Aklis, for the white antelope Gulrevaz, the Lily of the Lovely Light that groweth in the hollow of the crags over the Enchanted Sea: with these spells he will command the Sword of Aklis, and nothing can bar him passage. Moreover I will expend in his aid all my subtleties, my transformations, the stores of my wisdom. Many seek this Sword, and people the realms of Rabesqurat, or are beasts in Aklis, or crowned Apes, or go to feed the Roc, Kroojis, in the abyss beneath the Roc's-egg bridge; but there's virtue in Shibli Bagarag: wullahy! I am wistful in him of the hand of Destiny, and he will succeed in this undertaking if he dareth it."

Shibli Bagarag cried, "At thy bidding, O Noorna! Care I for dangers? I'm on fire to wield the Sword, and master the Event."

Thereupon, Noorna bin Noorka arose instantly, and took him by the cheeks a tender pinch, and praised him. Then drew she round him a circle with her forefinger that left a mark like the shimmering of evanescent green flame, saying, "White was the day I set eyes on thee!" Round the Vizier, her father, she drew a like circle; and she took an unguent, and traced with it characters on the two circles, and letters of strange form, arrowy, lance-like, like leaning sheaves, and crouching baboons, and kicking jackasses, and cocks a-crow, and lutes slack-strung; and she knelt and mumbled over and over words of magic, like the drone of a bee to hear, and as a roll of water, nothing distinguishable. After that she sought for an unguent of a red colour, and smeared it on a part of the floor by the corner of the room, and wrote on it in silver fluid a word that was the word "Eblis," and over that likewise she droned awhile. Presently she arose with a white-heated face, the sweat on her brow, and said to Shibli Bagarag and Feshnavat hurriedly and in a harsh tone, "How? have ye fear?"

They answered, "Our faith is in Allah, our confidence in thee."

Said she then, "I summon the Genie I hold in bondage. He will be wrathful; but ye are secure from him. He's this moment in the farthest region of earth, doing ill, as is his wont, and the wont of the stock of Eblis."

So the Vizier said, "He'll be no true helper, this Genie, and I care not for his company."

She answered, "O my father! leave thou that to me. What says the poet?—

*'It is the sapiency of fools,*
*To shrink from handling evil tools.'"*

Now, while she was speaking, she suddenly inclined her ear as to a distant noise; but they heard nothing. Then, after again listening, she cried in a sharp voice, "Ho! muffle your mouths with both hands, and stir not from the ring of the circles, as ye value life and its blessings."

So they did as she bade them, and watched her curiously. Lo! she swathed the upper and lower part of her face in linen, leaving the lips and eyes exposed; and she took water from an ewer, and sprinkled it on her head, and on her arms and her feet, muttering incantations. Then she listened a third time, and stooped to the floor, and put her lips to it, and called the name, "Karaz!" And she called this name seven times loudly, sneezing between whiles. Then, as it were in answer to her summons, there was a deep growl of thunder, and the palace rocked, tottering; and the air became smoky and full of curling vapours. Presently they were aware of the cry of a Cat, and its miaulings; and the patch of red unguent on the floor parted and they beheld a tawny Cat with an arched back. So Noorna bin Noorka frowned fiercely at the Cat, and cried, "This is thy shape, O Karaz; change! for it serves not the purpose."

The Cat changed, and was a Leopard with glowing yellow eyes, crouched for the spring. So Noorna bin Noorka stamped, and cried again, "This is thy shape, O Karaz; change! for it serves not the purpose."

And the Leopard changed, and was a Serpent with many folds, sleek, curled, venomous, hissing.

Noorna bin Noorka cried in wrath, "This is thy shape, O Karaz; change! or thou'lt be no other till Eblis is accepted in Paradise."

And the Serpent vanished. Lo! in its place a Genie of terrible aspect, black as a solitary tree seared by lightning; his forehead ridged and cloven with red streaks; his hair and ears reddened; his eyes like two hollow pits dug by the shepherd for the wolf, and the wolf in them. He shouted, "What work is it now, thou accursed traitress?"

Noorna replied, "I've need of thee!"

He said, "What shape?"

She answered, "The shape of an Ass that will carry two on its back, thou Perversity!"

Upon that, he cried, "O faithless woman, how long shall I be the slave of thy plotting? Now, but for that hair of my head, plucked by thy hand while I slept, I were free, no doer of thy tasks. Say, who be these that mark us?"

She answered, "One, the Vizier Feshnavat; and one, Shibli Bagarag of Shiraz, he that's destined to shave Shagpat, the son of Shimpoor, the son of Shoolpi, the son of Shullum; and the youth is my betrothed."

Now, at her words the whole Genie became as live coal with anger, and he panted black and bright, and made a stride toward Shibli Bagarag, and stretched his arm out to seize him; but Noorna, blew quickly on the circles she had drawn, and the circles rose up in a white flame high as the heads of those present, and the Genie shrank hastily back from the flame, and was seized with fits of sneezing. Then she said in scorn, "Easily, O Karaz, is a woman outwitted! Surely I could not guess what would be thy action! and I was wanting in foresight and insight! and I am a woman bearing the weight of my power as a woodman staggereth under the logs he hath felled!"

So she taunted him, and he still sneezing and bent double with the might of the sneeze. Then said Noorna in a stern voice, "No more altercation between us! Wait thou here till I reappear, Karaz!"

Thereupon, she went from them; and the two, Feshnavat and Shibli Bagarag, feared greatly being left with the Genie, for he became all colours, and loured on them each time that he ceased sneezing. He was clearly menacing them when Noorna returned, and in her hand a saddle made of hide, traced over with mystic characters and gold stripes.

So she cried, "Take this!" Then, seeing he hesitated, she unclosed from her left palm a powder, and scattered it over him; and he grew meek, and the bending knee of obedience was his, and he took the saddle. So she said, "'Tis well! Go now, and wait outside the city in the shape of an Ass, with this saddle on thy back."

The Genie groaned, and said, "To hear is to obey!" And he departed with those words, for she held him in bondage. Then she calmed down the white flames of the circles that enclosed Shibli Bagarag and the Vizier Feshnavat, and they stepped forth, marvelling at the greatness of her sorceries that held such a Genie in bondage.

# The Well of Paravid

N ow, there was haste in the movements of Noorna bin Noorka, and she arrayed herself and clutched Shibli Bagarag by the arm, and the twain departed from Feshnavat the Vizier, and came to the outside of the city, and lo! there was the Genie by a well under a palm, and he standing in the shape of an Ass, saddled. So they mounted him, and in a moment they were in the midst of the desert, and naught round them save the hot glimmer of the sands and the grey of the sky. Surely, the Ass went at such a pace as never Ass went before in this world, resting not by the rivulets, nor under the palms, nor beside the date-boughs; it was as if the Ass scurried without motion of his legs, so swiftly went he. At last the desert gave signs of a border on the low line of the distance, and this grew rapidly higher as they advanced, revealing a country of hills and rocks, and at the base of these the Ass rested.

So Noorna, said, "This desert that we have passed, O my betrothed, many are they that perish in it, and reach not the well; but give thanks to Allah that it is passed."

Then said she, "Dismount, and be wary of moving to the front or to the rear of this Ass, and measure thy distance from the lash of his tail."

So Shibli Bagarag dismounted, and followed her up the hills and the rocks, through ravines and gorges of the rocks, and by tumbling torrents, among hanging woods, over perilous precipices, where no sun hath pierced, and the bones of travellers whiten in loneliness; and they continued mounting upward by winding paths, now closed in by coverts, now upon open heights having great views, and presently a mountain was disclosed to them, green at the sides high up it; and Noorna bin Noorka said to Shibli Bagarag, "Mount here, for the cunning of this Ass can furnish him no excuse further for making thee food for the birds of prey."

So Shibli Bagarag mounted, and they ceased not to ascend the green slopes till the grass became scanty and darkness fell, and they were in a region of snow and cold. Then Noorna bin Noorka tethered the Ass to a stump of a tree and breathed in his ear, and the Ass became as a creature carved in stone; and she drew from her bosom two bags of silk, and blew in one and entered it, bidding Shibli Bagarag do likewise with the other bag; and he obeyed her, drawing it up to his neck, and the delightfulness of warmth came over him. Then said she, "To-morrow, at noon, we shall reach near the summit of the mountain and the Well of Paravid, if my power last over this Ass; and from that time thou wilt be on the high road to greatness, so fail not to remember what I have done for thee, and be not guilty of ingratitude when thy hand is the stronger."

He promised her, and they lay and slept. When he awoke the sun was half-risen, and he looked at Noorna bin Noorka in the silken bag, and she was yet in the peacefulness of pleasant dreams; but for the Ass, surely his eyes rolled, and his head and fore legs were endued with life, while his latter half seemed of stone. And the youth called to Noorna bin Noorka, and pointed to her the strangeness of the condition of the Ass. As she cast eyes on him she cried out, and rushed to him, and took him by the ears and blew up his nostrils, and the animal was quiet. Then she and Shibli Bagarag mounted him again, and she said to him, "It is well thou wert more vigilant than I, and that the sun rose not on this Ass while I slept, or my enchantment would have thawed on him, and he would have 'scaped us."

She gave her heel to the Ass, and the Ass hung his tail in sullenness and drooped his head; and she laughed, crying, "Karaz, silly fellow! do thy work willingly, and take wisely thine outwitting."

She jeered him as they journeyed, and made the soul of Shibli Bagarag merry, so that he jerked in his seat upon the Ass. Now, as they ascended the mountain they came to the opening of a cavern, and Noorna bin Noorka halted the Ass, and said to Shibli Bagarag, "We part here, and I wait for thee in this place. Take this phial, and fill it with the waters of the well, after thy bath. The way is before thee—speed on it."

He climbed the sides of the mountain, and was soon hidden in the clefts and beyond the perches of the vulture. She kept her eyes on the rocky point when he disappeared, awaiting his return; and the sun went over her head and sank on the yon-side of the mountain, and it was by the beams of the moon that she beheld Shibli Bagarag dropping from the crags and ledges of rock, sliding and steadying himself downward till he reached her with the phial in his hand, filled; and he was radiant, as it were divine with freshness, so that Noorna, before she spoke welcome to him, was lost in contemplating the warm shine of his visage, calling to mind the poet's words:

> *The wealth of light in sun and moon,*
> *All nature's wealth,*

*Hath mortal beauty for a boon*
*When match'd with health.*

Then said she, "O Shibli Bagarag, 'tis achieved, this first of thy tasks; for mutely on the fresh red of thy mouth, my betrothed, speaketh the honey of persuasiveness, and the children of Aklis will not resist thee." So she took the phial from him and led forth the Ass, and the twain mounted the Ass and descended the slopes of the mountain in moonlight; and Shibli Bagarag said, "Lo! I have marked wonders, and lived a life since our parting; and this well, 'tis a miracle to dip in it, and by it sit many maidens weeping and old men babbling, and youths that were idle youths striking bubbles from the surface of the water. The well is rounded with marble, and the sky is clear in it, cool in it, the whole earth imaged therein."

Then Noorna said, "Hadst thou a difficulty in obtaining the waters of the well?"

He answered, "Surely all was made smooth for me by thy aid. Now when I came to the well I marked not them by it, but plunged, and the depth of that well seemed to me the very depth of the earth itself, so went I ever downward; and when I was near the bottom of the well I had forgotten life above, and lo! no sooner had I touched the bottom of the well when my head emerged from the surface: 'twas wondrous! But for a sign that touched the bottom of the well, see, O Noorna bin Noorka, the Jewel, the one of myriads that glitter at the bottom, and I plucked it for a gift to thee."

So Noorna took the Jewel from his hand that was torn and crimson, and she cried, "Thou fair youth, thou bleedest with the plucking of it, and it was written, no hand shall pluck a jewel at the bottom of that well without letting of blood. Even so it is! Worthy art thou, and I was not mistaken in thee."

At her words Shibli Bagarag burst forth into praises of her, and he sang:

*"What is my worthiness*
*Match'd with thy worth?*
*Darkness and earthiness,*
*Dust and dearth!*

O Noorna, thou art wise above women: great and glorious over them."

In this fashion the youth lauded her that was his betrothed, but she exclaimed, "Hush! or the jealousy of this Ass will be aroused, and of a surety he'll spill us."

Then he laughed and she laughed till the tail of Karaz trembled.

# THE HORSE GARRAVEEN

Now, they descended leisurely the slopes of the mountain, and when they were again in the green of its base, Noorna called to the Ass, "Ho! Karaz! Sniff now the breezes, for the end of our journey by night is the meadows of Melistan. Forward in thy might, and bray not when we are in them, for thy comfort's sake!"

The Ass sniffed, turning to the four quarters, and chose a certain direction, and bore them swiftly over hills and streams eddying in silver; over huge mounds of sand, where the tents of Bedouins stood in white clusters; over lakes smooth as the cheeks of sleeping loveliness; by walls of cities, mosques, and palaces; under towers that rose as an armed man with the steel on his brows and the frown of battle; by the shores of the pale foaming sea it bore them, going at a pace that the Arab on his steed outstrippeth not. So when the sun was red and the dews were blushing with new light, they struggled from a wilderness of barren broken ground, and saw beneath them, in the warm beams, green, peaceful, deep, the meadows of Melistan. They were meadows dancing with flowers, as it had been fresh damsels of the mountain, fair with variety of colours that were so many gleams of changing light as the breezes of the morn swept over them; lavish of hues, of sweetness, of pleasantness, fir for the souls of the blest.

Then, after they had gazed awhile, Noorna bin Noorka said, "In these meadows the Horse Garraveen roameth at will. Heroes of bliss bestride him on great days. He is black to look on; speed quivers in his flanks like the lightning; his nostrils are wide with flame; there is that in his eye which is settled fire, and that in his hoofs which is ready thunder; when he paws the earth kingdoms quake: no animal liveth with blood like the Horse Garraveen. He is under a curse, for that he bore on his back one who defied the Prophet. Now, to make him come to thee thou must blow the call of battle, and to catch him thou must contrive to strike him on the fetlock as he runs with this musk-ball which I give thee; and to tame him thou must trace between his eyes a figure or the crescent with thy forenail. When that is done, bring him to me here, where I await thee, and I will advise thee further."

So she said, "Go!" and Shibli Bagarag showed her the breadth of his shoulders, and stepped briskly toward the meadows, and was soon brushing among the flowers and soft mosses of the meadows, lifting his nostrils to the joyful smells, looking about him with the broad eye of one that hungereth for a coming thing. The birds went up above him, and the trees shook and sparkled, and the waters of brooks and broad rivers flashed like waving mirrors waved by the slave-girls in sport when the beauties of the harem riot and dip their gleaming shoulders in the bath. He wandered on, lost in the gladness that lived, till the loud neigh of a steed startled him, and by the banks of a river before him he beheld the Horse Garraveen stooping to drink of the river; glorious was the look of the creature,—silver-hoofed, fashioned in the curves of beauty and swiftness. So Shibli Bagarag put up his two hands and blew the call of battle, and the Horse Garraveen arched his neck at the call, and swung upon his haunches, and sought the call, answering it, and tossing his mane as he advanced swiftly. Then, as he neared, Shibli Bagarag held the musk-ball in his fingers, and aimed at the fetlock of the Horse Garraveen, and flung it, and struck him so that he stumbled and fell. He snorted fiercely as he bent to the grass, but Shibli Bagarag ran to him, and grasped strongly the tuft of hair hanging forward between his ears, and traced between his fine eyes a figure of the crescent with his forenail, and the Horse ceased plunging, and was gentle as a colt by its mother's side, and suffered Shibli Bagarag to bestride him, and spurn him with his heel to speed, and bore him fleetly across the fair length of the golden meadows to where Noorna bin Noorka sat awaiting him. She uttered a cry of welcome, saying, "This is achieved with diligence and skill, O my betrothed! and on thy right wrist I mark strength like a sleeping leopard, and the children of Aklis will not resist thee."

So she bade him alight from the Horse, but he said, "Nay." And she called to him again to alight, but he cried, "I will not alight from him! By Allah! such a bounding wave of bliss have I never yet had beneath me, and I will give him rein once again; as the poet says:

> 'Divinely rings the rushing air
> When I am on my mettled mare:
> When fast along the plains we fly,
> A creature of the heavens am I.'"

Then she levelled her brows at him, and said gravely, "This is the temptation thou art falling into, as have thousands before thy time. Give him the rein a second time, and he will bear thee to the red pit, and halt upon the brink, and pitch thee into it among bleeding masses and skeletons of thy kind, where they lie who were men like to thee, and were borne away by the Horse Garraveen."

He gave no heed to her words, taunting her, and making the animal prance up and prove its spirit.

And she cried reproachfully, "O fool! is it thus our great aim will be defeated by thy silly conceit? Lo, now, the greatness and the happiness thou art losing for this idle vanity is to be as a dunghill cock matched with an ostrich; and think not to escape the calamities thou bringest on thyself, for as is said,

*No runner can outstrip his fate;*

and it will overtake thee, though thou part like an arrow from the bow."

He still made a jest of her remonstrance, trying the temper of the animal, and rejoicing in its dark flushes of ireful vigour.

And she cried out furiously, "How! art thou past counsel? then will we match strength with strength ere 'tis too late, though it weaken both."

Upon that, she turned quickly to the Ass and stroked it from one extremity to the other, crying, "Karaz! Karaz!" shouting, "Come forth in thy power!" And the Ass vanished, and the Genie stood in his place, tall, dark, terrible as a pillar of storm to travellers ranging the desert. He exclaimed, "What is it, O woman? Charge me with thy command!"

And she said, "Wrestle with him thou seest on the Horse Garraveen, and fling him from his seat."

Then he yelled a glad yell, and stooped to Shibli Bagarag on the horse and enveloped him, and seized him, and plucked him from the Horse, and whirled him round, and flung him off. The youth went circling in the air, high in it, and descended, circling, at a distance in the deep meadow-waters. When he crept up the banks he saw the Genie astride the Horse Garraveen, with a black flame round his head; and the Genie urged him to speed and put him to the gallop, and was soon lost to sight, as he had been a thunderbeam passing over a still lake at midnight. And Shibli Bagarag was smitten with the wrong and the folly of his act, and sought to hide his sight from Noorna; but she called to him, "Look up, O youth! and face the calamity. Lo, we have now lost the service of Karaz! for though I utter ten spells and one spell in a breath, the Horse Garraveen will ere that have stretched beyond the circle of my magic, and the Genie will be free to do his ill deeds and plot against us. Sad is it! but profit thou by a knowledge of thy weakness."

Then said she, "See, I have not failed to possess myself of the three hairs of Garraveen, and there is that to rejoice in."

She displayed them, and they were sapphire hairs, and had a flickering light; and they seemed to live, wriggling their lengths, and were as snakes with sapphire skins. Then she said, "Thy right wrist, O my betrothed!"

He gave her his right wrist, and she tied round it the three hairs of Garraveen, exclaiming, "Thus do skilful carpenters make stronger what has broken and indicated disaster. Surely, I confide in thy star? I have faith in my foresight?"

And she cried, "Eyes of mine, what sayest thou to me? Lo, we must part awhile: it is written."

Said he, "Leave me not, my betrothed: what am I without thy counsel? And go not from me, or this adventure will come to miserable issue."

So she said, "Thou beginnest to feel my worth?"

He answered, "O Noorna! was woman like thee before in this world? Surely 'tis a mask I mark thee under; yet art thou perforce of sheer wisdom and sweet manners lovely in my sight; and I have a thirst to hear thee and look on thee."

While he spake, a beam of struggling splendour burst from her, and she said, "O thou dear youth, yes! I must even go. But I go glad of heart, knowing thee prepared to love me. I must go to counteract the machinations of Karaz, for he's at once busy, vindictive, and cunning, and there's no time for us to lose; so farewell, my betrothed, and make thy wits keen to know me when we next meet."

So he said, "And I—whither go I?"

She answered, "To the City of Oolb straightway."

Then he, "But I know not its bearing from this spot: how reach it?"

She answered, "What! thou with the phial of Paravid in thy vest, that endoweth, a single drop of it, the flowers, the herbage, the very stones and desert sands, with a tongue to articulate intelligible talk?"

Said he, "Is it so?"

She answered, "Even so."

Ere Slubli Bagarag could question her further she embraced him, and blew upon his eyes, and he was blinded by her breath, and saw not her departure, groping for a seat on the rocks, and thinking her still by him. Sight returned not to him till long after weariness had brought the balm of sleep upon his eyelids.

# The Talking Hawk

N ow, when he awoke he found himself alone in that place, the moon shining over the low meadows and flower-cups fair with night-dew. Odours of night-flowers were abroad, filling the cool air with deliciousness, and he heard in the gardens below songs of the bulbul: it was like a dream to his soul, and he lay somewhile contemplating the rich loveliness of the scene, that showed no moving thing. Then rose he and bethought him of the words of Noorna, and of the City of Oolb, and the phial of the waters of Paravid in his vest; and he drew it forth, and dropped a drop of it on the rock where he had reclined. A deep harmony seemed suddenly to awake inside the rock, and to his interrogation as to the direction of Oolb, he heard, "The path of the shadows of the moon."

Thereupon he advanced to a prominent part of the rocks above the meadows, and beheld the shadows of the moon thrown forward into dimness across a waste of sand. And he stepped downward to the level of sand, and went the way of the shadows till it was dawn. Then dropped he a drop of the waters of the phial on a spike of lavender, and there was a voice said to him in reply to what he questioned, "The path of the shadows of the sun."

The shadows of the sun were thrown forward across the same waste of sand, and he turned and pursued his way, resting at noon beneath a date-tree, and refreshing himself at a clear spring beside it. Surely he was joyful as he went, and elated with high prospects, singing:

> *Sun and moon with their bright fingers*
> *Point the hero's path;*
>
> *If in his great work he lingers,*
> *Well may they be wroth.*

Now, the extent of the duration of his travel was four days and an equal number of nights; and it was on the fifth morn that he entered the gates of a city by the sea, even at that hour when the inhabitants were rising from sleep: fair was the sea beyond it, and the harbour was crowded with vessels, ships stored with merchandise—silks, dates, diamonds, Damascus steel, huge bales piled on the decks for the land of Roum and other lands. Shibli Bagarag thought, "There's scarce a doubt but that one of those sails will set for Oolb shortly. Wullahy! if I knew which, I'd board her and win a berth in her." Presently he thought, "I'll go to the public fountain and question it with the speech-winning waters." Thereupon he passed down the streets of the city and came to an open space, where stood the fountain, and sprinkled it with Paravid; and the fountain spake, saying, "Where men are, question not dumb things."

Cried he, "Faileth Paravid in its power? Have I done aught to baffle myself?"

Then he thought, "'Twere nevertheless well to do as the fountain directeth, and question men while I see them." And he walked about among the people, and came to the quays of the harbour where the ships lay close in, many of them an easy leap from shore, and considered whom to address. So, as he loitered about the quays, meditating on the means at the disposal of the All-Wise, and marking the vessels wistfully, behold, there advanced to him one at a quick pace, in the garb of a sailor. He observed Shibli Bagarag attentively a moment, and exclaimed as it were in the plenitude of respect and with the manner of one that is abashed, "Surely, thou art Shibli Bagarag, the nephew of the barber, him we watch for."

So Shibli Bagarag marvelled at this recognition, and answered, "Am I then already famous to that extent?"

And he that accosted him said, "'Tis certain the trumpet was blown before thy steps, and there is not a man in this city but knoweth of thy destination to the City of Oolb, and that thou art upon the track of great things, one chosen to bring about imminent changes."

Then said Shibli Bagarag, "For this I praise Noorna bin Noorka, daughter of Feshnavat, Vizier of the King that ruleth in the city of Shagpat! She saw me, that I was marked for greatness. Wullahy, the eagle knoweth me from afar, and proclaimeth me; the antelope of the hills scenteth the coming of one not as other men, and telleth his tidings; the wind of the desert shapeth its gust to a meaning, so that the stranger may wot Shibli Bagarag is at hand!"

He puffed his chest, and straightened his legs like the cock, and was as a man upon whom the Sultan has bestowed a dress of honour, even as the plumed peacock. Then the other said:

"Know that I am captain of yonder vessel, that stands farthest out from the harbour with her sails slackened; and she is laden with figs and fruits which I exchange for silks, spices, and other merchandise, with the people of Oolb. Now, what says the poet?—

> *'Delay in thine undertaking*
> *Is disaster of thy own making';*

and he says also:

> *'Greatness is solely for them that succeed;*
> *'Tis a rotten applause that gives earlier meed.'*

Therefore it is advisable for thee to follow me on board without loss of time, and we will sail this very night for the City of Oolb."

Now, Shibli Bagarag was ruled by the words of the captain albeit he desired to stay awhile and receive the homage of the people of that city. So he followed him into a boat that was by, and the twain were rowed by sailors to the ship. Then, when they were aboard the captain set sail, and they were soon in the hollows of deep waters. There was a berth in the ship set apart for Shibli Bagarag, and one for the captain. Shibli Bagarag, when he entered his berth, beheld at the head of his couch a hawk; its eyes red as rubies, its beak sharp as the curve of a scimitar. So he called out to the captain, and the captain came to him; but when he saw the hawk, he plucked his turban from his head, and dashed it at the hawk, and afterward ran to it, trying to catch it; and the hawk flitted from corner to corner of the berth, he after it with open arms. Then he took a sword, but the hawk flew past him, and fixed on the back part of his head, tearing up his hair by the talons, and pecking over his forehead at his eyes. And Shibli Bagarag heard the hawk scream the name "Karaz," and he looked closely at the Captain of the vessel, and knew him for the Genie Karaz. Then trembled he with exceeding terror, cursing his credulities, for he saw himself in the hands of the Genie, and nothing but this hawk friendly to him on the fearful waters. When the hawk had torn up a certain hair, the Genie stiffened, and glowed like copper in the furnace, the whole length of him; and he descended heavily through the bottom of the ship, and sank into the waters beneath, which hissed and smoked as at a bar of heated iron. Then Shibli Bagarag gave thanks to the Prophet, and praised the hawk, but the hawk darted out of the cabin, and he followed it on deck, and, lo! the vessel was in flames, and the hawk in a circle of the flames; and the flames soared with it, and left it no outlet. Now, as Shibli Bagarag watched the hawk, the flames stretched out towards him and took hold of his vestments. So he delayed not to commend his soul to the All-merciful, and bore witness to his faith, and plunged into the sea headlong. When he rose, the ship had vanished, and all was darkness where it had been; so he buffeted with the billows, thinking his last hour had come, and there was no help for him in this world; and the spray shaken from the billows blinded him, the great walls of water crumbled over him; strength failed him, and his memory ceased to picture images of the old time—his heart to beat with ambition; and to keep the weight of his head above the surface was becoming a thing worth the ransom of kings. As he was sinking and turning his eyes upward, he heard a flutter as of fledgling's wings, and the two red ruby eyes of the hawk were visible above him, like steady fires in the gloom. And the hawk perched on him, and buried itself among the wet hairs of his head, and presently taking the Identical in its beak, the hawk lifted him half out of water, and bore him a distance, and dropped him. This the hawk did many times, and at the last, Shibli Bagarag felt land beneath him, and could wade through the surges to the shore. He gave thanks to the Supreme Disposer, kneeling prostrate on the shore, and fell into a sleep deep in peacefulness as a fathomless well, unruffled by a breath.

Now, when it was dawn Shibli Bagarag awoke and looked inland, and saw plainly the minarets of a city shining in the first beams, and the front of yellow mountains, and people moving about the walls and on the towers and among the pastures round the city; so he made toward them, and inquired of them the name of their city. And they stared at him, crying, "What! know'st thou not the City of Oolb? the hawk on thy shoulder could tell thee that much." He looked and saw that the hawk was on his shoulder; and its left wing was scorched, the plumage blackened. So he said to the hawk, "Is it profitable, O preserving bird, to ask of thee questions?"

The hawk shook its wings and closed an eye.

So he said, "Do I well in entering this city?"

The hawk shook its wings again and closed an eye.

So he said, "To what house shall I direct my steps in this strange city for the attainment of the purpose I have?"

The hawk flew, and soared, and alighted on the topmost of the towers of Oolb. So when it returned he said, "O bird! rare bird! my counsellor! it is an indication, this alighting on the highest tower, that thou advisest me to go straight to the palace of the King?"

The hawk flapped its wings and winked both eyes; so Shibli Bagarag took forth the phial from his breast, remembering the virtues of the waters of the Well of Paravid, and touched his lips with them, that he might be endowed with flowing speech before the King of Oolb. As he did this the phial was open, and the hawk leaned to it and dipped its beak into the water; and he entered the city and passed through the long streets towards the palace of the King, and craved audience of him as one that had a thing marvellous to tell. So the King commanded that Shibli Bagarag should be brought before him, for he was a lover of marvels. As he went into the presence of the King, Shibli Bagarag listened to the hawk, for the hawk spake his language, and it said, "Proclaim to the King a new wonder—'the talking hawk.'"

So when he had bent his body to the King, he proclaimed the new wonder; and the King seemed not to observe the hawk, and said, "From what city art thou?"

He answered, "Native, O King, to Shiraz; newly from the City of Shagpat."

And the King asked, "How is it with that hairy wonder?"

He answered, "The dark forest flourisheth about him."

And the King said, "That is well! We of the City of Oolb take our fashions from them of the City of Shagpat, and it is but yesterday that I bastinadoed a barber that strayed among us."

Shibli Bagarag sighed when he heard the King, and thought to himself, "How unfortunate is the race of barbers, once honourable and in esteem! Surely it will not be otherwise till Shagpat is shaved!" And the King called out to him for the cause of his sighing; so he said, "I sigh, O King of the age, considering how like may be the case of the barber bastinadoed but yesterday, in his worth and value, to that of Roomdroom, the reader of planets, that was a barber."

And he related the story of Roomdroom for the edification of the King and the exaltation of barbercraft, delivering himself neatly and winningly and pointedly, so that the story should apply, which was its merit and its origin.

When Shibli Bagarag had finished his narration of the case of Roomdroom the barber, the King of Oolb said, "O thou, native of Shiraz, there is persuasion and sweetness and fascination on thy tongue, and I am touched with compassion for the soles of Baba Mustapha, that I bastinadoed but yesterday, and he was from Shiraz likewise."

Now, the heart of Shibli Bagarag leapt when he heard mention of Baba Mustapha; and he knew him for his uncle that was searching him. He would have cried aloud his relationship, but the hawk whispered in his ear. Then the hawk said to him, "There is danger in the King's muteness respecting me, for I am visible to him. Proclaim the spirit of prophecy."

So he proclaimed that spirit, and the King said, "Prophesy to me of barbercraft."

And he cried, "O King of the age, the barber is abased, trodden underfoot, given over to the sneers and the gibes of them that flatter the powerful ones; he is as the winter worm, as the crocodile in the slime of his sleep by the bank, as the sick eagle before moulting. But I say, O King, that he will come forth like the serpent in a new skin, shaming the old one; he slept a caterpillar, and will come forth a butterfly; he sank a star, and lo! he riseth a constellation."

Now, while he was speaking in the fervour of his soul, the King said something to one of the court officers surrounding him, and there was brought to the King a basin, a soap-bowl, and barber's tackle. When Shibli Bagarag saw these, the uses of the barber rushed upon his mind, and desire to sway the tackle pushed him forward and agitated him, so that he could not keep his hands from them.

Then the King exclaimed, "It is as I thought. Our passions betray themselves, and our habits; so is it written. By Allah! I swear thou art thyself none other than a barber, O youth."

Shibli Bagwrag was nigh fainting with terror at this discovery of the King, but the hawk said in his ear, "Proclaim speech in the tackle." So he proclaimed speech in the tackle; and the King smiled doubtfully, and said, "If this be a cheat, Shiraz will not see thy face more."

Then the hawk whispered in his ear, "Drop on the tackle secretly a drop from the phial." This he did, spreading his garments, and commanded the tackle to speak. And the tackle spake, each portion of it, confusedly as the noise of Babel. So the King marvelled greatly, and said, "'Tis a greater wonder than the talking hawk, the talking tackle. Wullahy! it ennobleth barbercraft! Yet it were well to comprehend the saying of the tackle."

Then the hawk flew to the tackle and fluttered about it, and lo! the blade and the brush stood up and said in a shrill tone, "It is ordained that Shagpat shall be shaved, and that Shibli Bagarag shall shave him."

The King bit the forefinger of amazement, and said, "What then ensueth, O talking tackle?"

And the brush and the blade stood up, and said in a shrill tone, "Honour to Shibli Bagarag and barbers! Shame unto Shagpat and his fellows!"

Upon that, the King cried, "Enough, O talking tackle; I will forestall the coming thing. I will be shaved! wullahy, that will I!"

Then the hawk whispered to Shibli Bagarag, "Forward and shear him!" So he stepped forth and seized the tackle, and addressed himself keenly to the shaving of the King of Oolb, lathering him and performing his task with perfect skill. And the courtiers crowded to follow the example of the King, and Shibli Bagarag shaved them, all of them. Now, when they were shaved, fear smote them, the fear of ridicule, and each laughed at the change that was in the other; but the King cried, "See that order is issued for the people of Oolb to be as we before to-morrow's sun. So is laughter taken in reverse." And the King said aside to Shibli Bagarag, "Say now, what may be thy price for yonder hawk?"

And the hawk bade him say, "The loan of thy cockleshell."

The King mused, and said, "That is much to ask, for it is that which beareth the Princess my daughter to the Lily of the Enchanted Sea, which she nourisheth; and if 'tis harmed, she will be stricken with ugliness, as was the daughter of the Vizier Feshnavat, who tended it before her. Yet is this hawk a bird of price. What be its qualities, besides the gift of speech?"

Shibli Bagarag answered, "To counsel in extremity; to forewarn; to counteract enchantments and foul magic."

Upon that the King said, "Follow me!"

And the King led the way from the hall, through many spacious chambers fair with mirrors and silks and precious woods, and smooth marble floors, down into a vault lit by a lamp that was shaped like an eye. Round the vault were hung helm-pieces, and swords, and rich-studded housings; and there were silken dresses, and costly shawls, and tall vases and jars of China, tapestries, and gold services. And the King said, "Take thy choice of these in exchange for the hawk."

But Shibli Bagarag said, "Nought save a loan of the cockle-shell, King!"

Then the King threatened him, saying, "There is a virtue in each of the things thou seest: the China jar is brimmed with wine, and remaineth so though a thousand drink of it; the dress of Samarcand rendereth the wearer invisible; yet thou refusest to exchange them for thy hawk!"

And the King swore by the beard of his father he would seize perforce the hawk and shut up Shibli Bagarag in the vault, if he fell not into his bargain. Shibli Bagarag was advised by the hawk to accept the China jar and the dress of Samarcand, and handed the hawk to the King in exchange for these things. So the King took the hawk upon his wrist and departed with it to the apartments of his daughter, and Shibli Bagarag went to the chamber prepared for him in the palace.

Now, when it was night, Shibli Bagarag heard a noise at his lattice, and he arose and peered through it, and lo! the hawk was fluttering without; so he let it in, and caressed it, and the hawk bade him put on his silken dress and carry forth his China jar, and go the round of the palace, and offer drink to the sentinels and the slaves. So he did as the hawk directed, and the sentinels and slaves were aware of a China jar brimmed with wine that was lifted to their lips, but him that lifted it they saw not: surely, they drank deep of the draught of astonishment.

Then the hawk flew before him, and he followed it to a chamber lit with golden lamps, gorgeously hung, and full of a dusky splendour and the faint sparkle of gems, ruby, amethyst, topaz, and beryl; in it there was the hush of sleep, and the heart of Shibli Bagarag told him that one beautiful was near. So he approached on tiptoe a couch of blue silk, bordered with gold-wire, and inwoven with stars of blue turquoise stones, as it had been the heavens of midnight. On the couch lay one, a woman, pure in loveliness; the dark fringes of her closed lids like living flashes of darkness, her mouth like an unstrung bow and as a double rosebud, even as two isles of coral between which in the clear transparent watery beds the pearls shine freshly.

And the hawk said to Shibli Bagarag, "This is the Princess Goorelka, the daughter of the King of Oolb, a sorceress, the Guardian of the Lily of the Enchanted Sea. Beneath her pillow is the cockle-shell; grasp it, but gaze not upon her."

He approached and slid his arm beneath the pillow of the Princess, and grasped the cockle-shell; but ere he drew it forth he gazed upon her, and the lustre of her countenance transfixed him as with a javelin, so that he could not stir, nor move his eyes from the contemplation of her sweetness of feature. The hawk darted at him fiercely, and pecked at him to draw his attention from her, and he stepped back, yet he continued taking fatal draughts from the magic cup of her beauty. Then the hawk screamed a loud scream of anguish, and the Princess awoke, and started half-way from the couch, and stared about her, and saw the bird in agitation. As she looked at the bird a shudder passed over her, and she snatched a veil and drew it over her face, murmuring, "I dream, or I am under the eye of a man." Then she felt beneath the pillow, and knew that the cockle-shell had been touched; and in a moment she leapt from her couch, and ran to a mirror and saw herself as she was, a full-moon made to snare the wariest and sit singly high on a throne in the hearts of men. At the sight of her beauty she smiled and seemed at peace, murmuring still, "I am under the eye of a man, or I dream." Now, while she so murmured she arrayed herself, and took the cockle-shell, and passed through the ante-room among her women sleeping; and Shibli Bagarag tracked her till she came to the vault; and she entered it and walked to the corner from which had hung the dress of Samarcand. When she saw it gone her face waxed pale, and she gazed slowly at all points, muttering, "There is no further doubt but that I am under the eye of a man!" Thereupon she ran hastily from the vault, and passed between the sentinels of the palace, and saw them where they lay drowsy with intoxication: so she knew that the China jar and the dress of Samarcand had been used that night, and for no purpose friendly to her wishes. Then she passed down the palace steps, and through the gates of the palace and the city, till she came to the shore of the sea; there she launched the cockle-shell and took the wind in her garments, and sat in it, filling it to overflowing, yet it floated. And Shibli Bagarag waded to the cockle-shell and took hold of it, and was drawn along by its motion swiftly through the waters, so that a foam swept after him; and Goorelka marked the foam. Now, they had passage over the billows smoothly, and soon the length of the sea was darkened with two high rocks, and between them there was a narrow channel of the sea, roughened with moonlight. So they sped between the rocks, and came upon a purple sea, dark-blue overhead, with large stars leaning to the waves. There was a soft whisperingness in the breath of the breezes that swung there, and many sails of charmed ships were seen in momentary gleams, flapping the mast idly far away. Warm as new milk from the full udders were the waters of that sea, and figures of fair women stretched lengthwise with the current, and lifted a head as they rushed rolling by. Truly it was enchanted even to the very bed!

# The Lily of the Enchanted Sea

Now, after the cockle-shell had skimmed calmly awhile, it began to pitch and grew unquiet, and came upon a surging foam, pale, and with scintillating bubbles. The surges increased in volume, and boiled, hissing as with anger, like savage animals. Presently, the cockle-shell rose upon one very lofty swell, and Shibli Bagarag lost hold of it, and lo! it was overturned and engulfed in the descent of the great mountain of water, and the Princess Goorelka was immersed in the depths. She would have sunk, but Shibli Bagarag caught hold of her, and supported her to the shore by the strength of his right arm. The shore was one of sand and shells, their wet cheeks sparkling in the moonlight; over it hung a promontory, a huge jut of black rock. Now, the Princess when she landed, seeing not him that supported her, delayed not to run beneath the rock, and ascended by steps cut from the base of the rock. And Shibli Bagarag followed her by winding paths round the rock, till she came to the highest peak commanding the circle of the Enchanted Sea, and glimpses of enthralled vessels, and mariners bewitched on board; long paths of starlight rippled into the distant gloom, and the reflection of the moon opposite was as a wide nuptial sheet of silver on the waters: islands, green and white, and with soft music floating from their foliage, sailed slowly to and fro. Surely, to dwell reclining among the slopes of those islands a man would forfeit Paradise! Now, the Princess, as she stood upon the peak, knew that she was not alone, and pretended to slip from her footing, and Shibli Bagarag called out and ran to her; but she turned in the direction of his voice and laughed, and he knew he was outwitted. Then, to deceive her, he dropped from the phial twenty drops round her on the rock, and those twenty drops became twenty voices, so that she was bewildered with their calls, and stopped her ears, and ran from them, and descended from the eminence nimbly, slipping over ledges and leaping the abysses. And Shibli Bagarag followed her, clutching at the trailers and tearing them with him, letting loose a torrent of stones and earth, till on a sudden they stood together above a greenswarded basin of the rock opening to the sea; and in the middle of the basin, lo! in stature like a maiden of the mountains, and one that droopeth her head pensively thinking of her absent lover, the Enchanted Lily. Wonder knocked at the breast of Shibli Bagarag when he saw that queenly flower waving its illumined head to the breeze: he could not retain a cry of rapture. As he did this the Princess stretched her hand to where he was and groped a moment, and caught him by the silken dress and tore in it a great rent, and by the rent he stood revealed to her. Then said she, "O youth, thou halt done ill to follow me here, and the danger of it is past computing; surely, the motive was a deep one, nought other than the love of me."

She spoke winningly, sweet words to a luted voice, and the youth fell upon his knees before her, smitten by her beauty; and he said, "I followed thee here as I would follow such loveliness to the gates of doom, O Princess of Oolb."

She smiled and said playfully, "I will read by thy hand whether thou be one faithful in love."

She took his hand and sprinkled on it earth and gravel, and commenced scanning it curiously. As she scanned it her forehead wrinkled up, and a shot like black lightning travelled across her countenance, withering its beauty: she cried in a forced voice, "Aha! it is well, O youth, for thee and for me that thou lovest me, and art faithful in love."

The look of the Princess of Oolb and her voice affrighted the soul of Shibli Bagarag, and he would have turned from her; but she held him, and went to the Lily, and emptied into the palm of her hand the dew that was in the Lily, and raised it to the lips of Shibli Bagarag, bidding him drink as a pledge for her sake and her love, and to appease his thirst. As he was about to drink, there fell into the palm of the Princess from above what seemed a bolt of storm scattering the dew; and after he had blinked with the suddenness of the action he looked and beheld the hawk, its red eyes inflamed with wrath. And the hawk screamed into the ear of Shibli Bagarag, "Pluck up the Lily ere it is too late, O fool!—the dew was poison! Pluck it by the root with thy right hand!"

So thereat he strode to the Lily, and grasped it, and pulled with his strength; and the Lily was loosened, and yielded, and came forth streaming with blood from the bulb of the root; surely the bulb of the root was a palpitating heart, yet warm, even as that we have within our bosoms.

Now, from the terror of that sight the Princess hid her eyes, and shrank away. And the lines of malice, avarice, and envy seemed ageing her at every breath. Then the hawk pecked at her three pecks, and perched on a corner of rock, and called shrilly the name "Karaz!" And the Genie Karaz came slanting down the night air, like a preying bird, and stood among them. So the hawk cried, "See, O Karaz, the freshness of thy Princess of Oolb"; and the Genie regarded her till loathing curled his lip, for she grew in ghastliness to the colour of a frog, and a frog's face was hers, a camel's back, a pelican's throat, the legs of a peacock.

Then the hawk cried, "Is this how ye meet, ye lovers,—ye that will be wedded?" And the hawk made his tongue as a thorn to them. At the last it exclaimed, "Now let us fight our battle, Karaz!"

But the Genie said, "Nay, there will come a time for that, traitress!"

The hawk cried, "Thou delayest, till the phial of Paravid, the hairs of Garraveen, and this Lily, my three helps, are expended, thinking Aklis, for which we barter them, striketh but a single blow? That is well! Go, then, and take thy Princess, and obtain permission of the King of Oolb, her father, to wed her, O Karaz!"

The hawk whistled with laughter, and the Genie was stung with its mockeries, and clutched the Princess of Oolb in a bunch, and arose from the ground with her, slanting up the night-air like fire, till he was seen high up even as an angry star reddening the seas beneath.

When he was lost to the eye, Shibli Bagarag drew a long breath and cried aloud, "The likeness of that Princess of Oolb in her ugliness to Noorna, my betrothed, is a thing marvellous, if it be not she herself." And he reflected, "Yet she seemed not to recognize and claim me"; and thought, "I am bound to her by gratitude, and I should have rescued her from Karaz, but I know not if it be she. Wullahy! I am bewildered; I will ask counsel of the hawk." He looked to the corner of the rock where the hawk had perched, but the hawk was gone; as he searched for it, his eyes fell upon the bed of earth where the Lily stood ere he plucked it, and lo! in the place of the Lily, there was a damsel dressed in white shining silks, fairer than the enchanted flower, straighter than the stalk of it; her head slightly drooping, like the moon on a border of the night; her bosom like the swell of the sea in moonlight; her eyes dark, under a low arch of darker lashes, like stars on the skirts of storm; and she was the very dream of loveliness, formed to freeze with awe, and to inflame with passion. So Shibli Bagarag gazed at her with adoration, his hands stretched half-way to her as if to clasp her, fearing she was a vision and would fade; and the damsel smiled a sweet smile, and lifted her antelope eyes, and said, "Who am I, and to whom might I be likened, O youth?"

And he answered, "Who thou art, O young perfection, I know not, if not a Houri of Paradise; but thou art like the Princess of Oolb, yet lovelier, oh lovelier! And thy voice is the voice of Noorna, my betrothed; yet purer, sweeter, younger."

So the damsel laughed a laugh like a sudden sweeping of wild chords of music, and said, "O youth, saw'st thou not the ascent of Noorna, thy betrothed, gathered in a bunch by Karaz?"

And he answered, "I saw her; but I knew not, O damsel of beauty; surely I was bewildered, amazed, without power to contend with the Genie."

Then she said, "Wouldst thou release her? So kiss me on the lips, on the eyes, and on the forehead, three kisses each time; and with the first say, 'By the well of Paravid'; and with the second, 'By the strength of Garraveen!' and with the third, 'By the Lily of the Sea!'"

Now, the heart of the youth bounded at her words, and he went to her, and trembling kissed her all bashfully on the lips, on the eyes, and on the forehead, saying each time as she directed. Then she took him by the hand, and stepped from the bed of earth, crying joyfully, "Thanks be to Allah and the Prophet! Noorna, is released from the sorceries that held her, and powerful."

So, while he was wondering, she said, "Knowest thou not the woman, thy betrothed?"

He answered, "O damsel of beauty, I am charged with many feelings; doubts and hopes are mixed in me. Say first who thou art, and fill my two ears with bliss."

And she said, "I will leave my name to other lips; surely I am the daughter of the Vizier Feshnavat, betrothed to a wandering youth,—a barber, who sickened at the betrothal, and consoled himself with a proverb when he gave me the kiss of contract, and knew not how with truth to pay me a compliment."

Now, Shibli Bagarag saw this was indeed Noorna bin Noorka, his betrothed, and he fell before her in love and astonishment; but she lifted him to her neck, and embraced him, saying, "Said I not truly when I said 'I am that I shall be'? My youth is not as that of Bhanavar the Beautiful, gained at another's cost, but my own, and stolen from me by wicked sorceries." And he cried, "Tell me, O Noorna, my betrothed, how this matter came to pass?"

She said, "On our way to Aklis."

She bade him grasp the Lily, and follow her; and he followed her down the rock and over the bright shells upon the sand, admiring her stateliness, her willowy lightness, her slimness as of the palm-tree. Then

GEORGE MEREDITH

she waded in the water, and began to strike out with her arms, and swim boldly,—he likewise; and presently they came to a current that hurried them off in its course, and carried them as weeds, streaming rapidly. He was bearing witness to his faith as a man that has lost hope of life, when a strong eddy stayed him, and whirled him from the current into the calm water. So he looked for Noorna, and saw her safe beside him flinging back the wet tresses from her face, that was like the full moon growing radiant behind a dispersing cloud. And she said, "Ask not for the interpretation of wonders in this sea, for they cluster like dates on a date branch. Surely, to be with me is enough?"

And she bewitched him in the midst of the waters, making him oblivious of all save her, so that he hugged the golden net of her smiles and fair flatteries, and swam with an exulting stroke, giving his breast broadly to the low billows, and shouting verses of love and delight to her. And while they swam sweetly, behold, there was seen a pearly shell of flashing crimson, amethyst, and emerald, that came scudding over the waves toward them, raised to the wind, fan-shaped, and in its front two silver seats. When she saw it, Noorna cried, "She has sent me this, Rabesqurat! Perchance is she favourable to my wishes, and this were well!"

Then she swayed in the water sideways, and drew the shell to her, and the twain climbed into it, and sat each on one of the silver seats, folded together. In its lightness it was as a foam-bubble before the wind on the blue water, and bore them onward airily. At his feet Shibli Bagarag beheld a stool of carved topaz, and above his head the arch of the shell was inlaid with wreaths of gems: never was vessel fairer than that.

Now, while they were speeding over the water, Noorna said, "The end of this fair sea is Aklis, and beyond it is the Koosh. So while the wind is our helmsman, and we go circled by the quiet of this sea, I'll tell thee of myself, if thou carest to hear."

And he cried with the ardour of love, "Surely, I would hear of nought save thyself, Noorna, and the music of the happy garden compareth not in sweetness with it. I long for the freshness of thy voice, as the desert camel for the green spring, O my betrothed!"

So she said, "And now give ear to the following":—

# And this is the Story of Noorna Bin Noorka, the Genie Karaz, and the Princess of Oolb

K now, that when I was a babe, I lay on my mother's bosom in the wilderness, and it was the bosom of death. Surely, I slept and smiled, and dreamed the infant's dream, and knew not the coldness of the thing I touched. So were we even as two dead creatures lying there; but life was in me, and I awoke with hunger at the time of feeding, and turned to my mother, and put up my little mouth to her for nourishment, and sucked her, but nothing came. I cried, and commenced chiding her, and after a while it was as decreed, that certain horsemen of a troop passing through the wilderness beheld me, and seeing my distress and the helpless being I was, their hearts were stirred, and they were mindful of what the poet says concerning succour given to the poor, helpless, and innocent of this world, and took me up, and mixed for me camel's milk and water from the bags, and comforted me, and bore me with them, after they had paid funeral rites to the body of my mother.

Now, the rose-bud showeth if the rose-tree be of the wilds or of the garden, and the chief of that troop seeing me born to the uses of gentleness, carried me in his arms with him to his wife, and persuaded her that was childless to make me the child of their adoption. So I abode with them during the period of infancy and childhood, caressed and cared for, as is said:

> *The flower a stranger's hand may gather,*
> *Strikes root into the stranger's breast;*
> *Affection is our mother, father,*
> *Friend, and of cherishers the best.*

And I loved them as their own child, witting not but that I was their child, till on a day while I played among some children of my years, the daughter of the King of Oolb passed by us on a mule, with her slaves and drawn swords, and called to me, "Thou little castaway!" and had me brought to her, and peered upon my face in a manner that frightened me, for I was young. Then she put me down from the neck of her mule where she had seated me, saying, "Child of a dead mother and a runaway father, what need I fear from thy like, and the dreams of a love-sick Genie?" So she departed, but I forgot not her words, and dwelt upon them, and grew fevered with them, and drooped. Now, when he saw my bloom of health gone, heaviness on my feet, the light hollowed from my eyes, my benefactor, Ravaloke—he that I had thought my father—took me between his knees, and asked me what it was and the cause of my ailing; and I told him.

Then said he, "This is so: thou art not my child; but I love thee as mine, O my little Desert-flower; and why the Princess should fancy fear of thee I like not to think; but fear thou her, for she is a mask of wiles and a vine trailing over pitfalls; such a sorceress the world knoweth not as Goorelka of Oolb."

Now, I was penetrated by what he said, and ceased to be a companion to them that loved childish games and romps, and meditated by myself in gardens and closets, feigning sleep when the elder ones discoursed, that I might learn something of this mystery, and all that was spoken perplexed me more, as the sage declareth:

*Who in a labyrinth wandereth without clue,*
*More that he wandereth doth himself undo.*

Though I was quick as the quick-eyed falcon, I discovered nought, flying ever at false game,—

*A follower of misleading beams,*
*A cheated soul, the mock of dreams.*

At times I thought that it was the King of Oolb was my father, and plotted to come in his path; and there were kings and princes of far countries whom I sought to encounter, that they might claim me; but none claimed me. O my betrothed, few gave me love beside Ravaloke, and when the wife that he cherished died, he solely, for I was lost in waywardness and the slave of moody imaginings. 'Tis said:

*If thou the love of the world for thyself wouldst gain,*
*mould thy breast*
*Liker the world to become, for its like the world loveth best;*

and this was not I then.

Now, the sons and daughters of men are used to celebrate the days of their birth with gifts and rejoicings, but I could only celebrate that day which delivered me from death into the hands of Ravaloke, as none knew my birth-hour. When it was the twelfth return of this event, Ravaloke, my heart's father, called me to him and pressed in my hand a glittering coin, telling me to buy with it in the bazaars what I would. So I went forth, attended by a black slave, after the mid-noon, for I was eager to expend my store, and cared not for the great heat. Scarcely had we passed the cheese-market and were hurrying on to shops of the goldsmiths and jewellers, when I saw an old man, a beggar, in a dirty yellow turban and pieced particoloured cloth-stuff, and linen in rags his other gear. So lean was he, and looked so weak that I wondered he did other than lay his length on the ground; and as he asked me for alms his voice had a piteousness that made me to weep, and I punished my slave for seeking to drive him away, and gave my one piece of gold into his hand. Then he asked me what I required of him in exchange, and I said, "What can a poor old man that is a beggar give?" He laughed, and asked me then what I had intended to buy with that piece of money. So, beginning to regret the power that was gone from me of commanding with my gold piece this and that fine thing, I mused, and said, "Truly, a blue dress embroidered with gold, and a gold crown, and gold bracelets set with turquoise stones,—these, and toys; but could I buy in this city a book of magic, that were my purchase."

The old fellow smiled, and said to my black slave, "And thou, hadst thou this coin, what were thy purchase therewith?"

He, scoffing the old beggar, answered, "A plaister for sores as broad as my back, and a camel's hump, O thou old villain!"

The old man grunted in his chest, and said, "Thou art but a camel thyself, to hinder a true Mussulman from passing in peace down a street of Oolb; so 'twere a good purchase and a fitting: know'st thou what is said of the blessing given by them that receive a charity?

*'Tis the fertilizing dew that streameth after the sun,*
*Strong as the breath of Allah to bless life well begun.'*

So is my blessing on the little damsel, and she shall have her wish, wullahy, thou black face! and thou thine."

This spake the old man, and hobbled off while my slave was jeering him. So I strolled through the bazaars and thought no more of the old man's words, and longed to purchase a hundred fineries, and came to the confectioner's, and smelt the smell of his musk-scented sweetmeats and lemon sweets and sugared pistachios that are delicious to crunch between the teeth. My mouth watered, and I said to my slave, "O Kadrab, a coin, though 'twere small, would give us privilege in yonder shop to select, and feast, and approve the skill of the confectioner."

He grinned, and displayed in his black fist a petty coin of exchange, but would not let me have it till I had sworn to give no more away to beggars. So even as we were hurrying into the shop, another old beggar wretcheder than the first fronted me, and I was moved, and forgot my promise to Kadrab, and gave him the money. Then was Kadrab wroth, and kicked the old beggar with his fore-foot, lifting him high in air, and lo! he did not alight, but rose over the roofs of the houses and beyond the city, till he was but a speck in the blue of the sky above. So Kadrab bit his forefinger amazed, and glanced at his foot, and at what was visible of the old beggarman, and again at his foot, thinking but of what he had done with it, and the might manifested in that kick, fool that he was! All the way homeward he kept scanning the sky and lifting his foot aloft, and I saw him bewildered with a strange conceit, as the poet has exclaimed in his scorn:

> *Oh, world diseased! oh, race empirical!*
> *Where fools are the fathers of every miracle!*

Now, when I was in my chamber, what saw I there but a dress of very costly blue raiment with gold-work broidery and a lovely circlet of gold, and gold bracelets set with stones of turquoise, and a basket of gold woven wire, wherein were toys, wondrous ones—soldiers that cut off each other's heads and put them on again, springing antelopes, palm-trees that turned to fountains, and others; and lo! a book in red binding, with figures on it and clasps of gold, a great book! So I clapped my hands joyfully, crying, "The old beggar has done it!" and robed myself in the dress, and ran forth to tell Ravaloke. As I ran by a window looking on the inner court, I saw below a crowd of all the slaves of Ravaloke round one that was seeking to escape from them, and 'twas Kadrab with a camel's hump on his back, and a broad brown plaister over it, the wretch howling, peering across his shoulder, and trying to bolt from his burden, as a horse that would run from his rider. Then I saw that Kadrab also had his wish, his camel's hump, and thought, "The old beggar, what was he but a Genie?" Surely Ravaloke caressed me when he heard of the adventure, and what had befallen Kadrab was the jest of the city; but for me I spared little time away from that book, and studied in it incessantly the ways and windings of magic, till I could hold communication with Genii, and wield charms to summon them, and utter spells that subdue them, discovering the haunts of talismans that enthral Afrites and are powerful among men. There was that Kadrab coming to me daily to call out in the air for the old beggarman to rid him of his hump; and he would waste hours looking up into the sky moodily for him, and cursing the five toes of his foot, for he doubted not the two beggars were one, and that he was punished for the kick, and lamented it direly, saying in the thick of his whimperings, "I'd give the foot that did it to be released from my hump, O my fair mistress." So I pitied him, and made a powder and a spell, and my first experiment in magic was to relieve Kadrab of his hump, and I succeeded in loosening it, and it came away from him, and sank into the ground of the garden where we stood. So I told Kadrab to say nothing of this, but the idle-pated fellow blabbed it over the city, and it came to the ears of Goorelka. Then she sent for me to visit her, and by the advice of Ravaloke I went, and she fondled me, and sought to get at the depth of my knowledge by a spell that tieth every faculty save the tongue, and it is the spell of vain longing. Now, because I baffled her arts she knew me more cunning than I seemed, and as night advanced she affected to be possessed with pleasure in me, and took me in her arms and sought to fascinate me, and I heard her mutter once, "Shall I doubt the warning of Karaz?" So presently she said, "Come with me"; and I went with her under the curtain of that apartment into another, a long saloon, wherein were couches round a fountain, and beyond it an aviary lit with lamps: when we were there she whistled, and immediately there was a concert of birds, a wondrous accord of exquisite piping, and she leaned on a couch and took me by her to listen; sweet and passionate was the harmony of the birds; but I let not my faculties lull, and observed that round the throat of every bird was a ringed mark of gold and stamps of divers gems similar in colour to a ring on the forefinger of her right hand, which she dazzled my sight with as she flashed it. When we had listened a long hour to this music, the Princess gazed on me as if to mark the effect of a charm, and I saw disappointment on her lovely face, and she bit her lip and looked spiteful, saying, "Thou art far gone in the use of magic, and wary, O girl!" Then she laughed unnaturally, and called slaves to bring

GEORGE MEREDITH

in sweet drinks to us, and I drank with her, and became less wary, and she fondled me more, calling me tender names, heaping endearments on me; and as the hour of the middle-night approached I was losing all suspicion in deep languor, and sighed at the song of the birds, the long love-song, and dozed awake with eyes half shut. I felt her steal from me, and continued still motionless without alarm: so was I mastered. What hour it was or what time had passed I cannot say, when a bird that was chained on a perch before me—a very quaint bird, with a topknot awry, and black, heavy bill, and ragged gorgeousness of plumage—the only object between my lids and darkness, suddenly, in the midst of the singing, let loose a hoarse laugh that was followed by peals of laughter from the other birds. Thereat I started up, and beheld the Princess standing over a brazier, and she seized a slipper from her foot and flung it at the bird that had first laughed, and struck him off his perch, and went to him and seized him and shook him, crying, "Dare to laugh again!" and he kept clearing his throat and trying to catch the tune he had lost, pitching a high note and a low note; but the marvel of this laughter of the bird wakened me thoroughly, and I thanked the bird in my soul, and said to Goorelka, "More wondrous than their singing, this laughter, O Princess!"

She would not speak till she had beaten every bird in the aviary, and then said in the words of the poet:

> *Shall they that deal in magic match degrees of wonder?*
> *From the bosom of one cloud comes the lightning and the thunder.*

Then said she, "O Noorna! I'll tell thee truly my intent, which was to enchant thee; but I find thee wise, so let us join our powers, and thou shalt become mighty as a sorceress."

Now, Ravaloke had said to me, "Her friendship is fire, her enmity frost; so be cold to the former, to the latter hot," and I dissembled and replied, "Teach me, O Princess!"

So she asked me what I could do. Could I plant a mountain in the sea and people it? could I anchor a purple cloud under the sun and live there a year with them I delighted in? could I fix the eyes of the world upon one head and make the nations bow to it; change men to birds, fishes to men; and so on—a hundred sorceries that I had never attempted and dreamed not of my betrothed! I had never offended Allah by a misuse of my powers. When I told her, she cried, "Thou art then of a surety she that's fitted for the custody of the Lily of the Light, so come with me."

Now, I had heard of the Lily, even this thou holdest may its influence be unwithering!—and desired to see it. So she led me from the palace to the shore of the sea, and flung a cockleshell on the waters, and seated herself in it with me in her lap; and we scudded over the waters, and entered this Enchanted Sea, and stood by the Lily. Then, I that loved flowers undertook the custody of this one, knowing not the consequences and the depth of her wiles. 'Tis truly said:

> *The overwise themselves hoodwink,*
> *For simple eyesight is a modest thing:*
> *They on the black abysm's brink*
> *Smile, and but when they fall bitterly think,*
> *What difference 'twixt the fool and me, Creation's King?*

Nevertheless for awhile nothing evil resulted, and I had great joy in the flower, and tended it with exceeding watchfulness, and loved it, so that I was brought in my heart to thank the Princess and think well of her.

Now, one summer eve as Ravaloke rested under the shade of his garden palm, and I studied beside him great volumes of magic, it happened that after I had read certain pages I closed one of the books marked on the cover "Alif," and shut the clasp louder than I intended, so that he who was dozing started up, and his head was in the sloped sun in an instant, and I observed the shadow of his head lengthen out along the grass-plot towards the mossed wall, and it shot up the wall, darkening it—then drawing back and lessening, then darting forth like a beast of darkness irritable for prey. I was troubled, for whatso is seen while the volume Alif is in use hath a portent; but the discovery of what this might be baffled me. So I determined to watch events, and it was not many days ere Ravaloke, who was the leader of the armies of the King of Oolb, was called forth to subdue certain revolted tributaries of the King, and at my entreaty took me with him, and I saw battles and encounters lasting a day's length. Once we were encamped in a fruitful country by a brook running with a bright eye between green banks, and I that had freedom and the password of the camp wandered down to it, and refreshed my forehead with its coolness. So, as I looked under the falling drops, lo! on the opposite bank the old beggar that

GEORGE MEREDITH

had given me such fair return for my alms and Kadrab his hump! I heard him call, "This night is the key to the mystery," and he was gone. Every incantation I uttered was insufficient to bring him back. Surely, I hurried to the tents and took no sleep, watching zealously by the tent of Ravaloke, crouched in its shadow. About the time of the setting of the moon I heard footsteps approach the tent within the circle of the guard, and it was a youth that held in his hand naked steel. When he was by the threshold of the tent, I rose before him and beheld the favourite of Ravaloke, even the youth he had destined to espouse me; so I reproached him, and he wept, denying not the intention he had to assassinate Ravaloke, and when his soul was softened he confessed to me, "'Twas that I might win the Princess Goorelka, and she urged me to it, promising the King would promote me to the vacant post of Ravaloke."

Then I said to him, "Lov'st thou Goorelka?"

And he answered, "Yea, though I know my doom in loving her; and that it will be the doom of them now piping to her pleasure and denied the privilege of laughter."

So I thought, "Oh, cruel sorceress! the birds are men!" And as I mused, my breast melted with pity at their desire to laugh, and the little restraint they had upon themselves notwithstanding her harshness; for could they think of their changed condition and folly without laughter? and the folly that sent them fresh mates in misery was indeed matter for laughter, fed to fulness by constant meditation on the perch. Meantime, I uncharmed the youth and bade him retire quickly; but as he was going, he said, "Beware of the Genie Karaz!" Then I held him back, and after a parley he told me what he had heard the Princess say, and it was that Karaz had seen me and sworn to possess me for my beauty. "Strangely smiled Goorelka when she spake that," said he.

Now, the City of Oolb fronts the sea, and behind it is a mountain and a wood, where the King met Ravaloke on his return victorious over the rebels. So, to escape the eye of the King I parted with Ravaloke, and sought to enter the city by a circuitous way; but the paths wound about and zigzagged, and my slaves suffered nightfall to surprise us in the entanglements of the wood. I sent them in different directions to strike into the main path, retaining Kadrab at the bridle of my mule; but that creature now began to address me in a familiar tone, and he said something of love for me that enraged me, so that I hit him a blow. Then came from him sounds like the neighing of mares, and lo! he seized me and rose with me in the air, and I thought the very heavens were opening to that black beast, when on a sudden he paused, and shot down with me from heights of the stars to the mouth of a cavern by the Putrid Sea, and dragged me into a cavern greatly illuminated, hung like a palace chamber, and supported on pillars of shining jasper. Then I fell upon the floor in a swoon, and awaking saw Kadrab no longer, but in his place a Genie. O my soul, thou halt seen him!—I thought at once, "'tis Karaz!" and when he said to me, "This is thy abode, O lady! and I he that have sworn to possess thee from the hour I saw thee in the chamber of Goorelka," then was I certain 'twas Karaz. So, collecting the strength of my soul, I said, in the words of the poet:

*"Woo not a heart preoccupied!*
*What thorn is like a loathing bride?*
*Mark ye the shrubs how they turn from the sea,*
*The sea's rough whispers shun?*
*But like the sun of heaven be,*
*And every flower will open wide.*
*Woo with the shining patience we*
*Beheld in heaven's sun."*

Then he sang:

*Exquisite lady! name the smart*
*That fills thy heart.*
*Thou art the foot and I the worm:*
*Prescribe the Term.*

Finding him compliant, I said, "O great Genie, truly the search of my life has been to discover him that is, my father, and how I was left in the wilderness. There's no peace for me, nor understanding the word of love, till I hear by whom I was left a babe on the bosom of a dead mother."

He exclaimed, and his eyes twinkled, "'Tis that? that shalt thou know in a span of time. O my mistress, hast thou seen the birds of Goorelka? Thy father Feshnavat is among them, perched like a bird."

So I cried, "And tell me how he may be disenchanted."

He said, "Swear first to be mine unreluctantly."

Then I said, "What is thy oath?"

He answered, "I swear, when I swear, by the Identical."

Thereupon I questioned him concerning the Identical, what it was; and he, not suspecting, revealed to me the mighty hair in his head now in the head of Shagpat, even that. So I swore by that to give myself to the possessor of the Identical, and flattered him. Then said he, "O lovely damsel, I am truly one of the most powerful of the Genii; yet am I in bondage to that sorceress Goorelka by reason of a ring she holdeth; and could I get that ring from her and be slave to nothing mortal an hour, I could light creation as a torch, and broil the inhabitants of earth at one fire."

I thought, "That ring is known to me!" And he continued, "Surely I cannot assist thee in this work other than by revealing the means of disenchantment, and it is to keep the birds laughing uninterruptedly an hour; then are they men again, and take the forms of men that are laughers—I know not why."

So I cried, "'Tis well! carry me back to Oolb."

Then the Genie lifted me into the air, and ceased not speeding rapidly through it, till I was on the roof of the house of Ravaloke. O sweet youth! moon of my soul! from that time to the disenchantment of Feshnavat, I pored over my books, trying experiments in magic, dreadful ones, hunting for talismans to countervail Goorelka; but her power was great, and 'twas not in me to get her away from the birds one hour to free them. On a certain occasion I had stolen to them, and kept them laughing with stories of man to within an instant of the hour; and they were laughing exultingly with the easy happy laugh of them that perceive deliverance sure, when she burst in and beat them even to the door of death. I saw too in her eyes, that glowed like the eyes of wild cats in the dark, she suspected me, and I called Allah to aid the just cause against the sinful, and prepared to war with her.

Now, my desire, which was to liberate my father and his fellows in tribulation, I knew pure, and had no fear of the sequel, as is declared:

> *Fear nought so much as Fear itself; for arm'd with Fear the Foe*
> *Finds passage to the vital part, and strikes a double blow.*

So one day as I leaned from my casement looking on the garden seaward, I saw a strange red and yellow-feathered bird that flew to the branch of a citron-tree opposite, with a ring in its beak; and the bird was singing, and with every note the ring dropped from its bill, and it descended swiftly in an arrowy slant downward, and seized it ere it reached the ground, and commenced singing afresh. When I had marked this to happen many times, I thought, "How like is this bird to an innocent soul possessed of magic and using its powers! Lo, it seeketh still to sing as one of the careless, and cannot relinquish the ring and be as the careless, and between the two there is neither peace for it nor pleasure." Now, while my eyes were on the pretty bird, dwelling on it, I saw it struck suddenly by an arrow beneath the left wing, and the bird fluttered to my bosom and dropped in it the ring from its beak. Then it sprang weakly, and sought to fly and soar, and fluttered; but a blue film lodged over its eyes, and its panting was quickly ended. So I looked at the ring and knew it for that one I had noted on the finger of Goorelka. Red blushed my bliss, and 'twas revealed to me that the bird was of the birds of the Princess that had escaped from her with the ring. I buried the bird, weeping for it, and flew to my books, and as I read a glow stole over me. O my betrothed, eyes of my soul! I read that the possessor of that ring was mistress of the marvellous hair which is a magnet to the homage of men, so that they crowd and crush and hunger to adore it, even the Identical! This was the power that peopled the aviary of Goorelka, and had well-nigh conquered all the resistance of my craft.

Now, while I read there arose a hubbub and noise in the outer court, and shrieks of slaves. The noise approached with rapid strides, and before I could close my books Goorelka burst in upon me, crying, "Noorna! Noorna!" Wild and haggard was her head, and she rushed to my books and saw them open at the sign of the ring: then began our combat. She menaced me as never mortal was menaced. Rapid lightning-flashes were her transformations, and she was a serpent, a scorpion, a lizard, a lioness in succession, but I leapt perpetually into fresh rings of fire and of witched water; and at the fiftieth transformation, she fell on the floor exhausted, a shuddering heap. Seeing that, I ran from her to the aviary in her palace, and hurried over a story of men to the birds, that rocked them on their perches with chestquakes of irresistible laughter. Then flew I back to the Princess, and she still puffing on the floor, commenced wheedling and begging the ring of me, stinting no promises. At last she cried, "Girl! what is this ring to thee without beauty? Thy beauty is in my keeping."

And I exclaimed, "How? how?" smitten to the soul.

She answered, "Yea; and I can wear it as my own, adding it to my own, when thou'rt a hag!"

My betrothed! I was on the verge of giving her the ring for this secret, when a violent remote laughter filled the inner hollow of my ears, and it increased, till the Princess heard it; and now the light of my casement was darkened with birds, the birds of Goorelka, laughing as on a wind of laughter. So I opened to them, and they darted in, laughing all of them, till I could hold out no longer, and the infection of laughter seized me, and I rolled with it; and the Princess, she too laughed a hyaena-laugh under a cat's grin, and we all of us remained in this wise some minutes, laughing the breath out of our bodies, as if death would take us. Whoso in the City of Oolb heard us, the slaves, the people, and the King, laughed, knowing not the cause. This day is still remembered in Oolb as the day of laughter. Now, at a stroke of the hour the laughter ceased, and I saw in the chamber a crowd of youths and elders of various ranks; but their visages were become long and solemn as that of them that have seen a dark experience. 'Tis certain they laughed little in their lives from that time, and the muscles of their cheeks had rest. So I caught down my veil, and cried to the Princess, "My father is among these; point him out to me."

Ere she replied one stepped forth, even Feshnavat, my father, and called me by name, and knew me by a spot on the left arm, and made himself known to me, and told me the story of my dead mother, how she had missed her way from the caravan in the desert, and he searching her was set upon by robbers, and borne on their expeditions. Nothing said he of the sorceries of Goorelka, and I, not wishing to provoke the Princess, suffered his dread to exist. So I kissed him, and bowed my head to him, and she fled from the sight of innocent happiness. Then took I the ring, and summoned Karaz, and ordered him to reinstate all those princes and chiefs and officers in their possessions and powers, on what part of earth soever that might be. Never till I stood as the Lily and thy voice sweetened the name of love in my ears, heard I aught of delicate delightfulness, like the sound of their gratitude. Many wooed me to let them stay by me and guard me, and do service all their lives to me; but this I would not allow, and though they were fair as moons, some of them, I responded not to their soft glances, speaking calmly the word of farewell, for I was burdened with other thoughts.

Now, when the Genie had done my bidding, he returned to me joyfully. My soul sickened to think myself his by a promise; but I revolved the words of my promise, and saw in them a loophole of escape. So, when he claimed me, I said, "Ay! ay! lay thy head in my lap," as if my mind treasured it. Then he lay there, and revealed to me his plans for the destruction of men. "Or," said he, "they shall be our slaves and burden-beasts, for there's now no restraint on me, now thou art mistress of the ring, and mine." Thereupon his imagination swelled, and he saw his evil will enthroned, and the hopes of men beneath his heel, crying, "And the more I crush them the thicker they crowd, for the Identical compelleth their very souls to adore in spite of distaste."

Then said I, "Tell me, O Genie! is the Identical subservient to me in another head save thine?"

He answered, "Nay I in another head 'tis a counteraction to the power of the Ring, the Ring powerless over it."

And I said, "Must it live in a head, the Identical?"

Cried he, "Woe to what else holdeth it!"

I whispered in his hairy pointed red ear, "Sleep! sleep!" and lulled him with a song, and he slept, being weary with my commissioning. Then I bade Feshnavat, my father, fetch me one of my books of magic, and read in it of the discovery of the Identical by means of the Ring; and I took the Ring and hung it on a hair of my own head over the head of the Genie, and saw one of the thin lengths begin to twist and dart and writhe, and shift lustres as a creature in anguish. So I put the Ring on my forefinger, and turned the hair round and round it, and tugged. Lo, with a noise that stunned me, the hair came out! O my betrothed, what shrieks and roars were those: with which the Genie awoke, finding himself bare of the Identical! Oolb heard them, and the sea foamed like the mouth of madness, as the Genie sped thunder-like over it, following me in mid-air. Such a flight was that! Now, I found it not possible to hold the Identical, for it twisted and stung, and was nigh slipping from me while I flew. I saw white on a corner of the Desert, a city, and I descended on it by the shop of a clothier that sat quietly by his goods and stuffs, thinking of fate less than of kabobs and stews and rare seasonings. That city hath now his name. Wullahy, had I not then sown in his head that hair which he weareth yet, how had I escaped Karaz, and met thee? Wondrous are the decrees of Providence! Praise be to Allah for them! So the Genie, when he found himself baffled by me, and Shagpat with the mighty hair in his head, the Identical, he yelled, and fetched Shagpat a slap that sent him into the middle of the street; but Kadza screamed after him, and there was immediately such lamentation in the city about Shagpat, and such tearing of hair about him, that I perceived at once the virtue that was in the Identical.

As for Karaz, finding his claim as possessor of the Identical no more valid, he vanished, and has been my rebellious slave since, till thou, O my betrothed, mad'st me spend him in curing thy folly on the horse Garraveen, and he escaped from my circles beyond the dominion of the Ring; yet had he his revenge, for I that was keeper of the Lily, had, I now learned ruefully, a bond of beauty with it, and whatever was a stain to one withered the other. Then that sorceress Goorelka stole my beauty from me by sprinkling a blight on the petals of the fair flower, and I became as thou first saw'st me. But what am I as I now am? Blissful! blissful! Surely I grew humble with the loss of beauty, and by humility wise, so that I assisted Feshnavat to become Vizier by the Ring, and watched for thy coming to shave Shagpat, as a star watcheth; for 'tis written, "A barber alone shall be shearer of the Identical"; and he only, my betrothed, hath power to plant it in Aklis, where it groweth as a pillar, bringing due reverence to Aklis.

# The Wiles of Rabesqurat

N ow, when Noorna bin Noorka had made an end of her narration, she folded her hands and was mute awhile; and to the ear of Shibli Bagarag it seemed as if a sweet instrument had on a sudden ceased luting. So, as he leaned, listening for her voice to recommence, she said quickly, "See yonder fire on the mountain's height!"

He looked and saw a great light on the summit of a lofty mountain before them.

Then said she, "That is Aklis! and it is ablaze, knowing a visitant near. Tighten now the hairs of Garraveen about thy wrist; touch thy lips with the waters of Paravid; hold before thee the Lily, and make ready to enter the mountain. Lo, my betrothed, thou art in possession of the three means that melt opposition, and the fault is thine if thou fail."

He did as she directed; and they were taken on a tide and advanced rapidly to the mountain, so that the waters smacked and crackled beneath the shell, covering it with silver showering arches of glittering spray. Then the fair beams of the moon became obscured, and the twain reddened with the reflection of the fire, and the billows waxed like riotous flames; and presently the shell rose upon the peak of many waves swollen to one, and looking below, they saw in the scarlet abyss of waters at their feet a monstrous fish, with open jaws and one baleful eye; and the fish was lengthy as a caravan winding through the desert, and covered with fiery scales. Shibli Bagarag heard the voice of Noorna shriek affrightedly, "Karaz!" and as they were sliding on the down slope, she stood upright in the shell, pronouncing rapidly some words in magic; and the shell closed upon them both, pressing them together, and writing darkness on their very eyeballs. So, while they were thus, they felt themselves gulped in, and borne forward with terrible swiftness, they knew not where, like one that hath a dream of sinking; and outside the shell a rushing, gurgling noise, and a noise as of shouting multitudes, and muffled multitudes muttering complaints and yells and querulous cries, told them they were yet speeding through the body of the depths in the belly of the fish. Then there came a shock, and the shell was struck with light, and they were sensible of stillness without motion. Then a blow on the shell shivered it to fragments, and they were blinded with seas of brilliancy on all sides from lamps and tapers and crystals, cornelians and gems of fiery lustre, liquid lights and flashing mirrors, and eyes of crowding damsels, bright ones. So, when they had risen, and could bear to gaze on the insufferable splendour, they saw sitting on a throne of coral and surrounded by slaves with scimitars, a fair Queen, with black eyes, kindlers of storms, torches in the tempest, and with floating tresses, crowned with a circlet of green-spiked precious stones and masses of crimson weed with flaps of pearl; and she was robed with a robe of amber, and had saffron sandals, loose silvery-silken trousers tied in at the ankle, the ankle white as silver; wonderful was the quivering of rays from the jewels upon her when she but moved a finger! Now, as they stood with their hands across their brows, she cried out, "O ye traversers of my sea! how is this, that I am made to thank Karaz for a sight of ye?"

And Noorna bin Noorka answered, "Surely, O Queen Rabesqurat, the haven of our voyage was Aklis, and we feared delay, seeing the fire of the mountain ablaze with expectations of us."

Then the Queen cried angrily, "'Tis well thou hadst wit to close the shell, O Noorna, or there would have been delay indeed. Say, is not the road to Aklis through my palace? And it is the road thousands travel."

So Noorna bin Noorka said, "O Queen, this do they; but are they of them that reach Aklis?"

And the Queen cried violently, purpling with passion, "This to me! when I helped ye to the plucking of the Lily?"

Now, the Queen muttered an imprecation, and called the name "Abarak!" and lo, a door opened in one of the pillars of jasper leading from the throne, and there came forth a little man, humped, with legs like bows, and arms reaching to his feet; in his hand a net weighted with leaden weights. So the Queen levelled her finger at Noorna, and he spun the net above her head, and dropped it on her shoulder, and dragged her with him to the pillar. When Shibli Bagarag saw that, the world darkened to him, and he rushed upon Abarak; but Noorna called swiftly in his ear, "Wait! wait! Thou by thy spells art stronger than all here save Abarak. Be true! Remember the seventh pillar!" Then, with a spurn from the hand of Abarak, the youth fell back senseless at the feet of the Queen.

Now, with the return of consciousness his hearing was bewitched with strange delicious melodies, the touch of stringed instruments, and others breathed into softly as by the breath of love, delicate, tender, alive with enamoured bashfulness. Surely, the soul that heard them dissolved like a sweet in the goblet, mingling with so much ecstasy of sound; and those melodies filling the white cave of the ear were even at once to drown the soul in delightfulness and buoy it with bliss, as a heavy-leaved flower is withered and refreshed by sun and dews. Surely, the youth ceased not to listen, and oblivion of cares and aught other in this life, save that hidden luting and piping, pillowed his drowsy head. At last there was a pause, and it seemed every maze of music had been wandered through. Opening his eyes hurriedly, as with the loss of the music his own breath had gone likewise, he beheld a garden golden with the light of lamps hung profusely from branches and twigs of trees by the glowing cheeks of fruits, apple and grape, pomegranate and quince; and he was reclining on a bank piled with purple cushions, his limbs clad in the richest figured silks, fringed like the ends of clouds round the sun, with amber fringes. He started up, striving to recall the confused memory of his adventures and what evil had befallen him, and he would have struggled with the vision of these glories, but it mastered him with the strength of a potent drug, so that the very name of his betrothed was forgotten by him, and he knew not whither he would, or the thing he wished for. Now, when he had risen from the soft green bank that was his couch, lo, at his feet a damsel weeping! So he lifted her by the hand, and she arose and looked at him, and began plaining of love and its tyrannies, softening him, already softened. Then said she, "What I suffer there is another, lovelier than I, suffering; thou the cause of it, O cruel youth!"

He said, "How, O damsel? what of my cruelty? Surely, I know nothing of it."

But she exclaimed, "Ah, worse to feign forgetfulness!"

Now, he was bewildered at the words of the damsel, and followed her leading till they entered a dell in the garden canopied with foliage, and beyond it a green rise, and on the rise a throne. So he looked earnestly, and beheld thereon Queen Rabesqurat, she sobbing, her dark hair pouring in streams from the crown of her head. Seeing him, she cleared her eyes, and advanced to meet him timidly and with hesitating steps; but he shrank from her, and the Queen shrieked with grief, crying, "Is there in this cold heart no relenting?"

Then she said to him winningly, and in a low voice, "O youth, my husband, to whom I am a bride!"

He marvelled, saying, "This is a game, for indeed I am no husband, neither have I a bride... yet have I confused memory of some betrothal..."

GEORGE MEREDITH

Thereupon she cried, "Said I not so? and I the betrothed."

Still he exclaimed, "I cannot think it! Wullahy, it were a wonder!"

So she said, "Consider how a poor youth of excellent proportions came to a flourishing Court before one, a widowed Queen, and she cast eyes of love on him, and gave him rule over her and all that was hers when he had achieved a task, and they were wedded. Oh, the bliss of it! Knit together with bond and a writing; and these were the dominions, I the Queen, woe's me!—thou the youth!"

Now, he was roiled by the enchantments of the Queen, caught in the snare of her beguilings; and he let her lead him to a seat beside her on the throne, and sat there awhile in the midst of feastings, mazed, thinking, "What life have I lived before this, if the matter be as I behold?" thinking, "'Tis true I have had visions of a widowed queen, and I a poor youth that came to her court, and espoused her, sitting in the vacant seat beside her, ruling a realm; but it was a dream, a dream,—yet, wah! here is she, here am I, yonder my dominions!" Then he thought, "I will solve it!" So, on a sudden he said to her beside him, "O Queen, sovereign of hearts! enlighten me as to a perplexity."

She answered, "The voice of my lord is music in the ear of the bride."

Then said he, in the tone of one doubting realities, "O fair Queen, is there truly now such a one as Shagpat in the world?"

She laughed at his speech and the puzzled appearance of his visage, replying, "Surely there liveth one, Shagpat by name in the world; strange is the history of him, his friends, and enemies; and it would bear recital."

Then he said, "And one, the daughter of a Vizier, Vizier to the King in the City of Shagpat?"

Thereat, she shook her head, saying, "I know nought of that one."

Now, Shibli Bagarag was mindful of his thwackings; and in this the wisdom of Noorna, is manifest, that the sting of them yet chased away doubts of illusion regarding their having been, as the poet says,

> *If thou wouldst fix remembrance—thwack!*
> *'Tis that oblivion controls;*
> *I care not if't be on the back,*
> *Or on the soles.*

He thought, "Wah! yet feel I the thong, and the hiss of it as of the serpent in the descent, and the smack of it as the mouth of satisfaction in its contact with tender regions. This, wullahy! was no dream."

Nevertheless, he was ashamed to allude thereto before the Queen, and he said, "O my mistress, another question, one only! This Shagpat—is he shaved?"

She said, "Clean shorn!"

Quoth he, astonished, grief-stricken, with drawn lips, "By which hand, chosen above men?"

And she exclaimed, "O thou witty one that feignest not to know! Wullahy! by this hand of thine, O my lord and king, daring that it is; dexterous! surely so! And the shaving of Shagpat was the task achieved,—I the dower of it, and the rich reward."

Now, he was meshed yet deeper in the net of her subtleties, and by her calling him "lord and king"; and she gave a signal for fresh entertainments, exhausting the resources of her art, the mines of her wealth, to fascinate him. Ravishments of design and taste were on every side, and he was in the lap of abundance, beguiled by magic, caressed by beauty and a Queen. Marvel not that he was dazzled, and imagined himself already come to the great things foretold of him by the readers of planets and the casters of nativities in Shiraz. He assisted in beguiling himself, trusting wilfully to the two witnesses of things visible; as is declared by him of wise sayings:

> *There is in every wizard-net a hole,*
> *So the entangler first must blind the soul.*

And it is again said by that same teacher:

> *Ye that the inner spirit's sight would seal,*
> *Nought credit but what outward orbs reveal.*

And the soul of Shibli Bagarag was blinded by Rabesqurat in the depths of the Enchanted Sea. She sang to him, luting deliriously; and he was intoxicated with the blissfulness of his fortune, and took a lute and sang to her love-verses in praise of her, rhyming his rapture. Then they handed the goblet to each other, and drank till they were on fire with the joy of things, and life blushed beauteousness. Surely, Rabesqurat was becoming forgetful of her arts through the strength of those draughts, till her eye marked the Lily by his side, which he grasped constantly, the bright flower, and she started and said, "One grant, O my King, my husband!"

So he said courteously, "All grants are granted to the lovely, the fascinating; and their grief will be lack of aught to ask for?"

Then said she, "O my husband, my King, I am jealous of that silly flower: laugh at my weakness, but fling it from thee."

Now, he was about to cast it from him, when a vanity possessed his mind, and he exclaimed, "See first the thing I will do, a wonder."

She cried, "No wonders, my life! I am sated with them."

And he said, "I am oblivious, O Queen, of how I came by this flower and this phial; but thou shalt hear a thing beyond the power of common magic, and see that I am something."

Now, she plucked at him to abstain from his action, but he held the phial to the flower. She signed imperiously to some slaves to stay his right wrist, and they seized on it; but not all of them together could withhold him from dropping a drop into the petals of the flower, and lo, the Lily spake, a voice from it like the voice of Noorna, saying, "Remember the Seventh Pillar." Thereat, he lifted his eyes to his brows and frowned back memory to his aid, and the scene of Karaz, Rabesqurat, Abarak, and his betrothed was present to him. So perceiving that, the Queen delayed not while he grasped the phial to take in her hands some water from a basin near, and flung it over him, crying, "Oblivion!" And while his mind was straining to bring back images of what had happened, he fell forward once more at the feet of Rabesqurat, senseless as a stone falls; such was the force of her enchantments.

Now, when he awoke the second time he was in the bosom of darkness, and the Lily gone from his hand; so he lifted the phial to make certain of that, and groped about till he came to what seemed an urn to the touch, and into this he dropped a drop, and asked for the Lily; and a voice said, "I caught a light from it in passing." And he came in the darkness to a tree, and a bejewelled bank, and other urns, and swinging lamps without light, and a running water, and a grassy bank, and flowers, and a silver seat, sprinkling each; and they said all in answer to his question of the Lily, "I caught a light from it in passing." At the last he stumbled upon the steps of a palace, and ascended them, endowing the steps with speech as he went, and they said, "The light of it went over us." He groped at the porch of the palace, and gave the door a voice, and it opened on jasper hinges, shrieking, "The light of it went through me." Then he entered a spacious hall, scattering drops, and voices exclaimed, "We glow with the light of it." He passed, groping his way through other halls and dusk chambers, scattering drops, and as he advanced the voices increased in the fervour of their replies, saying sequently: "We blush with the light of it; We beam with the light of it; We burn with the light of it." So, presently he found himself in a long low room, sombrely lit, roofed with crystals; and in a corner of the room, lo! a damsel on a couch of purple, she white as silver, spreading radiance. Of such lustrous beauty was she that beside her, the Princess Goorelka as Shibli Bagarag first beheld her, would have paled like a morning moon; even Noorna had waned as Both a flower in fierce heat; and the Queen of Enchantments was but the sun behind a sand-storm, in comparison with that effulgent damsel on the length of the purple couch. Well for him he wilt of the magic which floated through that palace; as is said,

> *Tempted by extremes,*
> *The soul is most secure;*
> *Too vivid loveliness blinds with its beams,*
> *And eyes turned inward perceive the lure.*

Pulling down his turban hastily, he stepped on tiptoe to within arm's reach of her, and, looking another way, inclined over her soft vermeil mouth the phial slowly till it brimmed the neck, and dropped a drop of Paravid between the bow of those sweet lips. Still not daring to gaze on her, he said then, "My question is of the Lily, the Lily of the Sea, and where is it, O marvel?"

And he heard a voice answer in the tones of a silver bell, clear as a wind in strung wires, "Where I lie, lies the Lily, the Lily of the Sea; I with it, it with me."

Said he, "O breather of music, tell me how I may lay hand on the flower of beauty to bear it forth."

And he heard the voice, "An equal space betwixt my right side and my left, and from the shoulder one span and half a span downward."

Still without power to eye her, he measured the space and the spans, his hand beneath the coverlids of the couch, and at a spot of the bosom his hand sank in, and he felt a fluttering thing, fluttering like a frighted bird in the midst of the fire. And the voice said, "Quick, seize it, and draw it out, and tie it to my feet by the twines of red silk about it."

He seized it and drew it out, and it was a heart—a heart of blood-streaming with crimson, palpitating. Tears flashed on his sight beholding it, and pity took the seat of fear, and he turned his eyes full on her,

GEORGE MEREDITH

crying, "O sad fair thing! O creature of anguish! O painful beauty! Oh, what have I done to thee?"

But she panted, and gasped short and shorter gasps, pointing with one finger to her feet. Then he took the warm living heart while it yet leapt and quivered and sobbed; and he held it with a trembling hand, and tied it by the red twines of silk about it to her feet, staining their whiteness. When that was done, his whole soul melted with pity and swelled with sorrow, and ere he could meet her eyes a swoon overcame him. Surely, when the world dawned to him a third time in those regions the damsel was no longer there, but in her place the Lily of Light. He thought, "It was a vision, that damsel! a terrible one; one to terrify and bewilder! a bitter sweetness! Oh, the heart, the heart!" Reflecting on the heart brought to his lids an overcharging of tears, and he wept violently awhile. Then was he warned by the thought of his betrothed to take the Lily and speed with it from the realms of Rabesqurat; and he stole along the halls of the palace, and by the plashing fountains, and across the magic courts, passing chambers of sleepers, fair dreamers, and through ante-rooms crowded with thick-lipped slaves. Lo, as he held the Lily to light him on, and the light of the Lily fell on them that were asleep, they paled and shrank, and were such as the death-chill maketh of us. So he called upon his head the protection of Allah, and went swifter, to chase from his limbs the shudder of awe; and there were some that slept not, but stared at him with fixed eyes, eyes frozen by the light of the Lily, and he shunned those, for they were like spectres, haunting spirits. After he had coursed the length of the palace, he came to a steep place outside it, a rock with steps cut in stairs, and up these he went till he came to a small door in the rock, and lying by it a bar; so he seized the bar and smote the door, and the door shivered, for on his right wrist were the hairs of Garraveen. Bending his body, he slipped through the opening, and behold, an orchard dropping blossoms and ripe golden fruits, streams flowing through it over sands, and brooks bounding above glittering gems, and long dewy grasses, profusion of scented flowers, shade and sweetness. So he let himself down to the ground, which was an easy leap from the aperture, and walked through the garden, holding the Lily behind him, for here it darkened all, and the glowing orchard was a desert by its light. Presently, his eye fell on a couch swinging between two almond trees, and advancing to it he beheld the black-eyed Queen gathered up, folded temptingly, like a swaying fruit; she with the gold circlet on her head, and she was fair as blossom of the almond in a breeze of the wafted rose-leaf. Sweetly was she gathered up, folded temptingly, and Shibli Bagarag refrained from using the Lily, thinking, "'Tis like the great things foretold of me, this having of Queens within the very grasp, swinging to and fro as if to taunt backwardness!" Then he thought, "'Tis an enchantress! I will yet try her." So he made a motion of flourishing the Lily once or twice, but forbore, fascinated, for she had on her fair face the softness of sleep, her lips closed in dimples, and the wicked fire shut from beneath her lids. Mastering his mind, the youth at last held the Lily to her, and saw a sight to blacken the world and all bright things with its hideousness. Scarce had he time to thrust the Lily in his robes, when the Queen started up and clapped her hands, crying hurriedly, "Abarak! Abarak!" and the little man appeared in a moment at the door by which Shibli Bagarag had entered the orchard. So, she cried still, "Abarak!" and he moved toward her. Then she said, "How came this youth here, prying in my private walks, my bowers? Speak!"

He answered, "By the aid of Garraveen only, O Queen! and there is no force resisteth the bar so wielded."

Rabesqurat looked under her brows at Shibli Bagarag and saw the horror on his face, and she cried out to Abarak in an agony, "Fetch me the mirror!" Then Abarak ran, and returned ere the Queen had drawn seven impatient breaths, and in one hand he bore a sack, in the other a tray: so he emptied the contents of the sack on the surface of the tray; surely they were human eyes! and the Queen flung aside her tresses, and stood over them. The youth saw her smile at them, and assume tender and taunting manners before them, and imperious manners, killing glances, till in each of the eyes there was a sparkle. Then she flung back her head as one that feedeth on a mighty triumph, exclaiming, "Yet am I Rabesqurat! wide is my sovereignty." Sideways then she regarded Shibli Bagarag, and it seemed she was urging Abarak to do a deed beyond his powers, he frowning and pointing to the right wrist of the youth. So she clenched her hands an instant with that feeling which knocketh a nail in the coffin of a desire not dead, and controlled herself, and went to the youth, breaking into beams of beauty; and an enchanting sumptuousness breathed round her, so that in spite of himself he suffered her to take him by the hand and lead him from that orchard through the shivered door and into the palace and the hall of the jasper pillars. Strange thrills went up his arm from the touch of that Queen, and they were as little snakes twisting and darting up, biting poison-bites of irritating blissfulness.

Now, the hall was spread for a feast, and it was hung with lamps of silver, strewn with great golden goblets, and viands, coloured meats, and ordered fruits on shining platters. Then said she to Shibli Bagarag, "O youth! there shall be no deceit, no guile between us. Thou art but my guest, I no bride to thee, so take the place of the guest beside me."

He took his seat beside her, Abarak standing by, and she helped the youth to this dish and that dish, from the serving of slaves, caressing him with flattering looks to starve aversion and nourish tender fellowship. And he was like one that slideth down a hill and can arrest his descent with a foot, yet faileth that freewill. When he had eaten and drunk with her, the Queen said, "O youth, no other than my guest! art thou not a prince in the country thou comest from?"

In a moment the pride of the barber forsook him, and he equivocated, saying, "O Queen! there is among the stars somewhere, as was divined by the readers of planets, a crown hanging for me, and I search a point of earth to intercept its fall."

She marked him beguiled by vanity, and put sweetmeats to his mouth, exclaiming, "Thy manners be those of a prince!" Then she sang to him of the loneliness of her life, and of one with whom she wished to share her state,—such as he. And at her signal came troops of damsels that stood in rings and luted sweetly on the same theme—the Queen's loneliness, her love. And he said to the Queen, "Is this so?"

She answered, "Too truly so!"

Now, he thought, "She shall at least speak the thing that is, if she look it not." So he took the goblet, and contrived to drop a drop from the phial of Paravid therein without her observing him; and he handed her the goblet, she him; and they drank. Surely, the change that came over the Queen was an enchantment, and her eyes shot lustre, her tongue was loosed, and she laughed like one intoxicated, lolling in her seat, lost to majesty and the sway of her magic, crying, "O Abarak! Abarak! little man, long my slave and my tool; ugly little man! And O Shibli Bagarag! nephew of the barber! weak youth! small prince of the tackle! have I not nigh fascinated thee? And thou wilt forfeit those two silly eyes of thine to the sack. And, O Abarak, Abarak! little man, have I flattered thee? So fetter I the strong with my allurements! and I stay the arrow in its flight! and I blunt the barb of high intents! Wah! I have drunk a potent stuff; I talk! Wullahy! I know there is a danger menacing Shagpat, and the eyes of all Genii are fixed on him. And if he be shaved, what changes will follow! But 'tis in me to delude the barber, wullahy! and I will avert the calamity. I will save Shagpat!"

While the Queen Rabesqrat prated in this wise with flushed face, Shibli Bagarag was smitten with the greatness of his task, and reproached his soul with neglect of it. And he thought, "I am powerful by spells as none before me have been, and 'twas by my weakness the Queen sought to tangle me. I will clasp the Seventh Pillar and make an end of it, by Allah and his Prophet (praised be the name!), and I will reach Aklis by a short path and shave Shagpat with the sword."

So he looked up, and Abarak was before him, the lifted nostrils of the little man wide with the flame of anger. And Abarak said, "O youth, regard me with the eyes of judgement! Now, is it not frightful to rate me little?—an instigation of the evil one to repute me ugly?"

The promptings of wisdom counselled Shibli Bagarag to say, "Frightful beyond contemplation, O Abarak! one to shame our species! Surely, there is a moon between thy legs, a pear upon thy shoulders, and the cock that croweth is no match for thee in measure."

Abarak cried, "We be aggrieved, we two! O youth, son of my uncle, I will give thee means of vengeance; give thou me means."

Shibli Bagarag felt scorn at the Queen, and her hollowness, and he said, "'Tis well; take this Lily and hold it to her."

Now, the Queen jeered Abarak, and as he approached her she shouted, "What! thou small of build! mite of creation! sour mixture! thou puppet of mine! thou! comest thou to seek a second kiss against the compact, knowing that I give not the well-favoured of mortals beyond one, a second."

Little delayed Abarak at this to put her to the test of the Lily, and he held the flower to her, and saw the sight, and staggered back like one stricken with a shaft. When he could get a breath he uttered such a howl that Rabesqrat in her drunkenness was fain to save her ears, and the hall echoed as with the bellows of a thousand beasts of the forest. Then, to glut his revenge he ran for the sack, and emptied the contents of it, the Queen's mirror, before her; and the sackful of eyes, they saw the sight, and sickened, rolling their whites. That done, Abarak gave Shibli Bagarag the bar of iron, and bade him smite the pillars, all save the seventh; and he smote them strengthily, crumbling them at a blow, and bringing down the great hall and its groves, and glasses and gems, lamps, traceries, devices, a heap of ruin, the seventh pillar alone standing. Then, while he pumped back breath into his body, Abarak said, "There's no delaying in this place now, O youth! Say, halt thou spells for the entering of Aklis?"

He answered, "Three!"

Then said Abarak, "'Tis well! Surely now, if thou takest me in thy service, I'll help thee to master the Event, and serve thee faithfully, requiring nought from thee save a sight of the Event, and 'tis I that myself missed one, wiled by Rabesqurat."

Quoth Shibli Bagarag, "Thou?"

He answered, "No word of it now. Is't agreed?"

So Shibli Bagarag cried, "Even so."

Thereupon, the twain entered the pillar, leaving Rabesqurat prone, and the waves of the sea bounding toward her where she lay. Now, they descended and ascended flights of slippery steps, and sped together along murky passages, in which light never was, and under arches of caves with hanging crystals, groping and tumbling on hurriedly, till they came to an obstruction, and felt an iron door, frosty to the touch. Then Abarak said to Shibli Bagarag, "Smite!" And the youth lifted the bar to his right shoulder, and smote; and the door obeyed the blow, and discovered an opening into a strange dusky land, as it seemed a valley, on one side of which was a ragged copper sun setting low, large as a warrior's battered shield, giving deep red lights to a brook that fell, and over a flat stream a red reflection, and to the sides of the hills a dark red glow. The sky was a brown colour; the earth a deeper brown, like the skins of tawny lions. Trees with reddened stems stood about the valley, scattered and in groups, showing between their leaves the cheeks of melancholy fruits swarthily tinged, and toward the centre of the valley a shining palace was visible, supported by massive columns of marble reddened by that copper sun. Shibli Bagarag was awed at the stillness that hung everywhere, and said to Abarak, "Where am I, O Abarak? the look of this place is fearful!"

And the little man answered, "Where, but beneath the mountains in Aklis? Wullahy! I should know it, I that keep the passage of the seventh pillar!"

Then the thought of his betrothed Noorna, and her beauty, and the words, "Remember the seventh pillar," struck the heart of Shibli Bagarag, and he exclaimed passionately, "Is she in safety? Noorna, my companion, my betrothed, netted by thee, O Abarak!"

Abarak answered sharply, "Speak not of betrothals in this place, or the sword of Aklis will move without a hand!"

But Shibli Bagarag waxed the colour of the sun that was over them, and cried, "By Allah! I will smite thee with the bar, if thou swear not to her safety, and point not out to me where she now is."

Then said Abarak, "Thou wilt make a better use of the bar by lifting it to my shoulder, and poising it, and peering through it."

Shibli Bagarag lifted the bar to the shoulder of Abarak, and poised it, and peered through the length of it, and lo! there was a sea tossing in tumult, and one pillar standing erect in the midst of the sea; and on the pillar, above the washing waves, with hair blown back, and flapping raiment, pale but smiling still, Noorna, his betrothed!

Now, when he saw her, he made a rush to the door of the passage; but Abarak blocked the way, crying, "Fool! a step backward in Aklis is death!"

And when he had wrestled with him and reined him, Abarak said, "Haste to reach the Sword from the sons of Aklis, if thou wouldst save her."

He drew him to the brink of the stream, and whistled a parrot's whistle; and Shibli Bagarag beheld a boat draped with drooping white lotuses that floated slowly toward them; and when it was near, he and Abarak entered it, and saw one, a veiled figure, sitting in the stern, who neither moved to them nor spake, but steered the boat to a certain point of land across the stream, where stood an elephant ready girt for travellers to mount him; and the elephant kneeled among the reeds as they approached, that they might mount him, and when they had each taken a seat, moved off, waving his trunk. Presently the elephant came to a halt, and went upon his knees again, and the two slid off his back, and were among black slaves that bowed to the ground before them, and led them to the shining gates of the palace in silence. Now, on the first marble step of the palace there sat an old white-headed man dressed like a dervish, who held out at arm's length a branch of gold with golden singing-birds between its leaves, saying, "This for the strongest of ye!"

Abarak exclaimed, "I am that one"; and he held forth his hand for the branch.

But Shibli Bagarag cried, "Nay, 'tis mine. Wullahy, what has not the strength of this hand overthrown?"

Then the brows of Abarak twisted; his limbs twitched, and he bawled, "To the proof!" waking all the echoes of Aklis. Shibli Bagarag was tempted in his desire for the golden branch to lift the iron bar upon

Abarak, when lo! the phial of Paravid fell from his vest, and he took it, and sprinkled a portion of the waters over the singing birds, and in a moment they burst into a sweet union of voices, singing, in the words of the poet:

> *When for one serpent were two asses match?*
> *How shall one foe but with wiles master double?*
> *So let the strong keep for ever good watch,*
> *Lest their strength prove a snare, and themselves a mere bubble;*
> *For vanity maketh the strongest most weak,*
> *As lions and men totter after the struggle.*
> *Ye heroes, be modest! while combats ye seek,*
> *The cunning one trippeth ye both with a juggle.*

Now, at this verse of the birds Shibli Bagarag fixed his eye on the old man, and the beard of the old man shrivelled; he waxed in size, and flew up in a blaze and with a baffled shout bearing the branch; surely, his features were those of Karaz, and Shibli Bagarag knew him by the length of his limbs, his stiff ears, and copper skin. Then he laughed a loud laugh, but Abarak sobbed, saying, "By this know I that I never should have seized the Sword, even though I had vanquished the illusions of Rabesqurat, which held me fast half-way."

So Shibli Bagarag stared at him, and said, "Wert thou also a searcher, O Abarak?"

But Abarak cried, "Rouse not the talkative tongue of the past, O youth! Wullahy! relinquish the bar that is my bar, won by me, for the Sword is within thy grip, and they await thee up yonder steps. Go! go! and look for me here on thy return."

# The Palace of Aklis

Now, Shibli Bagarag assured himself of his three spells, and made his heart resolute, and hastened up the reddened marble steps of the Palace; and when he was on the topmost step, lo! one with a man's body and the head of a buffalo, that prostrated himself, and prayed the youth obsequiously to enter the palace with the title of King. So Shibli Bagarag held his head erect, and followed him with the footing of a Sultan, and passed into a great hall, with fountains in it that were fountains of gems, pearls, chrysolites, thousand-hued jewels, and by the margin of the fountains were shapes of men with the heads of beasts-wolves, foxes, lions, bears, oxen, sheep, serpents, asses, that stretched their hands to the falls, and loaded their vestments with brilliants, loading them without cessation, so that from the vestments of each there was another pouring of the liquid lights. Then he with the buffalo's head bade Shibli Bagarag help himself from the falls; but Shibli Bagarag refused, for his soul was with Noorna, his betrothed; and he saw her pale on that solitary pillar in the tumult of the sea, and knew her safety depended on his faithfulness.

He cried, "The Sword of Aklis! nought save the Sword!"

Now, at these words the fox-heads and the sheep-heads and the ass-heads and the other heads of beasts were lifted up, and lo! they put their hands to their ears, and tapped their foreheads with the finger of reflection, as creatures seeking to bring to mind a serious matter. Then the fountains rose higher, and flung jets of radiant jewels, and a drenching spray of gems upon them, and new thirst aroused them to renew their gulping of the falls, and a look of eagerness was even in the eyes of the ass-heads and the silly sheep-heads; surely, Shibli Bagarag laughed to see them! Now, when he had pressed his lips to recover his sight from the dazzling of those wondrous fountains, he heard himself again addressed by the title of King, and there was before him a lofty cock with a man's head. So he resumed the majesty of his march, and followed the fine-stepping cock into another hall, spacious, and clouded with heavy scents and perfumes burning in censers and urns, musk, myrrh, ambergris, and livelier odours, gladdening the nostril like wine, making the soul reel as with a draught of the forbidden drink. Here, before a feast that would prick the dead with appetite, were shapes of beasts with heads of men, asses, elephants, bulls, horses, swine, foxes, river-horses, dromedaries; and they ate and drank as do the famished with munch and gurgle, clacking their lips joyfully. Shibli Bagarag remembered the condition of his frame when first he looked upon the City of Shagpat, and was incited to eat and accede to the invitation of the cock with the man's head, and sit among these merry feeders and pickers of mouth-watering morsels, when, with the City of Shagpat, lo! he had a vision of Shagpat, hairier than at their interview, arrogant in hairiness; his head remote in contemptuous waves and curls and frizzes, and bushy protuberances of hair, lost in it, like an idolatrous temple in impenetrable thickets. Then the yearning of the Barber seized Shibli Bagarag, and desire to shear Shagpat was as a mighty overwhelming wave in his bosom, and he shouted, "The Sword of Aklis! nought save the Sword!"

Now, at these words the beasts with men's heads wagged their tails, all of them, from right to left, and kept their jaws from motion, staring stupidly at the dishes; but the dishes began to send forth stealthy steams, insidious whispers to the nose, silver intimations of savouriness, so that they on a sudden set up a howl, and Shibli Bagarag puckered his garments from them as from devouring dogs, and hastened from that hall to a third, where at the entrance a damsel stood that smiled to him, and led him into a vast marbled chamber, forty cubits high, hung with draperies, and in it a hundred doors; and he was in the midst of a very rose-garden of young beauties, such as the Blest behold in Paradise, robed in the colours of the rising and setting sun; plump, with long, black, languishing, almond-shaped eyes, and undulating figures. So they cried to him, "What greeting, O our King?"

Now, he counted twenty and seven of them, and, fitting his gallantry to verse, answered:

> *Poor are the heavens that have not ye*
> *To swell their glowing plenty;*
> *Up there but one bright moon I see,*
> *Here mark I seven-and-twenty.*

The damsels laughed and flung back their locks at his flattery, sporting with him; and he thought, "These be sweet maidens! I will know if they be illusions like Rabesqurat"; so, as they were romping, he slung his right arm round one, and held the Lily to her, but there was no change in her save that she winked somewhat and her eyes watered; and it was so with the others, for when they saw him hold the Lily to one they made him do so to them likewise. Then he took the phial, and touched their lips with the waters, and lo! they commenced luting and laughing, and singing verses, and prattling, laughing betweenwhiles at each other; and one, a noisy one, with long, black, unquiet tresses, and a curved foot and roguish ankle, sang as she twirled:

> *My heart is another's, I cannot be tender;*
> *Yet if thou storm it, I fain must surrender.*

And another, a fresh-cheeked, fair-haired, full-eyed damsel, strong upon her instep and stately in the bearing of her shoulders, sang shrilly:

> *I'm of the mountains, and he that comes to me*
> *Like eagle must win, and like hurricane woo me.*

And another, reclining on a couch buried in dusky silks, like a butterfly under the leaves, a soft ball of beauty, sang moaningly:

> *Here like a fruit on the branch am I swaying;*
> *Snatch ere I fall, love! there's death in delaying.*

And another, light as an antelope on the hills, with antelope eyes edged with kohl, and timid, graceful movements, and small, white, rounded ears, sang clearly:

> *Swiftness is mine, and I fly from the sordid;*
> *Follow me, follow! and you'll be rewarded.*

And another, with large limbs and massive mould, that stepped like a cow leisurely cropping the pasture, and shook with jewels amid her black hair and above her brown eyes, and round her white neck and her wrists, and on her waist, even to her ankle, sang as with a kiss upon every word:

> *Sweet 'tis in stillness and bliss to be basking!*
> *He who would have me, may have for the asking.*

And another, with eyebrows like a bow, and arrows of fire in her eyes, and two rosebuds her full moist parted pouting lips, sang, clasping her hands, and voiced like the tremulous passionate bulbul in the shadows of the moon:

*Love is my life, and with love I live only;*
*Give me life, lover, and leave me not lonely.*

And a seventh, a very beam of beauty, and the perfection of all that is imagined in fairness and ample grace of expression and proportion, lo! she came straight to Shibli Bagarag, and took him by the hand and pierced him with lightning glances, singing:

*Were we not destined to meet by one planet?*
*Can a fate sever us?—can it, ah! can it?*

And she sang tender songs to him, mazing him with blandishments, so that the aim of existence and the summit of ambition now seemed to him the life of a king in that palace among the damsels; and he thought, "Wah! these be no illusions, and they speak the thing that is in them. Wullahy, loveliness is their portion; they call me King."

Then she that had sung to him said, "Surely we have been waiting thee long to crown thee our King! Thou hast been in some way delayed, O glorious one!"

And he answered, "O fair ones, transcending in affability, I have stumbled upon obstructions in my journey hither, and I have met with adventures, but of this crowning that was to follow them I knew nought. Wullahy, thrice have I been saluted King; I whom fate selecteth for the shaving of Shagpat, and till now it was a beguilement, all emptiness."

They marked his bewildered state, and some knelt before him, some held their arms out adoringly, some leaned to him with glistening looks, and he was fast falling a slave to their flatteries, succumbing to them; imagination fired him with the splendours due to one that was a king, and the thought of wearing a crown again took possession of his soul, and he cried, "Crown me, O my handmaidens, and delay not to crown me; for, as the poet says:

*'The king without his crown*
*Hath a forehead like the clown';*

and the circle of my head itcheth for the symbols of majesty."

At these words of Shibli Bagarag they arose quickly and clapped their hands, and danced with the nimble step of gladness, exclaiming, "O our King! pleasant will be the time with him!" And one smoothed his head and poured oil upon it; one brought him garments of gold and silk inwoven; one fetched him slippers like the sun's beam in brightness; others stood together in clusters, and with lutes and wood-instruments, low-toned, singing odes to him; and lo! one took a needle and threaded it, and gave the thread into the hands of Shibli Bagarag, and with the point of the needle she pricked certain letters on his right wrist, and afterwards pricked the same letters on a door in the wall. Then she said to him, "Is it in thy power to make those letters speak?"

He answered, "We will prove how that may be."

So he flung some drops from the phial over the letters, and they glowed the colour of blood and flashed with a report, and it was as if a fiery forked-tongue had darted before them and spake the words written, and they were, "This is the crown of him who bath achieved his aim and resteth here." Thereupon, she stuck the needle in the door, and he pulled the thread, and the door drew apart, and lo! a small chamber, and on a raised cushion of blue satin a glittering crown, thick with jewels as a frost, such as Ambition pineth to wear, and the knees of men weaken and bend beholding, and it lanced lights about it like a living sun. Beside the cushion was a vacant throne, radiant as morning in the East, ablaze with devices in gold and gems, a seat to fill the meanest soul with sensations of majesty and tempt dervishes to the sitting posture. Shibli Bagarag was intoxicated at the sight, and he thought, "Wah! but if I sit on this throne and am a king, with that crown I can command men and things! and I have but to say, Fetch Noorna, my betrothed, from yonder pillar in the midst of the uproarious sea!—Let the hairy Shagpat be shaved! and behold, slaves, thousands of them, do my bidding! Wullahy, this is greatness!" Now, he made a rush to the throne, but the damsels held him back, crying, "Not for thy life till we have crowned thee, our master and lord!"

Then they took the crown and crowned him with it; and he sat upon the throne calmly, serenely, like a Sultan of the great race accustomed to sovereignty, tempering the awfulness of his brows with benignant glances. So, while he sat the damsels hid their faces and started some paces from him, as unable to bear the splendour of his presence, and in a moment, lo! the door closed between him and them, and he was in darkness. Then he heard a voice of the damsels cry in the hall, "The ninety and ninth! Peace now for us and blissfulness with our lords, for now all are filled save the door of the Sword, which maketh the hundredth." After that he heard the same voice say, "Leave them, O my sisters!"

So he listened to the noise of their departing, and knew he had been duped. Surely his soul cursed him as he sat crowned and throned in that darkness! He seized the crown to dash it to the earth, but the crown was fixed on his forehead and would not come off; neither had he force to rise from the throne. Now, the thought of Noorna, his betrothed, where she rested waiting for him to deliver her, filled Shibli Bagarag with the extremes of anguish; and he lifted his right arm and dashed it above his head in the violence of his grief, striking in the motion a hidden gong that gave forth a burst of thunder and a roll of bellowings, and lo! the door opened before him, and the throne as he sat on it moved out of the chamber into the hall where he had seen the damsels that duped him, and on every side of the hall doors opened; and he marvelled to see men, old and young, beardless and venerable, sitting upon thrones and crowned with crowns, motionless, with eyes like stones in the recesses. He thought, "These be other dupes! Wallaby! a drop of the waters of Paravid upon their lips might reveal mysteries, and guide me to the Sword of my seeking." So, as he considered how to get at them from the seat of his throne, his gaze fell on a mirror, and he beheld the crown on his forehead what it was, bejewelled asses' ears stiffened upright, and skulls of monkeys grinning with gems! The sight of that crowning his head convulsed Shibli Bagarag with laughter, and, as he laughed, his seat upon the throne was loosened, and he pitched from it, but the crown stuck to him and was tenacious of its hold as the lion that pounceth upon a victim. He bowed to the burden of necessity, and took the phial, and touched the lips of one that sat crowned on a throne with the waters in the phial; and it was a man of exceeding age, whitened with time, and in the long sweep of his beard like a mountain clad with snow from the peak that is in the sky to the base that slopeth to the valley. Then he addressed the old man on his throne, saying, "Tell me, O King! how camest thou here? and in search of what?"

The old man's lips moved, and he muttered in deep tones, "When cometh he of the ninety-and-ninth door?"

So Shibli Bagarag cried, "Surely he is before thee, in Aklis."

And the old man said, "Let him ask no secrets; but when he hath reached the Sword forget not to flash it in this hall, for the sake of brotherhood in adventure."

After that he would answer no word to any questioning.

# THE SONS OF AKLIS

N ow, Shibli Bagarag thought, "The poet is right in Aklis as elsewhere, in his words:

> *'The cunning of our oft-neglected wit*
> *Doth best the keyhole of occasion fit';*

and whoso looketh for help from others looketh the wrong way in an undertaking. Wah! I will be bold and batter at the hundredth door, which is the door of the Sword." So he advanced straightway to the door, which was one of solid silver, charactered with silver letters, and knocked against it three knocks; and a voice within said, "What spells?"

He answered, "Paravid; Garraveen; and the Lily of the Sea!"

Upon that the voice said, "Enter by virtue of the spells!" and the silver door swung open, discovering a deep pit, lightened by a torch, and across it, bridging it, a string of enormous eggs, rocs' eggs, hollowed, and so large that a man might walk through them without stooping. At the side of each egg three lamps were suspended from a claw, and the shell passage was illumined with them from end to end. Shibli Bagarag thought, "These eggs are of a surety the eggs of the Roc mastered by Aklis with his sword!" Now, as the sight of Shibli Bagarag grew familiar to the place, he beheld at the bottom of the pit a fluttering mass of blackness and two sickly eyes that glittered below.

Then thought he, "Wah! if that be the Roc, and it not dead, will the bird suffer one to defile its eggs with other than the sole of the foot, naked?" He undid his sandals and kicked off the slippers given him by the damsels that had duped him, and went into the first egg over the abyss, and into the second, and into the third, and into the fourth, and into the fifth. Surely the eggs swung with him, and bent; and the fear of their breaking and he falling into the maw of the terrible bird made him walk unevenly. When he had come to the seventh egg, which was the last, it shook and swung violently, and he heard underneath the flapping of the wings of the Roc, as with eagerness expecting a victim to prey upon. He sustained his soul with the firmness of resolve and darted himself lengthwise to the landing, clutching a hold with his right hand; as he did so, the bridge of eggs broke, and he heard the feathers of the bird in agitation, and the bird screaming a scream of disappointment as he scrambled up the sides of the pit.

Now, Shibli Bagarag failed not to perform two prostrations to Allah, and raised the song of gratitude for his preservation when he found himself in safety. Then he looked up, and lo! behind a curtain, steps leading to an anteroom, and beyond that a chamber like the chamber of kings where they sit in state dispensing judgements, like the sun at noon in splendour; and in the chamber seven youths, tall and comely young men, calm as princes in their port, each one dressed in flowing robes, and with a large glowing pearl in the front of their turbans. They advanced to meet him, saying, "Welcome to Aklis, thou that art proved worthy! 'Tis holiday now with us"; and they took him by the hand and led him with them in silence past fountain-jets and porphyry pillars to where a service with refreshments was spread, meats, fowls with rice, sweetmeats, preserves, palateable mixtures, and monuments of the cook's art, goblets of wine like liquid rubies. Then one of the youths said to Shibli Bagarag, "Thou hast come to us crowned, O our guest! Now, it is not our custom to pay homage, but thou shalt presently behold them that will, so let not thy kingliness droop with us, but feast royally."

And Shibli Bagarag said, "O my princes, surely it is a silly matter to crown a mouse! Humility hath depressed my stature! Wullahy, I have had warning in the sticking of this crown to my brows, and it sticketh like an abomination."

They laughed at him, saying, "It was the heaviness of that crown which overweighted thee in the bridge of the abyss, and few be they that bear it and go not to feed the Roc."

Now, they feasted together, interchanging civilities, offering to each other choice morsels, dainties. And the anecdotes of Shibli Bagarag, his simplicity and his honesty, and his vanity and his airiness, and the betraying tongue of the barber, diverted the youths; and they plied him with old wine till his stores of merriment broke forth and were as a river swollen by torrents of the mountain; and the seven youths laughed at him, spluttering with laughter, lurching with it. Surely, he described to them the loquacity of Baba Mustapha his uncle, and they laughed so that their chins were uppermost; but at his mention of Shagpat greater gravity was theirs, and they smoothed their faces solemnly, and the sun of their merriment was darkened for awhile. Then they took to flinging about pellets of a sugared preparation, and reciting verses in praise of jovial living, challenging to drink this one and that one, passing the cup

GEORGE MEREDITH

with a stanza. Shibli Bagarag thought, "What a life is this led by these youths! a fair one! 'Tis they that be the sons of Aklis who sharpen the Sword of Events; yet live they in jollity, skimming from the profusion of abundance that which floateth!"

Now, marking him contemplative, one of the youths shouted, "The King lacketh homage!"

And another called, "Admittance for his people!"

Then the seven arose and placed Shibli Bagarag on an elevation in the midst of them, and lo! a troop of black slaves leading by the collar, asses, and by a string, monkeys. Now, for the asses they brayed to the Evil One, and the monkeys were prankish, pulling against the string, till they caught sight of Shibli Bagarag. Then was it as if they had been awestricken; and they came forward to him with docile steps, eyeing the crown on his head, and prostrated themselves, the asses and the monkeys, like creatures in whom glowed the lamp of reason and the gift of intelligence. So Shibli Bagarag drooped his jaw and was ashamed, and he cried, "my princes! am I a King of these?"

They answered, "A King in mightiness! Sultan of a race!"

So he said, "It is certain I shall need physic to support such a sovereignty! And I must be excused liberal allowances of old wine to sit in state among them. Wullahy! they were best gone for awhile. Send them from me, O my princes! I sicken."

And he called to the animals, "Away! begone!" frowning.

Then said the youths, "Well commanded! and like a King! See, they troop from thy presence obediently."

Now the animals fled from before the brows of Shibli Bagarag, and when the chamber was empty of them the seven young men said, "Of a surety thou wert flattered to observe the aspect of these animals at beholding thee."

But he cried, "Not so, O my princes; there is nought flattering in the homage of asses and monkeys."

Then they said, "O Sultan of asses, ruler of monkeys, better that than thyself an ass and an ape! As was said by Shah Kasirwan, 'I prefer being king of beasts worshipped by beasts, rather than a crowned beast worshipped by men'; and it was well said. Wullahy! the kings of Roum quote it."

Now Shibli Bagarag was not rendered oblivious of the Sword of his quest by the humour of these youths, or the wine-bibbings, and he exclaimed while they were turning up the heels of their cups, "O ye sons of Aklis, know that I have come hither for the Sword sharpened by your hands, for the releasing of my betrothed, Noorna bin Noorka, daughter of the Vizier Feshnavat, and for the shaving of Shagpat."

While he was proceeding to recount the story of his search for the Sword, they said, "Enough, O potentate of the braying class and of the scratching tribe! we have seen thee through the eye of Aklis since the time of thy first thwacking. What says the poet?

> *'A day for toil and a day for rest*
> *Gives labour zeal, and pleasure zest.'*

So, of thy seeking let us hear to-morrow; but now drink with us, and make merry, and touch the springs of memory; spout forth verses, quaint ones, suitable to the hour and the entertainment. Wullahy! drink with us! taste life! Let the humours flow."

Then they made a motion to some slaves, and presently a clattering of anklets struck the ear of Shibli Bagarag: and he beheld dancing-girls, moons of beauty and elegance, and they danced wild dances, and dances graceful and leopard-like and serpent-like in movement; and the youths flung flowers at them, applauding them. Then came other sets of dancers even lovelier, more languishing; and again others with tambourines and musical instruments, that sang ravishingly. So the senses of Shibli Bagarag were all taken with what he saw and heard, and ate and drank; and by degrees a mist came before his eyes, and the sweet sounds and voices of the girls grew distant, and it was with difficulty he kept his back from the length of the cushions that were about him. Then he thought of Noorna, and that she sang to him and danced, and when he rose to embrace her she was Rabesqrat by the light of the Lily! And he thought of Shagpat, and that in shaving him the blade was checked in its rapid sweep, and blunted by a stumpy twine of hair that waxed in size and became the head of Karaz that gulped at him a wide devouring gulp, and took him in, and flew up with him, leaving Shagpat half sheared. Then he thought himself struggling halfway down the throat of the monstrous Roc, and that, when he was wholly inside the Roc, he was in a wide-arched passage crowded with lamps, and at the end of the passage Noorna in the clutch of Karaz, she shouting, "The Sword, the Sword!"

Now, while he felt for the Sword wherewith to release her from the Genie, his eyes opened, and he saw day through a casement, and that he had reposed on an embroidered couch in the corner of a stately room ornamented with carvings of blue and gold. So while he wondered and yawned, gaping, slaves started up from the floor and led him to a bath of coloured marble, and bathed him in perfumed waters, and dressed him in a dress of yellow silk, rich and ample. Then they paraded before him through lesser apartments and across terraces, till they came to a great hall; loftier and more spacious than any he had yet beheld, with fountains at the two ends, and in the centre a tree with golden spreading branches and leaves of gold; among the leaves gold-feathered birds, and fruits of all seasons and every description—the drooping grape and the pleasant-smelling quince, and the blood-red pomegranate, and the apricot, and the green and rosy apple, and the gummy date, and the oily pistachio-nut, and peaches, and citrons, and oranges, and the plum, and the fig. Surely, they were countless in number, melting with ripeness, soft, full to bursting; and the birds darted among them like sun-flashes. Now, Shibli Bagarag thought, "This is a wondrous tree! Wullahy! there is nought like it save the tree in the hall of the Prophet in Paradise, feeding the faithful!" As he regarded it he heard his name spoken in the hall, and turning he beheld seven youths in royal garments, that were like the youths he had feasted with, and yet unlike them, pale, and stern in their manners, their courtesy as the courtesy of kings. They said, "Sit with us and eat the morning's meal, O our guest!"

So he sat with them under the low branches of the tree; and they whistled the tune of one bird and of another bird, and of another, and lo! those different birds flew down with golden baskets hanging from their bills, and in the baskets fruits and viands and sweetmeats, and cool drinks. And Shibli Bagarag ate from the baskets of the birds, watching the action of the seven youths and the difference that was in them. He sought to make them recognise him and acknowledge their carouse of the evening that was past, but they stared at him strangely and seemed offended at the allusion, neither would they hear mention of the Sword of his seeking. Presently, one of the youths stood upon his feet and cried, "The time for kings to sit in judgement!"

And the youths arose and led Shibli Bagarag to a hall of ebony, and seated him on the upper seat, themselves standing about him; and lo! asses and monkeys came before him, complaining of the injustice of men and their fellows, in brays and bellows and hoots. Now, at the sight of them again Shibli Bagarag was enraged, and he said to the youths, "How! do ye not mock me, O masters of Aklis!"

But they said only, "The burden of his crown is for the King."

He cooled, thinking, "I will use a spell." So he touched the lips of an animal with the waters of Paravid, and the animal prated volubly in our language of the kick this ass had given him, and the jibe of that monkey, and of his desire of litigation with such and such a beast for pasture; and the others when they spake had the same complaints to make. Shibli Bagarag listened to them gravely, and it was revealed to him that he who ruleth over men hath a labour and duties of hearing and judging and dispensing judgement similar to those of him who ruleth over apes and asses. Then said he, "O youths, my princes! methinks the sitting in this seat giveth a key to secret sources of wisdom; and I see what it is, the glory and the exaltation coveted by men." Now, he took from the asses and the monkeys one, and said to it, "Be my chief Vizier," and to another, "Be my Chamberlain!" and to another, "Be my Treasurer!" and so on, till a dispute arose between the animals, and jealousy of each other was visible in their glances, and they appealed to him clamorously. So he said, "What am I to ye?"

They answered, "Our King!"

And he said, "How so?"

They answered, "By the crowning of the brides of Aklis."

Then he said, "What be ye, O my subjects?"

They answered, "Men that were searchers of the Sword and plunged into the tank of temptation."

And he said, "How that?"

They answered, "By the lures of vanity, the blinding of ambition, and tasting the gall of the Roc."

So Shibli Bagarag leaned to the seven youths, saying, "O my princes, but for not tasting the gall of the Roc I might be as one of these. Wullahy! I the King am warned by base creatures." Then he said to the animals, "Have ye still a longing for the crown?"

And they cried, all of them, "O light of the astonished earth, we care for nought other than it."

So he said, "And is it known to ye how to dispossess the wearer of his burden?"

They answered, "By a touch of the gall of the Roc on his forehead."

Then he lifted his arms, crying, "Hie out of my presence! and whoso of ye fetcheth a drop of the gall, with that one will I exchange the crown."

At these words some moved hastily, but the most faltered, as doubting and incredulous that he would propose such an exchange; and one, an old monkey, sat down and crossed his legs, and made a study of Shibli Bagarag, as of a sovereign that held forth a deceiving bargain. But he cried again, "Hie and haste! as my head is now cased I think it not the honoured part."

Then the old monkey arose with a puzzled look, half scornful, and made for the door slowly, turning his head toward Shibli Bagarag betweenwhiles as he went, and scratching his lower limbs with the mute reflectiveness of age and extreme caution.

Now, when they were gone, Shibli Bagarag looked in the eyes of the seven youths, and saw they were content with him, and his countenance was brightened with approval. So he descended from his seat, and went with them from the hall of ebony to a court where horses were waiting saddled, and slaves with hawks on their wrists stood in readiness; and they mounted each a horse, but he loitered. The seven youths divined his feeling, and cried impatiently, "Come! no lingering in Aklis!" So he mounted likewise, and they emerged from the palace, and entered the hills that glowed under the copper sun, and started a milk-white antelope with ruby spots, and chased it from its cover over the sand-hills, a hawk being let loose to worry it and distress its timid beaming eyes. When the creature was quite overcome, one of the youths struck his heel into his horse's side and flung a noose over the head of the quarry, and drew it with them, gently petting it the way home to the palace. At the gates of the palace it was released, and lo! it went up the steps, and passed through the halls as one familiar with them. Now, when they were all assembled in the anteroom of the hall, where Shibli Bagarag had first seen the seven youths, sons of Aklis, in their jollity, one of them said to the Antelope, "We have need of thee to speak a word with Aklis, O our sister!"

So the same youth requested the use of the phial of Paravid, and Shibli Bagarag applied it carefully, tenderly, to the mouth of the Antelope. Then the Antelope spake in a silver-ringing voice, saying, "What is it, O my brothers?"

They answered, "Thou knowest we dare not attempt interchange of speech with Aklis, seeing that we disobeyed him in visiting the kingdoms of the earth: so it is for thee to question him as to the object of this youth, and it is the Shaving of Shagpat."

So she said, "'Tis well; I wot of it."

Then she advanced to the curtain concealing the abyss of the Roc and the bridge of its eggs, and went behind it. There was a pause, and they heard her say presently in a grave voice, toned with reverence, "How is it, O our father? is it a good thing that thy Sword be in use at this season?"

And they heard the Voice answer from a depth, "'Twere well it rust not!"

They heard her say, "O our father Aklis, and we wish to know if be held in favour by thee, and thou sanction it with thy Sword."

And they heard the Voice answer, "The Shaving of Shagpat is my Sword alone equal to, and he that shaveth him performeth a service to mankind ranking next my vanquishing of the Roc."

Then they heard her say, "And it is thy will we teach him the mysteries of the Sword, and that which may be done with it?"

And they heard the Voice answer, "Even so!"

After that the Voice was still, and soon the Antelope returned from behind the curtain, and the youths caressed her with brotherly caresses, and took a circle of hands about her, and so moved to the great Hall of the gorgeous Tree, and fed her from the branches. Now, while they were there, Shibli Bagarag advanced to the Antelope, and knelt at her feet, and said, "O Princess of Aklis, surely I am betrothed to one constant as a fixed star, and brighter; a mistress of magic, and innocent as the bleating lamb; and she is now on a pillar, chained there, in the midst of the white wrathful sea, wailing for me to deliver her with this Sword of my seeking. So, now, I pray thee help me to the Sword swiftly, that I may deliver her."

The youths, her brothers, clamoured and interposed, saying, "Take thy shape ere that, O Gulrevaz, our sister!"

But she cried, "He is betrothed! not till he graspeth the Sword. Tell him, the youth, our conditions, and for what exchange the Sword is yielded."

And they said, "The conditions are, thou part with thy spells, all of them, O youth!"

And he said, "There is no condition harsh that exchangeth the Sword; O ye Seven, I agree!"

Then she said, "'Tis well! nobility is in the soul of this youth. Go before us now to the Cave of Chrysolites, O my brothers."

So these departed before, and she in her antelope form followed footing gracefully, and made Shibli Bagarag repeat the story of his betrothal as they went.

# The Sword of Aklis

Now, when they had made the passage of many halls, built of different woods, filled with divers wonders, they descended a sloping vault, and came to a narrow way in the earth, hung with black, at the end of it a stedfast blaze like a sun, that grew larger as they advanced, and they heard the sea above them. The noise of it, and its plunging and weltering and its pitilessness, struck on the heart of Shibli Bagarag as with a blow, and he cried, "Haste, haste, O Princess! perchance she is even now calling to me with her tongue, and I not aiding her; delayed by the temptation of this crown and the guile of the Brides."

She checked him, and said, "In Aklis no haste!" Then she said, "Look!" And lo, fronting them the single blaze became two fires; and drawing nigh, Shibli Bagarag beheld them what they were, angry eyes in the head of a great lion, a model of majesty, and passion was in his mane and power was in his forepaws; so while he lashed his tail as a tempest whippeth the tawny billows at night, and was lifting himself for a roar, she said, "A hair of Garraveen, and touch him with it!"

Shibli Bagarag pushed up his sleeve and broke one of the three sapphire hairs and stepped forward to the lion, holding in his right hand the hair of vivid light. The lion crouched, and was in the vigour of the spring when that hair touched him, and he trembled, tumbling on his knees and letting the twain pass. So they advanced beyond him, and lo! the Cave of Chrysolites irradiate with beams, breaks of brilliance, confluences of lively hues, restless rays, meeting, vanishing, flooding splendours, now scattered in dazzling joints and spars, now uniting in momentary disks of radiance. In the centre of the cave glowed a furnace, and round it he distinguished the seven youths, swarthier and sterner than before, dark sweat standing on the brows of each. Their words were brief, and they wore each a terrible frown, saying to him, without further salutation, "Thrust in the flame of this furnace thy right wrist."

At the same moment, the Antelope said in his ear, "Do thou their bidding, and be not backward! In Aklis fear is ruin, and hesitation a destroyer."

He fixed his mind on the devotedness of Noorna, and held his nether lip tightly between his teeth, and thrust his right wrist in the flame of the furnace. The wrist reddened, and became transparent with heat, but he felt no pain, only that his whole arm was thrice its natural weight. Then the flame of the furnace fell, and the seven youths made him kneel by a brook of golden waters and dip his forehead up to his eyes in the waters. Then they took him to the other side of the cave, and his sight was strengthened to mark the glory of the Sword, where it hung in slings, a little way from the wall, outshining the lights of the cave, and throwing them back with its superior force and stedfastness of lustre. Lo! the length of it was as the length of crimson across the sea when the sun is sideways on the wave, and it seemed full a mile long, the whole blade sheening like an arrested lightning from the end to the hilt; the hilt two large live serpents twined together, with eyes like sombre jewels, and sparkling spotted skins, points of fire in their folds, and reflections of the emerald and topaz and ruby stones, studded in the blood-stained haft. Then the seven young men, sons of Aklis, said to Shibli Bagarag, "Surrender the Lily!" And when he had given into their hands the Lily, they said, "Grasp the handle of the Sword!"

Now, he beheld the Sword and the ripples of violet heat that were breathing down it, and those two venomous serpents twined together, and the size of it, its ponderousness; and to essay lifting it appeared to him a madness, but he concealed his thought, and, setting his soul on the safety of Noorna, went forward to it boldly, and piercing his right arm between the twists of the serpents, grasped the jewelled haft. Surely, the Sword moved from the slings as if a giant had swayed it! But what amazed him was the marvel of the blade, for its sharpness was such that nothing stood in its way, and it slipped through everything as we pass through still water, the stone columns, blocks of granite by the walls, the walls of earth, and the thick solidity of the ground beneath his feet. They bade him say to the Sword, "Sleep!" and it was no longer than a knife in the girdle. Likewise, they bade him hiss on the heads of the serpents, and say, "Wake!" and while he held it lengthwise it shot lengthening out. Then they bade him hold in one hand the sapphire hair that conquered the lion, and with the edge of the Sword touch one point of it. So he did that, and it split in half, and the two halves he also split; and he split those four, and those eight, till the hairs were thin as light and not distinguishable from it. When Shibli Bagarag saw the power of the Sword, he exulted and cried, "Praise be to the science of them that forecast events and the haps of life!" Now, in the meantime he marked the youths take those hairs of Garraveen that he had split, and tie them round the neck of the Antelope, and empty the contents of the phial down her throat; and they put the bulb of the Lily, that was a heart, in her mouth, and she swallowed it till the flower covered her face. Then they took each a handful of the golden waters of the brook flowing through the cave, and flung the waters over her, exclaiming, "By the three spells that have power in Aklis, and by which these waters are a blessing!"

In the passing of a flash she took her shape, and was a damsel taller than the tallest of them that descend from the mountains, a vision of loveliness, with queenly brows, closed red lips, and large full black eyes; her hair black, and on it a net of amber strung with pearls. To look upon her was to feel the tyranny of love, love's pangs of alarm and hope and anguish; and she was dressed in a dress of white silk, threaded with gold and sapphire, showing in shadowy beams her rounded figure and the stateliness that was hers. So she ran to her brothers and embraced them, calling them by their names, catching their hands, caressing them as one that had been long parted from them. Then, seeing Shibli Bagarag as he stood transfixed with the javelins of loveliness that flew from her on all sides, she cried: "What, O Master of the Event! halt thou nought for the Sword but to gaze before thee in silliness?"

Then he said, "O rare in beauty! marvel of Aklis and the world! surely the paradise of eyes is thy figure and the glory of thy face!"

But she shouted, "To work with the Sword! Shame on thee! is there not one, a bright one, a miracle in faithfulness, that awaiteth thy rescue on the pillar?"

And she repeated the praises he had spoken of Noorna bin Noorka, his betrothed. Then he grasped the Sword firmly, remembering the love of Noorna, and crying, "Lead me from this, O ye sons of Aklis, and thou, Princess Gulrevaz, lead me, that I may come to her."

So they said, "Follow us!" and he sheathed the Sword in his girdle with the word "Sleep!" and followed them, his heart beating violently.

# Koorookh

N ow, they sped from the Cave of Chrysolites by another passage than that by which they entered it, and nothing but the light of the Sword to guide them. By that light Shibli Bagarag could distinguish glimmering shapes, silent and statue-like, to the right and the left of them, their visages hidden in a veil of heavy webs; and he saw what seemed in the dusk broad halls, halls of council, and again black pools and black groves, and columns of crowded porticoes,—all signs of an underground kingdom. They came to some steps and mounted these severally, coming to a platform, in the middle of which leapt a fountain, the top spray of it touched with a beam of earth and the air breathed by men. Here he heard the youths dabble with the dark waters, and he discerned Gulrevaz tossing it in her two hands, calling, "Koorookh! Koorookh!" Then they said to him, "Stir this fountain with the Sword, O Master of the Event!" So he stirred the fountain, and the whole body of it took a leap toward the light that was like the shoot of a long lance of silver in the moon's rays, and lo! in its place the ruffled feathers of a bird. Then the seven youths and the Princess and Shibli Bagarag got up under its feathers like a brood of water-fowl; and the bird winged straight up as doth a blinded bee, ascending, and passing in the ascent a widening succession of winding terraces, till he observed the copper sun of Aklis and the red lands below it. Thrice, in the exuberance of his gladness, he waved the Sword, and the sun lost that dulness on its disk and took a bright flame, and threw golden arrows everywhere; and the pastures were green, the streams clear, the sands sparkling. The bird flew, and circled, and hung poised a moment, presently descending on the roof of the palace. Now, there was here a piece of solid glass, propped on two crossed bars of gold, and it was shaped like an eye, and might have been taken for one of the eyes inhabiting the head of some monstrous Genie. Shibli Bagarag ran to it when he was afoot, and peered through it. Surely, it was the first object of his heart that he beheld—Noorna, his betrothed, pale on the pillar; she with her head between her hands and her hair scattered by the storm, as one despairing. Still he looked, and he save swimming round the pillar that monstrous fish, with its sole baleful eye, which had gulped them both in the closed shell of magic pearl; and he knew the fish for Karaz, the Genie, their enemy. Then he turned to the Princess, with an imploring voice for counsel how to reach her and bring her rescue; but she said, "The Sword is in thy hands, none of us dare wield it"; and the seven youths answered likewise. So, left to himself, he drew the Sword from his girdle, and hissed on the heads of the serpents, at the same time holding it so that it might lengthen out inimitably. Then he leaned it over the eye of the glass, in the direction of the pillar besieged by the billows, and lo! with one cut, even at that distance, he divided the fishy monster, and with another severed the chains that had fettered Noorna; and she arose and smiled blissfully to the sky, and stood upright, and signalled him to lay the point of the blade on the pillar. When he had done this, knowing her wisdom, she put a foot boldly upon the blade and ran up it toward him, and she was half-way up the blade, when suddenly a kite darted down upon her, pecking at her eyes, to confuse her. She waxed unsteady and swayed this way and that, balancing with one arm and defending herself from the attacks of the kite with another. It seemed to Shibli Bagarag she must fall and be lost; and the sweat started on his forehead in great drops big as nuts. Seeing that and the agitation of his limbs, Gulrevaz cried, "O Master of the Event, let us hear it!"

But he shrieked, "The kite! the kite! she is running up the blade, and the kite is at her eyes! and she swaying, swaying! falling, falling!"

So the Princess exclaimed, "A kite! Koorookh is match for a kite!"

Then she smoothed the throat of Koorookh, and clasped round it a collar of bright steel, roughened with secret characters; and she took a hoop of gold, and passed the bird through it, urging it all the while with one strange syllable; and the bird went up with a strong whirr of the wing till he was over the sea, and caught sight of Noorna tottering beneath him on the blade, and the kite pecking fiercely at her. Thereat he fluttered eagerly a twinkle of time, and the next was down with his beak in the neck of the kite, crimsoned in it. Now, by the shouts and exclamations of Shibli Bagarag, the Princess and the seven youths, her brothers, knew that the bird had performed well his task, and that the fight was between Koorookh and the kite. Then he cried gladly to them, "Joy for us, and Allah be praised! The kite is dropping, and she leaneth on one wing of Koorookh!"

And he cried in anguish, "What see I? The kite is become a white ball, rolling down the blade toward her; and it will of a surety destroy her." And he called to her, thinking vainly his voice might reach her. So the Princess said, "A white ball? 'tis I that am match for a white ball!"

Now, she seized from the corner of the palace-roof a bow and an arrow, and her brothers lifted her to a level with the hilt of the Sword, leaning on the eye of glass. Then she planted one foot on the shoulder of Shibli Bagarag as he bent peering through the eye, and fitted the arrow to a level of the Sword, slanting its slant, and let it fly, doubling the bow. Shibli Bagarag saw the ball roll to within a foot of Noorna, when it was as if stricken by a gleam of light, and burst, and was a black cloud veined with fire, swathing her in folds. He lost all sight of Noorna; and where she had been were vivid flashes, and then a great flame, and in the midst a red serpent and a green serpent twisted as in the death-struggle. So he cried, "A red serpent and a green serpent!"

And the sons of Aklis exclaimed, "A red serpent? 'Tis we that are match for a red serpent!"

Thereupon they descended steps through the palace roof, and while the fight between those two serpents was rageing, Shibli Bagarag beheld seven small bright birds, bee-catchers, that entered the flame, bearing in their bills slips of a herb, and hovering about the heal of the red serpent, distracting it. Then he saw the red serpent hiss and snap at one, darting out its tongue, and lo! on the fork of its tongue the little bird let fall the slip of herb in its bill, and in an instant the serpent changed from red to yellow and from yellow to pale-spotted blue, and from that to a speckled indigo-colour, writhing at every change, and hissing fire from its open jaws. Meantime the green serpent was released and was making circles round the flame, seeking to complete some enchantment, when suddenly the whole scene vanished, and Shibli Bagarag again beheld Noorna steadying her steps on the blade, and leaning on one wing of Koorookh. She advanced up the blade, coming nearer and nearer; and he thought her close, and breathed quick and ceased looking through the glass. When he gazed abroad, lo! she was with Koorookh, on a far hill beyond the stream in outer Aklis. So he said to the Princess Gulrevaz, "O Princess, comes she not to me here in the palace?"

But the Princess shook her head, and said, "She hath not a spell! She waiteth for thee yonder with Koorookh. Now, look through the glass once more."

He looked through the glass, and there on a plain, as he had first seen it when Noorna appeared to him, was the City of Shagpat, and in the streets of the city a vast assembly, and a procession passing on, its front banner surmounted by the Crescent, and bands with curled and curved instruments playing, and slaves scattering gold and clashing cymbals, every demonstration and evidence of a great day and a high occasion in the City of Shagpat! So he peered yet keenlier through the

glass, and behold, the Vizier Feshnavat, father of Noorna, walking in
fetters, subject to the jibes and evil-speaking of the crowds of people,
his turban off, and he in a robe of drab-coloured stuff, in the scorned
condition of an unbeliever. Shibli Bagarag peered yet more earnestly
through the glass eye, and in the centre of the procession, clad gorgeously
in silks and stuffs, woven with gold and gems, a crown upon his head,
and the appanages of supremacy and majesty about him, was Shagpat.
He paced upon a yellow flooring that was unrolled before him from
a mighty roll; and there were slaves that swarmed on all sides of him,
supporting upon gold pans and platters the masses of hair that spread
bushily before and behind, and to the right and left of him. Truly the
gravity of his demeanour exceeded that which is attained by Sheiks and
Dervishes after much drinking of the waters of wisdom, and fasting,
and abnegation of the pleasures that betray us to folly in this world!
Now, when he saw Shagpat, the soul of Shibli Bagarag was quickened
to do his appointed work upon him, shear him, and release the Vizier
Feshnavat. Desire to shave Shagpat was as a salt thirst rageing in him,
as the dream of munching to one that starveth; even as the impelling
of violent tempests to skiffs on the sea; and he hungered to be at him,
crying, as he peered, "'Tis he! even he, Shagpat!"

Then he turned to the Princess Gulrevaz, and said, "'Tis Shagpat,
exalted, clothed with majesty, O thou morning star of Aklis!"

She said, "Koorookh is given thee, and waiteth to carry ye both; and
for me I will watch that this glass send forth a beam to light ye to that
city; so farewell, O thou that art loved! And delay in nothing to finish
the work in hand."

Now, when he had set his face from the Princess he descended
through the roof of the palace, and met the seven youths returning,
and they accompanied him through the halls of the palace to that hall
where the damsels had duped him. He was mindful of his promise to
the old man crowned, and flashed the Sword a strong flash, so that he
who looked on it would be seared in the eyelashes. Then the doors of the
recesses flew apart, eight-and-ninety in number, and he beheld divers
sitters on thrones, with the diadem of asses' ears stiffened upright, and
monkeys' skulls grinning with gems; they having on each countenance
the look of sovereigns and the serenity of high estate. Shibli Bagarag
laughed at them, and he thought, "Wullahy! was I one of these? I, the
beloved of Noorna, destined Master of the Event!" and he thought, "Of
a surety, if these sitters could but laugh at themselves, there would be

a release for them, and the crown would topple off which getteth the homage of asses and monkeys!" He would have spoken to them, but the sons of Aklis said, "They have seen the flashing of the Sword, and 'twere well they wake not." As they went from the hall the seven youths said, "Reflect upon the age of these sitters, that have been sitting in the chairs from three to eleven generations back! And they were searchers of the Sword like thee, but were duped! In like manner, the hen sitteth in complacency, but she bringeth forth and may cackle; 'tis owing to the aids of Noorna that thou art not one of these sitters, O Master of the Event!" Now, they paced through the hall of dainty provender, and through the hall of the jewel-fountains, coming to the palace steps, where stood Abarak leaning on his bar. As they advanced to Abarak, there was a clamour in the halls behind, that gathered in noise like a torrent, and approached, and presently the Master was ware of a sharp stroke on his forehead with a hairy finger, and then a burn, and the Crown that had clung to him toppled off; surely it fell upon the head of the old monkey, the cautious and wise one, he that had made a study of Shibli Bagarag. Thereupon that monkey stalked scornfully from them; and Abarak cried, "O Master of the Event! it was better for me to keep the passage of the Seventh Pillar, than be an ape of this order. Wah! the flashing of the Sword scorcheth them, and they scamper."

# The Veiled Figure

Verily there was lightning in Aklis as Shibli Bagarag flashed the Sword over the clamouring beasts: the shape of the great palace stood forth vividly, and a wide illumination struck up the streams, and gilded the large hanging leaves, and drew the hills glimmeringly together, and scattered fires on the flat faces of the rocks. Then the seven youths said quickly, "Away! out of Aklis, O Master of the Event! from city to city of earth this light is visible, and men will know that Fate is in travail, and an Event preparing for them, and Shagpat will be warned by the portent; wherefore lose not the happy point of time on which thy star is manifest." And they cried again, "Away! out of Aklis!" with gestures of impatience, urging his departure.

Then said he, "O youths, Sons of Aklis, it is written that gratitude is the poor man's mine of wealth, and the rich man's flower of beauty; and I have but that to give ye for all this aid and friendliness of yours."

But they exclaimed, "No aid or friendliness in Aklis! By the gall of the Roc! it is well for thee thou camest armed with potent spells, and hadst one to advise and inspirit thee, or thou wouldst have stayed here to people Aklis, and grazed in a strange shape."

Now, the seven waxed in impatience, and he laid their hands upon his head and moved from them with Abarak, to where in the dusk the elephant that had brought them stood. Then the elephant kneeled and took the twain upon his back, and bore them across the dark land to that reach of the river where the boat was moored in readiness. They entered the boat silently among its drapery of lotuses, and the Veiled Figure ferried them over the stream that rippled not with their motion. As they were crossing, desire to know that Veiled Figure counselled Shibli Bagarag evilly to draw the Sword again, and flash it, so that the veil became transparent. Then, when Abarak turned to him for the reason of the flashing of the Sword, he beheld the eyes of the youth fixed in horror, glaring as at sights beyond the tomb. He said nought, but as the boat's-head whispered among the reeds and long flowers of the opposite marge, he took Shibli Bagarag by the shoulders and pushed him out of the boat, and leaped out likewise, leading him from the marge forcibly, hurrying him forward from it, he at the heels of the youth propelling him; and crying in out-of-breath voice at intervals, "What sight? what sight?" But the youth was powerless of speech, and when at last he opened his lips, the little man shrank from him, for he laughed as do the insane, a peal of laughter ended by gasps; then a louder peal, presently softer; then a peal that started all the echoes in Aklis. After awhile, as Abarak still cried in his ear, "What sight?" he looked at him with a large eye, saying querulously, "Is it written I shall be pushed by the shoulder through life? And is it in the pursuit of further thwackings?"

Abarak heeded him not, crying still, "What sight?" and Shibli Bagarag lowered his tone, and jerked his body, pronouncing the name "Rabesqurat!" Then Abarak exclaimed, "'Tis as I weened. Oh, fool! to flash the Sword and peer through the veil! Truly, there be few wits will bear that sight!" On a sudden he cried, "No cure but one, and that a sleep in the bosom of the betrothed!"

Thereupon he hurried the youth yet faster across the dark lawns of Aklis toward the passage of the Seventh Pillar, by which the twain had entered that kingdom. And Shibli Bagarag saw as in a dream the shattered door, shattered by the bar, remembering dimly as a thing distant in years the netting of the Queen, and Noorna chained upon the pillar; he remembered Shagpat even vacantly in his mind, as one sheaf of barley amid other sheaves of the bearded field, so was he overcome by the awfulness of that sight behind the veil of the Veiled Figure!

As they advanced to the passage, he was aware of an impediment to its entrance, as it had been a wall of stone there; and seeing Abarak enter the passage without let, he kicked hard in front at the invisible obstruction, but there was no coming by. Abarak returned to him, and took his right arm, and raised the sleeve from his wrist, and lo, the two remaining hairs of Garraveen twisted round it in sapphire winds. Cried he, "Oh, the generosity of Gulrevaz! she has left these two hairs that he may accomplish swiftly the destiny marked for him! but now, since his gazing through that veil, he must part with them to get out of Aklis." And he muttered, "His star is a strange one! one that leadeth him to fortune by the path of frowns! to greatness by the aid of thwackings! Truly the ways of Allah are wonderful!" Shibli Bagarag resisted him in nothing, and Abarak loosed the two bright hairs from his wrist, and those two hairs swelled and took glittering scales, and were sapphire snakes with wings of intense emerald; and they rose in the air spirally together, each over each, so that to see them one would fancy in the darkness a fountain of sapphire waters flashed with the sheen of emerald. When they had reached a height loftier than the topmost palace-towers of Aklis, they descended like javelins into the earth, and in a moment re-appeared, in the shape of Genii when they are charitably disposed to them they visit; not much above the mortal size, nor overbright, save for a certain fire in their eyes when they turned them; and they were clothed each from head to foot in an armour of sapphire plates shot with steely emerald. Surely the dragon-fly that darteth all day in the blaze over pools is like what they were. Abarak bit his forefinger and said, "Who be ye, O sons of brilliance?"

They answered, "Karavejis and Veejravoosh, slaves of the Sword."

Then he said, "Come with us now, O slaves of the Sword, and help us to the mountain of outer Aklis."

They answered, "O thou, there be but two means for us of quitting Aklis: on the wrist of the Master, or down the blade of the Sword! and from the wrist of the Master we have been loosed, and no one of thy race can tie us to it again."

Abarak said, "How then shall the Master leave Aklis?"

They answered, "By Allah in Aklis! he can carve a way whither he will with the Sword."

But Abarak cried, "O Karavejis and Veejravoosh! he bath peered through the veil of the Ferrying Figure."

Now, when they heard his words, the visages of the Genii darkened, and they exclaimed sorrowfully, "Serve we such a one?"

And they looked at Shibli Bagarag a look of anger, so that he, whose wits were in past occurrences, imagined them his enemy and the foe of Noorna split in two, crying, "How? Is Karaz a couple? and do I multiply him with strokes of the Sword?"

Thereupon he drew the Sword from his girdle in wrath, flourishing it; and Karavejis and Veejravoosh felt the might of the Sword, and prostrated themselves to the ground at his feet. And Abarak said, "Arise, and bring us swiftly to the mountain of outer Aklis."

Then said they, "Seek a passage down yonder brook in the moonbeams; and it is the sole passage for him now."

Abarak went with them to the brook that was making watery music to itself between banks of splintered rock and over broad slabs of marble, bubbling here and there about the roots of large-leaved water-flowers, and catching the mirrored moon of Aklis in whirls, breaking it in lances. Then they waded into the water knee-deep, and the two Genii seized hold of a great slab of marble in the middle of the water, and under was a hollow brimmed with the brook, that the brook partly filled and flowed over. Then the Genii said to Abarak, "Plunge!" and they said the same to Shibli Bagarag. The swayer of the Sword replied, as it had been a simple occasion, a common matter, and a thing for the exercise of civility, "With pleasure and all willingness!" Thereupon he tightened his girth, and arrowing his two hands, flung up his heels and disappeared in the depths, Abarak following. Surely, those two went diving downward till it seemed to each there was no bottom in the depth, and they would not cease to feel the rushing of the water in their ears till the time anticipated by mortals.

GEORGE MEREDITH

# THE BOSOM OF NOORNA

Now, while a thousand sparks of fire were bursting on the sight of the two divers, and they speeded heels uppermost to the destiny marked out for them by the premeditations of the All-Wise, lo! Noorna was on the mountain in outer Aklis with Koorookh, waiting for the appearance of her betrothed, Sword in hand. She saw beams from the blazing eye of Aklis, and knew by the redness of it that one, a mortal, was peering on the earth and certain of created things. So she waited awhile in patience for the return of her betrothed, with the head of Koorookh in her lap, caressing the bird, and teaching it words of our language; and the bird fashioned its bill to the pronouncing of names, such as "Noorna" and "Feshnavat," and "Goorelka"; and it said "Karaz," and stuck not at the name "Shagpat," and it learnt to say even "Shagpat shall be shaved! Shagpat shall be shaved!" but no effort of Noorna could teach it to say, "Shibli Bagarag," the bird calling instead, "Shiparack, Shiplabarack, Shibblisharack." And Noorna chid it with her forefinger, crying, "O Koorookh! wilt thou speak all names but that one of my betrothed?"

So she said again, "Shibli Bagarag." And the bird answered, imitating its best, "Shibberacavarack." Noorna was wroth with it, crying, "Oh naughty bird! is the name of my beloved hateful to thee?"

And she chid Koorookh angrily, he with a heavy eye sulking, and keeping the sullen feathers close upon his poll. Now, she thought, "There is in this a meaning and I will fathom it." So she counted the letters in the name of her betrothed, that were thirteen, and spelt them backwards, afterwards multiplying them by an equal number, and fashioning words from the selection of every third and seventh letter. Then took she the leaf from a tree and bade Koorookh fly with her to the base of the mountain sloping from Aklis to the sea, and there wrote with a pin's point on the leaf the words fashioned, dipping the leaf in the salt ripple by the beach, till they were distinctly traced. And it was revealed to her that Shibli Bagarag bore now a name that might be uttered by none, for that the bearer of it had peered through the veil of the ferrying figure in Aklis. When she knew that, her grief was heavy, and she sat on the cold stones of the beach and among the bright shells, weeping in anguish, loosing her hair, scattering it wildly, exclaiming, "Awahy! woe on me! Was ever man more tired than he before entering Aklis, he that was in turns abased and beloved and exalted! yet his weakness clingeth to him, even in Aklis and with the Wondrous Sword in his grasp."

Then she thought, "Still he had strength to wield the Sword, for I marked the flashing of it, and 'twas he that leaned forward the blade to me; and he possesses the qualities that bring one gloriously to the fruits of enterprise!" And she thought, "Of a surety, if Abarak be with him, and a single of the three slaves of the Sword that I released from the tail of Garraveen, Ravejoura, Karavejis, and Veejravoosh, he will yet come through, and I may revive him in my bosom for the task." So, thinking upon that, the sweet crimson surprised her cheeks, and she arose and drew Koorookh with her along the beach till they came to some rocks piled ruggedly and the waves breaking over them. She mounted these, and stepped across them to the entrance of a cavern, where flowed a full water swiftly to the sea, rolling smooth bulks over and over, and with a translucent light in each, showing precious pebbles in the bed of the water below; agates of size, limpid cornelians, plates of polished jet, rubies, diamonds innumerable that were smitten into sheen by slant rays of the level sun, the sun just losing its circle behind lustrous billows of that Enchanted Sea. She turned to Koorookh a moment, saying, with a coax of smiles, "Will my bird wait here for me, even at this point?" Koorookh clapped both his wings, and she said again, petting him, "He will keep watch to pluck me from the force of water as I roll past, that I be not carried to the sea, and lost?"

Koorookh still clapped his wings, and she entered under the arch of the cavern. It was roofed with crystals, a sight of glory, with golden lamps at intervals, still centres of a thousand beams. Taking the sandal from her left foot and tucking up the folds of her trousers to the bend of her clear white knee, she advanced, half wading, up the winds of the cavern, and holding by the juts of granite here and there, till she came to a long straight lane in the cavern, and at the end of it, far down, a solid pillar of many-coloured water that fell into the current, as it had been one block of gleaming marble from the roof, without ceasing. Now, she made toward it, and fixed her eye warily wide on it, and it was bright, flawless in brilliancy; but while she gazed a sudden blot was visible, and she observed in the body of the fall two dark objects plumping downward one after the other, like bolts, and they splashed in the current and were carried off by the violence of its full sweep, shooting by her where she stood, rapidly; but she, knotting her garments round the waist to give her limbs freedom and swiftness, ran a space, and then bent and plunged, catching, as she rose, the foremost to her bosom, and whirled away under the flashing crystals like a fish scaled with splendours that hath darted and seized upon a prey, and is bearing it greedily to some secure corner of the deeps to swallow the quivering repast at leisure. Surely, the heart of Noorna was wise of what she bore against her bosom; and it beat exulting strokes in the midst of the rush and roar and gurgle of the torrent, and the gulping sounds and multitudinous outcries of the headlong water. That verse of the poet would apply to her where he says:

> Lead me to the precipice,
> And bid me leap the dark abyss:
> I care not what the danger be,
> So my beloved, my beauteous vision,
> Be but the prize I bear with me,
> For she to Paradise can turn Perdition.

Praise be to him that planteth love, the worker of this marvel, within us! Now, she sped in the manner narrated through the mazes of the cavern, coming suddenly to the point at the entrance where perched Koorookh gravely upon one leg, like a bird with an angling beak: he caught at her as she was hurling toward the sea, and drew her to the bank of rock, that burden on her bosom; and it was Shibli Bagarag, her betrothed, his eyes closed, his whole countenance colourless. Behind him like a shadow streamed Abarak, and Noorna kneeled by the waterside and fetched the little man from it likewise; he was without a change, as if drawn from a familiar element; and when he had prostrated himself thrice and called on the Prophet's name in the form of thanksgiving, he wrung his beard of the wet, and had wit to bless the action of Noorna, that saved him. Then the two raised Shibli Bagarag from the rock, and reclined him lengthwise under the wings of Koorookh, and Noorna stretched herself there beside him with one arm about his neck, the fair head of the youth on her bosom. And she said to Abarak, "He hath dreamed many dreams, my betrothed, but never one so sweet as that I give him. Already, see, the hue returneth to his cheek and the dimples of pleasure." So was it; and she said, "Mount, O thou of the net and the bar! and stride Koorookh across the neck, for it is nigh the setting of the moon, and by dawn we must be in our middle flight, seen of men, a cloud over them."

Said Abarak, "To hear is to obey!"

He bestrode the neck of Koorookh and sat with dangling feet, till she cried, "Rise!" and the bird spread its wings and flapped them wide, rising high in the silver rays, and flying rapidly forward with the three on him from the mountain in front of Aklis, and the white sea with its enchanted isles and wonders; flying and soaring till the earth was as what might be held in the hollow of the hand, and the kingdoms of the earth a mingled heap of shining dust in the midst.

# The Revival

Now, the feathers of Koorookh in his flight were ruffled by a chill breeze, and they were speeding through a light glow of cold rose-colour. Then said Noorna, "'Tis the messenger of morning, the blush. Oh, what changes will date from this day!"

The glow of rose became golden, and they beheld underneath them, on one side, the rim of the rising red sun, and rays streaming over the earth and its waters. And Noorna said, "I must warn Feshnavat, my father, and prepare him for our coming."

So she plucked a feather from Koorookh and laid the quill downward, letting it drop. Then said she, "Now for the awakening of my betrothed!"

Thereupon she hugged his head a moment, and kissed him on the eyelids, the cheeks, and the lips, crying, "By this means only!" Crying that, she pushed him, sliding, from the back of the bird, and he parted from them, falling headforemost in the air like a stricken eagle. Then she called to Koorookh, "Seize him!" and the bird slanted his beak and closed his wings, the two, Abarak and Noorna, clinging to him tightly; and he was down like an arrow between Shibli Bagarag and the ground, spreading beneath him like a tent, and Noorna caught the youth gently to her lap; then she pushed him off again, intercepting his descent once more, till they were on a level with one of the mountains of the earth, from which the City of Shagpat is visible among the yellow sands like a white spot in the yolk of an egg. So by this time the eyes of the youth gave symptoms of a desire to look upon the things that be, peeping faintly beneath the lashes, and she exclaimed joyfully, raising her white hands above her head, "One plunge in the lake, and life will be his again!"

Below them was a green lake, tinted by the dawn with crimson and yellow, deep, and with high banks. As they crossed it to the middle, she slipped off the youth from Koorookh, and he with a great plunge was received into the stillness of the lake. Meanwhile Koorookh quivered his wings and seized him when he arose, bearing him to an end of the lake, where stood one dressed like a Dervish, and it was the Vizier Feshnavat, the father of Noorna. So when he saw them, he shouted the shout of congratulation, catching Noorna to his breast, and Shibli Bagarag stretched as doth a heavy sleeper in his last doze, saying, in a yawning voice, "What trouble? I wot there is nought more for us now that Shagpat is shaved! Oh, I have had a dream, a dream! He that is among Houris in Paradise dreameth not a dream like that. And I dreamed—'tis gone!"

Then said he, staring at them, "Who be ye? What is this?"

Noorna, took him again to her bosom, and held him there; and she plucked a herb, and squeezed it till a drop from it fell on either of his lids, applying to them likewise a dew from the serpents of the Sword, and he awoke to the reality of things. Surely, then he prostrated himself and repeated the articles of his faith, taking one hand of his betrothed and kissing her; and he embraced Abarak and Feshnavat, saying to the father of Noorna, "I know, O Feshnavat, that by my folly and through my weakness I have lost time in this undertaking, but it shall be short work now with Shagpat. This thy daughter, the Eclipser of Reason, was ever such a prize as she? I will deserve her. Wullahy! I am now a new man, sprung like fire from ashes. Lo, I am revived by her for the great work."

Said Abarak: "O Master of the Event, secure now without delay the two slaves of the Sword, and lean the blade toward Aklis."

Upon that, he ran up rapidly to the summit of the mountain and drew the Sword from his girdle, and leaned it toward Aklis, and it lengthened out over lands, the blade of it a beam of solid brilliance. Presently, from forth the invisible remoteness they saw the two Genii, Karavejis and Veejravoosh, and they were footing the blade swiftly, like stars, speeding up till they were within reach of the serpents of the hilt, when they dropped to the earth, bowing their heads; so he commanded them to rise, crying, "Search ye the earth and its confines, and bring hither tidings of the Genie Karaz."

They said, "To hear is to obey."

Then they began to circle each round the other, circling more and more sharply till beyond the stretch of sight, and Shibli Bagarag said to Feshnavat, "Am I not awake, O Feshnavat? I will know where is Karaz ere I seek to operate on Shagpat, for it is well spoken of the poet:

> 'Obstructions first remove
> Ere thou thy cunning prove';

and I will encounter this Karaz that was our Ass, ere I try the great shave."

Then said he, turning quickly, "Yonder is the light from Aklis striking on the city, and I mark Shagpat, even he, illumined by it, singled out, where he sitteth on the roof of the palace by the market-place."

GEORGE MEREDITH

So they looked, and it was as he had spoken, that Shagpat was singled out in the midst of the city by the wondrous beams of the eye of Aklis, and made prominent in effulgence.

Said Abarak, climbing to the level of observation, "He hath a redness like the inside of a halved pomegranate."

Feshnavat stroked his chin, exclaiming, "He may be likened to a mountain goat in the midst of a forest roaring with conflagration."

Said Shibli Bagarag, "Now is he the red-maned lion, the bristling boar, the uncombed buffalo, the plumaged cock, but soon will he be like nothing else save the wrinkled kernel of a shaggy fruit. Lo, now, the Sword! it leapeth to be at him, and 'twill be as the keen icicle of winter to that perishing foliage, that doomed crop! So doth the destined minute destroy with a flash the hoarded arrogance of ages; and the destined hand doeth what creation failed to perform; and 'tis by order, destiny, and preordainment, that the works of this world come to pass. This know I, and I witness thereto that am of a surety ordained to the Shaving of Shagpat!"

Then he stood apart and gazed from Shagpat to the city that now began to move with the morning; elephants and coursers saddled by the gates of the King's palace were visible, and camels blocking the narrow streets, and the markets bustling. Surely, though the sun illumined that city, it was as a darkness behind Shagpat singled by the beams of Aklis.

# THE PLOT

N ow, while Shibli Bagarag gazed on Shagpat kindled by the beams of Aklis, lo, the Genii Karavejis and Veejravoosh circling each other in swift circles like two sapphire rings toward him, and they whirled to a point above his head, and fell and prostrated themselves at his feet: so he cried, "O ye slaves of the Sword, my servitors! how of the whereabout of Karaz?"

They answered, "O Master of the Event, we found him after many circlings far off, and 'twas by the borders of the Putrid Sea. We came not close on him, for he is stronger than we without the Sword, but it seemed he was distilling drops of an oil from certain substances, large thickened drops that dropped into a phial."

Then Shibli Bagarag said, "The season of weakness with me is over, and they that confide in my strength, my cunning, my watchfulness, my wielding of the Sword, have nought to fear for themselves. Now, this is my plot, O Feshnavat,—that part of it in which thou art to have a share. 'Tis that thou depart forthwith to the City yonder, and enter thy palace by a back entrance, and I will see that thou art joined within an hour of thy arrival there by Baba Mustapha, my uncle, the gabbler. He is there, as I guess by signs; I have had warnings of him. Discover him speedily. Thy task is then to induce him to make an attempt on the head of Shagpat in all wiliness, as he and thou think well to devise. He will fail, as I know, but what is that saying of the poet?

> *'Persist, if thou wouldst truly reach thine ends,*
> *For failures oft are but advising friends.'*

And he says:

> *'Every failure is a step advanced,*
> *To him who will consider how it chanced.'*

Wherefore, will I that this attempt be made, keeping the counsel that is mine. Thou must tell Baba Mustapha I wait without the city to reward him by my powers of reward with all that he best loveth. So, when he has failed in his attempt on Shagpat, and blows fall plenteously upon him, and he is regaled with the accustomed thwacking, as I have tasted it in this undertaking, do thou waste no further word on him, for his part is over, and as is said:

> 'Waste not a word in enterprise!
> Against—or for—the minute flies.'

'Tis then for thee, O Feshnavat, to speed to the presence of the King in his majesty, and thou wilt find means of coming to him by a disguise. Once in the Hall of Council, challenge the tongue of contradiction to affirm Shagpat other than a bald-pate bewigged. This is for thee to do."

Quoth Feshnavat plaintively, after thought, "And what becometh of me, O thou Master of the Event?"

Shibli Bagarag said, "The clutch of the executioner will be upon thee, O Feshnavat, and a clamouring multitude around; short breathing-time given thee, O father of Noorna, ere the time of breathing is commanded to cease. Now, in that respite the thing that will occur, 'tis for thee to see and mark; sure, never will reverse of things be more complete, and the other side of the picture more rapidly exhibited, if all go as I conceive and plot, and the trap be not premature nor too perfect for the trappers; as the poet has declared:

> 'Ye that intrigue, to thy slaves proper portions adapt;
> Perfectest plots burst too often, for all are not apt.'

And I witness likewise to the excellence of his saying:

> 'To master an Event,
> Study men!
> The minutes are well spent
> Only then.'

Also 'tis he that says:

> 'The man of men who knoweth men, the Man of men is he!
> His army is the human race, and every foe must flee.'

So have I apportioned to thee thy work, to Baba Mustapha his; reserving to myself the work that is mine!"

Thereat Feshnavat exclaimed, "O Master of the Event, may I be thy sacrifice! on my head be it! and for thee to command is for me to obey! but surely, this Sword of thine that is in thy girdle, the marvellous blade—'tis alone equal to the project and the shave; and the matter might be consummated, the great thing done, even from this point whence we behold Shagpat visible, as 'twere brought forward toward us by the beams! And this Sword swayed by thee, and with thy skill and strength and the hardihood of hand that is thine, wullahy! 'twould shear him now, this moment, taking the light of Aklis for a lather."

Shibli Bagarag knotted the brows of impatience, crying, "Hast thou forgotten Karaz in thy calculations? I know of a surety what this Sword will do, and I wot the oil he distilleth strengtheneth Shagpat but against common blades. Yet shall it not be spoken of me, Shibli Bagarag, that I was tripped by my own conceit; the poet counselleth:

> *'When for any mighty end thou hast the aid of heaven,*
> *Mount until thy strength shall match those great means which*
> *are given':*

nor that I was overthrown in despising mine enemy, forgetful of the saying of the sage:

> *'Read the features of thy foe, wherever he may find thee,*
> *Small he is, seen face to face, but thrice his size behind thee.'*

Wullahy! this Karaz is a Genie of craft and resources, one of a mighty stock, and I must close with Shagpat to be sure of him; and that I am not deceived by semblances, opposing guile with guile, and guile deeper than his, for that he awaiteth it not, thinking I have leaped in fancy beyond the Event, and am puffed by the after-breaths of adulation, I!— thinking I pluck the blossoms in my hunger for the fruit, that I eat the chick of the yet unlaid egg, O Feshnavat. As is said, and the warrior beareth witness to the wisdom of it:

> *'His weapon I'll study; my own conceal;*
> *So with two arms to his one shall I deal.'*

The same also testifieth:

> "'Tis folly of the hero, though resistless in the field,
> To stake the victory on his steel, and fling away the shield.'

And likewise:

> 'Examine thine armour in every joint,
> For slain was the Giant, and by a pin's point.'

Wah! 'tis certain there will need subtlety in this undertaking, and a plot plotted, so do thou my bidding, and fail not in the part assigned to thee."

Now, Feshnavat was persuaded by his words, and cried, "In diligence, discretion, and the virtues which characterize subordinates, I go, and I delay not! I will perform the thing required of me, O Master of the Event." And he repeated in verse:

> With danger beset, be the path crooked or narrow,
> Thou art the bow, and I the arrow.

Then embraced he his daughter, kissing her on the forehead and the eyes, and tightening the girdle of his robe, departed, with the name of Allah on his lips, in the direction of the City.

So Shibli Bagarag called to him the two Genii, and his command was, "Soar, ye slaves of the Sword, till the range of earth and its mountains and seas and deserts are a cluster in the orb of the eye, Shiraz conspicuous as a rose among garlands, and the ruby consorted with other gems in a setting. In Shiraz or the country adjoining ye will come upon one Baba Mustapha by name; and, if he be alone, ye may recognize him by his forlorn look and the hang of his cheeks, his vacancy as of utter abandonment; if in company, 'twill be the only talker that's he; seize on him, give him a taste of thin air, and deposit him without speech on the roof of a palace, where ye will see Feshnavat in yonder city: this do ere the shadows of the palm-tree by the well in the plain move up the mounds that enclose the fortified parts."

Cried Karavejis and Veejravoosh, "To hear is to obey."

Up into the sky, like two bright balls tossed by jugglers, the two Genii shot; and, watching them, Noorna bin Noorka said, "My life, there is a third wanting, Ravejoura; and with aid of the three, earth could have planted no obstruction to thy stroke; but thou wert tempted by the third temptation in Aklis, and left not the Hall in triumph, the Hall of the Duping Brides!"

He answered, "That is so, my soul; and the penalty is mine, by which I am made to employ deceits ere I strike."

And she said, "'Tis to the generosity of Gulrevaz thou owest Karavejis and Veejravoosh; and I think she was generous, seeing thee true to me in love, she that hath sorrows!"

So he said, "What of the sorrows of Gulrevaz? Tell me of them."

But she said, "Nay, O my betrothed! wouldst thou have this tongue blistered, and a consuming spark shot against this bosom?"

Then he: "Make it clear to me."

She put her mouth to his ear, saying, "There is a curse on whoso telleth of things in Aklis, and to tattle of the Seven and their sister forerunneth wretchedness."

Surely, he stooped to that fair creature, and folded her to his heart, his whole soul heaving to her; and he cried again and again, "Shall harm hap to thee through me? by Allah, no!"

And he closed the privileged arm of the bridegroom round her waist, that had the yieldingness of the willow-branchlet, the flowingness of the summer sea-wave, and seemed as 'twere melting honey-like at the first gentle pressure; she leaning her head shyly on his shoulder, yet confiding in his faithfulness; it was that she was shy of the great bliss in her bosom, and was made timid by the fervour of her affection; as is sung:

> *Deeper than the source of blushes*
> *Is the power that makes them start;*
> *Up in floods the red stream rushes,*
> *At one whisper of the heart.*

And it is sung in words present to the youth as he surveyed her:

> *O beauty of the bride! O beauty of the bride!*
> *Her bashful joys like serpents sting her tenderness*
> *to tears:*
> *Her hopes are sleeping eagles in the shining of the spheres;*
> *O beauty of the bride! O beauty of the bride!*
> *And she's a lapping antelope that from her image flees;*
> *And she's a dove caught in two hands, to pant as she*
> *shall please;*

*O beauty of the bride! O beauty of the bride!*
*Like torrents over Paradise her lengthy tresses roll:*
*She moves as doth a swaying rose, and chides her hasty soul;*
*The thing she will, that will she not, yet can no will control*
*O beauty, beauty, beauty of the bride!*

They were thus together, Abarak leaning under one wing of Koorookh for shade up the slope of the hill, and Shibli Bagarag called to him, "Ho, Abarak! look if there be aught impending over the City."

So he arose and looked, crying, "One with plunging legs, high up in air over the City, between two bright bodies." Shibli Bagarag exclaimed, "'Tis well! The second chapter of the Event is opened; so call it, thou that tellest of the Shaving of Shagpat. It will be the shortest."

Then he said, "The shadow of yonder palm is now a slanted spear up the looped wall of the City. Now, the time of Shagpat's triumph, and his greatest majesty, will be when yonder walls chase the shadow of the palm up this hill; and then will Baba Mustapha be joining the chorus of creatures that shriek toward even ere they snooze. There's not an ape in the woods, nor hyaena in the forest, nor birds on the branches, nor frogs in the marsh that will outnoise Baba Mustapha under the thong! Wullahy, 'twill grieve his soul in aftertime when he sitteth secure in honours, courted, with a thousand ears at his bidding, that so much breath 'scaped him without toll of the tongue! But as the poet says truly:

*'The chariot of Events lifteth many dusty heels,*
*And many, high and of renown, it crusheth with its wheels.'*

Wah! I have had my share of the thong, and am I, Master of the Event, to be squeamish in attaining an end by its means? Nay, by this Sword!"

Thereat, he strode once again to the summit of the hill, and in a moment the Genii fronted him like two shot arrows quivering from the flight. So he cried, "It is done?"

They answered, "In faithfulness."

So he beckoned to Noorna, and she came forward swiftly to him, exclaiming, "I read the plot, and the thing required of me; so say nought, but embrace me ere I leave thee, my betrothed, my master!"

He embraced her, and led her to where the Genii stood. Then said he to the Genii, "Convey her to the City, O ye slaves of the Sword, and watch over her there. If ye let but an evil wind ruffle the hair of her head, lo! I sever ye with a stroke that shaketh the under worlds. Remain by her till the shrieks of Baba Mustapha greet ye, and then will follow commotion among the crowd, and cries for Shagpat to show himself to the people, cries also of death to Feshnavat; and there will be an assembly in the King's Hall of Justice; thither lead ye my betrothed, and watch over her." And he said to Noorna, "Thou knowest my design?"

So she said, "When condemnation is passed on Feshnavat, that I appear in the hall as bride of Shagpat, and so rescue him that is my father." And she cried, "Oh, fair delightful time that is coming! my happiness and thy honour on earth dateth from it. Farewell, O my betrothed, beloved youth! Eyes of mine! these Genii will be by, and there's no cause for fear or sorrow, and 'tis for thee to look like morning that speeds the march of light. Thou, my betrothed, art thou not all that enslaveth the heart of woman?"

Cried Shibli Bagarag, "And thou, O Noorna, all that enraptureth the soul of man! Allah keep thee, my life!"

Lo! while they were wasting the rich love in their hearts, the Genii rose up with Noorna, and she, waving her hand to him, was soon distant and as the white breast of a bird turned to the sun. Then went he to where Abarak was leaning, and summoned Koorookh, and the twain mounted him, and rose up high over the City of Shagpat to watch the ripening of the Event, as a vulture watcheth over the desert.

# THE DISH OF POMEGRANATE GRAIN

Now, in the City of Shagpat, Kadza, spouse of Shagpat, she that had belaboured Shibli Bagarag, had a dream while these things were doing; and it was a dream of danger and portent to the glory of her eyes, Shagpat. So, at the hour when he was revealed to Shibli Bagarag, made luminous by the beams of Aklis, Kadza went to an inner chamber, and greased her hands and her eyelids, and drank of a phial, and commenced tugging at a brass ring fixed in the floor, and it yielded and displayed an opening, over which she stooped the upper half of her leanness, and pitching her note high, called "Karaz!" After that, she rose and retreated from the hole hastily, and in the winking of an eye it was filled, as 'twere a pillar of black smoke, by the body of the Genie, he breathing hard with mighty travel. So he cried to her between his pantings and puffings, "Speak! where am I wanted, and for what?"

Now, Kadza was affrighted at the terribleness of his manner, and the great smell of the Genie was an intoxication in her nostril, so that she reeled and could just falter out, "Danger to the Identical!"

Then he, in a voice like claps of thunder, "Out with it!"

She answered beseechingly, "'Tis a dream I had, O Genie; a dream of danger to him."

While she spake, the Genie clenched his fists and stamped so that the palace shook and the earth under it, exclaiming, "O abominable Kadza! a dream is it? another dream? Wilt thou cease dreaming awhile, thou silly woman? Know I not he that's powerful against us is in Aklis, crowned ape, and that his spells are gone? And I was distilling drops to defy the Sword and strengthen Shagpat from assault, yet bringest thou me from my labour by the Putrid Sea with thy accursed dream!" Thereat, he frowned and shot fire at her from his eyes, so that she singed, and the room thickened with a horrible smell of burning. She feared greatly and trembled, but he cooled himself against the air, crying presently in a diminished voice, "Let's hear this dream, thou foolish Kadza! 'Tis as well to hear it. Probably Rabesqurat hath sent thee some sign from Aklis, where she ferryeth a term. What's that saying:

*'A woman's at the core of every plot man plotteth,*
*And like an ill-reared fruit, first at the core it rotteth.'*

So, out with it, thou Kadza!"

Now, the urgency of that she had dreamed overcame fear in Kadza, and she said, "O great Genie and terrible, my dream was this. Lo! I saw an assemblage of the beasts of the forests and them that inhabit wild places. And there was the elephant and the rhinoceros and the hippopotamus, and the camel and the camelopard, and the serpent and the striped tiger; also the antelope, the hyena, the jackal, and above them, eminent in majesty, the lion. Surely, he sat as 'twere on a high seat, and they like suppliants thronging the presence: this I saw, the heart on my ribs beating for Shagpat. And there appeared among the beasts a monkey all ajoint with tricks, jerking with malice, he looking as 'twere hungry for the doing of things detestable; and the lion scorned him, and I marked him ridicule the lion: 'twas so. And the lion began to scowl, and the other beasts marked the displeasure of the lion. Then chased they that monkey from the presence, and for awhile he was absent, and the lion sat in his place gravely, with calm, receiving homage of the other beasts; and down to his feet came the eagle that's lord of air, and before him kneeled the great elephant, and the subtle serpent eyed him with awe. But soon did that monkey, the wretched animal! reappear, and there was no peace for the lion, he worrying till close within stretch of the lion's paw! Wah! the lion might have crushed him, but that he's magnanimous. And so it was that as the monkey advanced the lion roared to him, 'Begone!'"

"And the monkey cried, 'Who commandeth?'

"So the lion roared, 'The King of beasts and thy King!'

"Then that monkey cried, 'Homage to the King of beasts and my King! Allah keep him in his seat, and I would he were visible.'

"So the lion roared, 'He sitteth here acknowledged, thou graceless animal! and he's before thee apparent.'

"Then the monkey affected eagerness, and gazed about him, and peered on this beast and on that, exclaiming like one that's injured and under slight, 'What's this I've done, and wherein have I offended, that he should be hidden from me when pointed out?'

"So the lion roared, ''Tis I where I sit, thou offensive monkey!'

"Then that monkey in the upper pitch of amazement, 'Thou! Is it for created thing to acknowledge a king without a tail? And, O beasts of the forest and the wilderness, how say ye? Am I to blame that I bow not to one that hath it not?'

"Upon that, the lion rose, and roared in the extreme of wrath; but the word he was about to utter was checked in him, for 'twas manifest that where he would have lashed a tail he shook a stump, wagging it as the dog doth. Lo! when the lion saw that, the majesty melted from him, and in a moment the plumpness of content and prosperity forsook him, so that his tawny skin hung flabbily and his jaw drooped, and shame deprived him of stateliness; abashed was he! Now, seeing the lion shamed in this manner, my heart beat violently for Shagpat, so that I awoke with the strength of its beating, and 'twas hidden from me whether the monkey was punished by the lion, or exalted by the other beasts in his place, or how came it that the lion's tail was lost, witched from him by that villain of mischief, the monkey; but, O great Genie, I knew there was a lion among men, reverenced, and with enemies; that lion, he that espoused me and my glory, Shagpat! 'Twas enough to know that and tremble at the omen of my dream, O Genie. Wherefore I thought it well to summon thee here, that thou mightest set a guard over Shagpat, and shield him from the treacheries that beset him."

When Kadza had ceased speaking, the Genie glowered at her awhile in silence. Then said he, "What creature is that, Kadza, which tormenteth like the tongue of a woman, is small as her pretensions to virtue, and which showeth how the chapters of her history should be read by the holy ones, even in its manner of movement?"

Cried Kadza, "The flea that hoppeth!"

So he said, "'Tis well! Hast thou strength to carry one of my weight, O Kadza?"

She answered in squeamishness, "I, wullahy! I'm but a woman, Genie, though the wife of Shagpat: and to carry thee is for the camel and the elephant and the horse."

Then he, "Tighten thy girdle, and when tightened, let a loose loop hang from it."

She did that, and he gave her a dark powder in her hand, saying, "Swallow the half of this, and what remaineth mix with water, and sprinkle over thee."

That did she, and thereupon he exclaimed, "Now go, and thy part is to move round Shagpat; and a wind will strike thee from one quarter, and from which quarter it striketh is the one of menace and danger to Shagpat."

So Kadza was diligent in doing what the Genie commanded, and sought for Shagpat, and moved round him many times; but no wind struck her. She went back to the Genie, and told him of this, and the

Genie cried, "What? no wind? not one from Aklis? Then will Shagpat of a surety triumph, and we with him."

Now, there was joy on the features of Kadza and Karaz, till suddenly he said, "Halt in thy song! How if there be danger and menace above? and 'tis the thing that may be."

Then he seized Kadza, and slung her by him, and went into the air, and up it till the roofs of the City of Shagpat were beneath their feet, all on them visible. And under an awning, on the roof of a palace, there was the Vizier Feshnavat and Baba Mustapha, they ear to lip in consultation, and Baba Mustapha brightening with the matter revealed to him, and bobbing his head, and breaking on the speech of the Vizier. Now, when he saw them the Genie blew from his nostrils a double stream of darkness which curled in a thick body round and round him, and Kadza slung at his side was enveloped in it, as with folds of a huge serpent. Then the Genie hung still, and lo! two radiant figures swept toward the roof he watched, and between them Noorna bin Noorka, her long dark hair borne far backward, and her robe of silken stuff fluttering and straining on the pearl buttons as she flew. There was that in her beauty and the silver clearness of her temples and her eyes, and her cheeks, and her neck, and chin and ankles, that made the Genie shudder with love of her, and he was nigh dropping Kadza to the ground, forgetful of all save Noorna. When he recovered, and it was by tightening his muscles till he was all over hard knots, Noorna was seated on a cushion, and descending he heard her speak his name. Then sniffed he the air, and said to Kadza, "O spouse of Shagpat, a plot breweth, and the odour of it is in my nostril. Fearest thou a scorching for his sake thou adorest, the miracle of men?"

She answered, "On my head be it, and my eyes!"

He said, "I shall alight thee behind the pole of awning on yonder roof, where are the two bright figures and the dingy one, and the Vizier Feshnavat and Noorna bin Noorka. A flame will spring up severing thee from them; but thou'rt secure from it by reason of the powder I gave thee, all save the hair that's on thee. Thou'lt have another shape than that which is thine, even that of a slave of Noorna bin Noorka, and say to her when she asketh thy business with her, 'O my mistress, let the storm gather-in the storm-bird when it would surprise men.' Do this, and thy part's done, O Kadza!"

Thereupon he swung a circle, and alighted her behind the pole of awning on the roof, and vanished, and the circle of flame rose up,

GEORGE MEREDITH

and Kadza passed through it slightly scorched, and answered to the question of Noorna, "O my mistress, let the storm gather-in the storm-bird when it would surprise men." Now, when Noorna beheld her, and heard her voice, she pierced the disguise, and was ware of the wife of Shagpat, and glanced her large eyes over Kadza from head to sole till they rested on the loose loop in her girdle. Seeing that, she rose up, and stretched her arms, and spread open the palm of her hand, and slapped Kadza on the cheek and ear a hard slap, so that she heard bells; and ere she ceased to hear them, another, so that Kadza staggered back and screamed, and Feshnavat was moved to exclaim, "What has the girl, thy favourite, offended in, O my daughter?"

So Noorna continued slapping Kadza, and cried, "Is she not sluttish? and where's the point of decency established in her, this Luloo? Shall her like appear before thee and me with loose girdle!"

Then she pointed to the girdle, and Kadza tightened the loose loop, and fell upon the ground to avoid the slaps, and Noorna knelt by her, and clutched at a portion of her dress and examined it, peering intently; and she caught up another part, and knotted it as if to crush a living creature, hunting over her, and grasping at her; and so it was that while she tore strips from the garments of Kadza, Feshnavat jumped suddenly in wrath, and pinched over his garments, crying, "'Tis unbearable! 'Tis I know not what other than a flea that persecuteth me:"

Upon that, Noorna ran to him, and while they searched together for the flea, Baba Mustapha fidgeted and worried in his seat, lurching to the right and to the left, muttering curses; and it was evident he too was persecuted, and there was no peace on the roof of that palace, but pinching and howling and stretching of limbs, and curses snarled in the throat and imprecations on the head of the tormenting flea. Surely, the soul of Kadza rejoiced, for she knew the flea was Karaz, whom she had brought with her in the loose loop of her girdle through the circle of flame which was a barrier against him. She glistened at the triumph of the flea, but Noorna strode to her, and took her to the side of the roof, and pitched her down it, and closed the passage to her. Then ran she to Karavejis and Veejravoosh, whispering in the ear of each, "No word of the Sword?" and afterward aloud, "What think ye will be the term of the staying of my betrothed in Aklis, crowned ape?"

They answered, "O pearl of the morn, crowned ape till such time as Shagpat be shaved."

So she beat her breast, crying, "Oh, utter stagnation, till Shagpat be shaved! and oh, stoppage in the tide of business, dense cloud upon the face of beauty, and frost on the river of events, till Shagpat be shaved! And oh! my betrothed, crowned ape in Aklis till Shagpat be shaved!"

Then she lifted her hands and arms, and said, "To him where he is, ye Genii! and away, for he needeth comfort."

Thereat the glittering spirits dissolved and thinned, and were as taper gleams of curved light across the water in their ascent of the heavens. When they were gone Noorna, exclaimed, "Now for the dish of pomegrante grain, O Baba Mustapha, and let nothing delay us further."

Quoth Baba Mustapha, "'Tis ordered, O my princess and fair mistress, from the confectioner's; and with it the sleepy drug from the seller of medicaments—accursed flea!"

Now, she laughed, and said, "What am I, O Baba Mustapha?"

So he said, "Not thou, O bright shooter of beams, but I, wullahy! I'm but a bundle of points through the pertinacity of this flea! a house of irritabilities! a mere mass of fretfulness! and I've no thought but for the chasing of this unlucky flea: was never flea like it in the world before this flea; and 'tis a flea to anger the holy ones, and make the saintly Dervish swear at such a flea." He wriggled and curled where he sat, and Noorna cried, "What! shall we be defeated by a flea, we that would shave Shagpat, and release this city and the world from bondage?" And she looked up to the sky that was then without a cloud, blazing with the sun on his mid seat, and exclaimed, "O star of Shagpat! wilt thou constantly be in the ascendant, and defeat us, the liberators of men, with a flea?"

Now, whenever one of the twain, Baba Mustapha and the Vizier Feshnavat, commenced speaking of the dish of pomegranate grain, the torment of the flea took all tongue from him, and was destruction to the gravity of council and deliberation. The dish of pomegranate grain was brought to them by slaves, and the drug to induce sleep, yet neither could say aught concerning it, they were as jointy grasshoppers through the action of the flea, and the torment of the flea became a madness, they shrieking, "'Tis now with thee! 'Tis now with me! Fires of the damned on this flea!" In their extremity, they called to Allah for help, but no help came, save when they abandoned all speech concerning the dish of pomegranate grain, then were they for a moment eased of the flea. So Noorna recognized the presence of her enemy Karaz, and his malicious working; and she went and fetched a jar brimmed with water for the bath, and stirred it with her forefinger, and drew on it a flame from the rays of the sun till there rose up from the jar a white thick smoke. She rustled her raiment, making the wind of it collect round Baba Mustapha and Feshnavat, and did this till the sweat streamed from their brows and bodies, and they were sensible of peace and the absence of the flea. Then she whisked away the smoke, and they were attended by slaves with fresh robes, and were as new men, and sat together over the dish of pomegranate grain, praising the wisdom of Noorna and her power. Then Baba Mustapha revived in briskness, and cried, "Here the dish! and 'tis in my hands an instrument, an instrument of vengeance! and one to endow the skilful wielder of it with glory. And 'tis as I designed it,—sweet, seasoned, savoury,—a flattery to the eye and no deceiver to the palate. Wah! and such an instrument in the hands of the discerning and the dexterous, and the discreet and the judicious, and them gifted with determination, is't not such as sufficeth for the overturning of empires and systems, O my mistress, fair one, sapphire of this city? And is't not written that I shall beguile Shagpat by its means, and master the Event, and shame the King of Oolb and his Court? And I shall then sit in state among men, and surround myself with adornments and with slaves, mute, that speak not save at the signal, and are as statues round the cushions of their lord—that's myself. And I shall surround myself with the flatteries of wealth, and walk bewildered in silks and stuffs and perfumeries; and sweet young beauties shall I have about me, antelopes of grace, as I like them, and select them, long-eyed, lazy, fond of listening, and with bashful looks that timidly admire the dignity that's in man."

While he was prating Noorna took the dish in her lap, and folded her silvery feet beneath her, and commenced whipping into it the drug: and she whipped it dexterously and with equal division among the grain, whipping it and the flea with it, but she feigned not to mark the flea and whipped harder. Then took she colour and coloured it saffron, and laid over it gold-leaf, so that it glittered and was an enticing sight; and the dish was of gold, crusted over with devices and patterns, and heads of golden monsters, a ravishment of skill in him that executed it, cumbrous with ornate golden workmanship; likewise there were places round the dish for sticks of perfume and cups carved for the storing of perfumed pellets, and into these Noorna put myrrh and ambergris and rich incenses, aloes, sandalwood, prepared essences, divers keen and sweet scents. Then when all was in readiness, she put the dish upon the knee of Baba Mustapha, and awoke him from his babbling reverie with a shout, and said, "An instrument verily, O Baba Mustapha! and art thou a cat to shave Shagpat with that tongue of thine?"

Now, he arose and made the sign of obedience and said, "'Tis well, O lady of grace and bright wit! and now for the cap of Shiraz and the Persian robe, and my twenty slaves and seven to follow me to the mansion of Shagpat. I'll do: I'll act."

So she motioned to a slave to bring the cap of Shiraz and the Persian robe, and in these Baba Mustapha arrayed himself. Then called he for the twenty-and-seven slaves, and they were ranged, some to go before, some to follow him. And he was exalted, and made the cap of Shiraz nod in his conceit, crying, "Am I not leader in this complot? Wullahy! all bow to me and acknowledge it." Then, to check himself, he called out sternly to the slaves, "Ho ye! forward to the mansion of Shagpat; and pass at a slow pace through the streets of the city—solemnly, gravely, as before a potentate; then will the people inquire of ye, Who't is ye marshal, and what mighty one? and ye will answer, He's from the court of Shiraz, nothing less than a Vizier—bearing homage to Shagpat, even this dish of pomegranate grain."

So they said, "To hear is to obey."

Upon that he waved his hand and stalked majestically, and they descended from the roof into the street, criers running in front to clear the way. When Baba Mustapha was hidden from view by a corner of the street, Noorna shrank in her white shoulders and laughed, and was like a flashing pearl as she swayed and dimpled with laughter. And she cried, "True are those words of the poet, and I testify to them in the instance of Baba Mustapha:

> 'With feathers of the cock, I'll fashion a vain creature;
> With feathers of the owl, I'll make a judge in feature';

Is not the barber elate and lofty? He goeth forth to the mastery of this Event as go many, armed with nought other than their own conceit: and 'tis written:

> 'Fools from their fate seek not to urge:
> The coxcomb carrieth his scourge.'"

So Feshnavat smoothed his face, and said, "Is't not also written?—

*'Oft may the fall of fools make wise men moan!*
*Too often hangs the house on one loose stone!'*

'Tis so, O Noorna, my daughter, and I am as a reed shaken by the wind of apprehensiveness, and doubt in me is a deep root as to the issue of this undertaking, for the wrath of the King will be terrible, and the clamour of the people soundeth in my ears already. If Shibli Bagarag fail in one stroke, where be we? 'Tis certain I knew not the might in Shagpat when I strove with him, and he's powerful beyond the measure of man's subtlety; and yonder flies a rook without fellow—an omen; and all's ominous, and ominous of ill: and I marked among the troop of slaves that preceded Baba Mustapha one that squinted, and that's an omen; and, O my daughter, I counsel that thou by thy magic speed us to some remote point in the Caucasus, where we may abide the unravelling of this web securely, one way or the other way. 'Tis my counsel, O Noorna."

Then she, "Abandon my betrothed? and betray him on the very stroke of the Sword? and diminish him by a withdrawal of that faith in his right wrist which strengtheneth it more than Karavejis and Veejravoosh wound round it in coils?" And she leaned her head, and cried, "Hark! hear'st thou? there's shouting in the streets of Shiraz and of Shagpat! Shall we merit the punishment of Shahpesh the Persian on Khipil the builder, while the Event is mastering? I'll mark this interview between Baba Mustapha and Shagpat; and do thou, O my father, rest here on this roof till the King's guard of horsemen and soldiers of the law come hither for thee, and go with them sedately, fearing nought, for I shall be by thee in the garb of an old woman; and preserve thy composure in the presence of the King and Shagpat exalted, and allow not the thing that happeneth let fly from thee the shaft of speech, but remain a slackened bow till the strength of my betrothed is testified, fearing nought, for fear is that which defeateth men, and 'tis declared in a distich,—

*'The strongest weapon one can see*
*In mortal hands is constancy.'*

And for us to flee now would rank us with that King described by the poet:

*'A king of Ind there was who fought a fight*
*From the first gleam of morn till fall of night;*

*But when the royal tent his generals sought,*
*Proclaiming victory, fled was he who fought.*
*Despair possessed them, till they chanced to spy*
*A Dervish that paced on with downward eye;*
*They questioned of the King; he answer'd slow,*
*'Ye fought but one, the King a double, foe.'*

And, O my father, they interpreted of this that the King had been vanquished, he that was victor, by the phantom army of his fears."

Now, the Vizier cried, "Be the will of Allah achieved and consummated!" and he was silenced by her wisdom and urgency, and sat where he was, diverting not the arch on his brow from its settled furrow. He was as one that thirsteth, and whose eye hath marked a snake of swift poison by the water, so thirsted he for the Event, yet hung with dread from advancing; but Noorna bin Noorka busied herself about the roof, drawing circles to witness the track of an enemy, and she clapped her hands and cried, "Luloo!" and lo, a fair slave-girl that came to her and stood by with bent head, like a white lily by a milk-white antelope; so Noorna clouded her brow a moment, as when the moon darkeneth behind a scud, and cried, "Speak! art thou in league with Karaz, girl?"

Luloo strained her hands to her temples, exclaiming, "With the terrible Genie?—I?—in league with him? my mistress, surely the charms I wear, and the amulets, I wear them as a protection from that Genie, and a safeguard, he that carrieth off the maidens and the young sucklings, walking under the curse of mothers."

Said Noorna, "O Luloo, have I boxed those little ears of thine this day?"

The fair slave-girl smiled a smile of submissive tenderness, and answered, "Not this day, nor once since Luloo was rescued from the wicked old merchant by thy overbidding, and was taken to the arms of a wise kind sister, wiser and kinder than any she had been stolen from, she that is thy slave for ever."

She said this weeping, and Noorna mused, "'Twas as I divined, that wretched Kadza: her grief's to come!" Then spake she aloud as to herself, "Knew I, or could one know, I should this day be a bride?" And, hearing that, Luloo shrieked, "Thou a bride, and torn from me, and we two parted? and I, a poor drooping tendril, left to wither? for my life is round thee and worthless away from thee, O cherisher of the fallen flower."

And she sobbed out wailful verses and words, broken and without a meaning; but Noorna caught her by the arm and swung her, and bade her fetch on the instant a robe of blue, and pile in her chamber robes of amber and saffron and grey, bridal-robes of many-lighted silks, plum-coloured, peach-coloured, of the colour of musk mixed with pale gold, together with bridal ornaments and veils of the bride, and a jewelled circlet for the brow. When this was done, Noorna went with Luloo to her chamber, attended by slave-girls, and arrayed herself in the first dress of blue, and swayed herself before the mirror, and rattled the gold pieces in her hair and on her neck with laughter. And Luloo was bewildered, and forgot her tears to watch the gaiety of her mistress; and lo! Noorna, made her women take off one set of ornaments with every dress, and with every dress she put on another set; and after she had gone the round of the different dresses, she went to the bathroom with Luloo, and at her bidding Luloo entered the bath beside Noorna, and the twain dipped and shouldered in the blue water, and were as when a single star is by the full moon on a bright midnight pouring lustre about. And Noorna splashed Luloo, and said, "This night we shall not sleep together, O Luloo, nor lie close, thy bosom on mine."

Thereat, Luloo wept afresh, and cried, "Ah, cruel! and 'tis a sweet thought for thee, and thou'lt have no mind for me, tossing on my hateful lonely couch."

Tenderly Noorna eyed Luloo, and the sprinkles of the bath fell with the tears of both, and they clung together, and were like the lily and its bud on one stalk in a shower. Then, when Noorna had spent her affection, she said, "O thou of the long downward lashes, thy love was constant when I stood under a curse and was an old woman—a hag! Carest thou so little to learn the name of him that claimeth me?"

Luloo replied, "I thought of no one save myself and my loss, O my lost pearl; happy is he, a youth of favour. Oh, how I shall hate him that taketh thee from me. Tell me now his name, O sovereign of hearts!"

So Noorna smoothed the curves and corners of her mouth and calmed her countenance, crying in a deep tone and a voice as of reverence, "Shagpat!"

Now, at that name Luloo drank in her breath and was awed, and sank in herself, and had just words to ask, "Hath he demanded thee again in marriage, O my mistress?"

Said Noorna, "Even so."

Luloo muttered, "Great is the Dispenser of our fates!"

And she spake no further, but sighed and took napkins and summoned the slave-girls, and arrayed Noorna silently in the robe of blue and bridal ornaments. Then Noorna said to them that thronged about her, "Put on, each of ye, a robe of white, ye that are maidens, and a fillet of blue, and a sash of saffron, and abide my coming."

And she said to Luloo, "Array thyself in a robe of blue, even as mine, and let trinkets lurk in thy tresses, and abide my coming."

Then went she forth from them, and veiled her head and swathed her figure in raiment of a coarse white stuff, and was as the moon going behind a hill of dusky snow; and she left the house, and passed along the streets and by the palaces, till she came to the palace of her father, now filled by Shagpat. Before the palace grouped a great concourse and a multitude of all ages and either sex in that city, despite the blaze and the heat. Like roaring of a sea beyond the mountains was the noise that issued from them, and their eyes were a fire of beams against the portal of the palace. Now, she saw in the crowd one Shafrac, a shoemaker, and addressed him, saying, "O Shafrac, the shoemaker, what's this assembly and how got together? for the poet says:

> *'Ye string not such assemblies in the street,*
> *Save when some high Event should be complete.'"*

He answered, "'Tis an Event complete. Wullahy! the deputation from Shiraz to Shagpat, and the submission of that vain city to the might of Shagpat." And he asked her, jestingly, "Art thou a witch, to guess that, O veiled and virtuous one?"

Quoth she, "I read the thing that cometh ere 'tis come, and I read danger to Shagpat in this deputation from Shiraz, and this dish of pomegranate grain."

So Shafrac cried, "By the beard of my fathers and that of Shagpat! let's speak of this to Zeel, the garlic-seller."

He broadened to one that was by him, and said, "O Zeel, what's thy mind? Here's a woman, a wise woman, a witch, and she sees danger to Shagpat in this deputation from Shiraz and this dish of pomegranate grain."

Now, Zeel screwed his visage and gazed up into his forehead, and said, "'Twere best to consult with Bootlbac, the drum-beater."

The two then called to Bootlbac, the drum-beater, and told him the matter, and Bootlbac pondered, and tapped his brow and beat on his stomach, and said, "Krooz el Krazawik, the carrier, is good in such a case."

Now, from Krooz el Krazawik, the carrier, they went to Dob, the confectioner; and from Dob, the confectioner, to Azawool, the builder; and from Azawool, the builder, to Tcheik, the collector of taxes; and each referred to some other, till perplexity triumphed and was a cloud over them, and the words, "Danger to Shagpat," went about like bees, and were canvassing, when suddenly a shrill voice rose from the midst, dominating other voices, and it was that of Kadza, and she cried, "Who talks here of danger to Shagpat, and what wretch is it?"

Now, Tcheik pointed out Azawool, and Azawool Dob, and Dob Krooz el Krazawik, and he Bootlbac, and the drum-beater shrugged his shoulder at Zeel, and Zeel stood away from Shafrac, and Shafrac seized Noorna and shouted, "'Tis she, this woman, the witch!"

Kadza fronted Noorna, and called to her, "O thing of infamy, what's this talk of thine concerning danger to our glory, Shagpat?"

Then Noorna replied, "I say it, O Kadza! and I say it; there's danger threateneth him, and from that deputation and that dish of pomegranate grain."

Now, Kadza laughed a loose laugh, and jeered at Noorna, crying, "Danger to Shagpat! he that's attended by Genii, and watched over by the greatest of them, day and night incessantly?"

And Noorna said, "I ask pardon of the Power that seeth, and of thee, if I be wrong. Wah! am I not also of them that watch over Shagpat? So then let thou and I go into the palace and examine the doings of this deputation and this dish of pomegranate grain."

Now, Kadza remembered the scene on the roofs of the Vizier Feshnavat, and relaxed in her look of suspicion, and said, "'Tis well! Let's in to them."

Thereupon the twain threaded through the crowd and locked at the portals of the palace, and it was opened to them and they entered, and lo! the hand that opened the portals was the hand of a slave of the Sword, and against corners of the Court leaned slaves silly with slumber. So Kadza went up to them, and beat them, and shook them, and they yawned and mumbled, "Excellent grain! good grain! the grain of Shiraz!" And she beat them with what might was hers, till some fell sideways and some forward, still mumbling, "Excellent pomegranate grain!" Kadza was beside herself with anger and vexation at them, tearing them and cuffing them; but Noorna cried, "O Kadza! what said I? there's danger to Shagpat in this dish of pomegranate grain! and what's that saying:

> *'Tis much against the Master's wish*
> *That slaves too greatly praise his dish.'*

Wullahy! I like not this talk of the grain of Shiraz."

Now, while Noorna spake, the eyes of Kadza became like those of the starved wild-cat, and she sprang off and along the marble of the Court, and clawed a passage through the air and past the marble pillars of the palace toward the first room of reception, Noorna following her. And in the first room were slaves leaning and lolling like them about the Court, and in the second room and in the third room, silent all of them and senseless. So at this sight the spark of suspicion became a mighty flame in the bosom of Kadza, and horror burst out at all ends of her, and she shuddered, and cried, "What for us, and where's our hope if Shagpat be shorn, and he lopped of the Identical, shamed like the lion of my dream!"

And Noorna clasped her hands, and said, "'Tis that I fear! Seek for him, O Kadza!"

So Kadza ran to a window and looked forth over the garden of the palace, and it was a fair garden with the gleam of a fountain and watered plants and cool arches of shade, thick bowers, fragrant alleys, long sheltered terraces, and beyond the garden a summer-house of marble fanned by the broad leaves of a palm. Now, when Kadza had gazed a moment, she shrieked, "He's there! Shagpat! giveth he not the light of a jewel to the house that holdeth him? Awahy! and he's witched there for an ill purpose."

Then tore she from that room like a mad wild thing after its stolen cubs, and sped along corridors of the palace, and down the great flight of steps into the garden and across the garden, knocking over the ablution-pots in her haste; and Noorna had just strength to withhold her from dashing through the doors of the summer-house to come upon Shagpat, she straining and crying, "He's there, I say, O wise woman! Shagpat! let's into him."

But Noorna clung to her, and spake in her ear, "Wilt thou blow the fire that menaces him, O Kadza? and what are two women against the assailants of such a mighty one as he?" Then said she, "Watch, rather, and avail thyself of yonder window by the blue-painted pillar."

So Kadza crept up to the blue-painted pillar which was on the right side of the porch, and the twain peered through the window. Noorna beheld the Dish of Pomegranate Grain; and it was on the floor, empty of the grain, and Baba Mustapha was by it alone making a lather, and he was twitching his mouth and his legs, and flinging about his arms, and Noorna heard him mutter wrathfully, "O accursed flea! art thou at me again?" And she heard him mutter as in anguish, "No peace for thee, O pertinacious flea! and my steadiness of hand will be gone, now when I have him safe as the hawk his prey, mine enemy, this Shagpat that abused me: thou abominable flea! And, O thou flea, wilt thou, vile thing! hinder me from mastering the Event, and releasing this people and the world from enchantment and bondage? And shall I fail to become famous to the ages and the times because of such as thee, flea?"

So Kadza whispered to Noorna, "What's that he's muttering? Is't of Shagpat? for I mark him not here, nor the light by which he's girt."

She answered, "Listen with the ear and the eye and all the senses."

Now, presently they heard Baba Mustapha say in a louder tone, like one that is secure from interruption, "Two lathers, and this the third! a potent lather! and I wot there's not a hair in this world resisteth the sweep of my blade over such a lather as—Ah! flea of iniquity and abomination! what! am I doomed to thy torments?—so let's spread! Lo! this lather, is't not the pride of Shiraz? and the polish and smoothness it sheddeth, is't not roseate? my invention! as the poet says,—O accursed flea! now the knee-joint, now the knee-cap, and 'tis but a hop for thee to the arm-pit. Fires of the pit without bottom seize thee! is no place sacred from thee, and art thou a restless soul, infernal flea? So then, peace awhile, and here's for the third lather."

While he was speaking Baba Mustapha advanced to a large white object that sat motionless, upright like a snow-mound on a throne of cushions, and commenced lathering. When she saw that, Kadza tossed up her head and her throat, and a shriek was coming from her, for she was ware of Shagpat; but Noorna stifled the shriek, and clutched her fast, whispering, "He's safe if thou have but patience, thou silly Kadza! and the flea will defeat this fellow if thou spoil it not."

So Kadza said, looking up, "Is't seen of Allah, and be the Genii still in their depths?" but she constrained herself, peering and perking out her chin, and lifting one foot and the other foot, as on furnaces of fire in the excess of the fury she smothered. And lo, Baba Mustapha worked diligently, and Shagpat was behind an exulting lather, even as one pelted with wheaten flour-balls or balls of powdery perfume, and his hairiness was as branches of the forest foliage bent under a sudden fall of overwhelming snow that filleth the pits and sharpeneth the wolves with hunger, and teacheth new cunning to the fox. A fox was Baba Mustapha in his stratagems, and a wolf in the fierceness of his setting upon Shagpat. Surely he drew forth the blade that was to shear Shagpat, and made with it in the air a preparatory sweep and flourish; and the blade frolicked and sent forth a light, and seemed eager for Shagpat. So Baba Mustapha addressed his arm to the shearing, and inclined gently the edge of the blade, and they marked him let it slide twice to a level with the head of Shagpat, and at the third time it touched, and Kadza howled, but from Baba Mustapha there burst a howl to madden the beasts; and he flung up his blade, and wrenched open his robe, crying, "A flea was it to bite in that fashion? Now, I swear by the Merciful, a fang like that's common to tigers and hyaenas and ferocious animals."

Then looked he for the mark of the bite, plaining of its pang, and he could find the mark nowhere. So, as he caressed himself, eyeing Shagpat sheepishly and with gathering awe, Noorna said hurriedly to Kadza, "Away now, and call them in, the crowd about the palace, that they may behold the triumph of Shagpat, for 'tis ripe, O Kadza!"

And Kadza replied, "Thou'rt a wise woman, and I'll have thee richly rewarded. Lo, I'm as a camel lightened of fifty loads, and the glory of Shagpat see I as a new sun rising in the desert. Wullahy! thou'rt wise, and I'll do thy bidding."

Now, she went flying back to the palace, and called shrill calls to the crowd, and collected them in the palace, and headed them through the garden, and it was when Baba Mustapha had summoned courage for a second essay, and was in the act of standing over Shagpat to operate on him, that the crowd burst the doors, and he was quickly seized by them, and tugged at and hauled at and pummelled, and torn and vituperated, and as a wrecked vessel on stormy waters, plunging up and down with tattered sails, when the crew fling overboard freight and ballast and provision. Surely his time would have been short with that mob, but Noorna made Kadza see the use of examining him before the King, and there were in that mob sheikhs and fakirs, holy men who listened to the words of Kadza, and exerted themselves to rescue Baba Mustapha, and quieted the rage that was prevailing, and bore Baba Mustapha with them to the great palace of the King, which was in the centre of that City. Now, when the King heard of the attempt on Shagpat, and the affair of the Pomegranate Grain, he gave orders for the admission of the people, as many of them as could be contained in the Hall of Justice: and he set a guard over Baba Mustapha, and commanded that Shagpat should be brought to the palace even as he then was, and with the lather on him. So the regal mandate went forth, and Shagpat was brought in state on cushions, and the potency of the drug preserved his sedateness through all this, and he remained motionless in sleep, folded in the centre of calm and satisfaction, while this tumult was rageing and the City shook with uproar. But the people, when they saw him whitened behind a lather, wrath at Baba Mustapha's polluting touch and the audacity of barbercraft wrestled in them with the outpouring of reverence for Shagpat, and a clamour arose for the instant sacrifice of Baba Mustapha at the foot of their idol Shagpat. And the whole of the City of Shagpat, men, women, and children, and the sheikhs and the dervishes and crafts of the City besieged the King's palace in that middle hour of the noon, clamouring for the sacrifice of Baba Mustapha at the feet of their idol Shagpat.

# The Burning of the Identical

Now, the Great Hall for the dispensing of justice in the palace of the King was one on which the architect and the artificers had lavished all their arts and subtleties of design and taste and their conceptions of uniformity and grandeur, so that none entered it without a sense of abasement, and the soul acknowledged awfulness and power in him that ruled and sat eminent on the throne of that Hall. For, lo! the throne was of solid weighty gold, overhung with rich silks and purples; and the hall was lofty, with massive pillars, fifty on either side, ranging in stateliness down toward the blaze of the throne; and the pillars were pillars of porphyry and of jasper and precious marble, carven over all of them with sentences of the cunningest wisdom, distichs of excellence, odes of the poet, stanzas sharp with the incisiveness of wit, and that solve knotty points with but one stroke; and these pillars were each the gift of a mighty potentate of earth or of a Genie.

In the centre of the Hall a fountain set up a glittering jet, and spread abroad the breath of freshness, leaping a height of sixty feet, and shimmering there in a wide bright canopy with dropping silver sides. It was rumoured of the waters of this fountain that they were fed underground from the waters of the Sacred River, brought there in the reign of El Rasoon, a former sovereign in the City of Shagpat, by the labours of Zak,—a Genie subject to the magic of Azrooka, the Queen of El Rasoon; but, of a surety, none of earth were like to them in silveriness and sweet coolingness, and they were as wine to the weary.

Now, the King sat on his throne in the Hall, and around him his ministers, and Emirs, and chamberlains, and officers of state, and black slaves, and the soldiers of his guard armed with naked scimitars. And the King was as a sun in splendour, severely grave, and a frown on his forehead to darken kingdoms, for the attempt on Shagpat had stirred his kingly wrath, and awakened zeal for the punishment of all conspirators and offenders. So when Shagpat was borne in to the King upon his throne of cushions where he sat upright, smiling and inanimate, the King commanded that he should be placed at his side, the place of honour; and Shagpat was as a moon behind the whiteness of the lathers; even as we behold moon and sun together in the heavens, was Shagpat by the King.

There was great hubbub in the Hall at the entrance of Shagpat, and a hum of rage and muttered vehemence passed among the assembled people that filled the hall like a cavern of the sea, the sea roaring outside; but presently the King spake, and all hushed. Then said he, "O people! thought I to see a day that would shame Shagpat? he that has brought honour and renown upon me and all of this city, so that we shine a constellation and place of pilgrimage to men in remote islands and corners of the earth? Yea! and to Afrites and Genii? Have I not castigated barbers, and brought barbercraft to degradation, so that no youth is taught to exercise it? And through me the tackle of the barber, is't not a rusty and abominated weapon, and as a sword thrown by and broken, for that it dishonoured us? Surely, too, I have esteemed Shagpat precious."

While he spake, the King gazed on Shagpat, and was checked by passion at beholding him under the lather, so that the people praised Shagpat and the King. Then said he, "O people, who shall forecast disasters and triumphs? Lo, I had this day at dawn intelligence from recreant Oolb, and its King and Court, and of their return to do honour to Shagpat! And I had this day at dawn tidings, O people, from Shiraz, and of the adhesion of that vain city and its provinces to the might of Shagpat! So commenced the day, yet is he, the object of the world's homage, within a few hours defiled by a lather and the hand of an impious one!"

At these words of the King there rose a shout of vindictiveness and fury; but he cried, "Punishment on the offenders in season, O people! Probably we have not abased ourselves for the honour that has befallen us in Shagpat, and the distinction among nations and tribes and races, and creeds and sects, that we enjoy because of Shagpat. Behold! in abasement voluntarily undertaken there is exceeding brightness and exaltation; for how is the sun a sun save that daily he dippeth in darkness, to rise again freshly majestic? So then, be mine the example, O people of the City of Shagpat!"

Thereupon lo, the King descended from his throne, and stripped to the loins, flinging away his glittering crown and his robes, and abased himself to the dust with loud cries and importunities and howls, and penitential exclamations and sobbings; and it was in that Hall as when the sun goeth down in storm. Likewise the ministers of the King, and the Viziers and Emirs and officers of state, and slaves, and soldiers of the guard, bared their limbs, and fell beside the King with violent outcries and wailings; and the whole of the people in the

Hall prostrated their bodies with wailings and lamentations. And Baba Mustapha feigned to bewail himself, and Noorna bin Noorka knelt beside Kadza, and shrieked loudest, striking her breast and scattering her hair; and that Hall was as a pit full of serpents writhing, and of tigers and lions and wild beasts howling, each pitching his howl a note above his neighbours, so that the tone rose and sank, and there was no one soul erect in that Hall save Shagpat, he on his throne of cushions smiling behind the lathers, inanimate, serene as they that sin not. After an hour's lapse there came a pause, and the people hearkened for the voice of the King; but in the intervals a louder moan would strike their ears, and they whispered among themselves, "'Tis that of the fakir, El Zoop!" and the moaning and howling prevailed again. And again they heard another moan, a deep one, as of the earth in its throes, and said among themselves, "'Tis that of Bootlbac, the drumbeater!" and this led off to the howl of Areep, the dervish; and this was followed by the shriek of Zeel, the garlic-seller; and the waul of Krooz el Krazawik, the carrier; and the complainings of Dob, the confectioner; and the groan of Sallap, the broker; and the yell of Azawool, the builder. There would have been no end to it known; but the King rose and commenced plucking his beard and his hair,—they likewise in silence. When he had performed this ceremony a space, the King called, and a basin of water was brought to him, and handed round by slaves, and all dipped in it their hands, and renewed their countenances and re-arranged their limbs; and the Hall brightened with the eye of the King, and he cried, "O people, lo, the plot is revealed to me, and 'tis a deep one; but, by this beard, we'll strike at the root of it, and a blow of deadliness. Surely we have humiliated ourselves, and vengeance is ours! How say ye?"

A noise like the first sullen growl of a vexed wild beast which telleth that fury is fast travelling and the teeth will flash, followed these words; and the King called to his soldiers of the guard, "Ho! forth with this wretch that dared defile Shagpat, the holy one! and on your heads be it to fetch hither Feshnavat, the son of Feil, that was my Vizier, he that was envious of Shagpat, and whom we spared in our clemency."

Some of the guard went from the Hall to fulfil the King's injunction on Feshnavat, others thrust forth Baba Mustapha in the eyes of the King. Baba Mustapha was quaking as a frog quaketh for water, and he trembled and was a tongueless creature deserted of his lower limbs, and with eyeballs goggling, through exceeding terror. Now, when the King saw him, he contracted his brows as one that peereth on a small and minute object, crying, "How! is't such as he, this monster of audaciousness and horrible presumption? Truly 'tis said:

> *'For ruin and the deeds preluding change,*
> *Fear not great Beasts, nor Eagles when they range:*
> *But dread the crawling worm or pismire mean,*
> *Satan selects them, for they are unseen.'*

And this wretch is even of that sort, the select of Satan! Off with the top of the reptile, and away with him!"

Now, at the issue of the mandate Baba Mustapha choked, and horror blocked the throat of confession in him, so that he did nought save stagger imploringly; but the prompting of Noorna sent Kadza to the foot of the throne, and Kadza bent her body and exclaimed, "O King of the age! 'tis Kadza, the espoused of Shagpat thy servant, that speaketh; and lo! a wise woman has said in my ear, 'How if this emissary and instrument of the Evil One, this barber, this filthy fellow, be made to essay on Shagpat before the people his science and his malice? for 'tis certain that Shagpat is surrounded where he sitteth by Genii invisible, defended by them, and no harm can hap to him, but an illumination of glory and triumph manifest': and for this barber, his punishment can afterwards be looked to, O great King!"

The King mused awhile and sank in his beard. Then said he to them that had hold of Baba Mustapha watching for the signal, "I have thought over it, and the means of bringing double honour on the head of Shagpat. So release this fellow, and put in his hands the tackle taken from him."

This was done, and the people applauded the wisdom of the King, and crowded forward with sharpness of expectation; but Baba Mustapha, when he felt in his hands the tackle, the familiar instruments, strength and wit returned to him in petty measures, and he thought, "Perchance there'll yet be time for my nephew to strike, if he fail me not; fool that I was to look for glory, and not leave the work to him, for this Shagpat is a mighty one, powerful in fleas, and it needeth something other than tackle to combat such as he. A mighty one, said I? by Allah, he's awful in his mightiness!"

So Baba Mustapha kept delaying, and feigned to sharpen the blade, and the King called to him, "Haste! to the work! is it for thee, vile wretch, to make preparation for the accursed thing in our presence?"

And the people murmured and waxed impatient, and the King called again, "Thou'lt essay this, thou wretch, without a head, let but another minute pass." So when Baba Mustapha could delay no longer, he sighed heavily and his trembling returned, and the power of Shagpat smote him with an invisible hand, so that he could scarce move; but dread pricked him against dread, and he advanced upon Shagpat to shear him, and assumed the briskness of the barber, and was in the act of bending over him to bring the blade into play, when, behold, one of the chamberlains of the King stood up in the presence and spake a word that troubled him, and the King rose and hurried to a balcony looking forth on the Desert, and on three sides of the Desert three separate clouds of dust were visible, and from these clouds presently emerged horsemen with spears and pennons and plumes; and he could discern the flashing of their helms and the glistening of steel-plates and armour of gold and silver. Seeing this, the colour went from the cheeks of the King and his face became as a pinched pomegranate, and he cried aloud, "What visitation's this? Awahy! we are beset, and here's abasement brought on us without self-abasing!" Meantime these horsemen detached themselves from the main bodies and advanced at a gallop, wheeling and circling round each other, toward the walls of the city, and when they were close they lowered their arms and made signs of amity, and proclaimed their mission and the name of him they served. So tidings were brought to the King that the Lords of three cities, with vast retinues, were come, by reason of a warning, to pay homage to Shagpat, the son of Shimpoor; and these three cities were the cities of Oolb, and of Gaf, and of Shiraz, even these!

Now, when the King heard of it, he rejoiced with an exceeding joy, and arrayed himself in glory, and mounted a charger, the pride of his stables, and rode out to meet the Lords of the three cities surrounded by the horsemen of his guard. And it was within half-a-mile of the city walls that the four sovereigns met, and dismounted and saluted and embraced, and bestowed on one another kingly flatteries, and the titles of Cousin and Brother. So when the unctions of Royalty were over, these three Kings rode back to the city with the King that was their host, and the horsemen of the three kingdoms pitched their tents and camped outside the walls, making cheer. Then the King of the City of Shagpat related to the three Kings the story of Shagpat and the attempt that had been made on him; and in the great Hall of Justice he ordained the erecting of thrones for them whereon to sit; and they, when they had paid homage to Shagpat, sat by him there on either side. Then the King cried, "This likewise owe we to Shagpat, our glory! See, now, how the might that's in him shall defeat the machinations of evil, O my cousins of Oolb, and of Gaf, and of Shiraz." Thereupon he called, "Bring forth the barber!"

So Baba Mustapha was thrust forth by the soldiers of the guard; and the King of Shiraz, who was no other than the great King Shahpushan, exclaimed, when he beheld Baba Mustapha, "He? why, it is the prince of barbers and talkative ones! Hath he not operated on my head, the head of me in old time? Truly now, if it be in man to shave Shagpat, the hand of this barber will do it!"

And the King of Oolb peered on Baba Mustapha, crying, "Even this fellow I bastinadoed!"

And the King of Gaf, that was Kresnuk, famous in the annals of the time, said aloud, "I'm amazed at the pertinacity of this barber! To my court he came, searching some silly nephew, and would have shaved us all in spite of our noses; yea, talked my chief Vizier into a dead sleep, and so thinned him. And there was no safety from him save in thongs and stripes and lashes!"

Now, upon that the King of the City cried, "Be the will of Allah achieved, and the inviolacy of Shagpat made manifest! Thou barber, thou! do thy worst to contaminate him, and take the punishment in store for thee. And if it is written thou succeed, then keep thy filthy life: small chance of that!"

Baba Mustapha remembered the poet's words:

> *The abyss is worth a leap, however wide,*
> *When life, sweet life, is on the other side.*

And he controlled himself to the mastery of his members, and stepped forward to essay once more the Shaving of Shagpat. Lo, the great Hall was breathless, nought heard save the splashing of the fountain in its fall, and the rustle of the robe of Baba Mustapha as he aired his right arm, hovering round Shagpat like a bird about the nest; and he was buzzing as a bee ere it entereth the flower, and quivered like a butterfly when 'tis fluttering over a blossom; and Baba Mustapha sniffed at Shagpat within arm's reach, fearing him, so that the people began to hum with a great rapture, and the King Shahpushan cried, Aha! mark him! this monkey knoweth the fire!"

But the King of the City of Shagpat was wroth, and commanded his guards to flourish their scimitars, and the keen light cut the chords of indecision in Baba Mustapha, and drove him upon Shagpat with a dash of desperation; and lo! he stretched his hand and brought down the blade upon the head of Shagpat. Then was the might of Shagpat made manifest, for suddenly in his head the Identical rose up straight, even to a level with the roof of that hall, burning as it had been an angry flame of many fiery colours, and Baba Mustapha was hurled from him a great space like a ball that reboundeth, and he was twisting after the fashion of envenomed serpents, sprawling and spurning, and uttering cries of horror. Surely, to see that sight the four Kings and the people bit their forefingers, and winked till the water stood in their eyes, and Kadza, turning about, exclaimed, "This owe we to the wise woman! where lurketh she?" So she called about the hall, "wise woman! wise woman!"

Now, when she could find Noorna bin Noorka nowhere in that crowd, she shrieked exultingly, "'Twas a Genie! Wullahy! all Afrites, male and female, are in the service of Shagpat, my light, my eyes, my sun! I his moon!"

Meantime the King of the City called to Baba Mustapha, "Hast thou had enough of barbering, O vile one? Ho! a second essay on the head of Shagpat! so shall the might that's in him be indisputable, bruited abroad, and a great load upon the four winds."

Now, Baba Mustapha was persuaded by the scimitars of the guard to a second essay on the head of Shagpat, and the second time he was shot away from Shagpat through the crowd and great assemblage to the extreme end of the hall, where he lay writhing about, abandoned in loathliness; and he in his despondency, and despite of protestation and the slackness of his limbs, was pricked again by the scimitars of the guard to a third essay on the head of Shagpat, the people jeering at him, for they were joyous, light of heart; and lo! the third time he was shot off violently, and whirled away like a stone from a sling, even into the outer air and beyond the city walls, into the distance of waste places. And now a great cry rose from the people, as it were a song of triumph, for the Identical stood up wrathfully from the head of Shagpat, burning in brilliance, blinding to look on, he sitting inanimate beneath it; and it waxed in size and pierced through the roof of the hall, and was a sight to the streets of the city; and the horsemen camped without the walls beheld it, and marvelled, and it was as a pillar of fire to the solitudes of the Desert afar, and the wild Arab and wandering Bedouins and caravans of pilgrimage. Distant cities asked the reason of that appearance, and the cunning fakir interpreted it, and the fervent dervish expounded from it, and messengers flew from gate to gate and from land to land in exultation, and barbers hid their heads, and were friendly with the fox in his earth, because of that light. So the Identical burned on the head of Shagpat as in wrath, and with exceeding splendour of attraction, three nights and three days; and the fishes of the sea shoaled to the sea's surface and stared at it, and the fowls of the air congregated about the fury of the light with screams and mad flutters, till the streets and mosques and minarets and bright domes and roofs and cupolas of the City of Shagpat were blackened with scorched feathers of the vulture and the eagle and the rook and the raven and the hawk, and other birds, sacred and obscene; so was the triumph of Shagpat made manifest to men and the end of the world by the burning of the Identical three days and three nights.

# The Flashes of the Blade

Now, it was the morning of the fourth day, and lo! at the first leap of the sun of that day the flame of the Identical abated in its fierceness, and it dwindled and darkened, and tapered and flickered feebly, descending from its altitude in the heavens and through the ceiling of the Hall, and lay down to sleep among the intricate lengths and frizzled convolutions and undulating weights flowing from Shagpat, an undistinguished hair, even as the common hairs of his head. So, upon that, the four fasting Kings breathed, and from the people of the City there went up a mighty shout of gladness and congratulation at the glory they had witnessed; and they took the air deeply into their chests, and were as divers that have been long fathoms-deep under water, and ascend and puff hard and press the water from their eyes, that yet refuse to acknowledge with a recognition the things that be and the sights above, so mazed are they with those unmentionable marvels and treasures and profusion of jewels, and splendid lazy growths and lavish filmy illuminations, and multitudinous pearls and sheering shells, that lie heaped in the beds of the ocean. As the poet has said:

> *After too strong a beam,*
> *Too bright a glory,*
> *We ask, Is this a dream*
> *Or magic story?*

And he says:

> *When I've had rapturous visions such as make*
> *The sun turn pale, and suddenly awake,*
> *Long must I pull at memory in this beard,*
> *Ere I remember men and things revered.*

So was it with the people of the City, and they stood in the Hall and winked staringly at one another, shouting and dancing at intervals, capering with mad gravity, exclaiming on the greatness of that they had witnessed. And Zeel the garlic-seller fell upon Mob the confectioner, and cried, "Was this so, O Dob? Wullahy! this glory, was it verily?" And

Dob peered dimly upon Zeel, whispering solemnly, "Say, now, art thou of a surety that Zeel the garlic-seller known to me, my boon-fellow?" And the twain turned to Sallap the broker, and exchanged interjections with him, and with Azawool the builder, and with Krooz el Krazawik the carrier; and they accosted Bootlbac the drum-beater, where he stood apart, drumming the air as to a march of triumph, and no word would he utter, neither to Zeel, nor to Sallap, nor to Krooz el Krazawik, nor to Azawool his neighbour, nor to any present, but continued drumming on the air rapidly as in answer, increasing in the swiftness of his drumming till it was a rage to mark him, and the excitement about Bootlbac became as a mad eddy in the midst of a mighty stream, he drumming the air with exceeding swiftness to various measures, beating before him as on the tightened skin, lost to all presences save the Identical and Shagpat. So they edged away from Bootlbac in awe, saying, "He's inspired, Bootlbac! 'tis the triumph of Shagpat he drummeth." They feigned to listen to him till their ears deceived them, and they rejoiced in the velocity of the soundless tune of Bootlbac the drum-beater, and were stirred by it, excited to a forgetfulness of their fasting. Such was the force of the inspiration of Bootlbac the drum-beater, caused by the burning of the Identical.

Now, the four Kings, when they had mastered their wits, gazed in silence on Shagpat, and sighed and shook their heads, and were as they that have swallowed a potent draught and ponder sagely over the gulp. Surely, the visages of the Kings of Shiraz and of Gaf and of Oolb betokened dread of Shagpat and amazement at him; but the King of the City exulted, and the shining of content was on his countenance, and he cried, "Wondrous!" and again, "Wullahy, wondrous!" and "Oh, glory!" And he laughed and clucked and chuckled, and the triumph of Shagpat was to him as a new jewel in his crown outshining all others, and he was for awhile as the cock smitten with the pride of his comb, the peacock magnified by admiration of his tail. Then he cried, "For this, praise we Allah and the Prophet. Wullahy, 'twas wondrous!" and he went off again into a roll of cluckings and chucklings and exclamations of delight, crying, 'Need they further proof of the power in Shagpat now? Has he not manifested it? So true is that saying—

> *The friend that flattereth weakeneth at length;*
> *It is the foe that calleth forth our strength.'*

Wondrous! and never knew earth a thing to equal it in the range of marvels!"

Now, ere the last word was spoken by the King, there passed through the sky a mighty flash. Those in the Hall saw it, and the horsemen of the three cities encamped without the walls were nigh blinded by the keenness of its blaze. So they looked into the height, and saw straight over the City a speck of cloud, but no thunder came from it; and the King cried, "These be Genii! the issue of this miracle is yet to come! look for it, and exult." Then he turned to the other Kings, but they were leaning to right and left in their seats, as do the intoxicated, without strength to answer his questioning. So he exclaimed, "A curse on my head! have I forgotten the laws of hospitality? my cousins are famished!" He was giving orders for the spreading of a sumptuous banquet when there passed through the sky another mighty flash. They awaited the thunder this time confidently, yet none came. Suddenly the King exclaimed, "'Tis the wrath of Shagpat that his assailants remain uncastigated!" Then cried he to the eunuchs of the guard, "Hither with Feshnavat, the son of Feil!" And the King said to Feshnavat, "Thou plotter! envious of Shagpat!" Here the King, Kresnuk, fell forward at the feet of Shagpat from sheer inanition, and the King of the City ordered instantly wines and viands to be brought into the Hall, and commenced saying to Feshnavat, in the words of the wise entablature:

> *"Of reckless mercy thus the Sage declared:*
> *More culpable the sparer than the spared;*
> *For he that breaks one law, breaks one alone:*
> *But who thwarts Justice flouts Law's sovereign throne.'*

And have I not been over-merciful in thy case?"

As the King was haranguing Feshnavat, his nostril took in the steam of the viands and the fresh odours of the wines, and he could delay no longer to satisfy his craving, but caught up the goblet, and drank from it till his visage streamed the tears of contentment. Lo, while he put forth his hand tremblingly, as to continue the words of his condemnation of the Vizier, the heavens were severed by a third flash, one exceeding in fierceness the other flashes; and now the Great Hall rocked, and the pillars and thrones trembled, and the eyes of Shagpat opened. He made no motion, but sat like a wonder of stone, looking before him. Surely, Kadza shrieked, and rushed forward to him from the crowd, yet he said nothing, and was as one frozen. So the King cried, "He waketh! the flashes preceded his wakening! Now shall he see the vengeance of kings on his enemies." Thereupon he made a signal, and the scimitars of the guard were in air over the head of Feshnavat, when darkness as of the dropping of night fell upon all, and the darkness spake, saying, "I am Abarak of the Bar, preceder of the Event!"

Then it was light, but the ears of every soul present were pierced with the wailing of wild animals, and on all sides from the Desert hundreds of them were seen making toward the City, some swiftly, others at a heavy pace; and when they were come near they crouched and fawned, and dropped their dry tongues as in awe. There was the serpent, meek as before the days of sin, and the leopard slinking to get among the legs of men, and the lion came trundling along in utter flabbiness, raising not his head. Soon the streets were thronged with elephants and lions and sullen tigers, and wild cats and wolves, not a tail erect among them: great was the marvel! So the King cried, "We're in the thick of wonders; banquet we lightly while they increase upon us! What's yonder little man?" This was Abarak that stood before the King, and exclaimed, "I am the darkness that announceth the mastery of the Event, as a shadow before the sun's approach, and it is the Shaving of Shagpat!" The world darkened before the eyes of the King when he heard this, and in a moment Abarak was clutched by the soldiers of the guard, and dragged beside Feshnavat to await the final blow; and this would have parted two heads from two bodies at one stroke, but now Noorna bin Noorka entered the hall, veiled and in the bright garb of a bride, with veiled attendants about her, and the people opened to give her passage to the throne of the King. So she said, "Delay the stroke yet awhile, O Head of the Magnanimous! I am she claimed by Shagpat; surely, I am bride of him that is Master of the Event, and the hour of bridals is the hour of clemency."

The King looked at Shagpat, perplexed; but the eye of Shagpat gazed as into the distance of another world. Then said he, "We shall hear nought from the mouth of Shagpat till he is avenged, and till then he is silent with exceeding wrath." Hearing this, Noorna ran quickly to a window of the Hall, and let loose a white dove from her bosom.

Then came there that flash which is recorded in old traditions as the fourth of the flashes of thunderless lightnings, after the passing of which, hundreds of fakirs that had been awaiting it saw nothing further on this earth. Down through the Hall it swept; and lo! when the Kings and the people recovered their sight to regard Shagpat, he was, one side of him, clean shorn, the shaven side shining as the very moon!

Surely from that moment there was no longer aught mortal in the combat that ensued. For now, while amazement and horror palsied all present, the Genie Karaz, uttering a howl of fury, shot down the length of the Hall like a black storm-bolt, and caught up Shagpat, and whirled off with him into the air; and they beheld him dive and dodge the lightnings that beset him from upper heaven, catching Shagpat from them, now by the heels, now by the hair remaining one side his head. This lasted a full hour, when the Genie paused a second, and made a sheer descent into the earth. Then saw they the wings of Koorookh, each a league in length, overshadow the entire land, and on the neck of the bird sat Shibli Bagarag cleaving through the earth with his blade, and he sat on Koorookh as the moon sits on the midnight. There was no light save the light shed abroad by the flashes of the blade, and in these they beheld the air suffocated with Afrites and Genii in a red and brown and white heat, followers of Karaz. Strokes of the blade clove them, and their blood was fire that flowed over the feathers of Koorookh, lighting him in a conflagration; but the bird flew constantly to a fountain of earth below and extinguished it. Then the battle recommenced, and the solid earth yawned at the gashes made by the mighty blade, and its depths revealed how Karaz was flying with Shagpat from circle to circle of the under-regions, hurrying with him downward to the lowest circle, that was flaming to points, like the hair of vast heads. Presently they saw a wondrous quivering flash divide the Genie, and his heels and head fell together in the abysses, leaving Shagpat prone on great brasiers of penal flame. Then the blade made another hissing sweep over Shagpat, leaving little of the wondrous growths on him save a topknot.

But now was the hour struck when Rabesqurat could be held no longer serving the ferry in Aklis; and the terrible Queen streamed in the sky, like a red disastrous comet, and dived, eagle-like, into the depths, re-ascending with Shagpat in her arms, cherishing him; and lo, there were suddenly a thousand Shagpats multiplied about, and the hand of Shibli Bagarag became exhausted with hewing at them. The scornful laugh of the Queen was heard throughout earth as she triumphed over Shibli Bagarag with hundreds of Shagpats, Illusions; and he knew not where to strike at the Shagpat, and was losing all sleight of hand, dexterity, and cunning. Noorna shrieked, thinking him lost; but Abarak seized his bar, and leaning it in the direction of Aklis, blew a pellet from it that struck on the eye of Aklis, and this sent out a stretching finger of beams, and singled forth very Shagpat from the myriads of semblances, so that he glowed and was ruddy, the rest cowering pale, and dissolving like salt-grains in water.

Then saw earth and its inhabitants how the Genie Karaz re-ascended in the shape of a vulture with a fire beak, pecking at the eyes of him that wielded the Sword, so that he was bewildered and shook this way and that over the neck of Koorookh, striking wildly, languidly cleaving towers and palaces, and monuments of earth underneath him. Now, Shibli Bagarag discerned his danger, and considered, "The power of the Sword is to sever brains and thoughts. Great is Allah! I'll seek my advantage in that."

So he whirled Koorookh thrice in the crimson smoke of the atmosphere, and put the blade between the first and second thought in the head of Rabesqurat, whereby the sense of the combat became immediately confused in her mind, and she used her powers as the fool does, equally against all, for the sake of mischief solely—no longer mistress of her own Illusions; and she began doubling and trebling Shibli Bagarag on the neck of monstrous birds, speeding in draggled flightiness from one point of the sky to another. Even in the terror of the combat, Shibli Bagarag was fair to burst into a fit of violent laughter at the sight of the Queen wagging her neck loosely, perking it like a mad raven; and he took heart, and swept the blade rapidly over Shagpat as she dandled him, leaving Shagpat but one hair remaining on him; yet was that the Identical; and it arose, and was a serpent in his head, and from its jaws issued a river of fiery serpents: these and a host of Afrites besieged Shibli Bagarag; and now, to defend himself, he unloosed the twin Genii, Karavejis and Veejravoosh, from the wrist of that hand which wielded the Sword of Aklis, and these alternately interwound before and about him, and were even as a glittering armour of emerald plates, warding from him the assaults of the host; and lo! he flew, and the battle followed him over blazing cities and lands on fire with the slanting hail of sparkles.

By this time every soul in the City of Shagpat, kings and people, all save Abarak and Noorna bin Noorka, were overcome and prostrate with their faces to the ground; but Noorna watched the conflict eagerly, and saw the head of Shagpat sprouting incessant fresh crops of hair, despite the pertinacious shearing of her betrothed. Then she smote her hands, and cried, "Yea! though I lose my beauty and the love of my betrothed, I must join in this, or he'll be lost." So, saying to Abarak, "Watch over me," she went into the air, and, as she passed Rabesqurat, was multiplied into twenty damsels of loveliness. Then Abarak beheld a scorpion following the twenty in mid-air, and darting stings among them. Noorna tossed a ring, and it fell in a circle of flame round the scorpion. So, while the scorpion was shooting in squares to escape from the circle, the fire-beaked vulture flew to it, and fluttered a dense rain which swallowed the flame, and the scorpion and vulture assailed Noorna, that was changed to a golden hawk in the midst of nineteen other golden hawks. Now, as Rabesqurat came scudding by, and saw the encounter, she made the twenty hawks a hundred. The Genie Karaz howled at her, and pinioned her to a pillar below in the Desert, with Shagpat in her arms. But, as he soared aloft to renew the fight with Noorna, Shibli Bagarag loosed to her aid the Slaves of the Sword, and Abarak marked him slope to a distant corner of earth, and reascend in a cloud, which drew swiftly over the land toward the Great Hall. Lo, Shibli Bagarag stepped from it through a casement of the Hall, and with him Shagpat, a slack weight, mated out of all power of motion. Koorookh swooped low, on his back Baba Mustapha, and Shibli Bagarag flung Abarak beside him on the bird. Then Koorookh whirred off with them; and while the heavens raged, Shibli Bagarag prepared a rapid lather, and dashed it over Shagpat, and commenced shearing him with lightning sweeps of the blade. 'Twas as a racing wheel of fire to see him! Suddenly he desisted, and wiped the sweat from his face. Then calling on the name of Allah, he gave a last keen cunning sweep with the blade, and following that, the earth awfully quaked and groaned, as if speaking in the abysmal tongue the Mastery of the Event to all men. Aklis was revealed in burning beams as of a sun, and the trouble of the air ceased, vapours slowly curling to the four quarters. Shibli Bagarag had smitten clean through the Identical! Terribly had Noorna and those that aided her been oppressed by the multitude of their enemies; but, in a moment these melted away, and Karaz, together with the scorpion that was Goorelka, vanished. Day was on the baldness of Shagpat.

# CONCLUSION

S o was shaved Shagpat, the son of Shimpoor, the son of Shoolpi, the son of Shullum, by Shibli Bagarag, of Shiraz, according to preordainment.

The chronicles relate, that no sooner had he mastered the Event, than men on the instant perceived what illusion had beguiled them, and, in the words of the poet,—

> *The blush with which their folly they confess*
> *Is the first prize of his supreme success.*

Even Bootlbac, the drum-beater, drummed in homage to him, and the four Kings were they that were loudest in their revilings of the spouse of Kadza, and most obsequious in praises of the Master. The King of the City was fain to propitiate his people by a voluntary resignation of his throne to Shibli Bagarag, and that King took well to heart the wisdom of the sage, when he says:

> *Power, on Illusion based, o'ertoppeth all;*
> *The more disastrous is its certain fall!*

Surely Shibli Bagarag returned the Sword to the Sons of Aklis, flashing it in midnight air, and they, with the others, did reverence to his achievement. They were now released from the toil of sharpening the Sword a half-cycle of years, to wander in delight on the fair surface of the flowery earth, breathing its roses, wooing its brides; for the mastery of an Event lasteth among men the space of one cycle of years, and after that a fresh Illusion springeth to befool mankind, and the Seven must expend the concluding half-cycle in preparing the edge of the Sword for a new mastery. As the poet declareth in his scorn:

> *Some doubt Eternity: from life begun,*
> *Has folly ceased within them, sire to son?*
> *So, ever fresh Illusions will arise*
> *And lord creation, until men are wise.*

And he adds:

> *That is a distant period; so prepare*
> *To fight the false, O youths, and never spare!*
> *For who would live in chronicles renowned*
> *Must combat folly, or as fool be crowned.*

Now, for the Kings of Shiraz and of Gaf, Shibli Bagarag entertained them in honour; but the King of Oolb he disgraced and stripped of his robes, to invest Baba Mustapha in those royal emblems—a punishment to the treachery of the King of Oolb, as is said by Aboo Eznol:

> *When nations with opposing forces, rash,*
> *Shatter each other, thou that wouldst have stood*
> *Apart to profit by the monstrous feud,*
> *Thou art the surest victim of the crash.*
>
> *Take colours of whichever side thou wilt,*
> *And stedfastly thyself in battle range;*
> *Yet, having taken, shouldst thou dare to change,*
> *Suspicion hunts thee as a thing of guilt.*

Baba Mustapha, was pronounced Sovereign of Oolb, amid the acclamations of the guard encamped under the command of Ravaloke, without the walls.

No less did Shibli Bagarag honour the benefactor of Noorna, making him chief of his armies; and he, with his own hand, bestowed on the good old warrior the dress of honour presented to him by the Seven Sons, charactered with all the mysteries of Aklis, a marvel lost to men in the failure to master the Illusion now dominating earth.

So, then, of all that had worshipped Shagpat, only Kadza clung to him, and she departed with him into the realms of Rabesqurat, who reigned there, divided against herself by the stroke of the Sword. The Queen is no longer mighty, for the widening of her power has weakened it, she being now the mistress of the single-thoughted, and them that follow one idea to the exclusion of a second. The failure in the unveiling of her last-cherished Illusion was in the succumbing frailty of him that undertook the task, the world and its wise men having come to the belief that in thwackings there was ignominy to the soul of man, and a tarnish on the lustre of heroes. On that score, hear the words of the poet, a vain protest:

*Ye that nourish hopes of fame!*
*Ye who would be known in song!*
*Ponder old history, and duly frame*
*Your souls to meek acceptance of the thong.*

*Lo! of hundreds who aspire,*
*Eighties perish–nineties tire!*
*They who bear up, in spite of wrecks and wracks,*
*Were season'd by celestial hail of thwacks.*

*Fortune in this mortal race*
*Builds on thwackings for its base;*
*Thus the All-Wise doth make a flail a staff,*
*And separates his heavenly corn from chaff.*

*Think ye, had he never known*
*Noorna a belabouring crone,*
*Shibli Bagarag would have shaved Shagpat*
*The unthwack'd lives in chronicle a rat!*

*'Tis the thwacking in this den*
*Maketh lions of true men!*
*So are we nerved to break the clinging mesh*
*Which tames the noblest efforts of poor flesh.*

Feshnavat became the Master's Vizier, and Abarak remained at the right hand of Shibli Bagarag, his slave in great adventure. No other condition than bondage gave peace to Abarak. He was of the class enumerated by the sage:

*Who, with the strength of giants, are but tools,*
*The weighty hands which serve selected fools.*

Now, this was how it was in the case of Baba Mustapha, and the four Kings, and Feshnavat, and Abarak, and Ravaloke, and Kadza, together with Shagpat; but, in the case of Noorna bin Noorka, surely she was withering from a sting of the scorpion shot against her bosom, but the Seven Sons of Aklis gave her a pass into Aklis on the wings of Koorookh, and Gulrevaz, the daughter of Aklis, tended her, she that was alone capable of restoring her, and counteracting the malice of the scorpion by the hand of purity. So Noorna, prospered; but Shibli Bagarag drooped in uncertainty of her state, and was as a reaper in a field of harvest, around whom lie the yellow sheaves, and the brown beam of autumn on his head, the blaze of plenty; yet is he joyless and stands musing, for one is away who should be there, and without whom the goblet of Success giveth an unsweetened draught, and there is nothing pleasant in life, and the flower on the summit of achievement is blighted. At last, as he was listlessly dispensing justice in the Great Hall, seven days after the mastery of the Event, lo, Noorna, in air, borne by Gulrevaz, she fair and fresh in the revival of health and beauty, and the light of constant love. Of her entry into the Great Hall, to the embrace of her betrothed, the poet exclaims, picturing her in a rapture:

> *Her march is music, and my soul obeys*
> *Each motion, as a lute to cunning fingers*
> *I see the earth throb for her as she sways*
> *Wave-like in air, and like a great flower lingers*
> *Heavily over all, as loath to leave*
> *What loves her so, and for her loss would grieve.*

> *But oh, what other hand than heaven's can paint*
> *Her eyes, and that black bow from which their lightning*
> *Pierces afar! long lustrous eyes, that faint*
> *In languor, or with stormy passion brightening:*
> *Within them world in world lights up from sleep,*
> *And gives a glimpse of the eternal deep.*

> *Sigh round her, odorous winds; and, envious rose,*
> *So vainly envious, with such blushes gifted,*
> *Bow to her; die, strangled with jealous throes,*
> *O Bulbul! when she sings with brow uplifted;*
> *Gather her, happy youth, and for thy gain*
> *Thank Him who could such loveliness ordain.*

Surely the Master of the Event advanced to her in the glory of a Sultan, and seated her beside him in majesty, and their contract of marriage was read aloud in the Hall, and witnessed, and sealed: joyful was he! Then commenced that festival which lasted forty days, and is termed the Festival of the honours of hospitality to the Sons of Aldis, wherein the head-cook of the palace, Uruish, performed wonders in his science, and menaced the renown of Zrmack, the head-cook of King Shamshureen. Even so the confectioner, Dob, excelled himself in devices and inventions, and his genius urged him to depict in sugars and pastes the entire adventures of Shibli Bagarag in search of the Sword. Honour we Uruish and Do-b! as the poet sayeth:

> Divide not this fraternal twain;
> One are they, and one should for ever remain:
> As to sweet close in fine music we look,
> So the Confectioner follows the Cook.

And one of the Sons of Aklis, Zaragal, beholding this masterpiece of Dob, which was served to the guests in the Great Hall on the fortieth evening, was fair to exclaim in extemporaneous verse:

> Have I been wafted to a rise
> Of banquet spread in Paradise,
> Dower'd with consuming powers divine;—
> That I, who have not fail'd to dine,
> And greatly,
> Fall thus upon the cater and wine
> Sedately?

So there was feasting in the Hall, and in the City, and over Earth; great pledging the Sovereign of Barbers, who had mastered an Event, and become the benefactor of his craft and of his kind. 'Tis certain the race of the Bagarags endured for many centuries, and his seed were the rulers of men, and the seal of their empire stamped on mighty wax the Tackle of Barbers.

Now, of the promise made by the Sons of Aklis to visit Shibli Bagarag before their compulsory return to the labour of the Sword, and recount to him the marvel of their antecedent adventures; and of the love and grief nourished in the souls of men by the beauty and sorrowful eyes of Gulrevaz, that was mined the Bleeding Lily, and of her engagement to tell her story, on condition of receiving the first-born of Noorna to nurse for a season in Aklis; and of Shibli Bagarag's restoration of towns and monuments destroyed by his battle with Karaz; and of the constancy of passion of Shibli Bagarag for Noorna, and his esteem for her sweetness, and his reverence for her wisdom; and of the glory of his reign, and of the Songs and Sentences of Noorna, and of his Laws for the protection and upholding of women, in honour of Noorna, concerning which the Sage has said:

> *Were men once clad in them, we should create*
> *A race not following, but commanding, fate:*

—of all these records, and of the reign of Baba Mustapha in Oolb, surely the chronicles give them in fulness; and they that have searched say of them, there is matter therein for the amusement of generations.

# bookfinity™

## Discover more of your favorite classics with Bookfinity™.

- Track your reading with custom book lists.
- Get great book recommendations for your personalized Reader Type.
- Add reviews for your favorite books.
- AND MUCH MORE!

Visit **bookfinity.com** and take the fun Reader Type quiz to get started.

Enjoy our classic and modern companion pairings!

Printed in the USA
CPSIA information can be obtained
at www.ICGtesting.com
JSHW022326140824
68134JS00019B/1312